**NEW YORK REVIEW BOOKS**
CLASSICS

# NIGHTMARE ALLEY

WILLIAM LINDSAY GRESHAM (1909–1962) was born in Baltimore and went to high school in Brooklyn. Gresham's was a tortured mind and he led a tormented life; he sought to banish his demons through a maze of what turned out to be dead ends, from Marxism to psychoanalysis to Christianity to Alcoholics Anonymous to Rinzai Zen Buddhism. In addition to *Nightmare Alley* (1946), he wrote one other novel, *Limbo Tower* (1949), which went largely unnoticed. Three nonfiction books followed: *Monster Midway* (1953), *Houdini* (1959), and *The Book of Strength* (1961). Gresham married three times, and his second wife, the poet and novelist Joy Davidman, later (on her death-bed) became the wife of British author C. S. Lewis. Facing a diagnosis of terminal cancer, Gresham killed himself in New York City on September 14, 1962.

NICK TOSCHES (1949–2019) was the author of some twenty books of fiction, nonfiction, and poetry, including the celebrated *Hellfire: The Jerry Lee Lewis Story.* His book about William Lindsay Gresham, which he worked on for many years, remained unpublished at the time of his death.

# NIGHTMARE ALLEY

**WILLIAM LINDSAY GRESHAM**

*Introduction by*
**NICK TOSCHES**

NEW YORK REVIEW BOOKS

*New York*

THIS IS A NEW YORK REVIEW BOOK
PUBLISHED BY THE NEW YORK REVIEW OF BOOKS
435 Hudson Street, New York, NY 10014
www.nyrb.com

Library of Congress Cataloging-in-Publication Data

Gresham, William Lindsay, 1909–1962.
 Nightmare alley / by William Lindsay Gresham ; introduction by Nick Tosches.
   p. cm. — (New York Review Books classics)
 ISBN 978-1-59017-348-0 (alk. paper)
1. Circus performers—Fiction. 2. Mediums—Fiction. 3. Swindlers and
swindling—Fiction. I. Title.
 PS3513.R625N54 2010
 813'.52—dc22

                        2009051327


ISBN 978-1-59017-348-0
Available as an electronic book; 978-1-59017-428-9

Printed in the United States of America on acid-free paper.
10  9  8  7

# CONTENTS

# Introduction

Many who read this will have read *Nightmare Alley*. But it is to be hoped that others will be drawn to read this singular work for the first time. I envy the latter, and I don't want to interfere with the experience that awaits them by delving into matters that would reveal its plot, which grows increasingly more powerful and bizarre from beginning to end. But, to paraphrase Ezra Pound, a little knowledge can do us no harm.

This book, first published in 1946, was born in the winter of late 1938 and early 1939, in a village near Valencia, where William Lindsay Gresham, one of the international volunteers who had come to defend the Republic in the lost cause of the Spanish Civil War, was awaiting repatriation. He waited and he drank with a man, Joseph Daniel Halliday, who told him of something that took him aback with a scare: a carny attraction called a geek, a drunkard driven so low that he would bite off the heads of chickens and snakes just to get the booze he needed. Bill Gresham was only twenty-nine then. As he would later tell it, "the story of the geek haunted me. Finally, to get rid of it, I had to write it out. The novel, of which it was the frame, seemed to horrify readers as much as the original story had horrified me."

Upon his return from Spain, according to his own account, Gresham was not a well man. He became deeply involved in psychoanalysis, one of the many ways he sought throughout his life to banish his inner demons.

It was while writing *Nightmare Alley* that Gresham drifted away from psychoanalysis and became instead fascinated with the tarot, which he discovered while turning from Freud to, in the course of his research for *Nightmare Alley*, the Russian mystic P. D. Ouspensky (1878–1947).

Had only Gresham known of the paper Freud delivered at the Conference of the Central Committee of the International Psychoanalytical Association in September 1921. In it, Freud declared: "It no longer seems possible to brush aside the study of so-called occult facts; of things which seem to vouchsafe the real existence of psychic forces other than the known forces of the human and animal psyche, or which reveal mental faculties in which, until now, we did not believe." Freud and Ouspensky then might have walked even more closely together down Gresham's alley of nightmares.

Gresham used the tarot to structure his book. The tarot deck consists of twenty-two figured trump cards, of which twenty-one are numbered, and fifty-six cards divided into four suits of wands, cups, swords, and pentacles. The deck has been used for centuries for both gambling and fortune-telling. In the case of fortune-telling, it is the trump cards, also known as the Major Arcana, that are primarily employed, and these are the cards which give the titles to the chapters of *Nightmare Alley*. The first trump card is the Fool, which is the card that bears no number, and the final one is the World. Gresham begins his book with the Fool, but then shuffles the deck. His deck ends with the Hanged Man.

As piercing as the psychological probings of *Nightmare Alley* are, eerily the tarot alone is bestowed at times with a hint of ominous gravity and credence amid all the other spiritualist cons of the novel that are to Gresham and his characters nothing more than suckers' rackets.

It is interesting, too, that while still undergoing psychotherapy, Gresham crafted in *Nightmare Alley*, in the somewhat heavy-handedly named character of Dr. Lilith Ritter, the most viciously evil psychologist in the history of literature.

He would later say of this time that six years of therapy had both saved him and failed him: "Even then I was not a well man, for neurosis had left an aftermath. During years of analysis, editorial work, and the strain of small children in small rooms, I had controlled anxieties by deadening them with alcohol." He said, "I found that I could not stop drinking; I had become physically an alcoholic. And against alcoholism in this stage, Freud is powerless."

Nothing worth reading was ever written by anyone who was drunk while writing it; but *Nightmare Alley* evinces every sign that its writing was binge-riddled. Booze is so strong an element in the novel that it can almost be said to be a character, an essential presence like Fates in ancient Greek tragedy. The delirium tremens writhe and strike in this book like the snakes within. William Wordsworth's dictum that poetry was "emotion recollected in tranquillity" here finds a counterpart in Gresham's evocation in sobriety of what he calls in his novel "the horrors."

Surely "the horrors" in this sense had been part of colloquial speech, at least among drunks and opiate addicts, before Robert Louis Stevenson used it in *Treasure Island* (1883), and it is still very much current today.

The matter of language is paramount here. Gresham's cold blue steel prose is consummate, as is his use of slang in dialogue and interior monologue. Never affected, always natural and effective.

As noted in a little profile of him published in *The New York Times Book Review* soon after the novel's release: "Among the Gresham interests are confidence men, their wiles and argot, which he tosses off with a bland ease that, one executive at Rinehart was saying the other day, is enough to frighten an ordinary, law-abiding citizen."

The word "geek" (derived from "geck," a word for a fool, simpleton, or dupe, in use since from at least the early sixteenth through the nineteenth century) was generally unknown in its carnival sense of a "wild man" who bites the heads off live chickens or snakes, until Gresham introduced it to the general public in *Nightmare Alley*. In November 1947 the popular Nat "King" Cole Trio made a record called "The Geek."

As an elaboration of "cinch," the phrase "lead-pipe cinch," to denote a sure thing, had been around since the nineteenth century, and it would stay around a good while more. It could be found in 1949 in Nelson Algren's *The Man with the Golden Arm* and in 1974 in a *New York Times* financial report.

Some of the enchanting slang Gresham used seems to have appeared in print for the first time in *Nightmare Alley*. Geek, in its sideshow sense, may have been one of them. The earliest instance to be found thus far in *Billboard*'s carnival section occurs in a want ad of August 31, 1946, after the novel was already for sale: "No Geek or Girl Shows" stated a notice that Howard Bros. Shows was seeking acts and concessions. (Want ads for geeks in the carnival section of *Billboard* continued until at least 1960. An advertisement placed by Johnny's United Shows in the issue of June 17, 1957, was blunt: "Want outstanding Geek for Geek Show. Must know snakes.")

The phrase "cold reading" almost certainly appeared in print for the first time here, as did the unforgettable "spook racket." (We become aware of the meaning of these slang terms as we encounter them. Gresham never stoops to explication through forced dialogue.)

Both phrases next show up, almost immediately and in the same sentence, in Julien J. Proskauer's 1946 *The Dead Do Not Talk*, which was received by the Library of Congress almost four months after Gresham's novel and was assigned a later control number. After that, "cold reading" is found the following year in C. L. Boarde's slim, self-printed, spiral-bound guide to the spiritualist's craft, *Mainly Mental*, then begins to appear more widely, while "spook racket" seems to vanish to its well-deserved solitary throne beyond the veil.

The passage in which "cold reading" first appears, in the fourth chapter, "The World," also contains one of the novel's turning points, when the tale's central character, Stan, reading in the long-fallen mentalist Pete's old notebook, comes upon the words "Can control anybody by finding out what he's afraid of" and "Fear is the key to human nature."

Stan "looked past the pages to the garish wallpaper and through it into the world. The geek was made by fear. He was afraid of sobering up and getting the horrors. But what made him a drunk? Fear. Find out what they are afraid of and sell it back to them. That's the key."

Here too in "The World" is Stan's, and Gresham's, view of the language that enthralled. As Stan enters the remote piney deep South, where the fortune-teller did a better trade in John the Conqueror Root than in the horoscope cards she peddled at the close of her show:

> The speech fascinated him. His ear caught the rhythm of it and he noted their idioms and worked some of them into his patter. He had found the reason behind the peculiar, drawling language of the old carny hands—it was a composite of all the sprawling regions of the country. A language which sounded Southern to Southerners, Western to Westerners. It was the talk of the soil and its drawl covered the agility of the brains that poured it out. It was a soothing, illiterate, earthy language.

This is the language of *Nightmare Alley*, and many urbane critics of the time found it shocking and brutal as well. Gresham's wicked lyricism is unique: a gutter literacy that probes the stars, at times a celestial literacy that probes the gutter.

The nightmare alley into which William Lindsay Gresham leads us is not one of moral depravity, for the nicety of morality has nothing to do with it.

Gresham's novel is a tale of many things: the folly of faith and the cunning of those who peddle it; alcoholism and the destructive terror of delirium tremens; the playing deck of fate, which allots its death-bound destines without rhyme and without reason. What it is not is a tale of crime and punishment, sin and retribution. To see it as such is to misread it. What we consider to be crime and sin pervade this alley, but the punishment and retribution here seem more the wages of life itself.

"It was the dark alley, all over again," Stan tells himself in *Nightmare Alley*. "Ever since he was a kid Stan had had the dream. He was running down a dark alley, the buildings vacant and menacing on either side. Far down at the end of it a light burned, but there was something behind him, close behind him, getting closer until he woke up trembling and never reached the light." Stan reflects of his marks, of everyone: "They have it too—a nightmare alley." Yes, as Stan—that is to say, Gresham—observes elsewhere, fear is the key to human nature.

And Stan and Gresham were indeed one. There is a bizarre letter, frayed and torn, preserved in the collection of the Wade Center of Wheaton College, written by Gresham in 1959, when the end was near. In it he wrote: "Stan is the author."

Upon its publication, in September 1946, *Nightmare Alley* was an acclaimed and successful novel, and a damned and banned one. For thirty years after the first edition of 1946, every edition remained corrupt and censored. To use but one example, instead of "society dames with the clap, bankers that take it up the ass," readers encountered "society dames with a dose, bankers that have fishy eyes."

Within little more than a decade, it was all but forgotten. Sixteen autumns later, in September 1962, Gresham's body was found, self-killed, in a hotel room off Times Square. He has just turned fifty-

three a few weeks before. In his possession were business cards that
read:

```
┌─────────────────────────────────────────────┐
│  NO ADDRESS                    NO PHONE       │
│                                              │
│                                              │
│                   RETIRED                    │
│                                              │
│                                              │
│  NO BUSINESS                   NO MONEY       │
└─────────────────────────────────────────────┘
```

And so the alley, and the running, and the light beyond reach
came to an end—for the man who wrote of that alley, if not for us
who read of it.

—NICK TOSCHES

# NIGHTMARE ALLEY

*To*

**JOY DAVIDMAN**

Madame Sosostris, famous clairvoyante,
Had a bad cold, nevertheless
Is known to be the wisest woman in Europe,
With a wicked pack of cards. Here, said she,
Is your card, the drowned Phoenician Sailor,
(Those are pearls that were his eyes. Look!)
Here is Belladonna, the Lady of the Rocks,
The lady of situations.
Here is the man with three staves, and here the Wheel,
And here is the one-eyed merchant, and this card,
Which is blank, is something he carries on his back,
Which I am forbidden to see. I do not find
The Hanged Man. Fear death by water . . .

—*The Waste Land*


For at Cumae I saw with my own eyes the Sibyl hanging
in a bottle. And when the boys asked her, "What do you
want, Sibyl?" she answered, "I want to die."

—*The Satyricon*

# The Fool

*who walks in motley, with his eyes closed, over a precipice at the end of the world.*

STAN CARLISLE stood well back from the entrance of the canvas enclosure, under the blaze of a naked light bulb, and watched the geek.

This geek was a thin man who wore a suit of long underwear dyed chocolate brown. The wig was black and looked like a mop, and the brown greasepaint on the emaciated face was streaked and smeared with the heat and rubbed off around the mouth.

At present the geek was leaning against the wall of the pen, while around him a few—pathetically few—snakes lay in loose coils, feeling the hot summer night and sullenly uneasy in the glare. One slim little king snake was trying to climb up the wall of the enclosure and was falling back.

Stan liked snakes; the disgust he felt was for them, at their having to be penned up with such a specimen of man. Outside the talker was working up to his climax. Stan turned his neat blond head toward the entrance.

". . . where did he come from? God only knows. He was found on an uninhabited island five hundred miles off the coast of Florida. My friends, in this enclosure you will see one of the unexplained mysteries of the universe. Is he man or is he beast?

3

You will see him living in his natural habitat among the most venomous rep-tiles that the world provides. Why, he fondles those serpents as a mother would fondle her babes. He neither eats nor drinks but lives entirely on the atmosphere. And we're going to feed him one more time! There will be a slight additional charge for this attraction but it's not a dollar, it's not a quarter—it's a cold, thin dime, ten pennies, two nickels, the tenth part of a dollar. Hurry, hurry, hurry!"

Stan shifted over to the rear of the canvas pen.

The geek scrabbled under a burlap bag and found something. There was the wheet of a cork being drawn and a couple of rattling swallows and a gasp.

The "marks" surged in—young fellows in straw hats with their coats over their arms, here and there a fat woman with beady eyes. Why does that kind always have beady eyes, Stan wondered. The gaunt woman with the anemic little girl who had been promised she would see everything in the show. The drunk. It was like a kaleidoscope—the design always changing, the particles always the same.

Clem Hoately, owner of the Ten-in-One show and its lecturer, made his way through the crowd. He fished a flask of water from his pocket, took a swig to rinse his throat, and spat it on the ground. Then he mounted the step. His voice was suddenly low and conversational, and it seemed to sober the audience.

"Folks, I must ask ya to remember that this exhibit is being presented solely in the interests of science and education. This creature which you see before ya . . ."

A woman looked down and for the first time spied the little king snake, still frantically trying to climb out of the pit. She drew in her breath shrilly between her teeth.

". . . this creature has been examined by the foremost scientists of Europe and America and pronounced a man. That is to say: he has two arms, two legs, a head and a body, like a man. But under that head of hair there is the brain of a beast. See how he feels more at home with the rep-tiles of the jungle than with humankind."

The geek had picked up a black snake, holding it close behind the head so it couldn't snap at him, and was rocking it in his arms like a baby, muttering sounds.

The talker waited while the crowd rubbered.

"You may well ask how he associates with poisonous serpents without harm. Why, my friends, their poison has no effect whatsoever upon him. But if he were to sink his teeth in my hand nothing on God's green earth could save me."

The geek gave a growl, blinking stupidly up into the light from the bare bulb. Stan noticed that at one corner of his mouth there was a glint from a gold tooth.

"But now, ladies and gentlemen, when I told you that this creature was more beast than man I was not asking you to take my word for it. Stan—" He turned to the young man, whose brilliant blue eyes had not a trace of revelation in them. "Stan, we're going to feed him one more time for this audience alone. Hand me the basket."

Stanton Carlisle reached down, gripped a small covered market basket by the handle, and boosted it over the heads of the crowd. They fell back, jamming and pushing. Clem Hoately, the talker, laughed with a touch of weariness. "It's all right, folks; nothing you haven't seen before. No, I reckon you all know what this is." From the basket he drew a half-grown leghorn pullet, complaining. Then he held it up so they could see it. With one hand he motioned for silence.

The necks craned down.

The geek had leaned forward on all fours, his mouth hanging open vacantly. Suddenly the talker threw the pullet into the pit with a whirl of feathers.

The geek moved toward it, shaking his black cotton mop of wig. He grabbed for the chicken, but it spread its stumpy wings in a frenzy of self-preservation and dodged. He crawled after it.

For the first time the paint-smeared face of the geek showed some life. His bloodshot eyes were nearly closed. Stan saw his lips shape words without sound. The words were, "You son of a bitch."

Gently the youth eased himself out of the crowd, which was straining, looking down. He walked stiffly around to the entrance, his hands in his pockets.

From the pit came a panicky clucking and cackling and the crowd drew its breath. The drunk beat his grimy straw hat on the rail. "Get 'at ole shicken, boy! Go get 'at ole shicken!"

Then a woman screamed and began to leap up and down jerkily; the crowd moaned in an old language, pressing their bodies tighter against the board walls of the pit and stretching. The cackling had been cut off short, and there was a click of teeth and a grunt of someone working hard.

Stan shoved his hands deeper in his pockets. He moved through the flap entrance back into the main ring of the Ten-in-One show, crossed it to the gate and stood looking out on the carnival midway. When his hands came from his pockets one of them held a shiny half-dollar. He reached for it with his other hand and it vanished. Then with a secret, inner smile of contempt and triumph, he felt along the edge of his white flannel trousers and produced the coin.

Against the summer night the ferris wheel lights winked with the gaiety of rhinestones, the calliope's blast sounded as if the very steam pipes were tired.

"Christ a-mighty, it's hot, huh, kid?"

Clem Hoately, the talker, stood beside Stan, wiping the sweat from the band of his panama with a handkerchief. "Say, Stan, run over and get me a bottle of lemon soda from the juice joint. Here's a dime; get yourself one too."

When Stan came back with the cold bottles, Hoately tilted his gratefully. "Jesus, my throat's sore as a bull's ass in fly time."

Stan drank the pop slowly. "Mr. Hoately?"

"Yeah, what?"

"How do you ever get a guy to geek? Or is this the only one? I mean, is a guy born that way—liking to bite the heads off chickens?"

Clem slowly closed one eye. "Let me tell you something, kid. In the carny you don't ask nothing. And you'll get told no lies."

"Okay. But did you just happen to find this fellow—doing—doing this somewhere behind a barn, and work up the act?"

Clem pushed back his hat. "I like you, kid. I like you a lot. And just for that I'm going to give you a treat. I'm *not* going to give you a boot in the ass, get it? That's the treat."

Stan grinned, his cool, bright blue eyes never leaving the older man's face. Suddenly Hoately dropped his voice.

"Just because I'm your pal I ain't going to crap you up. You want to know where geeks came from. Well, listen—you don't find 'em. You *make* 'em."

He let this sink in, but Stanton Carlisle never moved a muscle. "Okay. But how?"

Hoately grabbed the youth by the shirt front and drew him nearer. "Listen, kid. Do I have to draw you a damn blueprint? You pick up a guy and he ain't a geek—he's a drunk. A bottle-a-day booze fool. So you tell him like this: 'I got a little job for you. It's a temporary job. We got to get a new geek. So until we do you'll put on the geek outfit and fake it.' You tell him, 'You don't have to do nothing. You'll have a razor blade in your hand and when you pick up the chicken you give it a nick with the blade and then make like you're drinking the blood. Same with rats. The marks don't know no different.'"

Hoately ran his eye up and down the midway, sizing up the crowd. He turned back to Stan. "Well, he does this for a week and you see to it that he gets his bottle regular and a place to sleep it off in. He likes this fine. This is what he thinks is heaven. So after a week you say to him like this, you say, 'Well, I got to get me a real geek. You're through.' He scares up at this because nothing scares a real rummy like the chance of a dry spell and getting the horrors. He says, 'What's the matter? Ain't I doing okay?' So you say, 'Like crap you're doing okay. You can't draw no crowd faking a geek. Turn in your outfit. You're through.' Then you walk away. He comes following you, begging for another chance and you say, 'Okay. But after tonight out you go.' But you give him his bottle.

"That night you drag out the lecture and lay it on thick. All the while you're talking he's thinking about sobering up and getting the crawling shakes. You give him time to think it over, while you're talking. Then throw in the chicken. He'll geek."

The crowd was coming out of the geek show, gray and listless and silent except for the drunk. Stan watched them with a strange, sweet, faraway smile on his face. It was the smile of a prisoner who has found a file in a pie.

# The Magician

*who holds toward heaven the wand of fire and points with his other hand toward earth.*

"IF YOU'LL step right over this way, folks, I want to call your attention to the attraction now appearing on the first platform. Ladies and gentlemen, you are about to witness one of the most spectacular performances of physical strenth the world has ever seen. Now some of you young fellows in the crowd look pretty husky but I want to tell you, gents, the man you are about to see makes the ordinary blacksmith or **athlete** look like a babe in arms. The power of an African gorilla in the body of a Greek god. Ladies and gents, Herculo, the world's most perfect man."

*Bruno Hertz:* If only once she would over here look while I have the robe off I would be glad to drop dead that minute. *Um Gotteswillen*, I would cut my heart out and hand it to her on a plate. Cannot she ever see that? I cannot get up courage to hold her hand in the kinema. Why has a man always to feel over some woman like this? I cannot even tell Zeena how crazy I am for her because then Zeena would try to put us together and then I would feel a *dummkopf* from not knowing how to say to her. Molly—a beautiful *Amerikanische* name. She will never love me. I know it in my heart. But I can tear to pieces any of the wolves in the show such as would hurt that girl. If one of them would try, then maybe Molly could see it. Perhaps then she could guess the way I feel and would give me one word for me to remember always. To remember, back in Wien.

". . . right over here, folks. Will you step in a little closer? On account of this exhibit ain't the biggest thing you ever seen; how about it, Major? Ladies and gentlemen, I now present for your edification and amusement Major Mosquito, the tiniest human being on record. Twenty inches, twenty pounds, and twenty years—and he's got plenty of big ideas for his age. Any of you girls would like to date him after the show, see me and I'll fix ya up. The Major will now entertain you with a little specialty number of his own, singing and tap-dancing to that grand old number, 'Sweet Rosie O'Grady.' Take it away, Major."

*Kenneth Horsefield:* If I lit a match and held it right close under that big ape's nose I wonder if I'd see the hairs in his nose-holes catch fire. Christ, what an ape! I'd like to have him tied up with his mouth propped open and then I'd sit back smoking my cigar and shoot his teeth out one after another. Apes. They're all apes. Especially the women with their big moon faces. I'd like to sink a hammer in 'em and watch 'em splash like pumpkins. Their great, greasy red mouths open like tunnels. Grease and filth, all of them.

Christ, there it goes. That same crack. The one woman makes it to the other behind her hand. If I see that same hand come up and that same routine once more I'll yell the goddamned place down. A million dames and always the same goddamned crack behind the same goddamned hand and the other one always champing on gum. Some day I'll blast 'em. I don't keep that equalizer in my trunk to play Boy Scout with. And that's the dame I'll blast. I'd of done it before now. Only they'd laugh at seeing me hold the butt with one hand and work the trigger with the other.

*Joe Plasky:* "Thank you, professor. Ladies and gents, I am known as the Half-man Acrobat. As you can see, my legs are both here but they're not much good to me. Infantile paralysis when I was a kid—they just naturally never growed. So I just made up my mind to tie 'em in a knot like this and forget about 'em and go on about my business. This is the way I get upstairs. Up on the hands. Steady. Here we go with a hop, skip, and a jump. Turn around and down we go, easy as pie. Thank you, folks.

"Now here's another little number I worked out by myself. Sometimes in a crowded trolley car I don't have room enough to stand on both hands. So up we go. Steady. And I stand on one! Thank you very much.

"Now then, for my next number I'm going to do something that no other acrobat in the world has ever attempted. A full somersault from a handstand back onto the hands. Are we all set? Let's go. It's a good trick—if I do it. Maybe some of you folks in the front row had better move back a couple steps. Don't bother. I'm just kidding. I've never missed yet, as you can see, for I'm still in the land of the living. All right, here we go— up—and *over!* Thank you very much, folks.

"And now if you'll just step right in close I'm going to give away a few little souvenirs. Naturally, I can't get rich giving away merchandise, but I'll do my best. I have here a little book-let full of old songs, recitations, jokes, wheezes, and parlor games. And I'm not going to charge you a dollar for it, nor even a half, but a cold, thin dime. That's all it costs, folks, a dime for a full evening of fun and fancy. And with it I'm going to give away, as a special inducement at this performance only, this little paper shimmy-dancer. Hold a match behind the paper: you see her shadow; and this is how you make her shake.

"You want one? Thank you, bud. Here you are, folks—brim-ful of assorted poems, dramatic readings, and witty sayings by the world's wisest men. And only a dime. . . ."

Sis wrote me the kids are both down with whooping cough. I'll send them a box of paints to help keep them quiet. Kids love paints. I'll send them some crayons, too.

"Sailor Martin, the living picture gallery. Ladies and gents, this young man that you see before you went to sea at an early age. He was shipwrecked on a tropical island which had only one other inhabitant—an old seafaring man, who had been there most of his life—a castaway. All he had managed to save from the wreck of his ship was a tattoo outfit. To pass the time he taught Sailor Martin the art and he practiced on himself. Most of the patterns you see are his own work. Turn around, Sailor. On his back, a replica of that world-famous painting, the Rock of Ages. On his chest—turn around, Sailor—the Battleship *Maine*, blowing up in Havana Harbor. Now if any of you young fellows in the audience would like an anchor, American flag, or sweetheart's initials worked on your arm in three beautiful colors, step right up to the platform and see the Sailor. No sissies need apply."

*Francis Xavier Martin:* Boy, that brunette working the electric-chair act is a beaut. Have I got what would make her happy and moan for more! Only Bruno would land on me like a ton of tomcats. I wonder if I'll hear from that redhead in Waterville. God, I can get one on thinking about her yet. What a shape—and knowing right where to put it, too. But this brunette kid, Molly, is the nuts. What a pair of bubbies! High and pointed—and that ain't no cupform either, brother; that's God.

I wish to Christ that kraut Bruno would bust a blood vessel some day, bending them horseshoes. Goddamn, that Molly kid's got legs like a racehorse. Maybe I could give her one jump and then blow the show. Jesus, it would be worth it, to get into that.

"Over here, folks, right over here. On this platform you see one of the most amazing little ladies the wide world has ever known. And right beside her we have an exact replica of the electric chair at Sing Sing prison. . . ."

*Mary Margaret Cahill:* Don't forget to smile; Dad always said that. Golly, I wish Dad was here. If I could only look out there and see him grinning up at me everything would be hunky dory. Time to drop the robe and give them an eyeful. Dad, honey, watch over me. . . .

Dad taught Molly all kinds of wonderful things while she was growing up and they were fun, too. For instance, how to walk out of a hotel in a dignified manner with two of your best dresses wrapped around you under the dress you had on. They had to do that once in Los Angeles and Molly got all of her clothes out. Only they nearly caught Dad and he had to talk fast. Dad was wonderful at talking fast and whenever he got in a tight place Molly would go all squirmy inside with thrill and fun because she knew her dad could always wiggle out just when the others thought he was cornered. Dad was wonderful.

Dad always knew nice people. The men were sometimes soused a little but the ladies that Dad knew were always beautiful and they usually had red hair. They were always wonderful to Molly and they taught her to put on lipstick when she was eleven. The first time she put it on by herself she got on too much and Dad burst out laughing loud and said she looked like something from a crib house—and jail bait at that.

The lady that Dad was friendly with at the time—her name was Alyse—shushed Dad and said, "Come over here, darling. Alyse'll show you. Let's take this off and start over. The idea is to keep people from knowing that you have any makeup on at all—especially at your age. Now watch." She looked at Molly's face carefully and said, "This is where you start. And don't let anybody talk you into putting rouge on anywhere else. You have a square face and the idea is to soften it and make it look round." She showed Molly just how to do it and then took it all off and made her do it herself.

Molly wanted Dad to help her but he said it wasn't his business—getting it off was more in his line, especially on the collars of shirts. Molly felt awful, having to do it all by herself because she was afraid she wouldn't do it right and finally she cried a little and then Dad took her on his lap and Alyse showed her again and after that it was all right and she always used makeup, only people didn't know about it. "My, Mr. Cahill—what a lovely child! Isn't she the picture of health! Such lovely rosy cheeks!" Then Dad would say, "Indeed, ma'am, lots of milk and early to bed." Then he would wink at Molly because she didn't like milk and Dad said beer was just as good for you and she didn't like beer very much but it was always nice and cold and besides you got pretzels with it and everything. Also Dad said it was a shame to go to bed early and miss everything when you could sleep late the next day and catch up—unless you had to be at the track for an early workout, to hold the clock on a horse, and then it was better to stay up and go to bed later.

Only, when Dad had made a real killing at the track he always got lit and when he got lit he always tried to send her off to bed just when everything was going swell and because other people in the crowd were always trying to get her to take some, Molly never cared for liquor. Once, in a hotel where they were stopping, there was a girl got terribly drunk and began to take her clothes off and they had to put her to bed in the room next to Molly's. There were a lot of men going in and coming out all night and the next day the cops came and arrested the girl, and Molly heard people talking about it and somebody said later that they let the girl go but she had to go to the hospital because she had been hurt inside someway. Molly couldn't bear the thought of getting drunk after that because anything might happen to you and you shouldn't let anything happen to you with a man unless you were in love with him. That was what everybody said and people who made love but weren't really in love were called tramps. Molly knew several ladies who were tramps and she asked Dad one time why they were tramps and that's what he said: that they'd let anybody hug and kiss them either for presents or money. You shouldn't do that unless the guy was a swell guy and not likely to cross you up or take a powder on you if you were going to have a baby. Dad said you should never let anybody make love to you if you couldn't use his toothbrush, too. He said that was a safe rule and if you followed that you couldn't go wrong.

Molly could use Dad's toothbrush and often did, because one of their brushes was always getting left behind in the hotel or sometimes Dad needed one to clean his white shoes with.

Molly used to wake up before Dad and sometimes she would run in and hop into his bed and then he would grunt and make funny snorey noises—only they sounded all funny and horrible— and then he would make believe he thought there was a woodchuck in the bed and he would blame the hotel people for letting woodchucks run around in their joint and then he would find out it was Molly and no woodchuck and he would kiss her and tell her to hurry up and get dressed and then go down and get him a racing form at the cigar stand.

One morning Molly ran in and there was a lady in bed with Dad. She was a very pretty lady and she had no nightie on and neither did Dad. Molly knew what had happened: Dad had been lit the night before and had forgotten to put on his pajamas and the girl had been lit and he had brought her up to their rooms to sleep on account of she was too tight to go home and he had intended to have her sleep with Molly but they had just fallen asleep first. Molly lifted the sheet up real, real careful and then she found out how she would look when she got big.

Then Molly got dressed and went down and got the racing form on the cuff and came back and they were still asleep, only the lady had snuggled in closer to Dad. Molly stood quiet in a corner a long time and kept still, hoping they would wake up and find her and she would run at them and go "Woo!" and scare them. Only the lady made a low noise like a moan and Daddy opened one eye and then put his arms around her. She opened her eyes and said, "Hello, sugar," all slow and sleepy, and then Dad started kissing her and she woke up after a while and started to kiss back. Finally Dad got on top of the lady and began to bounce up and down in the bed and Molly thought that was so funny that she burst out laughing and the lady screamed and said, "Get that kid out of here."

Dad was wonderful. He looked over his shoulder in one of his funny ways and said, "Molly, how would you like to sit in the lobby for about half an hour and pick me a couple of winners out of that racing form? I have to give Queenie here her exercise. You don't want to startle her and make her sprain a tendon." Dad kept still until Molly had gone but when she was outside the door she could hear the bed moving and she wondered if this lady could use Dad's toothbrush and she hoped she wouldn't because Molly wouldn't want to use it afterwards. It would make her sick to use it.

When Molly was fifteen one of the exercise boys at the stable asked her to come up in the hay loft and she went and he grabbed her and started kissing her and she didn't like him enough to kiss him and besides it was all of a sudden and she started wrestling with him and then she called, "Dad! Dad!" because the boy was touching her and Dad came bouncing up into the loft and he hit the boy so hard he fell down on the hay as if he was dead, only he wasn't. Dad put his arm around Molly and said, "You all right, baby?" And Dad kissed her and held her close to him for a minute and then he said, "You got to watch yourself, kidlet. This world's full of wolves. This punk won't bother you no more. Only watch yourself." And Molly smiled and said:

"I couldn't have used his toothbrush anyhow." Then Dad grinned and rapped her easy under the chin with his fist. Molly wasn't scared any more only she never strayed very far from Dad or from other girls. It was awful that had to happen because she could never feel right around the stables any more, and couldn't talk to the exercise boys and the jockeys any more in the old way and even when she did they were always looking at her breasts and that made her feel all weak and scarey inside somehow even when they were polite enough.

She was glad she was beginning to have breasts, though, and she got used to boys looking at them. She used to pull the neck of her nightie down and make like the ladies in evening dresses and once Dad bought her an evening dress. It was beautiful and one way you looked at it it was light rose and the other way it was gold and it came down off the shoulders and was cut low and it was wonderful. Only that was the year Centerboard ran out of the money and Dad had the bankroll on him to show and they had to sell everything they had to get a grubstake. That was when they went back to Louisville. That was the last year.

Dad got a job with an old friend who ran a gambling place down by the river, and Dad was his manager and wore a tuxedo all the time.

Things were going fine after a while and as soon as Dad squared up some of his tabs he registered Molly at a dancing school and she started to learn acrobatic and tap. She had a wonderful time, showing him the steps as she learned them. Dad could dance a lot of softshoe himself and he never had a lesson.

He said he just had Irish feet. Also he wanted her to take music lessons and sing, only she never could sing—she took after Mother that way. When the school gave a recital Molly did a Hawaiian number with a real hula skirt somebody had sent Dad from Honolulu and her hair falling over her shoulders like a black cloud and flowers in her hair and dark makeup and everybody applauded and some of the boys whistled and that made Dad mad because he thought they were getting fresh but Molly loved it because Dad was out there and as long as he was there she didn't care what happened.

She was sixteen and all grown up when things went to smash. Some fellows from Chicago had come down and there was trouble at the place where Dad worked. Molly never did find out what it was, only a couple of big men came to the house one night about two o'clock and Molly knew they were cops and she went all weak, thinking Dad had done something and they wanted him but he had always told her that the way to deal with cops was to smile at them, act dumb, and give them an Irish name.

One said, "You Denny Cahill's daughter?" Molly said yes. He said, "I got some mighty tough news for you, kid. It's about your dad." That was when Molly felt her feet slip on glass, like the world had suddenly tilted and it was slippery glass and she was falling off it into the dark and would fall and fall forever because there was no end to the place where she was falling.

She just stood there and she said, "Tell me."

The cop said, "Your dad's been hurt, girlie. He's hurt real bad." He wasn't like a shamus now; he was more like the sort of man who might have a daughter himself. She went up close to him because she was afraid of falling.

She said, "Is Dad dead?" and he nodded and put his arm around her and she didn't remember anything more for a while, only she was in the hospital when she came to and somehow she was all groggy and sleepy and she thought she had been hurt and kept asking for Dad and a cross nurse said she had better keep quiet and then she remembered and Dad was dead and she started to scream and it was like laughing, only it felt horrible and she couldn't stop and then they came and stuck her arm with a hype gun and she went out again and it was that way for a couple of times and finally she could stop crying and they told her she would have to get out because other people needed the bed.

Molly's grandfather, "Judge" Kincaid, said she could live with him and her aunt if she would take a business course and get a job in a year and Molly tried but she couldn't ever get it into her head somehow, although she could remember past performances of horses swell. The Judge had a funny way of looking at her and several times he seemed about to get friendly and then he would chill up. Molly tried being nice to him and calling him Granddad but he didn't like that and once, just to see what would happen, she ran up to him when he came in and threw her arms around his neck. He got terribly mad that time and told her aunt to get her out of the house, he wouldn't stand having her around.

It was terrible without Dad to tell her things and talk to and Molly wished she had died along with Dad. Finally she got a scholarship to the dancing school and she worked part time there with the young kids and Miss La Verne, who ran the school, let her stay with her. Miss La Verne was very nice at first and so was her boy friend, Charlie, who was a funny-looking man, kind of fat, who used to sit and look at Molly and he reminded her of a frog, the way he used to spread his fingers out on his knees, pointing in, and pop his eyes.

Then Miss La Verne got cross and said Molly better get a job, but Molly didn't quite know how to begin and finally Miss La Verne said, "If I get you a job will you stick with it?" Molly promised.

It was a job with a carny. There was a Hawaiian dance show, what they called a kooch show—two other girls and Molly. The fellow who ran it and did the talking was called Doc Abernathy. Molly didn't like him a bit and he was always trying to make the girls. Only Jeannette, one of the dancers, and Doc were steady and Jeannette was crazy-mad jealous of the other two. Doc used to devil her by horsing around with them.

Molly always liked Zeena, who ran the mental act in the Ten-in-One show across the midway. Zeena was awfully nice and she knew more about life and people than anybody Molly had ever met except Dad. Zeena had Molly bunk in with her, when she stayed in hotels, for company, because Zeena's husband slept in the tent to watch the props, he said. Really it was because he was a souse and he couldn't make love to Zeena any more. Zeena and Molly got to be real good friends and Molly didn't wish she was dead any more.

Then Jeannette got nastier and nastier about Doc's paying so much attention to Molly and she wouldn't believe that Molly didn't encourage him. The other girl told her, "With a chassis like that Cahill kid's got you don't have to do no encouraging." But Jeannette thought Molly was a stinker. One day Doc whispered something to her about Molly and Jeannette started for her looking like a wild animal with her lips pulled back over her teeth. She smacked Molly in the face and before Molly knew what was going on she had pulled off her shoe and was swinging at her, beating her in the face with it. Doc came rushing over and he and Jeannette had a terrible battle. She was cursing and screaming and Doc told her to shut up or he would smash her in the tits. Molly ran out and went over to the Ten-in-One and the boss fired Doc out of the carny and the kooch show went back to New York.

"Fifteen thousand volts of electricity pass through her body without hurting a hair of the little lady's head. Ladies and gentlemen, Mamzelle Electra, the girl who, like Ajax of Holy Writ, defies the lightning. . . ."

Glory be to God, I hope nothing happens to that wiring. I want Dad. God, how I want him here. I've got to remember to smile. . . .

"Stand over here, Teddy, and hold onto Ma's hand. So's you won't git tromped on and kin see. That there's a 'lectric chair, same's they got in the penitentiary. No, they ain't going to hurt the lady none, leastways I hope not. See? They strap her in that chair—only there's something about her body that don't take 'lectricity. Same's rain rolls right off the old gander's back. Don't be scared, Teddy. Ain't nothing going to happen to her. See how the 'lectricity makes her hair stand out stiff? Lightning'll do the same thing I heard tell. There. See? She's holding a 'lectric bulb in one hand and grabbing the wire with the other. See the bulb light? That means the 'lectricity is passing right through her 'thout hurting her none. I wisht your pa was that way with 'lectricity. He got a powerful bad burn last winter, time the wires blowed down and he was helping Jim Harness get his road cleared. Come along, Teddy. That's all they're going to do over here."

Now I can get up. Sailor Martin's looking at me again. I can't keep saying no to him every time he asks me to go out with him. But he can always think faster than I can. Only I mustn't let him, ever. I mustn't be a tramp; I don't want it this way, the first time. Dad . . .

*Stanton Carlisle:* The great Stanton stood up and smiled, running his glance over the field of upturned faces. He took a deep breath. "Well, folks, first of all I'm going to show you how to make money. Is there anybody in the crowd who's willing to trust me with the loan of a dollar bill? You'll get it back—if you can run fast. Thanks, bud. Now then—nothing in either hand, nothing up the sleeves."

Showing his hands empty, save for the borrowed bill, Stan gave a hitch to his sleeves. In the folds of his left sleeve was a roll of bills which he acquired deftly. "Now then, one dollar— Wait a minute, bud. Are you sure you gave me only one? You're sure. Maybe that's all you got with you, eh? But here are two— one and two. Count 'em. It's a good trick, especially along toward the end of the week."

Which one will smile at the oldest gag? One out of every five. Remember that. One in five is a born chump.

He produced the bills one after another, until he had a green fan of them. He returned the bill to the lad. In doing so he turned his left side from the crowd, got a metal cup in his hand. It hung by an elastic from his left hip.

"Now then, out of nowhere they came. Let's see what happens to them when we roll them up. One, two, three, four, five, six. All present and accounted for. Into a roll—" He placed the bills in his left hand, slipping them into the vanisher. "Blow on the hand—" The vanisher, released, thudded softly against his hip under his coat. "Lo and behold! Gone!"

There was a scattering of applause, as if they were a little ashamed of it. The chumps.

"Where did they go? You know, day after day I stand here—wondering just where they do go!" That's Thurston's gag. By God, I'm going to use it until I see one face—just one—in this bunch of rubes that gets the point. They never do. But that dollar bill production goes over. Poverty-struck bastards—they all wish they could do it. Make money out of the air. Only that's not the way I make mine. But it's better than real estate. My old man and his deals. Church vestryman on Sundays, con man the rest of the week. Frig him, the Bible-spouting bastard.

"Now then, if I can have your attention for a moment. I have here a bunch of steel rings. Each and every one of them a separate, solid hoop of steel. I have one, two, three-four, five, six-seveneight. Right? Now I take two. Tap 'em. Joined together! Would you take these, madam, and tell me if you can find any joints or signs of an opening? No? Thank you. All solid. And again, two separate rings. Go! Joined!"

Better speed it up, they're getting restless. This is the life, though. Everyone looking at you. How does he do it? Gosh, that's slick. Trying to figure it out. It's magic to them, all right. This is the life. While they're watching and listening you can tell 'em anything. They believe you. You're a magician. Pass solid rings through each other. Pull dollars out of the air. Magic. You're top man—while you keep talking.

"And now, folks, eight separate and distinct rings; yet by a magic word they fly together and are joined inextricably into a solid mass. There you are! I thank you for your kind attention. Now I have here a little booklet that's worth its weight in gold. Here is a collection of magic tricks that you can do—an hour's performance before your club, lodge, or church gathering or in your own parlor. An hour's practice—a lifetime of fun, magic, and mystery. This book formerly sold for a dollar, but for today I'm going to let you have it for two bits—a quarter of a dollar. Let's hurry it up, folks, because I know you all want to see and hear Madam Zeena, the seeress, and her act does not go on until everyone who wants one of these great books gets one. Thank you, sir. And you. Any more? Right.

"Now then, folks, don't go 'way. The next complete show will not start for twenty minutes. I call your attention to the next platform. Madam Zeena—miracle woman of the ages. She sees, she knows, she tells you the innermost secrets of your past, your present, and your future. Madam Zeena!"

Stan jumped down lightly from his own small platform and pushed through the crowd to a miniature stage draped in maroon velvet. A woman had stepped out from between the curtains. The crowd flowed over and stood waiting, looking up at her, some of the faces absently chewing, hands cupping popcorn into mouths.

The woman was tall, dressed in flowing white with astrological symbols embroidered on the hem of her robe. A cascade of brassy blond hair fell down her back and a band of gilt leather studded with glass jewels was around her forehead. When she raised her arms the loose sleeves fell back. She had large bones, but her arms were white and capable-looking, with a spattering of freckles. Her eyes were blue, her face round, and her mouth a shade too small, so that she looked a trifle like an elaborate doll. Her voice was low-pitched with a hearty ring to it.

"Step right up, folks, and don't be bashful. If there's any of you that want to ask me a question Mr. Stanton is now passing among you with little cards and envelopes. Write your question on the card; be careful not to let anybody else see what you write, because that's your business. I don't want anybody asking me about somebody else's business. Just let's all mind our own and we'll stay out of trouble. When you've written your question, sign your initials to the card or write your name as a token of good faith. Then give the sealed envelope to Mr. Stanton. You'll see what I'm going to do next.

"Meantime, while we're waiting for you to write your questions, I'm going to start right in. It isn't necessary for you to write anything, but that helps you to fix it firmly in mind and keeps your mind from wandering off it, same as if you want to remember somebody's name you just met it helps to jot it down. Isn't that so?"

One out of every five heads nodded, entranced, and the rest looked on, some with dull eyes, but most of them with questions written on their faces.

Questions? They've all got questions, Stan thought, passing out cards and envelopes. Who hasn't? Answer their questions and you can have them, body and soul. Or just about. "Yes, madam, you can ask her anything. The questions are held in strictest confidence. No one will know but yourself."

"First of all," Zeena began, "there's a lady worried about her mother. She's asking me mentally, 'Is mother going to get better?' Isn't that so? Where is that lady?"

Timidly a hand went up. Zeena pounced on it. "Well, madam, I'd say your mother has had a lot of hard work in her life and she's had a lot of trouble, mostly about money. But there's something else in there that I don't see quite clear yet." Stan looked at the woman who had raised her hand. Farmer's wife. Sunday best, ten years out of style. Zeena could go to town on this one— a natural.

"I'd say, ma'am, that what your mother needs is a good long rest. Mind, I'm not saying how she's going to get it—what with taxes and sickness in the family and doctor's bills piling up. I know how it is because I've had my share of troubles, same as all of us, until I learned how to govern my life by the stars. But I think if you and your brothers—no, you have a couple of sisters, though, haven't you? One sister? Well, if you and your sister can work out some way to let her get a couple weeks' rest I think her health ought to improve mighty quick. But you just keep following a doctor's orders. That is, you better get her to a doctor. I don't think them patent medicines will do her much good. You got to get her to a doctor. Maybe he'll take a few bushels of potatoes or a shoat as part of the bill. Anyhow, I think she'll be all right if you have plenty of faith. If you'll see me right after the demonstration, maybe I can tell you more. And you want to watch the stars and make sure you don't do anything at the wrong time of the month.

"I see now that Mr. Stanton has got a good handful of questions, so if he'll bring them right up here on the stage we'll continue with the readings."

Stan pushed through the crowd to a curtained door on one side of the little proscenium. He passed through. Inside there was a flight of rough board steps leading to the stage. It was dark and smelled of cheap whisky. Under the steps there was a square window opening into the low, boxlike compartment beneath the stage. At the window a bleary, unshaven face blinked out over a spotlessly clean white shirt. One hand held out a bunch of envelopes. Without a word Stan handed the man the envelopes he had collected, received the dummy batch, and in a second was onstage with them. Zeena moved forward a little table containing a metal bowl and a dark bottle.

"We'll ask the gentleman to drop all the questions into this bowl. Now then, people ask me if I have spirit aid in doing what I do. I always tell them that the only spirits I control are the ones in this bottle—spirits of alcohol. I'm going to pour a little on your questions and drop a match into the bowl. Now you can see them burning, and that's the last of them. So anybody who was afraid someone would find out what he wrote or that I was going to handle his question can just forget it. I've never touched them. I don't have to because I get an impression right away."

Stan had backed to one corner of the stage and stood watching the audience quietly as they strained their necks upward, hanging on every word of the seeress. In the floor, which was a few inches above their eye level, was a square hole. Zeena stroked her forehead, covering her eyes with her hand. At the opening appeared a pad of paper, a grimy thumb holding it, on which was scrawled in crayon, "What to do with wagon? J. E. Giles."

Zeena looked up, folding her arms with decision. "I get an impression— It's a little cloudy still but it's getting clearer. I get the initials *J . . . E . . . G.* I believe it's a gentleman. Is that right? Will the person who has those initials raise his hand, please?"

An old farmer lifted a finger as gnarled as a grapevine. "Here, ma'am."

"Ah, there you are. Thank you, Mr. *Giles*. The name *is* Giles, isn't it?"

The crowd sucked in its breath. "I thought so. Now then, Mr.

Giles, you have a problem, isn't that right?" The old man's head wagged solemnly. Stan noted the deep creases in his red neck. Old sodbuster. Sunday clothes. White shirt, black tie. What he wears at funerals. Tie already tied—he hooks it onto his collar button. Blue serge suit—Sears, Roebuck or a clothing store in town.

"Let me see," Zeena went on, her hand straying to her forehead again. "I see— Wait. I see green trees and rolling land. It's plowed land. Fenced in."

The old man's jaw hung open, his eyes frowning with concentration, trying not to miss a single word.

"Yes, green trees. Probably willow trees near a crick. And I see something under those trees. A— It's a wagon."

Watching, Stan saw him nod, rapt.

"An old, blue-bodied wagon under those trees."

"By God, ma'am, it's right there this minute."

"I thought so. Now you have a problem on your mind. You are thinking of some decision you have to make connected with that wagon, isn't that so? You are thinking about what to do with the wagon. Now, Mr. Giles, I would like to give you a piece of advice: don't sell that old blue-bodied wagon."

The old man shook his head sternly. "No, ma'am, I won't. Don't belong to me!"

There was a snicker in the crowd. One young fellow laughed out loud. Zeena drowned him out with a full-throated laugh of her own. She rallied, "Just what I wanted to find out, my friend. Folks, here we have an honest man and that's the only sort I want to do any business with. Sure, he wouldn't think of selling what wasn't his, and I'm mighty glad to hear it. But let me ask you just one question, Mr. Giles. Is there anything the matter with that wagon?"

"Spring's broke under the seat," he muttered, frowning.

"Well, I get an impression that you are wondering whether to get that spring fixed before you return the wagon or whether to return it with the spring broken and say nothing about it. Is that it?"

"That's it, ma'am!" The old farmer looked around him triumphantly. He was vindicated.

"Well, I'd say you had just better let your conscience be your guide in that matter. I would be inclined to talk it over with the man you borrowed it from and find out if the spring was weak when he loaned it to you. You ought to be able to work it out all right."

Stan quietly left the stage and crept down the steps behind the draperies. He squeezed under the steps and came out beneath the stage. Dead grass and the light coming through chinks in the box walls, with the floor over his head. It was hot, and the reek of whisky made the air sweetly sick.

Pete sat at a card table under the stage trap. Before him were envelopes Stan had passed him on his way up to the seeress; he was snipping the ends off with scissors, his hands shaking. When he saw Stan he grinned shamefacedly.

Above them Zeena had wound up the "readings" and gone into her pitch: "Now then, folks, if you really want to know how the stars affect your life, you don't have to pay a dollar, nor even a half; I have here a set of astrological readings, all worked out for each and every one of you. Let me know your date of birth and you get a forecast of future events complete with character reading, vocational guidance, lucky numbers, lucky days of the week, and the phases of the moon most conducive to your prosperity and success. I've only a limited amount of time, folks, so let's not delay. They're only a quarter, first come, first served and while they last, because I'm getting low."

Stan slipped out of the sweatbox, quietly parted the curtains, stepped into the comparatively cooler air of the main tent, and sauntered over toward the soft drink stand.

Magic is all right, but if only I knew human nature like Zeena. She has the kind of magic that ought to take anybody right to the top. It's a convincer—that act of hers. Yet nobody can do it, cold. It takes years to get that kind of smooth talk, and she's never stumped. I'll have to try and pump her and get wised up. She's a smart dame, all right. Too bad she's tied to a rumdum like Pete who can't even get his rhubarb up any more; so everybody says. She isn't a bad-looking dame, even if she is a little old.

Wait a minute, wait a minute. Maybe here's where we start to climb. . . .

CARD III

# The High Priestess

*Queen of borrowed light who guards a shrine between the pillars Night and Day.*

BEYOND the flowing windshield the taillight of the truck ahead wavered ruby-red in the darkness. The windshield wiper's tock-tock-tock was hypnotic. Sitting between the two women, Stan remembered the attic at home on a rainy day—private, shut off from prying eyes, close, steamy, intimate.

Molly sat next to the door on his right, leaning her head against the glass. Her raincoat rustled when she crossed her legs. In the driver's seat Zeena bent forward, peering between the swipes of the wiper, following blindly the truck that held the snake box and the gear for the geek show, Bruno's weights, and Martin's baggage with the tattoo outfit. The geek, with his bottle, had crawled into a little cavern made by the piled gear and folded canvas.

In her own headlights, when the procession stopped at a crossing, Zeena could see Bruno's chunky form in a slicker swing from the cab and plod around to the back to look at the gear and make sure the weights were fast. Then he came over and stepped on the running board. Zeena cranked down the window on her side. "Hi, Dutchy—wet enough for you?"

"Joost about," he said softly. "How is things back here? How is Pete?"

"Right in back of us here having a snooze on the drapes. You reckon we'll try putting up in this weather?"

Bruno shook his head. His attention crept past Zeena and Stan, and for a moment his eyes lingered sadly on Molly, who had not turned her head.

"I joost want to make sure everything is okay." He turned back into the rain, crossing the streaming beam of the headlights and vanishing in the dark. The truck ahead began to move; Zeena shifted gears.

"He's a fine boy," she said at last. "Molly, you ought to give Bruno a chance."

Molly said, "No, thanks. I'm doing okay. No, thanks."

"Go on—you're a big girl now. Time you was having some fun in this world. Bruno could treat you right, by the looks of him. When I was a kid I had a beau that was a lumberjack—he was built along the lines of Bruno. And oh, boy!"

As if suddenly aware that her thigh was pressed close to Stan's, Molly squeezed farther into the corner. "No, thanks. I'm having fun now."

Zeena sighed gustily. "Take your time, kid. Maybe you just ain't met the right fella. And Stan here ought to be ashamed of himself. Why, me and Pete was married when I was seventeen. Pete wasn't much older'n Stan. How old are you, Stan?"

"Twenty-one," Stan said, keeping his voice low.

Approaching a curve, Zeena braced herself. Stan could feel the muscles of her thigh tighten as she worked the wheel. "Them was the days. Pete was working a crystal act in vaudeville. God, he was handsome. In a soup and fish he looked about two feet taller than in his street clothes. He wore a little black beard and a turban. I was working in the hotel when he checked in and I was that green I asked him when I brought in the towels if he'd tell my fortune. I'd never had my fortune told. He looked in my hand and told me something very exciting was going to happen to me involving a tall, dark man. I got the giggles. It was only because he was so good-looking. I wasn't bashful around men. Never was. I couldn't have kept that hotel job a minute if I had been. But the best I'd been hoping for was to hook some gambler or race-track man—hoping he would help me get on the stage."

Suddenly Molly spoke. "My dad was a race-track man. He knew a lot about horses. He didn't die broke."

"Well, now," Zeena said, taking her eyes from the point of ruby light ahead long enough to send Molly a warm look in the darkness. "What d'you know. Oh, the gamblers was the great sheiks in my day. Any gal who could knock herself off a gambling man was doing something. We started when we were fourteen or fifteen. Lordy, that was fifteen years ago! Seems like yesterday some ways and like a million years in others. But the gamblers were the heartbreakers. Say, honey—I'll bet your dad was handsome, eh? Girls generally take after their fathers."

"You bet he was handsome. Daddy was the best-looking man I ever saw. I always said I'd never get married until I found a man as good-looking as Daddy—and as sweet. He was grand."

"Umm. Tall, dark, and handsome. Guess that lets you out, Stan. I don't mean about being tall. You're tall enough. But Molly likes 'em dark."

"I could get some hair dye," Stan said.

"Nope. Nope, never do. That might fool the public, Goldy Locks, but it would never fool a wife. Less'n you wanted to dye all over." She threw back her head and laughed. Stan found himself laughing too, and even Molly joined in.

"Nope," Zeena went on, "Pete was a real brunette all over; and, boy, could he love. We got married second season I traveled with him. He had me doing the back-of-the-house steal with the envelopes at first, in an usherette's uniform. Then we worked out a two-person act. He worked the stage, with his crystal, and I worked the audience. We used a word code at first and he used to ring in that part of the act as a stall while another girl was copying out the questions backstage. I'd go out and have people give me articles and Pete would look into his crystal and describe them. When we started we only used about ten different things and it was simple, but half the time I would get mixed up and then Pete would do some tall ad-libbing. But I learned. You should of seen our act when we were working the Keith time. By God, we could practically send a telegram word by word, and nobody could tumble, it was that natural, what we said."

"Why didn't you stay in vaudeville?" Stan asked intently. Suddenly he knew he had said the wrong thing; but there was no way to recall it, so he kept quiet.

Zeena paid close attention to her driving for a moment and then she rallied. "Pete's nerve began to go back on him." She turned and looked back into the rear of the van at the curled, sleeping figure, covered with a raincoat. Then she went on, dropping her voice. "He began muffing the code and he always needed a few shots before going on. Booze and mentalism don't mix. But we do as well in the carny, figuring up the net at the end of the year. And we don't have to cut no dash—living in swell hotels and all that. Horoscopes are easy to pitch and cost you about twenty-five a thousand. And we can take it easy in the winter. Pete don't drink much then. We got a shack down in Florida and he likes it down there. I do a little tea-leaf reading and one winter I worked a mitt camp in Miami. Palmistry always goes good in a town like Miami."

"I like Miami," Molly said softly. "Dad and I used to go there for the races at Hialeah and Tropical Park. It's a grand place."

"Any place is grand, long as you got the old do-re-mi in the grouch bag," Zeena said. "Say, this must be it. They're turning. I can tell you I ain't going to sleep in the truck tonight. Little Zeena's going to get her a room with a bathtub if they got any in this town. What say, kid?"

"Anything suits me," Molly said. "I'd love to have a hot bath."

Stan had a vision of what Molly would look like in the bathtub. Her body would be milk-white and long-limbed there in the water and a black triangle of shadow and her breasts with rosy tips. He would stand looking down at her and then bend over and she would reach soapy arms up but she would have to be someone else and he would have to be someone else, he thought savagely, because he had never managed to do it yet and always something held him back or the girl seemed to freeze up or suddenly he didn't want her any more once it was within reach and besides there was never the time or the place was wrong and besides it took a lot of dough and a car and all kinds of stuff and then they would expect you to marry them right away and they would probably get a kid the first thing. . . .

"Here we are, chillun," Zeena said.

The rain had slackened to a drizzle. In the lights of headlamps the roughnecks were busy tearing canvas from the trucks. Stan threw his slicker over his shoulders, went around to open the rear doors of the truck. He crawled in and gently shook Pete by the ankle. "Pete, wake up. We're here. We've got to put up."

"Oh, lemme sleep five minutes more."

"Come on, Pete. Zeena says to give us a hand putting up."

He suddenly threw off the raincoat which covered him and sat up shivering. "Just a minute, kid. Be right with you." He crawled stiffly from the truck and stood shaking, tall and stooped, in the cool night air. From one pocket he drew a bottle, offering it to Stan, who shook his head. Pete took a pull, then another, and corked the bottle. Then he drew the cork out, finished it, and heaved it into the night. "Dead soldier."

The floodlights were up and the carny boss had laid out the midway with his marking stakes. Stan shouldered planks that fitted together to make Zeena's stage and drew one bundle of them from the van.

The top of the Ten-in-One was going up. Stan gave a hand on the hoist, while watery dawn showed over the trees and in houses on the edge of the fair grounds lights began to snap on in bedrooms, then in kitchens.

In the growing lavender of daybreak the carny took shape. Booths sprang up, the cookhouse sent the perfume of coffee along the dripping air. Stan paused, his shirt stuck to him with sweat, a comfortable glow in the muscles of his arms and back. And his old man had wanted him to go into real estate!

Inside the Ten-in-One tent Stan and Pete set up the stage for the mental act. They got the curtains hung, moved the bridge table and a chair under the stage, and stowed away the cartons of horoscopes.

Zeena returned. In the watery gold light of morning lines showed around her eyes, but she held herself as straight as a tent pole. "Got me a whole damn bridal suite—two rooms and bawth. C'mon over, both of you, and have a good soak."

Pete needed a shave, and his gaunt, angular face seemed stretched tighter over his bones. "I'd like to, sugar. Only I got to do a few little chores first in town. I'll see you later on."

"It's 28 Locust Lane. You got enough dough?"

"You might let me have a couple of dollars from the treasury."

"Okay, honey. But get some coffee into you first. Promise Zeena you'll have breakfast."

Pete took the money and put it carefully away in a billfold. "I shall probably have a small glass of iced orange juice, two three-minute eggs, melba toast and coffee," he said, his voice suddenly vibrant. Then he seemed to fade. He took out the billfold and looked in it. "Must make sure I got my money safe," he said in an off-key, strangely childish tone. He started off across the lot toward a shack at the edge of the village. Zeena watched him go.

"I'll bet that joint is a blind pig," she said to Stan. "Pete's sure a real clairvoyant when it comes to locating hidden treasure—long as it gurgles when you shake it. Well, you coming back and clean up? Look at you! Your shirt's sticking to you with sweat!"

As they walked, Stan breathed in the morning. Mist hung over the hills beyond the town, and from a slope rising from the other side of the road came the gentle tonk of a cowbell. Stan stopped and stretched his arms.

Zeena stopped too. "Never get nothing like this working the two-a-day. Honest, you know, Stan, I'd get homesick just to hear a cow moo."

The sun, breaking through, sparkled in wagon ruts still deep with rain. Stan took her arm to help her across the puddles. Under the warm, smooth rubber of the raincoat he pressed the soft bulge of her breast. He could feel the heat steaming up over his face where the cool wind struck it.

"You're awful nice to have around, Stan. You know that?"

He stopped walking. They were out of sight of the carnival grounds. Zeena was smiling at something inside herself. Awkwardly his arm went around her and he kissed her. It was lots different from kissing high-school girls. The warm, intimate searching of her mouth left him weak and dizzy. They broke apart and Stan said, "Wow."

Zeena let her hand stay for an instant pressed against his cheek; then she turned and they walked on, hand in hand.

"Where's Molly?" he asked after a while.

"Pounding her ear. I talked the old gal that has the house into giving us the two rooms for the price of one. While I was waiting for her to put up her husband's lunch I took a quick peek in the family Bible and got all their birth dates down pat. I told her right off that she was Aries—March 29th. Then I gave her a reading that just set her back on her heels. We got a real nice room. Always pays to keep your eyes open, I always say. The kid had her a good soak and hit the hay. She'll be pounding her ear. She's a fine kid, if she could only grow up some and stop yelping for her daddy every time she has a hangnail. But she'll get over it, I reckon. Wait till you see the size of these rooms."

The room reminded Stan of home. The old house on Linden Street and the big brass bedstead in his parents' room, where it was all tumbled and smelling of perfume on Mother's pillow and of hair restorer on his father's side.

Zeena threw off her raincoat, rolled a newspaper into a tight bar, tied it with string in the middle and hung the coat up on a hook in the closet. She pulled off her shoes and stretched out on the bed, reaching her arms wide. Then she drew out her hairpins and the brassy hair which had been in a neat double roll around her head fell in pigtails. Swiftly she unbraided them and let the hair flow around her on the pillow.

Stan said, "I guess I'd better get that bath. I'll see if there's any hot water left. He hung his coat and vest on a chairback. When he looked up he saw that Zeena had her eyes on him. Her lids were partly closed. One arm was bent under her head and she was smiling, a sweet, possessive smile.

He came over to her and sat beside her on the edge of the bed. Zeena covered his hand with hers and suddenly he bent and kissed her. This time there was no need for them to stop and they didn't. Her hand slid inside his shirt and felt the smooth warmth of his back tenderly.

"Wait, honey. Not yet. Kiss me some more."

"What if Molly should wake up?"

"She won't. She's young. You couldn't wake that kid up. Don't worry about things, honey. Just take it easy and slow."

All the things Stan had imagined himself saying and doing at such a time did not fit. It was thrilling and dangerous and his heart beat so hard he felt it would choke him.

"Take all your things off, honey, and hang 'em on the chair, neat."

Stan wondered that he didn't feel in the least ashamed now that this was it. Zeena stripped off her stockings, unhooked her dress and drew it leisurely over her head. Her slip followed.

At last she lay back, her bent arm under her head, and beckoned him to come to her. "Now then, Stan honey, you can let yourself go."

"It's getting late."

"Sure is. You got to get your bath and get back. Folks'll think Zeena's gone and seduced you."

"They'd be right."

"Damned if they wouldn't." She raised herself on her elbows and let her hair fall down on each side of his face and kissed him lightly. "Get along with you. Skat, now."

"Can't. You're holding me pinned down."

"Try'n get away."

"Can't. Too heavy."

"See'f you can wiggle loose."

There was a knock at the door, a gentle, timid tapping. Zeena threw her hair out of her eyes. Stan started but she laid one finger on his lips. She swung off the bed gracefully and pulled Stan up by one hand. Then she handed him his trousers, underwear, and socks and pushed him into the bathroom.

Behind the bathroom door Stan crouched, his ear to the panel, his heart hammering with alarm. He heard Zeena get her robe out of a bag and take her time about answering the tap. Then the hall door opened. Pete's voice.

"Sorry t'wake you, sugar. Only—" His voice sounded thicker.

"Only, had little shopping to do. I sorta forgot 'bout getting breakfast."

There was the snap of a pocketbook opening. "Here's a buck, honey. Now make sure it's breakfast."

"Cross my heart, hope die."

Stan heard Zeena's bare feet approach the bathroom. "Stan," she called, "hurry up in there. I want to get some sleep. Get out of that tub and fall into your pants." To Pete she said, "The kid's had a hard night, tearing down and putting up in all that rain. I expect he's fallen asleep in the tub. Maybe you better not wait for him."

The door closed. Stan straightened up. She had never turned a hair, lying to Pete about him being in the bathtub. It comes natural in women, he thought. That's the way they all do when they have guts enough. That's the way they would all like to do. He found himself trembling. Quietly he drew a tub of hot water.

When it was half full he lay in it and closed his eyes. Well, now he knew. This was what all the love-nest murderers killed over and what people got married to get. This was why men left home and why women got themselves dirty reputations. This was the big secret. Now I know. But there's nothing disappointing about the feeling. It's okay.

He let his hands trail in the hot water and splashed little ripples over his chest. He opened his eyes. Drawing his hand out of the steamy warmth he gazed at it a moment and then carefully took from the back of it a hair that gleamed brassy-gold, like a tiny, crinkled wire. Zeena was a natural blonde.

The weeks went by. The Ackerman-Zorbaugh Monster Shows crawled from town to town, the outline of the sky's edge around the fair grounds changing but the sea of upturned faces always the same.

The first season is always the best and the worst for a carny. Stan's muscles hardened and his fingers developed great surety, his voice greater volume. He put a couple of coin sleights in the act that he would never have had the nerve to try in public before.

Zeena taught him many things, some of them about magic. "Misdirection is the whole works, honey. You don't need no fancy production boxes and trap doors and trick tables. I've always let on that a man that will spend his time learning misdirection can just reach in his pocket and put something in a hat and then go ahead and take it out again and everybody will sit back and gasp, wondering where it came from."

"Did you ever do magic?" he asked her.

Zeena laughed. "Not on your sweet life. There's very few girls goes in for magic. And that's the reason. A gal spends all her time learning how to attract attention to herself. Then in magic she has to unlearn all that and learn how to get the audience to look at something else. Strain's too great. The dolls can never make it. I couldn't. I've always stuck to the mental business. It don't hurt anybody—makes plenty of friends for you wherever you go. Folks are always crazy to have their fortunes told, and what the hell— You cheer 'em up, give 'em something to wish and hope for. That's all the preacher does every Sunday. Not much different, being a fortuneteller and a preacher, way I look at it. Everybody hopes for the best and fears the worst and the worst is generally what happens but that don't stop us from hoping. When you stop hoping you're in a bad way."

Stan nodded. "Has Pete stopped hoping?"

Zeena was silent and her childish blue eyes were bright. "Sometimes I think he has. Pete's scared of something—I think he got good and scared of himself a long time ago. That's what made him such a wiz as a crystal-reader—for a few years. He wished like all get out that he really could read the future in the ball. And when he was up there in front of them he really believed he was doing it. And then all of a sudden he began to see that there wasn't no magic anywhere to lean on and he had nobody to lean on in the end but himself—not me, not his friends, not Lady Luck—just himself. And he was scared he would let himself down."

"So he did?"

"Yeah. He did."

"What's going to happen to him?"

Zeena bristled. "Nothing's going to happen to him. He is a sweet man, down deep. Long as he lasts I'll stick to him. If it hadn't been for Pete I'd of probably ended up in a crib house. Now I got a nice trade that'll always be in demand as long as there's a soul in the world worried about where next month's rent is coming from. I can always get along. And take Pete right along with me."

Across the tent the talker, Clem Hoately, had mounted the platform of Major Mosquito and started his lecture. The Major drew back one tiny foot and aimed a kick with deadly accuracy at Hoately's shin. It made the talker stammer for a moment. The midget was snarling like an angry kitten.

"The Major is a nasty little guy," Stan said.

"Sure he is. How'd you like to be shut up in a kid's body that way? With the marks all yawping at you. It's different in our racket. We're up head and shoulders above the marks. We're better'n they are and they know it. But the Major's a freak born."

"How about Sailor Martin? He's a made freak."

Zeena snorted. "He's just a pecker carrying a man around with it. He started by having a lot of anchors and nude women tattooed on his arms to show the girls how tough he was or something. Then he got that battleship put on his chest and he was off. He was like a funny paper, with his shirt off, and he figured he might as well make his skin work for him. If he was ever in the Navy, I was born in a convent."

"He doesn't seem to be making much time with your Electric Chair pal."

Zeena's eyes flashed. "He better not. That kid's not going to get it until she runs into some guy that'll treat her right. I'll see to that. I'd beat the be-Jesus out of any snot-nose that went monkeying around Molly."

"You and who else?"

"Me and Bruno."

Evansburg, Morristown, Linklater, Cooley Mills, Ocheketawney, Bale City, Boeotia, Sanders Falls, Newbridge.

Coming: Ackerman-Zorbaugh Monster Shows. Auspices Tall

Cedars of Zion, Caldwell Community Chest, Pioneer Daughters of Clay County, Kallakie Volunteer Fire Department, Loyal Order of Bison.

Dust when it was dry. Mud when it was rainy. Swearing, steaming, sweating, scheming, bribing, bellowing, cheating, the carny went its way. It came like a pillar of fire by night, bringing excitement and new things into the drowsy towns—lights and noise and the chance to win an Indian blanket, to ride on the ferris wheel, to see the wild man who fondles those rep-tiles as a mother would fondle her babes. Then it vanished in the night, leaving the trodden grass of the field and the debris of popcorn boxes and rusting tin ice-cream spoons to show where it had been.

Stan was surprised, and gnawed by frustration. He had had Zeena—but how few chances ever came his way for him to have her again. She was the wise one, who knew all the ropes of the carny and everywhere else. She knew. And yet, in the tight world of the carnival, she could find very few opportunities to do what her eyes told Stan a dozen times a day that she would take pleasure in doing.

Pete was always there, always hanging around, apologetic, crestfallen, hands trembling, perfumed with bootleg, always a reminder of what he had been.

Zeena would beg off from a rendezvous with Stan to sew a button on Pete's shirt. Stan couldn't understand it; the more he thought about it the more confused and bitter he got. Zeena was using him to satisfy herself, he kept repeating. Then the thought struck him that maybe Zeena played a game of make-believe with him, and actually saw over his shoulder a shadow of Pete as he had been—handsome and straight and wearing his little black beard.

The thought would strike him right in the middle of his act and his patter would turn into a snarl.

One day Clem Hoately was waiting beside the platform when he came down after the last show. "Whatever's eating you, kid, you better turn it off while you're on the box. If you can't be a trouper, pack up your junk and beat it. Magicians come two for a nickel."

Stan had acquired enough carny to reach over, take a half dollar from Hoately's lapel, and vanish it in his other hand before walking away. But the call-down by the older man burnt into him. No woman or man his own age could drive the gall into his system like that. It took an old bastard, particularly when the stubble on his face looked silvery like fungus growing on a corpse. The bastard.

Stan went to sleep that night on his cot in the Ten-in-One tent with fantasies of slowly roasting Hoately over a fire, inquisition fashion.

Next day, just as they were about to open, Hoately stopped by his platform while Stan was opening a carton of pitch books.

"Keep them half-dollar tricks in the act, son. They got a nice flash. The marks love it."

Stan grinned and said, "You bet." When the first tip came wandering in he gave them all he had. His sale of the magic books almost doubled. He was on top of the world all day. But then came night.

By night Zeena's body plagued his dreams and he lay under the blanket, worn out and with his eyes burning for sleep, thinking back and having her over and over in memory.

Then he waited until closing one night. He stepped back of the curtains on her miniature stage. Zeena had taken off the white silk robe and was putting her hair up, her shoulders white and round and tantalizing over her slip. He took her roughly in his arms and kissed her and she pushed him away. "You beat it out of here. I got to get dressed."

"All right. You mean we're washed up?" he said.

Her face softened and she laid her palm gently against his cheek. "Got to learn to call your shots, honey. We ain't married folks. We got to be careful. Only one person I'm married to and that's Pete. You're a sweet boy and I'm fond as all hell of you. Maybe a little too fond of you. But we got to have some sense. Now you be good. We'll get together one of these days—or nights. And we'll have fun. That's a promise. I'll lay it on the line just as soon as ever we can."

"I wish I could believe it."

She slid her cool arms around his neck and gave him the promise between his lips, warm, sweet, and searching. His heart began to pound.

"Tonight?"

"We'll see."

"Make it tonight."

She shook her head. "I got to make Pete write some letters. He can't if he gets too loaded and he's got some that need answering. You can't let your friends down in show business. You find that out when you get on your uppers and have to hit 'em for a loan. Maybe tomorrow night."

Stan turned away, rebellious and savage, feeling as if the whole surface of his mind had been rubbed the wrong way. He hated Zeena and her Pete.

On his way over to the cookhouse for his supper he passed Pete. Pete was sober and shaky and profane. Zeena would have hidden his bottle in view of the letter-writing session. His eyes had begun to pop.

"Got a spare dollar on you, kid?" Pete whispered.

Zeena came up behind them. "You two boys stay right here and have your supper," she said, pushing them toward the cookhouse. "I've got to find a drugstore in this burg that keeps open late. Nothing like a girl's being careful of her beauty, huh? I'll be right back, honey," she said to Pete, fastening a loose button of his shirt. "We got to catch up on our correspondence."

Stan ate quickly, but Pete pushed the food around, wiped his mouth on the back of his hand, and wiped his hand carefully with his napkin.

He crushed the napkin into a hard, paper wad and aimed it at the cook's back with a curse.

"You got a spare fin, kid?"

"No. Let's get on back to the tent. You got the new Billboard to read. Zeena left it under the stage."

They walked back in silence.

Stan put up his cot and watched the Ten-in-One settle down

for the night. Under the astrology stage a single light burned, winking through the cracks of the boards. Inside Pete was sitting at the table, trying to read the Billboard and going over and over the same paragraph.

Why couldn't Zeena have let him accompany her to the store, Stan asked himself. Then, on the way, maybe they could have warmed up and she would have forgotten about Pete and writing letters.

Zeena had slipped the bottle under the seat of Major Mosquito's chair. Stan jumped down from his own platform and crossed the tent softly. The Major's tiny cot was just above his head; he could hear above him the quick breathing which sounded soprano. His hand found the bottle, drew it out.

There was only an inch or two left in it. Stan turned back and crept up the steps of Zeena's theater. A few moments later he came down and squeezed into the understage compartment. The bottle, more than half full now, was in his hand.

"How about a drink, Pete?"

"Glory be to God!" The flask was nearly snatched from his hand. Pete jerked the cork, holding it out to Stan automatically. The next instant he had it in his mouth and his Adam's apple was working. He drained it and handed it back. "God almighty. A friend in need as the saying goes. I'm afraid I didn't leave much for you, Stan."

"That's all right. I don't care for any right now."

Pete shook his head and seemed to pull himself together. "You're a good kid, Stan. You got a fine act. Don't let anything ever keep you out of the big time. You can go places, Stan, if you don't get bogged down. You should have seen us when we were on top. Used to pack 'em in. They'd sit through four other acts just to see us. Boy, I can remember all the times we had our names on the marquee in letters a foot high—top billing —everywhere we went. We had plenty fun, too.

"But you— Why, kid, the greatest names in the business started right where you are now. You're the luckiest kid in the world. You got a good front—you're a damn good-looking kid and I wouldn't crap you up. You can talk. You can do sleights. You got everything. Great magician someday. Only don't let the carny . . ." His eyes were glazing over. He stopped speaking and sat rigid.

"Why don't you turn out the light and take it easy until Zeena gets back?" Stan suggested.

A grunt was his only answer. Then the man stood up and threw back his shoulders. "Kid, you should have seen us when we played the Keith time!"

Good God, is this idiot never going to pass out, Stan thought. Beyond the wooden walls of the understage compartment and the canvas of the tent was the sound of a car's engine starting, the whirr of the starter rising through the night as the nameless driver pressed it. The motor caught and Stan heard the gears.

"You know, kid—" Pete drew himself up until his head nearly touched the boards of the ceiling. The alcohol seemed to stiffen his back. His chin came up commandingly. "Stan, lad like you could be a great mentalist. Study human nature!" He took a long, last pull at the bottle and finished it. Barely swaying, he opened his eyes wide and swallowed.

"Here—chord from the orchestra, amber spot—and I'm on. Make my spiel, give 'em one laugh, plenty mystery. Then I jump right into the reading. Here's m'crystal." He focused his eyes on the empty whisky bottle and Stan watched him with an uneasy twinge. Pete seemed to be coming alive. His eyes became hot and intent.

Then his voice altered and took on depth and power. He passed his left hand slowly over the bottle's surface. "Since the dawn of history," he began, his words booming in the wooden box-room, "mankind has sought to see behind the veil which hides him from tomorrow. And through the ages certain men have gazed into the polished crystal and seen. Is it some property of the crystal itself? Or does the gazer use it merely to turn his eyes inward? Who can tell? But visions come. Slowly, shifting their form, visions come . . ."

Stan found himself watching the empty bottle in which a single pale drop slanted across the bottom. He could not take his eyes away, so contagious was the other's absorption.

"Wait! The shifting shapes begin to clear. I see fields of

grass and rolling hills. And a boy—a boy is running on bare feet through the fields. A dog is with him."

Too swiftly for his wary mind to check him, Stan whispered the words, "Yes. Gyp."

Pete's eyes burned down into the glass. "Happiness then . . . but for a little while. Now dark mists . . . sorrow. I see people moving . . . one man stands out . . . evil . . . the boy hates him. Death and the wish of death . . ."

Stan moved like an explosion. He snatched for the bottle; it slipped and fell to the ground. He kicked it into a corner, his breath coming quick and rapid.

Pete stood for a moment, gazing at his empty hand, then dropped his arm. His shoulders sagged. He crumpled into the folding chair, resting his elbows on the card table. When he raised his face to Stan the eyes were glazed, the mouth slack. "I didn't mean nothing, boy. You ain't mad at me, are ya? Just fooling around. Stock reading—fits everybody. Only you got to dress it up." His tongue had thickened and he paused, his head drooping, then snapping up again. "Everybody had some trouble. Somebody they wanted to kill. Usually for a boy it's the old man. What's childhood? Happy one minute, heartbroke the next. Every boy had a dog. Or neighbor's dog—"

His head fell forward on his forearms. "Just old drunk. Just lush. Lord . . . Zeena be mad. Don't you let on, son, you gimme that little drink. She be mad at you, too." He began to cry softly.

Stan felt his stomach heave with disgust. He turned without a word and left the steaming compartment. In comparison, the air of the Ten-in-One tent, darkened now and still, felt cool.

It seemed as if half the night had worn away before Zeena did come back. Stan met her, talking in whispers so as not to disturb the others in the tent, now snoring heavily in their bunks.

"Where's Pete?"

"Passed out."

"Where'd he get it?"

"I—I don't know. He was over by the geek's layout."

"God damn it, Stan, I told you to watch him. Oh, well, I'm

tuckered out myself. Might as well let him sleep it off. Tomorrow's another day."

"Zeena."

"What is it, honey?"

"Let me walk you home."

"It ain't far and I don't want you getting ideas. The landlady of this dump has a face like a snapping turtle. We don't want to start no trouble in this burg. We've had enough trouble with the wheels pretty near getting shut down for gambling. This is bluenose."

They had left the tent and the darkened midway stretched out ahead of them, light still streaming from the cookhouse. "I'll walk you over," Stan said. There was a leaden feeling in his chest and he fought to throw it off. He laced his fingers in hers and she did not draw her hand away.

In the shadow of the first trees on the edge of the lot they stopped and kissed and Zeena clung to him. "Gosh, honey, I've missed you something awful. I guess I need more loving than I thought. But not in the room. That old battle-ax is on the prowl."

Stan took her arm and started along the road. The moon had set. They passed a field on a little rise and then the road dipped between clay banks with fields above road level. "Let's go up there," Stan whispered.

They climbed the bank and spread their coats out on the grass.

Stan reached the Ten-in-One tent just before light. He crept into his bunk and was out like a shot. Then something was chirping in his ear and tugging at his shoulder. A voice like a fiddle's E string was cutting through the layers of fatigue and the void which was in him from having emptied his nerves.

"Kid, wake up! Wake up, you big lump!" The shrill piping got louder.

Stan growled and opened his eyes. The tent was tawny gold with sun on the outside of it above him. The pestiferous force at his shoulder was Major Mosquito, his blond hair carefully dampened and brushed over his bulging baby forehead.

"Stan, get up! Pete's dead!"

"What?"

Stan shot off the bunk and felt for his shoes. "What happened to him?"

"Just croaked—the stinking old rum-pot. Got into that bottle of wood alcohol Zeena keeps to burn the phoney questions. It was all gone or pretty near. And Pete's dead as a herring. His mouth's hanging open like the Mammoth Cave. Come on, take a look. I kicked him in the ribs a dozen times and he never moved. Come and look at him."

Without speaking Stan laced up his shoes, carefully, correctly, taking great pains with them. He kept fighting back the thought that wouldn't stay out of his mind. Then it broke over him like a thunder storm: They'll hang me. They'll hang me. They'll hang me. Only I didn't mean it. I only wanted to pass him out. I didn't know it was wood— They'll hang me. I didn't mean it. They'll—"

He leaped from the platform and pressed through the knot of show people around the seeress's stage. Zeena stepped out and stood facing them, tall and straight and dry-eyed.

"He's gone all right. He was a good guy and a swell trouper. I told him that alky was bad. Only last night I hid his bottle on him—" She stopped and suddenly ducked back through the curtains.

Stan turned and pushed through the crowd. He walked out of the tent into the early sun and kept on to the edge of the grounds where the telephone poles beside the road carried their looping strands off into the distance.

His foot clinked against something bright and he picked up a burned-out electric bulb which lay in the ashes of a long-dead fire. It was iridescent and smoky inside, dark as a crystal ball on a piece of black velvet. Stan kept it in his hand, looking for a rock or a fence post. His diaphragm seemed to be pressing up around his lungs and keeping him from drawing his breath. On one of the telephone poles was a streaked election poster, carrying the gaunt face of the candidate, white hair falling dankly over one eyebrow, lines of craft and rapacity around the mouth that the photographer couldn't quite hide.

"Elect MACKINSEN for SHERIFF. HONEST—INCOR-
RUPTIBLE—FEARLESS."

Stan drew back his arm and let the bulb fly. "You son-of-a-
bitch whoremonger!" Slowly, as if by the very intensity of his
attention he had slowed down time itself, the bulb struck the
printed face and shattered, the sparkling fragments sailing high
in the air and glittering as they fell.

As if an abscess inside him had broken, Stan could breathe
again and the knot of fear loosened. He could never fear again
with the same agony. He knew it. It would never come again as
bad as that. His mind, clear as the bright air around him, took
over, and he began to think.

CARD IV

# The World

*Within a circling garland a girl dances; the beasts of the Apocalypse look on.*

SINCE morning, Stan's brain had been full of whirring wheels, grinding away at every possible answer. Where were you when he was over by the geek? On my platform, setting up my cot. What did you do then? Practiced a new move with cards. What move? Front-and-back-hand palm. Where did he go? Under the stage, I guess. You were watching him? Only that he didn't go outside. Where were you when Zeena came back? At the entrance waiting for her. . . .

Now the crowd was thinning out. Outside the stars had misted over and there was a flash of lightning behind the trees. At eleven Hoately stopped the bally. The last marks left and the inhabitants of the Ten-in-One smoked while they dressed. At last they gathered with sober faces around Hoately. Only Major Mosquito seemed unaffected. He started to whistle gaily, someone told him to pipe down.

When the last one was ready they filed out and got into cars. Stan rode with Hoately, the Major, Bruno, and Sailor Martin toward the center of town where the undertaker's parlor was located.

"Lucky break the funeral happened on a slow night," the Sailor said. No one answered him.

Then Major Mosquito chirruped, "O death, where is thy sting? O grave, where is thy victory?" He spat. "Why do they have to crap it up with all that stuff? Why can't they just shovel 'em under and let 'em start falling apart?"

"You shut up!" Bruno said thickly. "You talk too much for little fellow."

"Go frig a rubber duck."

"Tough on Zeena," Bruno said to the others. "She is fine woman."

Clem Hoately, driving with one hand carelessly on the wheel, said, "That rum-pot ain't going to be missed by nobody. Not even Zeena after a while. But it makes you take a good think for yourself. I remember that guy when he was big stuff. I ain't touched a drop in over a year now and I ain't going to, either. Seen too much of it."

"Who's going to work the act with Zeena?" Stan asked after a time. "She going to change her act? She could handle the questions herself and work one ahead."

Hoately scratched his head with his free hand. "That ain't too good nowadays. She don't have to change the act. You could work the undercover part. I'll take the house collection. We'll throw the Electric Girl between your spot and Zeena's, give you time to slip in and get set."

"Suits me."

He said it, Stan kept repeating. It wasn't my idea. The Major and Bruno heard him. He said it.

The street was empty and the light from the funeral parlor made a golden wedge on the sidewalk. Behind them the other car drew up. Old Maguire, the Ten-in-One's ticket seller and grinder, got out, then Molly; then Joe Plasky swung himself out on his hands and crossed the sidewalk. He reminded Stan of a frog, moving deliberately.

Zeena met them at the door. She was wearing a new black outfit, a dress with enormous flowers worked on it in jet. "Come on in, folks. I—I got Pete all laid out handsome. I just phoned a reverend and he's coming over. I thought it was nicer to get a reverend if we could, even if Pete wasn't no church man."

They went inside. Joe Plasky fumbled in his pocket and held an envelope up to Zeena. "The boys chipped in for a stone, Zeena. They knew you didn't need the dough but they wanted to do something. I wrote the Billboard this afternoon. They'll carry a box. I just said, 'Mourned by his many friends in show business.'"

She bent down and kissed him. "That's—that's damn sweet of you all. I guess we better get into the chapel. This looks like the reverend coming."

They took their places on folding chairs. The clergyman was a meek, dull little old man, looking sleepy. Embarrassed, too, Stan figured. As if carny folks were not quite human—like they had all left their pants off only he was too polite to let on he noticed.

He put on his glasses. ". . . we brought nothing into this world and it is certain we can carry nothing out. The Lord gave, and the Lord hath taken . . ."

Stan, sitting beside Zeena, tried to concentrate on the words and guess what the reverend was going to say next. Anything to keep from thinking. It's not my fault he's dead. I didn't mean to kill him. I killed him. There it starts again and all day I wasn't feeling anything and I thought I'd lost it.

"Lord, let me know my end, and the number of my days; that I may be certified how long I have to live . . ."

Pete never knew his end. Pete died happy. I did him a favor. He had been dying for years. He was afraid of living and he was trying to ease himself out only I had to go and kill him. I didn't kill him. He killed himself. Sooner or later he would have taken a chance on that wood alky. I only helped him a little. Christ, will I have to think about this damn thing the rest of my life?

Stan slowly turned his head and looked at the others. Molly was sitting with the Major between her and Bruno. In the back row Clem Hoately had his eyes shut. Joe Plasky's face held the shadow of a smile that was too deeply cut into it ever to vanish completely. It was the sort of smile Lazarus must have had afterwards, Stan thought. Sailor Martin had one eye closed.

The sight of the Sailor rushed Stan back to normal. He had done that a hundred times himself, sitting beside his father on the hard pew, watching his mother in a white surplice there in the choir stall with the other ladies. There's a blind spot in your eye and if you shut one eye and then let the gaze of the other travel in a straight line to one side of the preacher's head there will be a point where his head seems to disappear and he seems to be standing there preaching without any head.

Stan looked at Zeena beside him. Her mind was far away somewhere. The reverend speeded up.

"Man that is born of woman hath but a short time to live, and is full of misery. He cometh up and is cut down, like a flower; he fleeth as it were a shadow, and never continueth in one stay. In the midst of life we are in death . . ."

Behind them Major Mosquito heaved a sharp sigh and wriggled, the chair creaking. Bruno said, "Shoosh!"

When they got to the Lord's Prayer Stan found his voice with relief. Zeena must hear it. If she heard it she couldn't suspect him of having anything to do with— Stan lowered his voice and the words came automatically. She mustn't ever think—and yet she had looked at him sharp when he had said Pete was hanging around the geek. She mustn't think. Only he mustn't overplay it. God damn it, this was the time for misdirection if ever there was one. ". . . *for thine is the kingdom, the power and the glory for ever and ever.*"

"Amen."

The undertaker was silently brisk. He removed the coffin lid and set it noiselessly behind the casket. Zeena brought her handkerchief up to her face and turned away. They formed a line and passed by.

Clem Hoately came first, his furrowed face showing nothing. Then Bruno, holding Major Mosquito on his forearm so he could look down and see. Molly came next and Sailor Martin fell in behind her, moving close. Then old Maguire, his cap crushed in his hand. Joe Plasky hopped across the floor, pushing one of the folding chairs. When it came his turn to view the remains he moved the chair into place by the head of the coffin and swung himself up on the seat. He looked down and the smile was still around the corners of his eyes although his mouth was sober. Without thinking he made the sign of the cross.

Stan swallowed hard. It was his turn and there was no way of getting out of it. Joe had hopped to the floor and pushed the chair against the wall; Stan shoved both hands deep into his pockets and approached the casket. He had never seen a corpse; the skin of his scalp prickled at the thought.

He drew his breath and forced himself to look.

It seemed at first like a wax figure in a dress suit. One hand rested easily on the white waistcoat, the other was by the side. It held a round, clear glass ball. The face was rosy—the undertaker had filled out the drawn cheeks and painted the skin until it glowed with a waxen counterfeit of life. But there was something else that hit Stan like a blow between the ribs. Carefully fashioned of crêpe hair and stuck to the chin was a lifelike, neatly trimmed, little black beard.

"For the last demonstration Mamzelle Electra will perform a feat never attempted since Ben Franklin harnessed the lightning with his kite string. Holding the two filaments of a carbon arc light, she will allow the death-dealing current to pass through her body. . . ."

Stan quietly slipped into the compartment below the stage of Zeena, the Woman Who Knows. It no longer smelled of whisky. Stan had installed a piece of canvas as a ground sheet and had cut ventilation scrolls in the sides of the boxlike little room. Over the bridge table and on three sides of it he had erected a cardboard shield so he could open the envelopes and copy the questions on the pad by the light of a flashlight.

The rustle of feet surging around the stage outside, then Zeena's voice in her opening spiel. Stan took a bundle of dummy questions—blank cards in small envelopes—and stood by the window where Hoately would pass behind the curtains.

They parted at the side of the stage; Hoately's hand appeared. Quickly Stan took the collected questions and placed the dummy batch in the hand which vanished upward. Stan heard the creak of feet on the boards above him. He sat down at the table, switched on the shaded flashlight bulb, squared up the pack of envelopes and cut the ends from them with one snip of the scissors. Moving quickly, he shook out the cards and arranged them before him on the table.

Question: "Where is my son?" Handwriting old-fashioned. Woman over sixty, he judged. A good one to open with—the signature was clear and spelled out in full—Mrs. Anna Briggs Sharpley. Stan looked for two more complete names. One was signed to a wiseacre question which he put aside. He reached for the black crayon and the pad, wrote, "Where son?" printed the name swiftly but plainly, and held the pad up to the hole in the stage at Zeena's feet.

"I get the impression of the initial S. Is there a Mrs. Sharpley?"

Stan found himself listening to the answers as if they held a revelation.

"You think of your boy as still a little fellow, the way you knew him when he used to come asking you for a piece of bread with sugar on it. . . ."

Where the hell did Zeena get all that stuff from? She was no more telepathic than that kid, Molly, was electricity proof. The Electric Chair act was gaffed like everything in the carny. But Zeena—

"My dear lady, you must remember that he's a man grown now and probably has children of his own to worry about. You want him to write to you. Isn't that so?"

It was uncanny how Zeena could fish out things just by watching the person's face. Stan got a sudden thrust of cold fear. Of all the people in the world for him to hide anything from, it had to be a mind reader. He laughed a little in spite of his anxiety. But there was something which pulled him toward Zeena more strongly than his fear that she would find out and make him a murderer. How do you get to know so much that you can tell people what they are thinking about just by looking at them? Maybe you had to be born with the gift.

"Is Clarissa here? Clarissa, hold up your hand. That's a good girl. Now Clarissa wants to know if the young fellow she's been going around with is the right one for her to marry. Well, Clarissa, I may disappoint you but I have to speak the truth. You wouldn't want me to tell you no fibs. I don't think this boy is the one for you to marry. Mind, he may be and I don't doubt that he's a mighty fine young man. But something tells me that when the right young fellow comes along you won't ask me, you won't ask anybody—you'll just up and marry him."

That question had come up before and Zeena nearly always answered it the same way. The thought struck Stan that it was not genius after all. Zeena knew people. But people were a lot alike. What you told one you could tell nine out of ten. And there was one out of five that would believe everything you told them and would say yes to anything when you asked them if it was correct because they were the kind of marks that can't say no. Good God, Zeena is working for peanuts! Somewhere in this racket there is a gold mine!

Stan picked up another card and wrote on the pad: "Advise important domestic step, Emma." By God, if she can answer that one she must be a mind reader. He held it up to the trap and listened.

Zeena pattered on for a moment, thinking to herself and then her voice lifted and her heel knocked gently. Stan took down the pad and knew that this would be the blow-off question and he could relax. After this one she would go into the pitch.

"I have time for just one more question. And this is a question that I'm not going to ask anybody to acknowledge. There's a lady here whose first name begins with E. I'm not going to tell her full name because it's a very personal question. But I'm going to ask Emma to think about what she is trying to tell me mentally."

Stan switched off the flashlight, crept out of the understage compartment and tiptoed up the stairs behind the side curtains. Parting them carefully with his fingers he placed his eye to the crack. The marks' faces were a mass of pale circles below him. But at the mention of the name "Emma" he saw one face—a pale, haggard woman who looked forty but might be thirty. The lips parted and the eyes answered for an instant. Then the lips were pressed tight in resignation.

Zeena lowered her voice. "Emma, you have a serious problem. And it concerns somebody very near and dear to you. Or somebody who used to be very near and dear, isn't that right?" Stan saw the woman's head nod involuntarily.

"You are contemplating a serious step—whether to leave this person. And I think he's your husband." The woman bit her under lip. Her eyes grew moist quickly. That kind cries at the drop of a hat, Stan thought. If only she had a million bucks instead of a greasy quarter.

"Now there are two lines of vibration working about this problem. One of them concerns another woman." The tension left the woman's face and a sullen frown of disappointment drew over it. Zeena changed her tack. "But now the impressions get stronger and I can see that while there may have been some woman in the past, right now the problem is something else. I see cards . . . playing cards falling on a table . . . but no, it isn't your husband who's playing. It's the place . . . I get it now, clear as daylight. It's the back room of a saloon."

A sob came from the woman, and people twisted their heads this way and that; but Emma was watching the seeress, unmindful of the others.

"My dear friend, you have a mighty heavy cross to bear. I know all about it and don't you think I don't. But the step that confronts you now is a problem with a good many sides. If your husband was running around with other women and didn't love you that would be one thing. But I get a very strong impression that he does love you—in spite of everything. Oh, I know he acts nasty-mean sometimes but you just ask yourself if any of the blame is yours. Because here's one thing you must never forget: a man drinks because he's unhappy. Isn't anything about liquor that makes a man bad. A man that's happy can take a drink with the boys on Saturday night and come home with his pay safe in his pocket. But when a man's miserable about something he takes a drink to forget it and one isn't enough and he takes another snort and pretty soon the week's pay is all gone and he gets home and sobers up and then his wife starts in on him and he's more miserable than he was before and then his first thought is to go get drunk again and it runs around and around in a circle." Zeena had forgotten the other customers, she had forgotten the pitch. She was talking out of herself. The marks knew it and were hanging on every word, fascinated.

"Before you take that step," she went on, suddenly coming back to the show, "you want to be sure that you've done all you can to make that man happy. Maybe you can't learn what's bothering him. Maybe he don't quite know himself. But try to find it. Because if you leave him you'll have to find some way to take care of yourself and the kids anyhow. Well, why not start in tonight? If he comes home drunk put him to bed. Try talking to him friendly. When a man's drunk he's a lot like a kid. Well, treat him like a son and don't go jumping on him. To-morrow morning let him know that you understand and mother him up a little. Because if that man loves you—" Zeena paused for breath and then rushed on. "If that man loves you it don't matter whether he makes a living or not. It don't matter if he stays sober or not. If you've got a man that really loves you, you hang on to him like grim death for better or worse." There was a catch in her voice and for a long moment silence hung in the air over the waiting crowd. "Hang on—because you'll never regret it as much as you'll regret sending him away and now folks if you really want to know how the stars affect your life you don't have to pay five dollars or even one dollar I have here a set of astrological readings all worked out for each and every one of you let me know your date of birth and you get a forecast of future events complete with character reading, vocational guidance, lucky numbers. . . ."

For the long haul the Ackerman-Zorbaugh Monster Shows took to the railroad. Trucks loaded on flatcars, the carnies themselves loaded into old coaches, the train boomed on through darkness—tearing past solitary jerk towns, past sidings of dark freight empties, over trestles, over bridges where the rivers lay coiling their luminous way through the star-shadowed country-side.

In the baggage car, among piles of canvas and gear, a light burned high up on the wall. A large packing case with auger holes bored in its sides to admit air, stood in the middle of a cleared space. From inside it came intermittent scrapings. At one end of the car the geek lay on a pile of canvas, his ragged, over-alled knees drawn up to his chin.

Around the snake box men made the air gray with smoke.

"I'm staying." Major Mosquito's voice had the insistence of a cricket's.

Sailor Martin screwed up the left side of his face against the smoke of his cigarette and dealt.

"I'm in," Stan said. He had a Jack in the hole. The highest card showing was a ten in the Sailor's hand.

"I'm with you," Joe Plasky said, the Lazarus smile never changing.

Behind Joe sat the hulk of Bruno, his shoulders rounding under his coat. He watched intently, his mouth dropping open as he concentrated on Joe's hand.

"I'm in, too," Martin said. He dealt. Stan got another Jack and pushed in three blues.

"Going to cost you to string along," he said casually.

Martin had dealt himself another ten. "I'll string along."

Major Mosquito, his baby head close to the boxtop, stole another glance at his hole card. "Nuts!"

"Guess it's between you gents," Joe said placidly. Bruno, from behind him, said, "Ja. Let them fight it out. We take it easy this time."

Martin dealt. Two little ones fell between them. Stan threw more blues in. Martin met him and raised him two more.

"I'll see you."

The Sailor threw over his hole card. A ten. He reached for the pot.

Stan smiled and counted his chips. At a sound from the Major all of them jumped. "Hey!" It was like a long-drawn fiddle scrape.

"What's eating you, Big Noise?" Martin asked, grinning.

"Lemme see them tens!" The Major reached toward the center of the snake box with his infant's hand and drew the cards toward him. He examined the backs.

Bruno got up and moved over behind the midget. He picked up one of the cards and held it at an angle toward the light.

"What's eating you guys?" Martin said.

"Daub!" Major Mosquito wailed, taking his cigarette from the edge of the box and puffing it rapidly. "The cards are marked with daub. They're smeared to act like readers. You can see it if you know where to look."

Martin took one and examined it. "Damn! You're right."

"They're your cards," the Major went on in his accusing falsetto.

Martin bristled. "What d'ya mean, my cards? Somebody left 'em around the cookhouse. If I hadn't thought to bring 'em we wouldn't have had no game."

Stan took the deck and riffled them under his thumb. Then he riffled again, throwing cards face down on the table. When he reversed them they were all high ones, picture cards and tens. "That's daub, all right," he said. "Let's get a new deck."

"You're the card worker," Martin said aggressively. "What do you know about this? Daub is stuff you smear on the other fellow's cards during the game."

"I know enough not to use it," Stan said easily. "I don't deal. I never deal. And if I wanted to work any angles I'd stack them on the pick up until I got the pair I wanted on top the deck, undercut and injog the top card of the top half, shuffle off eight, outjog and shuffle off. Then I'd undercut to the outjog—"

"Let's get a new deck," Joe Plasky said. "We won't any of us get rich arguing about how the cards got marked. Who's got a deck?"

They sat silent, the expansion joints of the rails clicking by beneath them. Then Stan said, "Zeena has a deck of fortune-telling cards we can play with. I'll get them."

Martin took the marked deck, stepped to the partly open door and sent the cards flying into the wind. "Maybe a new deck will change my luck," he said. "I been going bust every hand except the last one."

The car shook and pounded on through the dark. Behind the open door they could see the dark hills and a sliver of moon setting behind them with a scattering of stars.

Stan returned and with him came Zeena. Her black dress was relieved by a corsage of imitation gardenias, her hair caught up on top of her head with a random collection of blond hairpins.

"Howdy, gents. Thought I'd take a hand myself if I wouldn't be intruding. Sure gets deadly back in that coach. I reckon I've read every movie magazine in the outfit by this time." She opened her purse and placed a deck of cards on the box. "Now you boys let me see your hands. All clean? 'Cause I don't want you smooching up these cards and getting 'em dirty. They're hard enough to get hold of."

Stan took the deck carefully and fanned them. The faces were an odd conglomeration of pictures. One showed a dead man, his back skewered with ten swords. Another had a picture of three women in ancient robes, each holding a cup. A hand reaching out of a cloud, on another, held a club from which green leaves sprouted.

"What do you call these things, Zeena?" he asked.

"That's the Tarot," she said impressively. "Oldest kind of cards in the world. They go all the way back to Egypt, some say. And they're sure a wonder for giving private readings. Every time I have something to decide or don't know which way to turn I run them over for myself. I always get some kind of an answer that makes sense. But you can play poker with 'em. They got four suits: wands are diamonds, cups are hearts, swords are clubs, and coins are spades. This bunch of pictures here—that's the Great Arcana. They're just for fortunetelling. But there's one of 'em—if I can find it—we can use for a joker. Here it is." She threw it out and placed the others back in her purse.

Stan picked up the joker. At first he couldn't figure out which end was the top. It showed a young man suspended head down by one foot from a T-shaped cross, but the cross was of living wood, putting out green shoots. The youth's hands were tied behind his back. A halo of golden light shone about his head and on reversing the card Stan saw that his expression was one of peace—like that of a man raised from the dead. Like Joe Plasky's smile. The name of the card was printed in old-fashioned script at the bottom. *The Hanged Man.*

"Holy Christ, if these damn things don't change my luck, nothing will," the Sailor said.

Zeena took a pile of chips from Joe Plasky, ante'd, then shuffled and dealt the hole cards face down. She lifted hers a trifle and frowned. The game picked up. Stan had an eight of cups in the hole and dropped out. Never stay in unless you have a Jack or better in the hole and drop out when better than a Jack shows on the board. Unless you've got the difference.

Zeena's frown deepened. The battle was between her, Sailor Martin, and the Major. Then the Sailor dropped out. The Major's hand showed three Knights. He called. Zeena held a flush in coins.

"Ain't you the bluffer," the Major piped savagely. "Frowning like you had nothing and you sitting on top a flush."

Zeena shook her head. "I wasn't meaning to bluff, even. It was the hole card I was frowning at—the ace of coins, what they call pentacles. I always read that 'Injury by a trusted friend.'"

Stan uncrossed his legs and said, "Maybe the snakes have something to do with it. They're scraping around under the lid here like they were uncomfortable."

Major Mosquito spat on the floor, then poked his finger in one of the auger holes. He withdrew it, chirruping. From the hole flicked a forked thread of pink. The Major drew his lips back from his tiny teeth and quickly touched the lighted ember of his cigarette to the tongue. It flashed back into the box and there was the frenzied scraping of coils twisting and whipping inside.

"Jesus!" Martin said. "You shouldn't of done that, you little stinker. Them damn things'll get mad."

The Major threw back his head. "Ho, ho, ho, ho! Next time I'll do it to you—I'll make a hit on the Battleship *Maine*."

Stan stood up. "I've had enough, gents. Don't let me break up the game, though."

Balancing against the rock of the train, he pushed through the piled canvas to the platform of the next coach. His left hand slid under the edge of his vest and unpinned a tiny metal box the size and shape of a five-cent piece. He let his hand drop and the container fell between the cars. It had left a dark smudge on his finger. Why do I have to frig around with all this chickenshit stuff? I didn't want their dimes. I wanted to see if I could take them. Jesus, the only thing you can depend on is your brains!

In the coach, under the dimmed lights, the crowd of carnival performers and concessioners sprawled, huddled, heads on each others' shoulders; some had stretched themselves on newspapers in the aisles. In the corner of a seat Molly slept, her lips slightly parted, her head against the glass of the black window.

How helpless they all looked in the ugliness of sleep. A third of life spent unconscious and corpselike. And some, the great majority, stumbled through their waking hours scarcely more awake, helpless in the face of destiny. They stumbled down a dark alley toward their deaths. They sent exploring feelers into the light and met fire and writhed back again into the darkness of their blind groping.

At the touch of a hand on his shoulder Stan jerked around. It was Zeena. She stood with her feet apart, braced easily against the train's rhythm. "Stan, honey, we don't want to let what's happened get us down. God knows, I felt bad about Pete. And I guess you did too. Everybody did. But this don't stop us from living. And I been wondering . . . you still like me, don't you, Stan?"

"Sure—sure I do, Zeena. Only I thought—"

"That's right, honey. The funeral and all. But I can't keep up mourning for Pete forever. My mother, now—she'd of been grieving around for a year but what I say is, it's soon enough we'll all be pushing 'em up. We got to get some fun. Tell you what. When we land at the next burg, let's us ditch the others and have a party."

Stan slid his arm around her and kissed her. In the swaying, plunging gait of the train their teeth clicked and they broke apart, laughing a little. Her hand smoothed his cheek. "I've missed you like all hell, honey." She buried her face in the hollow of his throat.

Over her shoulder Stan looked into the car of sleepers. Their faces had changed, had lost their hideousness. The girl Molly had waked up and was eating a chocolate bar. There was a smudge of chocolate over her chin. Zeena suspected nothing.

Stan raised his left hand and examined it. On the ball of the ring finger was a dark streak. Daub. He touched his tongue to it and then gripped Zeena's shoulder, wiping the stain on the black dress.

They broke apart and pushed down the aisle to a pile of suitcases where they managed to sit. In her ear Stan said, "Zeena, how does a two-person code work? I mean a good one—the kind you and Pete used to work." Audiences in evening clothes. Top billing. The Big Time.

Zeena leaned close, her voice suddenly husky. "Wait till we get to the burg. I can't think about nothing except you right now, honey. I'll tell you some time. Anything you want to know. But now I want to think about what's coming between the sheets." She caught one of his fingers and gave it a squeeze.

In the baggage coach Major Mosquito turned over his hole card. "Three deuces of swords showing and one wild one in the hole makes four of a kind. Ha, ha, ha, ha. *The Hanged Man!*"

When Stan woke up it was still dark. The electric sign which had been flaring on and off with blinding regularity, spelling out the name of Ayres' Department Store, was quiet at last and the smeared windowpane was dark. Something had wakened him. The mattress was hard and sagging; against his back he felt the warmth of Zeena's body.

Silently the bed shook and Stan's throat tightened with a reflex of fear at the unknown and the darkness until he felt the shake again and then a muffled gasp. Zeena was crying.

Stan turned over and slid his arm around her and cupped her breast with his hand. She had to be babied when she got this way.

"Stan, honey—"

"What's the matter, baby?"

Zeena turned heavily and pressed a damp cheek against his bare chest. "Just got to thinking about Pete."

There was nothing to say to this so Stan tightened his arms around her and kept quiet.

"You know, today I was going through some of the stuff in the little tin trunk—Pete's stuff. His old press books and old letters and all kinds of stuff. And I found the notebook he used to keep. The one he had the start of our code in. Pete invented that code himself and we were the only people that ever knew it. Pete was offered a thousand dollars for it by Allah Kismet—that was Syl Rappolo. He was one of the biggest crystal-workers in the country. But Pete just laughed at him. That old book was just like a part of Pete. He had such nice handwriting in them days . . ."

Stan said nothing but turned her face up and began kissing her. He was fully awake now and could feel the pulse jumping in his throat. He mustn't seem too eager. Better love her up first, all the way if he could do it again.

He found that he could.

It was Zeena's turn to keep quiet. Finally Stan said, "What are we going to do about your act?"

Her voice was suddenly crisp. "What about the act?"

"I thought maybe you were thinking of changing it."

"What for? Ain't we taking in more on the pitch than ever? Look, honey, if you feel you ought to be cut in for a bigger percentage don't be bashful—"

"I'm not talking about that," he interrupted her. "In this damn state nobody can write. Every time I stick a card and a pencil under the nose of some mark he says, 'You write it for me.' If I could remember all that stuff I could let 'em keep the cards in their pockets."

Zeena stretched leisurely, the bed creaking under her. "Don't you worry about Zeena, honey. When they can't write their names they're even more receptive to the answers. Why, I could quit the question-answering part of the act and just get up there and spiel away and then go into the pitch and still turn 'em."

A thrill of alarm raced along Stan's nerves at the thought of Zeena's being able to do without him before he could do without her. "But I mean, couldn't we work a code act? You could still do it, couldn't you?"

She chuckled. "Listen, schniggle-fritz, I can do it in my sleep. But it takes a hell of a lot of work to get all them lists and things learned. And the season's more than half over."

"I could learn it."

She thought for a while and then she said, "It's all right with me, honey. It's all down in Pete's book. Only don't you lose that book or Zeena'll cut your ears off."

"You have it here?"

"Wait a minute. Where's the fire? Sure I've got it here. You'll see it. Don't go getting sizzle-britches."

More silence. At last Stan sat up and swung his feet to the floor. "I better get back to that pantry they rented me for a room. We don't want the townies here to get any more ideas than they've got already." He snapped on the light and began to put on his clothes. In the garish light overhead Zeena looked haggard and battered like a worn wax doll. She had the sheet pulled over her middle but her breasts sagged over it. Her hair was in two brassy braids and the ends were uneven and spiky. Stan put on his shirt and knotted his tie. He slipped on his jacket.

"You're a funny fella."

"Why?"

"Getting all dressed up to walk thirty feet down the hall of a fleabag like this at four in the morning."

Somehow Stan felt this to be a reflection on his courage. His face grew warm. "Nothing like doing things right."

Zeena yawned cavernously. "Guess you're right, kiddo. See you in the morning. And thanks for the party."

He made no move to turn out the light. "Zeena, that notebook— Could I see it?"

She threw off the sheet, got up and squatted to snap open the suitcase. Does a woman always look more naked after you've had her, Stan wondered. Zeena rummaged in the bag and drew out a canvas-covered book marked "Ledger."

"Now run along, honey. Or come back to bed. Make up your mind."

Stan tucked the book under his arm and switched off the light. He felt his way to the door and with caution turned back the bolt. Yellow light from the hall sliced over the patchy wallpaper as he opened the door.

There was a whisper from the bed. "Stan—"

"What is it?"

"Come kiss your old pal good night."

He stepped over, kissed her cheek and left without another word, closing the door softly behind him.

The lock of his own door sounded like a rifle shot.

He looked each way along the hall but nothing stirred.

Inside, he tore off his clothes, went to the washbowl and washed and then threw himself down on the bed, propping the book on his bare stomach.

The first pages were taken up with figures and notations: "Evansport. July 20th. Books—$33.00 taken in. Paid—Plants at $2—$6.00. Plants: Mrs. Jerome Hotchkiss. Leonard Keely, Josiah Boos. All okay. Old spook workers. Boos looks like deacon. Can act a little. Worked the found ring in the coat lining . . ."

"Spook workers" must refer to the local confederates employed by traveling mediums. Swiftly Stan flipped the pages. More expenses: "F. T. rap squared. Chief Pellett. $50." That would be an arrest on a charge of fortune telling.

Stan felt like Ali Baba in the cavern of riches left by the Forty Thieves.

Impatiently he turned to the back of the book. On the last page was a heading: "Common Questions." Beneath it was a list, with figures:

"Is my husband true to me? 56, 29, 18, 42.

"Will mother get well? 18, 3, 7, 12.

"Who poisoned our dog? 3, 2, 3, 0, 3." Beside this was the notation, "Not a big item but a steady. Every audience. Can pull as cold reading during stall part of act."

The figures, then, were a record of the number of similar questions collected from the same audience. The question "Is my wife faithful?" had only about a third the number of entries as the one about the husband.

"The chumps," Stan whispered. "Either too bashful to ask or too dumb to suspect." Bet they were anxious to find out, all of them. As if jazzing wasn't what they all want, the goddamned hypocrites. They all want it. Only nobody else must have it. He turned the page.

"There is a recurring pattern followed by the questions asked. For every unusual question there will be fifty that you have had before. Human nature is the same everywhere. All have the same troubles. They are worried. Can control anybody by finding out what he's afraid of. Works with question-answering act. Think out things most people are afraid of and hit them right where they live. Health, Wealth, Love. And Travel and Success. They're all afraid of ill health, of poverty, of boredom, of failure. Fear is the key to human nature. They're afraid. . . ."

Stan looked past the pages to the garish wallpaper and through it into the world. The geek was made by fear. He was afraid of sobering up and getting the horrors. But what made him a drunk? Fear. Find out what they are afraid of and sell it back to them. That's the key. The key! He had known it when Clem Hoately had told him how geeks are made. But here was Pete saying the same thing:

Health. Wealth. Love. Travel. Success. "A few have to do with domestic troubles, in-laws, kids, pets. And so on. A few wisenheimers but you can ditch them easily enough. Idea: combine question-answering act with code act. Make list of questions, hook up with code numbers. Answer vague at first, working toward definite. If can see face of spectator and tell when hitting."

On the following pages was a neatly numbered list of questions. There were exactly a hundred. Number One was "Is my husband true to me?" Number Two was "Will I get a job soon?"

Outside the front of Ayres' Department Store had turned rosy-red with the coming sun. Stan paid it no heed. The sun slid up, the sound of wagon tires on concrete told of the awakening city. At ten o'clock there was a tap on the door. Stan shook himself. "Yes?"

Zeena's voice. "Wake up, sleepy head. Rise and shine."

He unlocked the door and let her in.

"What you got the light on for?" She turned it out, then saw the book. "Lord's sake, kid, ain't you been to bed at all?"

Stan rubbed his eyes and stood up. "Ask me a number. Any number up to a hundred."

"Fifty-five."

"Will my mother-in-law always live with us?"

Zeena sat down beside him and ran her fingers through his hair. "You know what I think, kid? I think you're a mind reader."

The carny turned south and the pines began to line sandy roads. Cicadas drummed the late summer air and the crowds of white people were gaunter, their faces filled with desolation, their lips often stained with snuff.

Everywhere the shining, dark faces of the South's other nation caught the highlights from the sun. They stood in quiet wonder, watching the carny put up in the smoky morning light. In the Ten-in-One they stood always on the fringe of the crowd, an invisible cordon holding them in place. When one of the whites turned away sharply and jostled them the words "Scuse me," fell from them like pennies balanced on their shoulders.

Stan had never been this far south and something in the air made him uneasy. This was dark and bloody land where hidden war traveled like a million earthworms under the sod.

The speech fascinated him. His ear caught the rhythm of it and he noted their idioms and worked some of them into his patter. He had found the reason behind the peculiar, drawling language of the old carny hands—it was a composite of all the sprawling regions of the country. A language which sounded Southern to Southerners, Western to Westerners. It was the talk of the soil and its drawl covered the agility of the brains that poured it out. It was a soothing, illiterate, earthy language.

The carny changed its tempo. The outside talkers spoke more slowly.

Zeena cut the price of her horoscopes to a dime each but sold "John the Conqueror Root" along with them for fifteen cents. This was a dried mass of twisting roots which was supposed to attract good fortune when carried in a bag around the neck. Zeena got them by the gross from an occult mail-order house in Chicago.

Stan's pitch of the magic books took a sudden drop and Zeena knew the answer. "These folks down here don't know nothing about sleight-of-hand, honey. Half of 'em figure you're doing real magic. Well, you got to have something superstitious to pitch."

Stan ordered a gross of paper-backed books, "One Thousand and One Dreams Interpreted." He threw in as a free gift a brass lucky coin stamped with the Seal of Love from the Seventh Book of Moses, said to attract the love of others and lead to the confusion of enemies. His pitch picked up in fine style. He learned to roll three of the lucky coins over his fingers at once. The tumbling, glittering cascade of metal seemed to fascinate the marks, and the dream books went fast.

He had learned the verbal code for questions not a day too soon, for the people couldn't write or were too shy to try.

"*Will* you *kindly* answer this lady's question *at once?*" Stan had cued the question, "Is my daughter all right?"

Zeena's voice had taken on a deeper southern twang. "Well, now, I get the impression that the lady is worried about someone near and dear to her, someone she hasn't heard from in a long time, am I right? Strikes me it's a young lady— It's your daughter you're thinking of, isn't it? Of course. And you want to know if she's well and happy and if you'll see her again soon. Well, I believe you will get some news of her through a third person before the month is out. . . ."

There was one question that came up so often that Stan worked out a silent signal for it. He would simply jerk his head in Zeena's direction. The first time he used it the question had come to him from a man—massive and loose-jointed with clear eyes smoldering in a handsome ebony face. "Am I ever going to make a trip?"

Zeena picked it up. "Man over there is wondering about something that's going to happen to him and I want to say right here and now that I believe you're going to get your wish. And I think it has something to do with travel. You want to make a trip somewheres. Isn't that so? Well, I see some troubles on the road and I see a crowd of people—men, they are, asking a lot of questions. But I see the journey completed after a while, not as soon as you want to make it but after a while. And there's a job waiting for you at the end of it. Job with good pay. It's somewhere to the north of here; I'm positive of that."

It was sure-fire. All of 'em want North, Stan thought. It was the dark alley, all over again. With a light at the end of it. Ever since he was a kid Stan had had the dream. He was running down a dark alley, the buildings vacant and black and menacing on either side. Far down at the end of it a light burned; but there was something behind him, close behind him, getting closer until he woke up trembling and never reached the light. They have it too—a nightmare alley. The North isn't the end. The light will only move further on. And the fear close behind them. White and black, it made no difference. The geek and his bottle, staving off the clutch of the thing that came following after.

In the hot sun of noon the cold breath could strike your neck. In having a woman her arms were a barrier. But after she had fallen asleep the walls of the alley closed in on your own sleep and the footsteps followed.

Now the very country simmered with violence, and Stan looked enviously at the sculptured muscles of Bruno Hertz. It wasn't worth the time and backbreaking effort it took to get that way. There must be an easier way. Some sort of jujitsu system where a man could use his brains and his agility. The Ackerman-Zorbaugh Monster Shows had never had a "Hey-rube" since Stan had been with them, but the thought of one ate at his peace of mind like a maggot. What would he do in a mob fight? What would they do to him?

Then Sailor Martin nearly precipitated one.

It was a steaming day of late summer. The South had turned out: hollow-eyed women with children in their arms and clinging to their skirts, lantern-jawed men, deadly quiet.

Clem Hoately had mounted the platform where Bruno sat quietly fanning himself with a palm-leaf fan. "If you'll step right this way, folks, I want to call your attention to one of the miracle men of all time—Herculo, the strongest man alive."

Stan looked back to the rear of the tent. In the corner by the geek's enclosure Sailor Martin had a couple of local youths engrossed in the strap on the barrelhead. He took a leather strap, folded it in the middle, then coiled it on the top of a nail keg. He placed his own finger in one of the two loops in the center and pulled the strap. His finger had picked the real loop in the strap. Then he bet one of the marks he couldn't pick the real loop. The mark bet and won and the Sailor handed him a silver dollar.

Zeena drew the curtains of the little stage and came out at the side. She drew a handkerchief from her bosom and touched her temples with it. "Whew, ain't it a scorcher today?" She followed Stan's glance to the rear of the tent. "The Sailor better go easy. Hoately don't like anybody to case the marks on the side this far south. Can't blame him. Too likely to start a rumpus. I say, if you can't make a living with your pitch you don't belong in no decent Ten-in-One. I could pick up plenty of honest dollars if I wanted to give special private readings and remove evil influences and all that stuff. But that just leads to trouble."

She stopped speaking and her hand tightened on Stan's arm. "Stan, honey, you better take a walk over there and see what's going on."

Stan made no move to go. On the platform he was king; the marks in their anonymous mass were below him and his voice held them, but down on their level, jammed in among their milling, collective weight, he felt smothered.

Suddenly one of the youths drew back his foot and kicked over the nail keg on which Martin had wound the strap with the elusive loop. The Sailor's voice was raised just a fraction above conversational level and he seemed to be speaking to the mark when he said, clearly and coolly, "Hey, rube!"

"Go on, Stan. Hurry. Don't let 'em get started."

As if he had a pistol pointed at his back, Stan marched across the tent to the spot where trouble was simmering. From the corner of his eye he saw Joe Plasky hop on his hands down the steps behind his own platform and swing his way toward the corner. He would not be alone, at least.

Plasky got there first. "Hello, gents. I'm one of the owners of the show. Everything all right?"

"Like hell it is," blustered one of the marks. A young farmer,

Stan judged. "This here tattooed son-of-a-bitch got five dollars of my money by faking. I seen this here strap swindle afore. I aims to get my money back."

"If there's any doubt in your mind about the fairness of any game of chance in the show I'm sure the Sailor here will return your original bet. We're all here to have a good time, mister, and we don't want any hard feelings."

The other mark spoke up. He was a tall, raw-boned sodbuster with a mouth which chronically hung open, showing long yellow teeth. "I seen this here trick afore, too, mister. Cain't fool me. Cain't nobody pick out that loop, way this feller unwinds it. A feller showed me how it works one time. It's a gahdamned swindle."

Joe Plasky's smile was broader than ever. He reached in the pocket of his shirt and drew out a roll of bills and took off a five. He held it up to the farmer. "Here's the money out of my own pocket, son. If you can't afford to lose you can't afford to bet. I'm just returning your bet because we want everybody to have a good time and no hard feelings. Now you boys better mosey along."

The youth shoved the five into the pocket of his pants and the two of them slouched out. Plasky turned to the Sailor. His smile was still there, but a hard, steady light shone in his eyes. "You dumb bastard! This is a tough town. The whole damn state is tough. And you haven't any more sense than to start a Heyrube. For Christ's sake watch your step! Now give me the five."

Sailor Martin spat between his teeth into the dust. "I won that fin and I could of handled them two jakes. Who elected you Little Tin Jesus around here?"

Plasky put his fingers in his mouth and whistled a single blast. The tip around the last platform was on its way out and Hoately turned back. Joe waved his hand in an arc and Hoately signaled back and let the canvas drop to close the front entrance. Outside old Maguire began to grind, trying to gather a tip and hold them until the show was opened again.

Bruno dropped lightly from his platform and strode over. Stan felt Zeena beside him. Major Mosquito was running back on his infant's legs, shrilling something incoherent.

Joe Plasky said evenly, "Sailor, you been leaving a trail of busted hearts and busted cherries all along the route. Now you're going to hand me that fin and pack up your gear. You're quitting the show. Hoately will back me up."

Stan's knees were weak. Zeena's hand was on his arm, her fingers gripping it. Would he be expected to take on the Sailor? Joe was a cripple, Bruno a superman. Stan was broader and heavier than the Sailor but the thought of a fight sickened him. He never felt that fists were good enough. He would have carried a gun except that it was a lot of trouble and he was afraid of killing with it.

Martin eyed the group. Bruno stood quietly in the background. "I don't fight no cripples, polack. And I don't owe you no five." The Sailor's lips were pale, his eyes hot.

The half-man acrobat reached up and took him by the hand, gripping the fingers together and bending them so that the tattooed man quickly sank to his knees. "Hey, leggo, you bastard!"

Silently and with his face a blank, Plasky crossed his forearms. He let go of Martin's hand and seized the collar of his robe in both fists. Then he levered his wrists together, forcing the backs of his hands into the Sailor's throat. Martin was caught in a human vise. His mouth dropped. He clawed frantically at the crossed arms of the half-man but the more he tugged, the tighter they crushed him. His eyes began to bulge and his hair fell over them.

Major Mosquito was leaping up and down, making fighting motions and shadowboxing. "Kill him! Kill him! Kill him! Choke him till he's dead! Kill the big ape!" He rushed in and began hammering the Sailor's staring face with tiny fists. Bruno picked him up, wriggling, and held him at arm's length by the collar of his jacket.

Joe began to shake the tattoo artist, gently at first and then harder. The calm deadliness of that ingenious and unbreakable hold filled Stan with terror and wild joy.

Clem Hoately came running up. "Okay, Joe. Guess he's educated. Let's break it up. We got a good tip waiting."

Joe smiled his smile of one raised from the dead. He released Sailor, who sat up rubbing his throat and breathing hard. Plasky reached into the pocket of the robe and found a wad of bills, took out a five and put the rest back.

Hoately picked the Sailor up and stood him on his feet. "You knock off, Martin. I'll pay you up to the end of the month. Pack up your stuff and leave whenever you want to."

When Martin was able to speak his voice was a hoarse whisper. "Okay. I'm on my way. I can take my needles into any barber shop and make more dough than in this crummy layout. But watch out, all of you."

Middle evening and a good crowd. Beyond the canvas and the gaudily painted banners Hoately's voice was raspy.

"Hi, look! Hi, look! Hi, look! Right this way for the monster aggregation of nature's mistakes, novelty entertainments, and the world-renowned museum of freaks, marvels, and curiosities. Featuring Mamzelle Electra, the little lady who defies the lightning."

Stan looked across at Molly Cahill. When she held the sputtering arc points together she always flinched; the last day or two, whenever he saw it, a little thrill leaped up his spine. Now she bent over and placed her compact behind the electric chair. Bending stretched her sequinned trunks tight over her buttocks.

It's funny how you can see a girl every day for months and yet not see her, Stan thought. Then something will happen—like the way Molly's mouth presses together when she holds the arc points and the fire starts to fly. Then you see her all different.

He dragged his glance away from the girl. Across the tent the massive chest of Bruno Hertz shone pink with sweat as he flexed the muscles of his upper arms, rippling under the pink skin, and the crowd rubbered.

Molly was sitting demurely in a bentwood chair beside the heavy, square menace with its coiled wires, its straps and its chilling suggestion of death which was as phoney as everything else in the carny. She was studying a green racing form. Absorbed, she reached down and scratched one ankle and Stan felt the ripple go up his back again.

Molly's eyes were on the racing sheet but she had stopped looking at it and was looking through it, her mind in the dream she always dreamed.

There was a man in it and his face was always in shadow. He was taller than she and his voice was low and intense and his hands were brown and powerful. They walked slowly, drinking in the summer reflected from every grass blade, shining from every pebble in fields singing with summer. An old rail fence and beyond it a field rising like a wave, a pasture where the eyes of daisies looked up at a sky so blue it made you ache.

His face was shadowy still, as his arms stole about her. She pressed her hands against the hardness of his chest, but his mouth found hers. She tried to turn her head away; but then his fingers were caressing her hair, his kisses falling upon the hollow of her throat while his other hand found her breast . . .

"Over here, folks, right over here. On this platform we have a little lady who is one of the marvels and mysteries of the age —Mamzelle Electra!"

Stan came up the steps behind Joe Plasky's platform and sat on the edge of it. "How they going?"

Joe smiled and went on assembling the novelties in his joke books, slipping the free gifts between the pages. "Can't complain. Good crowd tonight, ain't it?"

Stan shifted his seat. "I wonder if the Sailor will try to do us any dirt?"

Joe swung himself closer on his calloused knuckles and said, "Can't tell. But I don't think so. After all, he is carny. He's a louse, too. But we just want to keep our eyes open. I don't think he'll try to call me in spades—not after he's felt the *nami juji*."

Stan frowned. "Felt what?"

"*Nami juji*. That's the Jap name for it—that crosshanded choke I slipped on him. That takes some of the starch out of 'em."

The blond head was alert. "Joe, that was terrific, what you did. How in hell did you ever learn that?"

"Jap showed me. We had a Jap juggler when I was with the Keyhoe Shows. It's easy enough to do. He taught me a lot of ju-jit stuff only that's one of the best."

Stan moved closer. "Show me how you do it."

Plasky reached over and slid his right hand up Stan's right coat lapel until he was grasping the collar at the side of Stan's throat. He crossed his left arm over his right and gripped the left side of the collar. Suddenly Stan felt his throat caught in an iron wedge. It loosened immediately; Plasky dropped his hands and smiled. Stan's knees were trembling.

"Let me see if I can do it." He gripped Plasky's black turtle-neck sweater with one hand.

"Higher up, Stan. You got to grab it right opposite the big artery in the neck—here." He shifted the younger man's hand slightly. "Now cross your forearms and grab the other side. Right. Now then, bend your wrists and force the backs of your hands into my neck. That cuts off the blood from the brain."

Stan felt a surge of power along his arms. He did not know that his lips had drawn back over his teeth. Plasky slapped his arm quickly and he let go.

"Christ a-mighty, kid, you want to be careful with that! If you leave it on just a mite too long you'll have a corpse on your hands. And you got to practice getting it quick. It's a little hard to slip on but once you've got it the other fella can't break it—unless he knows the real Jap stuff."

Both men looked up as Maguire, the ticket seller, hurried toward them.

"She-ess-oo flee-ess-eyes!" He ducked past them to where Hoately stood on the Electric Girl's platform.

Plasky's smile widened as it always did in the face of trouble. "Shoo flies, kid. Cops. Just take it easy and you'll be all right. Here's where Hoately will have to do some real talking. And the fixer will have to earn his pay. I been expecting they'd slough the whole joint one of these days."

"What happens to us?" Stan's mouth had gone dry.

"Nothing, kid, if everybody keeps his head. Never argue with a cop. That's what you pay a mouthpiece for. Treat 'em polite and yes 'em to death and send for a mouthpiece. Hell, Stan, you got a lot to learn yet about the carny."

A whistle sounded from the entrance. Stan's head spun toward it.

A big, white-haired man with a badge pinned to his denim shirt stood there. His hat was pushed back and he had his thumbs hooked in his belt. A holster containing a heavy revolver hung from a looser belt on a slant. Hoately raised his voice, grinning down at the marks below Molly's platform.

"That will conclude our performance for the time being, folks. Now I guess you're all kind of dry and could stand a nice cold drink so I call your attention to the stand directly across the midway where you can get all the nice cold soda pop you can drink. That's all for now, folks. Come back tomorrow night and we'll have a few surprises for you—things you didn't see tonight."

The marks obediently began to drift out of the tent and Hoately approached the law. "What can I do for you, Chief? My name's Hoately and I'm owner of this attraction. You're welcome to inspect every inch of it and I'll give you all the co-operation you want. We've got no girl shows and no games of skill or chance."

The old man's hard little colorless eyes rested on Hoately as they would on a spider in the corner of a backhouse. "Stand here."

"You're the boss."

The old man's gaze flickered over the Ten-in-One tent. He pointed to the geek's enclosure. "What you got in there?"

"Snake charmer," Hoately said casually. "Want to see him?"

"That ain't what I heard. I heard you got an obscene and illegal performance going on here with cruelty to dumb animals. I got a complaint registered this evening."

The showman pulled out a bag of tobacco and papers and began to build a cigarette. His left hand made a quick twist, and the cigarette took form. He licked the paper with his tongue and struck a match. "Why don't you stay as my guest and view the entire performance, Chief? We'd be glad—"

The wide mouth tightened. "I got orders from the marshal to close down the show. And arrest anybody I see fit. I'm arresting you and—" He slid his eyes over the performers: Bruno placid in his blue robe, Joe Plasky smilingly assembling his pitch items, Stan making a half dollar vanish and reappear, Molly still sitting in the Electric Chair, the sequins of her skimpy bodice winking as her breasts rose and fell. She was smiling tautly. "And I'm taking that woman there—indecent exposure. We got decent women in this town. And we got daughters; growin' girls. We don't allow no naked women paradin' around and makin' exposes of 'emselves. The rest of you stay right here in case we need you. All right, you two, come along. Put a coat on that girl first. She ain't decent enough to come down to the lockup thataway."

Stan noticed that the stubble on the deputy marshal's chin was white—like a white fungus on a dead man, he thought savagely. Molly's eyes were enormous.

Hoately cleared his throat and took a deep breath. "Looky here, Chief, that girl's never had no complaints. She's got to wear a costume like that on account of she handles electric wires and ordinary cloth might catch fire and . . ."

The deputy reached out one hand and gripped Hoately by the shirt. "Shut up. And don't try offering me any bribes, neither. I ain't none o' your thievin' northern police, kissin' the priest's toe on Sundays and raking in the graft hell-bent for election six days a week. I'm a church deacon and I aim to keep this a clean town if I have to run every Jezebel out of it on a fence rail."

His tiny eyes were fastened on Molly's bare thighs. He raised his glance ever so slightly to take in her shoulders and the crease between her breasts. The eyes grew hot and the slack mouth raised at the corners. Beside the Electric Girl's platform he noticed a neat young man with corn-yellow hair saying something to the girl who nodded and then darted her attention back to the deputy.

The law lumbered over, dragging Hoately with him. "Young lady, git off that contraption." He reached up a red-knuckled hand toward Molly. Stan was on the other side of the platform feeling for the switch. There was an ominous buzzing and crackling: Molly's black hair stood straight up like a halo around her head. She brought her finger tips together. Blue fire flowed between them. The deputy stopped, stony. The girl reached out, and sparks jumped in a flashing stream from her fingers to the deputy's. With a shout he drew back, releasing Hoately. The buzz of the static generator stopped and a voice drew his attention; it was the blond youth.

"You can see the reason, Marshal, for the metal costume the young lady is forced to wear. The electricity would ignite any ordinary fabric and only by wearing the briefest of covering can she avoid bursting into flame. Thousands of volts of electricity cover her body like a sheath. Pardon me, Marshal, but there seem to be several dollar bills coming out of your pocket."

In spite of himself, the deputy followed Stan's pointing finger. He saw nothing. Stan reached out and one after another five folded dollar bills appeared from the pocket of the denim shirt. He made them into a little roll and pressed them into the old man's hand. "Another minute and you'd have lost your money, Marshal."

The deputy's eyes were half shut with disbelief and hostile suspicion; but he shoved the cash into his shirt pocket.

Stan went on, "And I see that you have bought your wife a little present of a few silk handkerchiefs." From the cartridge belt Stan slowly drew out a bright green silk, then another of purple. "These are very pretty. I'm sure your wife will like them. And here's a pure white one—for your daughter. She's about nineteen now, isn't she, Marshal?"

"How'd you know I got a daughter?"

Stan rolled the silks into a ball and they vanished. His face was serious, the blue eyes grave. "I know many things, Marshal. I don't know exactly how I know them but there's nothing supernatural about it, I am sure. My family was Scotch and the Scotch are often gifted with powers that the old folks used to call 'second sight.' "

The white head with its coarse, red face, nodded involuntarily.

"For instance," Stan went on, "I can see that you have carried a pocket piece or curio of some kind for nearly twenty years. Probably a foreign coin."

One great hand made a motion toward the pants pocket. Stan felt his own pulse racing with triumph. Two more hits and he'd have him.

"Several times you have lost that luck-piece but you've found it again every time; and it means a lot to you, you don't exactly know why. I'd say that you should always carry it."

The deputy's eyes had lost some of their flint.

From the tail of his eye Stan saw that the Electric Chair above them was empty; Molly had disappeared. So had everyone else except Hoately who stood slightly to the rear of the deputy, nodding his head wisely at every word of the magician's.

"Now this isn't any of my business, Marshal, because I know you are a man who is fully capable of handling his own affairs and just about anything else that is liable to come along. But my Scotch blood is working right this minute and it tells me that there is one thing in your life that is worrying you and it's something you find it difficult to handle. Because all your strength and your courage and your authority in the town seem to be of no avail. It seems to slip through your grasp like water—"

"Wait a minute, young fella. What are you talkin' 'bout?"

"As I said, it's absolutely none of my business. And you are a man in the prime of life and old enough to be my father and by rights you should be the one to give me good advice and not the other way round. But in this case I may be able to do you a good turn. I sense that there are antagonistic influences surrounding you. Someone near to you is jealous of you and your ability. And while part of this extends to your work as a peace officer and your duties in upholding the law, there is another part of it that has to do with your church . . ."

The face had changed. The savage lines had ironed out and now it was simply the face of an old man, weary and bewildered. Stan hurried on, panicky for fear the tenuous spell would break, but excited at his own power. If I can't read a Bible-spouting, whoremongering, big-knuckled hypocrite of a church deacon, he told himself, I'm a feeblo. The old son-of-a-bitch.

Stan's eyes misted over as if they had turned inward. His voice grew intimate. "There is someone you love very dearly. Yet there is an obstacle in the way of your love. You feel hemmed-in and trapped by it. And through it all I seem to hear a woman's voice, a sweet voice, singing. It's singing a beautiful old hymn. Wait a moment. It's 'Jesus, Savior, Pilot Me.' "

The deputy's mouth was open, his big chest was lifting and falling with his breath.

"I see a Sunday morning in a peaceful, beautiful little church. A church into which you have put your energy and your labor. You have labored hard in the Lord's vineyard and your labor has borne fruit in the love of a woman. But I see her eyes filled with tears and somehow your own heart is touched by them . . ."

Christ, how far do I dare go with this? Stan thought behind the running patter of his words.

"But I feel that all will come out well for you. Because you have strength. And you'll get more. The Lord will give you strength. And there are malicious tongues about you, ready to do you an injury. And to do this fine woman an injury if they can. Because they are like whited sepulchers which appear beautiful outward but are full of dead men's bones and all uncleanness and . . ."

The deacon's eyes were hot again but this time not at Stan. There was a hunted look in them too as the youth bore down:

"And the spirit of our Lord and Savior, Jesus Christ, has shined upon them but in vain, because they see as through a glass, darkly, and the darkness is nothing but a reflection of their own blackness and sin and hypocrisy and envy. But deep inside yourself you will find the power to combat them. And defeat them. And you will do it with the help of the God you believe in and worship.

"And while I feel the spirit talking to me straight out, like a father to his son, I must tell you that there's a matter of some money coming to you that will cause you some disappointment and delay but you will get it. I can see that the people in this town have been pretty blind in the past but something in the near future will occur which will wake them up and make them realize that you are a more valuable man than they ever would admit. There's a surprise for you—about this time next year or a little later, say around November. Something you've had your heart set on for a long time but it will come true if you follow the hunches you get and don't let anybody talk you out of obeying your own good judgment which has never let you down yet —whenever you've given it a free rein."

Hoately had evaporated. Stan turned and began to move slowly toward the gate. The midway outside was buzzing with little groups of talk. The entire carny had been sloughed and the deputies had chased the townies off the lot. Stan walked slowly, talking still in a soft, inward voice. The old man followed beside him, his eyes staring straight ahead.

"I'm very glad to have met you, Marshal. Because I expect to be back here again some day and I'd like to see if my Scotch blood had been telling me true, as I'm sure it has. I'm sure you don't mind a young fellow like myself presuming to tell you these things, because, after all, I'm not pretending to advise you. I know you've lived a lot longer than I and have more knowledge of the ways of the world than I could ever have. But when I first set eyes on you I thought to myself, 'Here's a man and a servant of the law who is troubled deep in his mind,' and then I saw that you had no reason to be because things are going to turn out just the way you want them to, only there will be a little delay . . ."

How the hell shall I finish this off, Stan wondered. I can talk myself right back into the soup if I don't quit.

They reached the entrance and Stan paused. The deputy's red, hard face turned toward him; the silence seemed to pour over Stan and smother him. This was the pay-off, and his heart sank. There was nothing more to be said now. This was where action started. Stan felt out of his depth. Then he suddenly knew the business that would work, if anything would. He turned away from the old man. Making his face look as spiritual as possible, he raised one hand and rested it easily in a gesture of peace and confidence against the looped canvas. It was a period at the end of the sentence.

The deputy let out a long, whistling breath, hooked his thumbs in his belt, and stood looking out on the darkening midway. Then he turned back to Stan and his voice was just an ordinary old man's voice. "Young fella, I wisht I'd met you a long time ago. Tell the others to go easy in this town because we aim to keep it clean. But, by God, when—if I'm ever elected marshal you ain't got nothing to worry about, long as you have a good, clean show. Good night, son."

He plodded away slowly, his shoulders squared against the dark, authority slapping his thigh on a belt heavy with cartridges.

Stan's collar was tight with the blood pounding beneath it. His head was as light as if he had a fever.

The world is mine, God damn it! The world is mine! I've got 'em across the barrel and I can shake them loose from whatever I want. The geek has his whisky. The rest of them drink something else: they drink promises. They drink hope. And I've got it to hand them. I'm running over with it. I can get anything I want. If I could hand this old fart a cold reading and get away with it I could do it to a senator! I could do it to a governor!

Then he remembered where he had told her to hide.

In the black space where the trucks were parked, Zeena's van was behind the others, dark and silent. He opened the cab door softly and crept in, his blood hammering.

"Molly!"

"Yes, Stan." The whisper came from the black cavern behind the seat.

"It's okay, kid. I stalled him. He's gone."

"Oh, Stan, gee, you're great. You're great."

Stan crawled back over the seat and his hand touched a soft, hot shoulder. It was trembling. His arm went about it. "Molly!"

Lips found his. He crushed her back on a pile of blankets.

"Stan, you won't let anything happen to me—will you?"

"Certainly not. Nothing's ever going to happen to you while I'm around."

"Oh, Stan, you're so much like my dad."

The hooks which held the sequinned bodice came open in his shaking fingers. The girl's high, pointed breasts were smooth under his hands, and his tongue entered her lips.

"Don't hurt me, Stan, honey. Don't." His collar choked him, the blood hammering in his throat. "Oh. Stan—hurt me, hurt me, hurt me—"

# CARD V

# The Empress

*who sits on Venus' couch amid the ripening grain and rivers of the earth.*

THE NIGHT was quiet at last, with only the katydids. The ferris wheel stood as gaunt as a skeleton against the stars; the cookhouse lights were lonely in the dark.

Stan stepped down into the grass beside the van and held his hand up to help Molly. Her palm was hot and damp. When she stood beside him she clung to him for a moment and pressed her forehead against his cheek. They were almost the same height. Her hair smelled sweet and tickled his lips. He shook his head impatiently.

"Stan, honey, you do love me—don't you?"

"Sure I do, baby."

"And you won't tell a soul. Promise me you won't tell. Because I never let any man do it to me before, honest."

"Are you sure?" Stan thrilled at his power over her. He wanted to hear her voice with fear in it.

"Yes, honey. Yes. Honest. You hurt me something terrible at first. You know—"

"Yes."

"Darling, if I'd ever done it before you wouldn't have hurt me. Only I'm glad you hurt me, honey, I'm glad. Because you were the first."

The air was chilly; she began to shiver. Stan slipped off his jacket and put it around her shoulders. "Gee, you're good to me, Stan."

"I'll always be."

"Always?" Molly stopped and turned to face him, resting both hands on his forearm. "What do you mean, Stan?"

"Just always."

"You mean until the season's over and we all split up?" Her voice held a deeper question.

Stan had decided. In his mind he saw the blaze of the foots, with himself standing there straight. In command. Molly was in the audience in an evening gown, walking slowly down the aisle. The marks—the audience—craned their necks to look at her. She was an eyeful. The placards at each side of the stage said simply, STANTON. The big time.

"Molly, you like show business, don't you?"

"Why, sure, Stan. Daddy always wanted to see me in show business."

"Well, what I mean is— Well, let's head for the big time. Together."

Her arm slid around his waist and they walked on again, slowly. "Darling, that's wonderful. I was hoping you'd say that to me."

"I mean it. Together we can get right to the top. You've got the class and the shape. I mean, you're beautiful and we can work up a two-person code act that'll knock 'em dead."

Molly's arm tightened around him. "Stan, that's what I always wanted. Daddy would be awful proud of us. I know he would. He'd be crazy about you, Stan. The way you can talk your way out of a tight place. That's what he admired most in anybody. That and not double-crossing a pal, ever. Daddy said he wanted on his tombstone, 'Here lies Denny Cahill. He never crossed up a pal.' "

"Did he get it?"

"No. My grandfather wouldn't hear of it. The stone just says, 'Dennis Cahill' and under it the dates when he was born and when he passed away. Only one night, just before I left Louisville, I went out and wrote it below the dates with chalk. I'll bet some of the chalk is still there."

They had reached the Ten-in-One. Inside a single bulb glowed. Stan peered in. "All clear, kid. Get into your things. I wonder where the others are?"

While Molly was dressing behind the curtains of Zeena's stage Stan walked over to the cookhouse and found the cook cleaning coffee urns. "Where's the bunch?"

"Scattered. The bulls run in a couple of fellows on the wheels and games. They even sloughed the cat rack. The fixer'll get 'em sprung tomorrow. And I'll have to put on a tub of water so they can boil up and get the crumbs out of their clothes. Want a cup o' java?"

"No, thanks. I want to find my bunch. Got any idea where they went?"

The cook wiped his hands and lit a cigarette. "Hoately's gone up the road to a lunch wagon or something. Roadside joint. You can't miss it. He said he didn't want to hang around the lot to-night. Can't blame him. Seems somebody put in a beef to the cops about the geek show you fellows got. And about the wheels. Way I heard it, that tattooed guy used to be in the Ten-in-One and had the run-in with Plasky was in town shooting off his mouth."

"Sailor Martin?"

"That's the son-of-a-bitch. What I heard, he worked on the townies and got them to beef to the cops. Can you imagine a carny doing that? Somebody ought to stick a butcher knife up his rear end and kick the handle off."

Stan heard a low whistle from outside and said good night to the cook. Molly was standing in the shadow of the Ten-in-One, looking prim and neat in a dark suit and a white silk blouse. He took her arm and they set off down the road.

It was a chicken-dinner shack; from inside came voices and laughs. He pushed open the screen door.

At a table with a red-checkered tablecloth the bunch was gathered. Pints of whisky stood among plates of chicken bones. Hoately was talking:

". . . and the minute I heard the kid go into that jerk-'em-to-

Jesus routine I knowed we was all set. I want to tell you, it was something to watch. That old buzzard's trap was hanging open a mile—lapping up every word the kid handed him."

He paused and let out a whoop at the sight of Stan and Molly.

The others helloed; Zeena bustled up and put her arms around Molly and kissed her. "Sakes alive, honey, I'm glad to see you. You come over and sit down right by Zeena. Where on earth did you skedaddle to? We knew they didn't pinch you or Stan because Clem hung around and watched. But I was looking all over for you."

"I hid in the van," Molly said. She looked down at her purse and ran her finger over the clasp.

"And Stan!" Zeena enveloped him in a hug and kissed him warmly on the mouth. "Stan, boy, you sure done noble. I always knew you were a mentalist. Imagine that—giving a cold reading to a cop and getting away with it! Oh, I just love you."

The rasping, fiddle voice of Major Mosquito cut through. "Come on over and have a drink. Hoately's treat. Come on over. I'm getting stinko."

They took their seats, and a gangling youth with spiky hair brought in two more plates of chicken. "Watch them bottles, folks. Town's hell on enforcement."

Stan and Molly sat together. Suddenly they were ravenous and dug into the chicken.

Joe Plasky said, "Nice going, kid. You kept your head. You're real carny, and no mistake."

Bruno said nothing. He had been about to start on his fourth plate of chicken but now it lay in front of him, neglected. Molly caught Stan's hand and squeezed it under the tablecloth. They exchanged a quick look.

Zeena poured herself a drink and took it in two swallows. "Liquor's terrible, Clem. It's that bad, I nearly left some—as the Scotch fella says."

Clem Hoately was picking his teeth with a sharpened match. "Short notice. I asked one of the deputies—young fellow who looked okay—where I could pick up a pint. He sent me to his brother-in-law. Town's all right if you case it careful. We won't have no trouble after tonight. That old son-of-a-bitch that sloughed us was the toughest they got. We'll open tomorrow night and pack 'em in. Best advertising in the world."

Molly looked startled. "I—I shouldn't think it would be safe."

Hoately grinned. "You can wear riding boots and breeches. That'll be all right. You got the shape to look good in 'em. Don't worry about it."

Zeena took a chicken bone from her mouth and said, "I think we all ought to give Stan a great big hand. We might have got into a peck of trouble if it hadn't been for him. I always say, there's nothing like the second sight. Anybody who can give a good reading'll never starve. Only, gosh"—she turned to face Stan—"I never knew you could spout the Bible, the way Clem's been telling us." She paused, chewing, and then went on, "Stan, 'fess up. Were you ever really a preacher?"

He shook his head, hard lines at the corners of his mouth. "That was my old man's idea once—to make me one. Only I couldn't see it. Then he wanted me to go into real estate. But that's too slow a turn. I wanted magic. But the old gent was a great hand at quoting scripture. I guess a lot of it rubbed off onto me."

Major Mosquito, holding a tumbler in both hands, lifted it. "Here's to the Great Stanton, purveyor of fun, magic, mystery and bullshit! He's a jolly good fellow, he's a jolly good . . ."

Bruno Hertz said, "You shut up. You talk too much for little fellow." His sad steer's eyes were on Molly. Suddenly he blurted out, "Molly, you and Stan going to get married?"

The room got as quiet as if a needle had been lifted off a record. Molly choked and Zeena slapped her on the back. Her face was red when she answered, "Why—what makes you think—"

Bruno, bold and desperate, stumbled on. "You and Stan been together! You going to get married?"

Stan looked up and met the strongman's gaze levelly. "As a matter of fact, Molly and I are going to head for vaudeville. We've got it all figured out. In the two-a-day nobody's going to run her in for wearing skimpies."

Zeena set down her glass. "Why—why, I think that's just splendid. Clem, did you hear? They're going to try the two-a-day. I think it's perfectly fine. I think it's great." She crushed

Molly in another hug. Then she reached out and rumpled Stan's hair. "Stan,—ain't—ain't you the foxy one! And you all the time —making out like you never—never knew the child was on the face of the earth." She dumped more whisky in her glass and said, "All right, folks, here's a toast to the bride and groom. Long life and may all your troubles be little ones—eh, Molly?"

Hoately lifted his coffee cup. Major Mosquito said, "Hooray! Let me hide under the bed, the first night. I'll be quiet. Just let me—"

Bruno Hertz poured a small drink for himself and gazed at Molly over the glass. "*Prosit, Liebchen.*" Under his breath he muttered, "Better wish luck. You going to need luck. Maybe some day you going to need—"

Joe Plasky's Lazarus smile was like a lamp. "All the best, kids. Glad to see it. I'll give you a letter to a couple of booking agents in New York."

Zeena cleared the plates and glasses from before her with an unsteady sweep. She reached into her purse and drew out a pack of cards. "Here you are, kids. Now's a good time to see what the Tarot has for you. The Tarot's always got an answer." She shuffled. "Go ahead, honey. Cut 'em. Let's see what you cut."

Molly cut the cards and Zeena grabbed them and turned them over. "Well, what d'you know—The Empress! That's her, honey. See, she's sitting on a couch and it's got the sign of Venus on it. That's for love. And she's got stars in her hair. That's for all the good things your husband's going to give you."

Major Mosquito squeaked with laughter, and Bruno hissed at him to keep quiet.

"The Empress is a good fortune card in love, honey. Couldn't be better 'cause it means you'll get what you want most." She shuffled again and held them up to Stan, who had stood up and moved in behind Molly's chair. Molly had taken his hand and was holding it near her cheek.

"Go on, Stan. You cut 'em, see what comes out."

Stan released Molly's hand. In the stacked cards, the edge of one showed darker than the others from handling and Stan cut to it without thinking, turning his half of the deck face up.

Major Mosquito let out a squall. Zeena knocked over the bottle and Hoately caught it before it had gurgled away. Bruno's stolid face was alight with something like triumph. Molly looked puzzled and Stan laughed. The midget across the table was beating the cloth with a spoon and crying out in an ecstasy of drunken glee:

"Ha! Ha! Ha! Ha! *The Hanged Man!*"

# Resurrection
# of the Dead

*At the call of an angel with
fiery wings, graves open, cof-
fins burst, and the dead are
naked.*

". . . I CAN see, madam, that there are many persons surrounding
you who are envious of your happiness, your culture, your good
fortune and—yes, I must be frank—your good looks. I would advise you, madam, to go your own way, doing those things which
you know down deep in your heart of hearts is right. And I am
sure your husband, who sits beside you in the theater now, will
agree with me. There is no weapon you can use against malicious
envy except the confidence in your way of life as the moral and
righteous one, no matter what the envious say. And it is one of
these, madam, and I believe you know of whom I am speaking,
who has poisoned your dog."

The applause was slow in starting. They were baffled; they
were awe-struck. Then it began from the back of the theater
and traveled forward, the people whose questions had been whispered to Molly and whose questions he had answered, clapping
last. It was a storm of sound. And Stan, hearing it through the
heavy drop curtain, breathed it in like mountain air.

The curtains parted for his second bow. He took it, bowing
slowly from the waist and then he extended his hand and Molly
swept from the wings where she had arrived by the door back-

stage behind the boxes. They bowed together, hand in hand, and then the curtains cut down again and they moved off through the wings and up the concrete stairs that led to the dressing rooms.

Stan opened the dressing-room door, stood aside for Molly to go in, then followed and shut the door. He sat for a moment on the wicker couch, then whipped off his white tie and unbuttoned the neckband of his stiff shirt and lit a cigarette.

Molly had stepped out of the skin-tight evening gown she wore and hung it on a hanger. She stood for a moment without a stitch on, scratching her ribs under the arms. Then she slipped on a robe, caught up her hair in a knot and began to dab cold cream on her face.

Finally Stan spoke. "Two nights running is too much."

Her hand stopped, pressed against her chin. Her head was turned away from him. "I'm sorry, Stan. I guess I was tired."

He got up and moved over, looking down at her. "After five years you still fluff it. My God, what do you use for brains anyway? What's eighty-eight?"

Her wide, smoky-gray eyes were brilliant with tears. "Stan, I—I'll have to think about it. When you come at me all of a sudden that way I have to think. I—just have to think," she finished lamely.

He went on, his voice cool. "Eighty-eight!"

"Organization!" she said, smiling quickly. "Shall I join some club, fraternity, or organization? Of course. I hadn't forgotten it, Stan. Honest, honey."

He went over to the couch and lay back on it. "You'll say it backwards and forwards a hundred times before you go to sleep tonight. Right?"

"Sure, Stan."

She brightened, relieved that the tension had passed. The towel came away from her face pink from the makeup. Molly patted powder on her forehead, started to put on her street lipstick. Stan took off his shirt and threw a robe around his shoulders. With a few practiced swipes he cold-creamed his face, frowning at his reflection. The blue eyes had grown frosty. There were lines, faint ones, at the corners of his mouth. They had always been there when he smiled but now he noticed for the first time

that they stayed there when his face was relaxed. Time was passing over his head.

Molly was fastening the snaps of her skirt. "Glory be, but I'm
tired. I don't want to go anywhere tonight but to bed. I could
sleep for a week."

Stan sat gazing at his image in the mirror, made hard by the
lights blazing around the edge. He was like a stranger to himself.
He wondered what went on behind that familiar face, the square
jaw, the corn-yellow hair. It was a mystery, even to himself. For
the first time in months he thought of Gyp and could see him
clearly through the mist of years, bounding through fields grown
lush with neglected weeds of late summer.

"Good boy," he muttered. "Good old boy."

"What was it, honey?" Molly was sitting on the wicker couch
reading a movie magazine while she waited for him to dress.

"Nothing, kid," he said over his shoulder. "Just mumbling in
my beard."

Who poisoned our dog? People around you who envy you.
Number fourteen. One: Will. Four: Tell. *Will* you *tell* this lady
what she is thinking about?

Stan shook his head and rubbed his face evenly with the towel.
He hung up his suit of tails and stepped into his tweed trousers.
He ran a comb through his hair and knotted his tie.

Outside the snow was falling lightly, lingering on the dark
surface of the dirty window of the dressing room.

At the stage door the winter met them with an icy breath.
They found a cab and got in and Molly slipped her arm through
his and rested her cheek against his shoulder and stayed that way.

"Here y'are, buddy. Hotel Plymouth."

Stan handed the driver a dollar and helped Molly out.

They passed through the revolving door into the drowsy heat
of the lobby and Stan stopped by the cigar counter for cigarettes.
He lifted his eyes to the desk and then he stopped and Molly,
turning back to see if he was coming, hurried up. She put her
hand on his arm. "Stan, darling—what's the matter with you?
God, you look terrible. Are you sick, honey? Answer me. Are
you sick? You're not mad at me, are you, Stan?"

Abruptly he turned away and strode out of the lobby into

the wind and the winter night. The cold air felt good and his face and neck needed the cold. He turned to the girl. "Molly, don't ask any questions. I just saw somebody I'm trying to duck. Go upstairs and pack our stuff. We're checking out. Got any dough? Well, square up the bill and have the bellhop bring the stuff out."

Without asking any more questions she nodded and went in.

When she came down the woman at the desk, the night clerk, smiled up at her from a detective story. "Will you make up my bill, please? Mr. and Mrs. Stanton Carlisle."

The woman smiled again. She was white-haired and Molly wondered why so many white-haired women insist on bright lip-stick. It makes them look like such crows, she thought. If I ever get white-haired I'll never wear anything darker than Passion Flower. Yet this woman had been quite a chick in her day, Molly decided. And she had lived. There was something about her that made you think she had been in show business. But then lots of good-looking people had when they were young and that really didn't mean a thing. It was managing to stay in show business and stay at the top that counted. Never getting to be a has-been and washed-up. That was the worst thing, to be washed-up. Only you had to save a pile of money while you were in the chips. And what with staying at the best places and buying dinners and drinks for managers and newspapermen and people they never seemed to get much ahead at the end of a season on the road. That is, the more the act was worth, the more it seemed to take to sell it.

"That will be eighteen dollars and eighty-five cents," the woman said. She looked searchingly at Molly. "Is—is your husband coming back to the hotel?"

Molly thought fast. "No. As a matter of fact, he's already waiting for me further downtown. We have to make a train."

The woman's face was not smiling any more. It had a hunted, hopeful look which was, at the same time, strangely hungry. Molly didn't like it a blessed bit. She paid and went out.

Stan was pacing up and down savagely. A cab was standing by the curb with its meter ticking. They put the bags in and rode off.

All hotels are the same place, Molly thought later, lying beside Stan in the partial darkness. Why do they always have street lights outside the windows and car lines in the street and elevators in the wall right beside your head and people upstairs who bang things? But anyhow it was better than never getting around or seeing anything.

Watching Stan undress had stirred her and made her remember so many good times and she had hoped he would feel like it even if they were both as tired as dogs. He had been so cross lately and they always seemed to be tired when they went to bed. With a little flare of panic she wondered if she were losing her looks or something. Stan could be so wonderful. It made her go all wriggly and scarey inside to think about it. God, it was worth waiting for—when he really wanted a party. But then she remembered something else and she began saying to herself, "Eighty-eight—organization. Shall I join some club, union, fraternity, or organization? Shall I join some club, union, fraternity, or organization?" She repeated it three times before she fell asleep with her lips slightly open and her cheek on one palm, her black hair tumbled over the pillow.

Stan reached out and felt around on the bedside table for the cigarettes. He found one and his match flared. Below them a late car whined into hearing from the distance, the steel rails carrying the sound. But he let it slip from his mind.

A memory was coming back. A day when he was eleven years old.

It was like other days of early summer. It began with a rattle of locusts in the trees outside the bedroom window. Stan Carlisle opened his eyes, and the sun was shining hotly.

Gyp sat on the chair beside the bed, whining gently deep in his throat and touching the boy's arm with one paw.

Stan reached out lazily and rubbed the mongrel's head while the dog writhed in delight. In a moment he had leaped onto the bed joyfully wagging all over. Then Stan was fully awake and remembered. He pushed Gyp off and began brushing violently at the streaks of dried clay left on the sheets by the dog's paws. Mother always got mad when Gyp Jumped Up.

Stan stole to the door, but the door to his parents' room across the hall was still closed. He tiptoed back and idly pulled on his underwear and the corduroy knickers. He stuffed a paper-backed book inside his shirt and laced up his shoes.

Down in the yard he could see the garage doors open. Dad had left for the office.

Stan went downstairs. Being careful not to make any noise he got a bottle of milk from the ice box, a loaf of bread and a jar of jelly. Gyp got bread and milk in a saucer on the floor.

While Stan sat in the early morning stillness of the empty kitchen, cutting off slices of bread and loading them with jelly, he read the catalog:

". . . a real professional outfit, suitable for theater, club, or social gathering. An hour's performance complete. With beautiful cloth-bound instruction book. Direct from us or at your toy or novelty dealer's. $15.00."

After his eighth slice of bread and jelly he put the remains of his breakfast away and went out on the back porch with the catalog. The sun was growing hotter. The brightness of the summer morning filled him with a pleasant sadness, as if at the thought of something noble and magic which had happened long ago in the days of knights and lonely towers.

Upstairs he heard the sharp rap of small heels on the floor and then the roar of water in the bathtub. Mother had gotten up early.

Stan hurried upstairs. Above the rush of the water he could make out his mother's voice, singing in a hard, glittering soprano, "Oh, my laddie, my laddie, I luve the kent you carry. I luve your very bonnet with the silver buckle on it . . ."

He was disturbed and resentful of the song. Usually she sang it after he had been sent up to bed, when the parlor was full of people and Mark Humphries, the big dark man who taught singing, was playing the accompaniment while Dad sat in the dining room, smoking a cigar and talking in low tones about deals with one of his own friends. It was part of the grown-up world with its secrets, its baffling changes from good temper to bad without warning. Stan hated it.

He stepped into the bedroom that always smelled of perfume.

The shining brass bedstead was glittering big and important in the bar of sunlight through the blind. The bed was rumpled.

Stan went over and buried his face in the pillow that smelled faintly of perfume, drawing in his breath through it again and again. The other pillow smelled of hair tonic.

He knelt beside the bed, thinking of Elaine and Lancelot—how she came floating down on a boat and Lancelot stood by the bank looking at her and being sorry she was dead.

The rush of water in the bathroom had given way to splashing and snatches of singing. Then the chung of the stopper and the water gurgling out.

Beyond the window, with its shades making the room cool and dark, a cicada's note sounded, starting easy and getting loud and dying away, sign of hot weather coming.

Stan took one more breath of the pillow, pushing it around his face to shut out sound and everything except its yielding softness and its sweetness.

There was a sharp click from the latch of the bathroom door. The boy frantically smoothed out the pillow; he tore around the big brass bed and out into the hall and across to his own room.

Downstairs he heard Jennie's slow step on the back porch and the creak of the kitchen chair as she slumped her weight into it to rest before she took off her hat and her good dress. It was the day for Jennie to do the wash.

Stan heard his mother come out of the bathroom; then he heard the bedroom door close. He crept out into the hall and paused beside it.

Inside there was a pat of bare feet on the floor and the catch of the bedroom door quietly slipped on. Grownups were always locking themselves in places. Stan got a sudden shiver of mystery and elation. It started in his lower back and rippled up between his shoulder blades.

Through the closed door came the soft clink of a perfume bottle being set down on the dressing table and then there was the scrape of chair legs. The chair creaked ever so little; it scraped the floor again; the bottle clinked as the stopper was put in.

When she came out she would be dressed up and ready to go

downtown and she would have a lot of jobs for him to do while she was gone—like cleaning up the closet in his room or cutting the grass on the terrace.

He moved stealthily along the hall and eased open the door to the attic stairs, closed it behind him gently and went up. He knew the creaky steps and skipped them. The attic was hot and heavy with the smell of wood and old silk.

Stan stretched out on an iron bed covered with a silk patchwork quilt. It was made of strips of silk sewn in squares, different colors on each side and a single square of black silk in the center of each. Grandma Stanton made it the winter before she died.

The boy lay face down. The sounds of the house filtered up to him from far away. The whining scrape of Gyp, banished to the back porch. Jennie in the cellar and the chug of the new washing machine. The brisk clatter of Mother's door opening and the tap of her high heels on the stairs. She called his name once sharply and then called something down to Jennie.

Jennie's voice came out the cellar window, mournful and rich. "Yes, Mis' Carlisle. If I see him I tell him."

For a moment Stan was afraid Mother would go out the back door and that Gyp would Jump Up and make her cross and then she would start talking about getting rid of him. But she went out the front door instead. Stan heard the mail box rattle. Then she went down the steps.

He leaped up and ran over to the attic window where he could see the front lawn through the maple tops below him.

Mother was walking quickly away toward the car line.

She would be going downtown to Mr. Humphries for her singing lesson. And she would not be back for a long time. Once she paused before the glass signboard on the lawn of the church. It told what Dr. Parkman would preach about next Sunday, but it was so black, and with the glass in front of it, it was like looking into a mirror. Mother stopped, as if reading about next Sunday's sermon; turning her head first one way and then another, she pulled her hat a little more forward and touched her hair.

She went on then, walking slower. The boy watched her until she was out of sight.

On every hilltop and rise Stan turned and gazed back across the fields. He could spy the roof of his own house rising among the bright green of the maples.

The sun beat down.

The air was sweet with the smell of summer grasses. Gyp bounded through the hummocks, chasing away almost out of sight and bouncing back again.

Stan climbed a fence, crossed a pasture, and then mounted a stone wall, boosting Gyp over. On the other side of the wall the fields were thicker with brush and little oak bushes and pines and beyond it the woods began.

When he stepped into their dark coolness he felt again that involuntary shudder, which was part pleasure and part apprehension, rise between his shoulder blades. The woods were a place to kill enemies in. You fought them with a battle-ax and you were naked and nobody dared say anything about it because you had the ax always hanging from your wrist by a piece of leather. Then there was an old castle deep in the forest. It had green moss in the cracks between the stones and there was a moat around it full of water and it stood there deep and still as death and from the castle there was never a sound or a sign of life.

Stan trod softly now and held his breath, listening to the green silence. The leaves were tender under his feet. He stepped over a fallen tree and then looked up through the branches to where the sun made them bright.

He began to dream. He and Lady Cynthia rode through the forest. Cynthia was Mother's name, only Lady Cynthia was not like Mother except that she looked like her. She was just a beautiful lady on a white palfrey and the bridle was set with gems and jewels that winked in the dappled light through the branches. Stan was in armor and his hair was long and cut straight across and his face was tanned dark and with no freckles. His horse was a powerful charger as black as midnight. That was its name—Midnight. He and Lady Cynthia had come to the forest to seek an adventure, for in the forest was a powerful old magician.

Stan came out on a long-disused timber road where he slipped out of the dream, for he remembered that they had been here on the picnic. That was the time they had come out with Mr.

and Mrs. Morris and Mark Humphries had driven Mother and Dad and Stan in his car with the top down. They brought the food in baskets.

Sudden anger rose up in him when he thought how his dad had had to spoil the day by having a fuss with Mother about something. He had spoken in low tones but then Mother had said, "Stan and I are going for a walk all by ourselves, aren't we, Stan?" She was smiling at the others the way she did when something was wrong. Stan had felt that delicious shudder go up between his shoulders.

That was the time they found the Glade.

It was a deep cleft in a ridge and you would never know it was there unless you stumbled on it. He had been back since but on that day Mother had been there and all of a sudden, as if she had felt the magic of the place, she had knelt and kissed him. He remembered the perfume she had on. She had held him off at arm's length and she was really smiling this time, as if at something deep inside herself, and she said, "Don't tell anybody. This place is a secret just between us."

He had been happy all the way back to the others.

That night when they were back home and he was in bed, the sound of his father's voice, rasping and rumbling through the walls, had made him sick with rebellion. What did he have to always be fussing with Mother for? Then the thought of the Glade, and of how she looked when she kissed him, made him wriggle with delight.

But the next day it was all gone and she spoke sharp to him about everything and kept finding jobs for him to do.

Stan started down the loggers' road. In a damp spot he stooped and then knelt like a tracker examining a spoor. The spot was fed by a trickle of spring. Across it were the tracks of auto tires, their clear and sacrilegious imprints just beginning to fill with water.

Stan hated them—the grownups were everywhere. He hated their voices most of all.

Cautiously he crossed the road, calling Gyp to him to keep him from rustling through the brush. He held the dog's collar and went on, taking care not to tread on any dead twigs. The

Glade had to be approached with the reverence of silence. He climbed the last bank on his hands and knees and then on looking over the crest he froze.

Voices were coming from the Glade.

He peered further over. Two people were lying on an Indian blanket and with a hot rush Stan knew that one was a man and the other was a woman and this was what men and women did secretly together that everybody stopped talking about when he came around, only some grownups never talked about it at all. Curiosity leaped inside of him at the thought of spying on them when they didn't know he was there. He was seeing it all—all of it—the thing that made babies grow inside of women. He could hardly breathe.

The woman's face was hidden by the man's shoulder, and only her hands could be seen pressing against his back. After a while they were still. Stan wondered if they were dead—if they ever died doing it and if it hurt them but they had to do it even so.

At last they stirred and the man rolled over on his back. The woman sat up, holding her hands to her hair. Her laughter rang up the side of the Glade, a little harsh but still silvery.

Stan's fingers tightened on the grass hummock under his hand. Then he spun around, dragging Gyp by the collar, and stumbled, sliding and bumping, down the slope to the road. He ran with his breath scorching his throat, his eyes burning with tears. He ran all the way back and then went up in the attic and lay on the iron bed and tried to cry, but then he couldn't.

He heard Mother come in after a while. The light outside began to darken and shadows got longer.

Then he heard the car drive up. Dad got out. Stan could tell by the way he slammed the car door that he was mad. Downstairs he heard his father's voice, rasping through the floors, and his mother's raised, the way she spoke when she was exasperated.

Stan came downstairs, one step at a time, listening.

His father's voice came from the living room. ". . . I don't care for any more of your lies. I tell you, Mrs. Carpenter saw the two of you turning up the road into Mills' Woods. She recognized you and she saw Mark and she recognized the car."

Mother's tone was brittle. "Charles, I should think you would have a little more—*pride*, shall we say?—than to take the word of anyone as malicious and as common as your *friend*, Mrs. Carpenter."

Dad was hammering on the mantelpiece with his fist; Stan could hear the metal thing that covered the fireplace rattle. "New York hats! A nigger to clean up the house! Washing machines! Music lessons! After all I've given you, you turn around and hand me something like this. You! I ought to horse-whip that snake-in-the-grass within an inch of his life!"

Mother spoke slowly. "I rather think Mark Humphries can take care of himself. In fact, I should dearly love to see you walk right up to him on the street and tell him the things you've been saying to me. Because he would tell you that you are a liar. And you would get just what you're asking for; just what you're asking for. Besides that, Charles, you have a filthy mind. You mustn't judge others by yourself, dear. After all, it is quite possible for a person with some breeding to enjoy an hour's motoring in friendship and nothing more. But I realize that if you and—Clara Carpenter, shall we say? . . ."

Dad let out a noise that was something like a roar and something like a sob. "By the Eternal, I've sworn never to take the Lord's name in vain, but you're enough to try the patience of a saint. God *damn* you! D'you hear? *God damn you and all—*"

Stan had reached the ground floor and stood with his fingers running up and down the newel post of the stairs, looking in through the wide double doors of the living room. Mother was sitting very straight on the sofa without leaning back. Dad was standing by the mantel, one hand in his pocket and the other beating against the wood. When he looked up and saw Stan he stopped short.

Stan wanted to turn and run out the front door but his father's eyes kept him fastened to the floor. Mother turned her head and saw him and smiled.

The telephone rang then.

Dad started and plunged down the hall to answer it, his savage "Hello!" bursting like a firecracker in the narrow hallway.

Stan moved painfully, like walking through molasses. He

crossed the room and came near his mother whose smile had hardened and grown sick-looking. She whispered, "Stan, Dad is upset because I went riding with Mr. Humphries. We wanted to take you riding with us but Jennie said you weren't here. But —Stan—let's make believe you did go with us. You'll go next time. I think it would make Dad feel better if he thought you were along."

From the hall his father's voice thundered, "By the Eternal, why did the fool have to be told in the first place? I was against telling him. It's the Council's business to vote on the committee's recommendation. We had it in the bag, sewed up tight. Now every idiot in town will know just where the streets will be cut and that property will shoot sky-high by tomorrow morning. . . ."

As Mother leaned close to Stan he smelled the perfume she had on her hair. She always put it on when she went downtown to take her singing lesson. Stan felt cold inside and empty. Even when she kissed him. "Whose boy are you, Stan? You're Mother's boy, aren't you, dear?"

He nodded and walked clumsily to the double doors. Dad was coming back. He took Stan roughly by the shoulder and shoved him toward the front door. "Run along, now. Your mother and I are talking."

Mother was beside them. "Let him stay, Charles. Why don't you ask Stanton what—what he did this afternoon?"

Dad stood looking at her with his mouth shut tight. He still had Stan by the shoulder. Slowly he turned his head. "Stan, what's your mother talking about?"

Stan swallowed. He hated that slack mouth and the stubble of pale yellow on the chin that came out when Dad hadn't shaved for several hours. Mark Humphries did a trick with four little wads of newspaper and a hat and had showed Stan how to do it. And he used to ask riddles.

Stan said, "We went riding with Mr. Humphries in his automobile." Over his father's arm, still holding him, Stan saw Mother's face make a little motion at him as if she were kissing the air.

Dad went on, his voice quiet and dangerous. "Where did you go with Mr. Humphries, son?"

Stan's tongue felt thick. Mother's face had gotten white, even her mouth. "We—we went out where we had the picnic that time."

Dad's fingers loosened and Stan turned and ran out into the falling dusk. He heard the front door close behind him.

Someone switched on the living-room lamp. After a while Dad came out, got in his car and went downtown. Mother had left some cold meat and bread and butter on the kitchen table and Stan ate it alone, reading the catalog. Only it had lost its flavor and there seemed to be something terribly sad about the blue willow-pattern plate and the old knife and fork. Gyp whined under the table. Stan handed him all his own meat and got some jelly and ate it on the bread. Mother was upstairs in the spare bedroom with the door locked.

The next day Mother got breakfast for him. He said nothing and neither did she. But she wasn't a grownup any more. Or he wasn't a kid any more. There were no more grownups. They lied when they got scared, just like anybody. Everybody was alike only some were bigger. He ate very little and wiped his mouth and said, "Excuse me," politely. Mother didn't ask him to do any jobs. She didn't say anything at all.

He tied Gyp up to the kennel and set out for the woods where the old loggers' road cut into them. He moved in a dream and the shine of the sun seemed to hold back its warmth. At the top of the Glade he paused and then slid doggedly down its slope. Around him the trees rose straight and innocent in the sun and the sound of a woodpecker came whirring through them. The grass was crushed in one place; close by Stan found a handkerchief with "C" embroidered in a corner.

He looked at it with a crawling kind of fascination and then scooped out a hole in the earth and buried it.

When he got back he kept catching himself thinking about things as if nothing had happened, then stopping and the wave of desolation would sweep over him.

Mother was in her room when he came upstairs.

But something was lying big and square on his bed. He raced in.

There it was. The "Number 3" set—Marvello Magic. A full hour's entertainment, suitable for stage, club, or social gathering, $15.00. Its cover was gay with a picture of Mephistopheles making cards rise from a glass goblet. On the side of the box was a paper sticker which read, "Myers' Toy and Novelty Mart" and the address downtown. The corners of the box were shiny with imitation metal bindings, printed on the paper.

Stan knelt beside the bed, gazing at it. Then he threw his arms around it and beat his forehead against one of the sharp corners until the blood came.

Outside the trolley had approached and slid under the hotel window, groaning its lonely way through the night. Stan was trembling. He threw back the covers, switched on the bed light and stumbled into the bathroom. From his fitted case he took a vial and shook a white tablet into his hand. He found the tooth glass, swallowed the tablet with a gulp of tepid water.

When he got back in bed it was several minutes before the sedative began to work and he felt the peaceful grogginess stealing up to his brain.

"Christ, why did I have to go thinking of that?" he said aloud. "After all these years, why did I have to see her? And Christmas only a week off."

CARD VII

# The
# Emperor

*carved on his throne the name of power and on his scepter the sign of power.*

"STAN, honey, I'm scared."

He slowed the car and bent to look at the road signs. Sherwood Park—8 miles. "We're nearly there. What are you scared of? Because these people have a lot of jack? Whistle the eight bars of our opener and you'll snap out of it."

"I've tried that, Stan. Only—gosh, it's silly. But how'll I know which fork to grab? The way they lay out these fancy dinners looks like Tiffany's window."

The Great Stanton turned off the highway. Late light of summer evening lay over the sky; his headlights threw back the pale undersides of leaves as the roadster sped up the lane. On either side elms stood in columns of dignity.

"Nothing to it. Watch the old dame at the head of the table. Just stall until she dives in and she'll cue you on the hardware. My mother's folks had barrels of jack once. The old lady knew her way around. That's what she used to tell my old man whenever they went anywhere."

The house rose out of the dusk behind a sweep of lawn as big as a golf course. At the door a Negro butler with tiny brass buttons said, "Let me rest your coat and hat, sir."

103

"My name is Stanton. Stanton the Mentalist."

"Oh. Mis' Harrington say to show you right upstairs. She say you be wanting to have dinner upstairs, sir."

Stan and Molly followed him. Through an archway they could see women in evening dresses. A man in a dinner jacket stood with his back to a dark, enormous fireplace. He held a cocktail glass, gripping it by the foot instead of the stem.

The room was on the top floor, rear; the ceiling slanted.

"Dinner'll be served right soon, sir. Anything you want, just pick up that phone and push button eight on the box. That's butler's pantry."

When he had closed the door Stan locked it. "Relax, kid," he said wryly, "we're eating private. Let's get loaded first and try out the batteries."

He opened their traveling bags; Molly drew her dress over her head and hung it in a closet. From one of the bags she shook out a black net evening gown laden with sequins. "Hold the wires, honey, so they won't catch in my hair."

Expertly Stan eased the dress over her head. It was high-cut in the back with a ruff. He took a curved metal band attached to a flat earphone and slipped it over her head while the girl held her hair forward. When she threw it back the hair covered her ears so that the compact headset was completely hidden. Stan reached into the low V of the neck, found a miniature plug, and connected the headset. From his own suitcase he took his tails and began to stud a dress shirt.

"Go slow on that makeup, kid. Remember—you're not working behind foots now. And don't do any bumps or grinds while you're supposed to be hypnotized."

Standing in his underwear, he put on a linen vest with pockets like a hunting jacket's. They bulged with flat flashlight batteries. A wire dangled; strapping it to his leg in three places, he carried it down and drew on a black silk sock, feeding the wire through a tiny hole. His shoe followed, then the wire plugged into a socket at the side of the shoe. Finally he put on his shirt. Moistening his fingers, he rubbed them on a handkerchief, took from a wax paper envelope a spotless white tie, and tied it, frowning in the mirror of the dresser. In his coat a spider web of fine wire was sewed into the lining as an aerial; another plug connected it with the hidden vest which held the transmitter.

The Great Stanton adjusted his suspenders, then buttoned his waistcoat; he gave his hair a touch with the brushes and handed Molly a whiskbroom so that she could dust his shoulders for him.

"Gee, honey, you look handsome."

"Consider yourself kissed good and hard. I don't want to get smeared up. For God's sake take some of that lipstick off."

Under the toes of his left foot was the reassuring bulge of the contact key. Stan reached under his white vest and threw an invisible switch. He walked across the floor. "Get any buzz?"

"Not yet."

"Now." He pressed hard with his toes inside his shoe; but Molly made no sign. "God damn! If I'd been able to get a line on who was going to be at this shindig I'd have worked a straight crystal routine. There's too many things to come loose in this damn wireless gimmick." He ran his hands over the girl's dress, checking. Then he said, "Hold up your hair." The head-set plug had slipped out. Stan spread its minute prongs with the point of a nail file and rasped them bright with irritable strokes. He connected it and Molly rearranged her hair.

On the other side of the room he again pressed with his left toes.

"I've got it, honey. Nice and clear. Now walk and see if it buzzes when you don't want it to."

Stan paced back and forth, keeping his weight off his toes, and Molly said she couldn't hear a thing, only when he wiggled his toes and made the contact.

"Okay. Now I'm in another room. What are the tests?"

"A card, a color, and a state."

"Right. What's this?"

Molly closed her eyes. From the earphone came a faint buzz three times—spades. Then a long buzz and three short ones—five plus three is eight. "Eight of spades."

"Right."

A tap from the door made Stan hiss for her to keep quiet.

"Dinner is served, sir. Mis' Harrington send her respects. She'll let you know on the phone when it's time for you all to come down. Better let me open up this bottle now, sir; we's powerful busy downstairs." He eased the cork out, his polished fingers dark against the napkin.

Stan felt in his pocket for a quarter and caught himself just in time. The butler bowed out.

"Gee, lookit, Stan! Champagne!"

"One glass for you, Cahill. We're working. If you load up on that stuff you'll be calling the old girl 'dearie.'"

"Aw, Stan."

He poured, put a few drops in his own glass, then carried the bottle into the bathroom and emptied the rest, bubbling gaily, down the drain of the washbowl.

From the rear Mrs. Bradburn Harrington looked like a little girl, but, Christ, what a crow when you see her head-on, Stan thought. She tapped a brass gong until the babble died. "Now I have a real treat for us. Mr. Stanton, whom I'm sure many of us have seen in the theater, will show us some wonderful things. I don't know just what they're going to do so I'll let Mr. Stanton tell you all about it himself."

Stan stood in the hall beside Molly. He took a deep breath and smoothed down his hair with both hands. The butler suddenly appeared beside him, holding a silver plate. On it was a slip of paper, folded. "Mis' Harrington tell me to give you this, sir."

Stan took it, unfolded it deftly with one hand, and read it at a single glance. He crushed it and swept it into his pocket, his face darkening. Molly whispered, "What's the matter, hon? What's happened?"

"Nothing!" he spat out savagely. "It's in the bag."

From the drawing room Mrs. Harrington's voice continued, ". . . and it will all be very exciting, I'm sure. May I present Mr. Stanton."

Stan drew a breath and walked in. He bowed to the hostess, again to the guests. "Ladies and gentlemen, what we are about to do may have many explanations. I shall offer none. In the realm of the human mind science has hardly scratched the surface. Most of its mysteries lie hidden from us yet. But down through the years certain people have had unusual gifts. I take no credit for mine." This time his bow was hardly more than a lowering of the eyes. This audience was the top. This was class. With a momentary shock Stan recognized a famous novelist, tall, slightly stooped, half bald. One of the season's debutantes, who had already made the papers with an affair involving a titled émigré, sat primly holding a highball on her knee, her white dress so low-cut that Stan fancied he could see the aureoles of her nipples.

"My family was Scotch originally, and the Scotch are said to possess strange faculties." The gray head of a stern-faced old judge nodded. "My ancestors used to call it 'second sight.' I shall call it simply—mentalism. It is a well-known fact that the minds of two people can establish a closer communication than words. A *rapport*. I discovered such a person several years ago. Ladies and gentlemen, allow me to present my assistant, Miss Cahill."

Molly swept in smiling, with her long stride, and rested her hand lightly on Stan's bent forearm. The debutante turned to a young man sitting on the arm of her chair. "Friend of yours, Diggie?" He closed her lips with his hand, staring fascinated at Molly.

Her eyes were half closed, her lips slightly parted. The old judge quietly took off his reading glasses.

"If I may trouble you, I should like to have Miss Cahill recline on that sofa."

There was a scurry of people finding other seats and a man snickered. Stan led Molly to the sofa and arranged a pillow behind her. She lifted her feet and he tucked the folds of the sequinned gown up from the floor. Reaching into his waistcoat pocket he drew out a ball of rock crystal the size of a marble and held it above the level of her eyes. "Concentrate."

The room was still at last.

"Your eyelids are growing heavy. Heavy. Heavy. You cannot lift them. You are falling asleep. Sleep. Sleep . . ."

Molly let her breath out in a long sigh and the lines about her mouth relaxed. Stan picked up her hand and laid it in her lap.

She was limp. He turned to the company: "I have placed her in deep hypnosis. It is the only way I know by which telepathy can be made sure. I shall now pass among you, and I shall ask you to show me a number of objects, such as jewels, theater tickets, anything you wish."

He turned back to the reclining girl. "Miss Cahill, I shall touch a number of objects in this room. As I touch them you are to describe them. Is that clear?"

Dreamily she nodded. Her voice was a whisper. "Yes. Objects. Describe . . ."

Stan crossed the room and the old judge held out a gold fountain pen. Stan took it, focused his attention on it, his eyes widening. His back was to Molly and her head was turned toward the back of the sofa. She could see nothing. But her voice came as from a distance, just clear enough for them to hear if they listened hard. "A pen. A fountain pen. Gold. And something's . . . engraved. *A . . . G . . . K.*"

There was a ripple of applause, which Stan stopped with a lifted hand.

The hostess pointed to the spray of little brown orchids she wore as a corsage. Molly's voice went on, far away. "Flowers . . . beautiful flowers . . . they're . . . they're . . . or . . . orchids, I think."

The crowd sucked in its breath.

The debutante with the scarlet lips and the low-cut dress beckoned to Stan. When he drew near she reached into the pocket of the young man beside her and took out a gold mesh vanity case. Throwing open the cover, she held it so that only Stan could see what it contained. He frowned and she giggled up at him. "Go on, Mister Mindreader. Read my mind."

Stan stood motionless. He took a deep breath and by straining it against his throat forced the color to rise in his face.

"Look. He blushes too," said the girl.

The Great Stanton never moved but Molly's voice went on. "Something . . . something . . . do I have to tell what it is?"

Over his shoulder Stan said softly, "No, never mind it."

The girl snapped the bag shut and replaced it in the man's

pocket. "You win, brother. You win." She gulped down the rest of her drink.

The Great Stanton bowed. "Lest I be accused of using trickery and signaling Miss Cahill, I should like a committee to follow me from the room for a few moments. Five or six persons will do nicely. And I shall ask someone here to take a slip of paper and record what Miss Cahill says while I am out of the room."

The hostess volunteered, and three couples followed Stan across the hall and into the library. When they were inside he closed the door. Something touched his hand; it was cold and made him jump. The guests laughed. Beside him stood a harlequin Great Dane, gazing up with eyes that held mastery in their steadiness and an odd loneliness too. The dog nudged Stan's leg with his paw and the mentalist began to scratch him idly behind the ears while he spoke to the others.

"I should like one of you now to choose some card in a pack of fifty-two."

"Deuce of clubs."

"Fine. Remember it. Now will someone select a color?"

"Chartreuse."

"That's a little difficult to visualize, but we'll try. Now will one of the ladies think of a state—any state in the union."

"That's easy," the girl spoke with a drawl. "There's only one state worth thinking about—Alabama."

"Alabama. Excellent. But would you care to change your mind?"

"No, indeedy. It's Alabama for sure."

Stanton bowed. "Shall we join the others?"

He held the door for them and they filed out. Stan knelt and laid his cheek against that of the Great Dane. "Hello, beautiful. Bet you wish you were my dog, don't you?"

The Dane whined softly.

"Don't let 'em get you down, boy. Bite 'em in their fat asses."

He rose, brushed his lapel, and strolled back to the lights and the voices.

Molly still lay on the couch, looking like a sleeping princess waiting for the kiss of a deliverer. The room was in a hubbub.

"The deuce of clubs! And the color—they picked chartreuse

and she couldn't decide whether it was yellow or green! Isn't it amazing! And Alabama!"

"How would you like to have him for a husband, darling? Someone I know would have to scoot back to Cannes."

"Miraculous. Nothing short of miraculous."

Stan sat beside Molly, took one of her hands in his and said, "Wake up! Come now, wake up!"

She sat up, passing the back of her hand over her eyes. "Why —what's happened? Oh! Was I all right?"

"You were splendid," he said, looking into her eyes. "Every test was perfect."

"Oh, I'm so glad."

Still holding her hand, he drew her to her feet. They walked to the door, turned and bowed slightly and passed through it, applause clattering behind them.

"Stan, don't we stay for the party? I mean, the rest of it?"

"Shut up!"

"But—Stan—"

"I said shut up! I'll tell you later. Beat it upstairs. I'll be up in a little while and we'll get to hell out of here."

Obediently she went, pressing her lips together, fighting back an impulse to cry. This was nothing more than any other show; she had hoped there would be a party afterwards and dancing and more champagne.

Stan crossed over to the library, and the dog met him, jumping up. Heedless of his starched shirt bosom, Stan let him. "You know a pal, don't you, boy."

"Mr. Stanton—"

It was the old man who looked like a judge.

"I couldn't let you go without telling you how miraculous your work is."

"Thank you."

"I mean it, my boy. I'm afraid you don't realize what you've stumbled onto here. This goes deeper than you realize."

"I have no explanation for it," Stan said abruptly, still scratching the dog behind the ears.

"But I think I know your secret."

Silence. Stan could feel the blood surging up over his face.

Good Christ, another amateur magician, he thought, raging. I've got to ditch him. But I've got to get him on my side, first. At last he said, smiling, "Perhaps you have the solution. A few persons of unusual intelligence and scientific knowledge might be able to guess at the main principle."

The old man nodded sagely. "I've guessed it, my boy. I've guessed it. This is no code act."

Stan's smile was intimate and his eyes danced with fellowship. God, here it comes. But I'll handle him somehow.

"Yes, my boy. I know. And I don't blame you for keeping your secret. It's the young lady."

"Yes?"

The judge lowered his voice. "I know it isn't telepathy. You have *spirit aid!*"

Stan felt like shouting. Instead he closed his eyes, the shadow of a smile passing over his mouth.

"They don't understand, my boy. I know why you have to present it as second sight. They're not ready to receive the glorious truth of survival. But our day will come, my boy. It will come. Develop your gift—the young lady's mediumship. Cherish it, for it is a fragile blossom. But what a soul-stirring thing it is! Oh, to think of it—this precious gift of mediumship, this golden bridge between us and those who have joined the ranks of the liberated, there to dwell on ever-ascending planes of spiritual life—"

The door opened and both men turned. It was Molly. "Oh. I'm sorry. I didn't know you were busy. Say, Stan—"

"Miss Cahill, I should like you to meet Judge Kimball. It *is* Judge Kimball, I am certain of it, although I do not recall ever having seen your photograph."

The old man nodded, smiling as if he and Stan shared a secret. He patted Molly's hand. "A great gift, my dear child, a great gift."

"Yeah, it's a gift all right, Judge. Well, I guess I'll be going back upstairs."

Stan took both her hands in his and shook them. "You were splendid tonight, my dear. Splendid. Now run along and I'll join you shortly. You had better lie down and rest for a few minutes."

When he released her Molly said, "Oops," and looked at her left hand; but Stan urged her toward the door, closing it gently behind her. He turned back to the judge.

"I'll confess, Judge. But"—he tilted his head toward the room across the hall—"they wouldn't understand. That is why I dropped in here for a moment. Someone here does understand." He looked down at the dog. "Don't you, boy?"

The Dane whined softly and crept closer.

"You know, Judge, they can sense things that are beyond all human perception. They can see and hear presences about us which we can never detect." Stan had moved toward a reading lamp beside an armchair. "For instance, I received a very faint but clear impression just now that someone from the Other Side is in the room. I am sure it is a young girl, that she is trying to get through to us. But I can tell nothing more about her; I cannot see her. If only our handsome friend here could talk he might be able to tell us."

The dog was staring into a dark corner of the book-lined room. He growled questioningly. Then, while the old man watched, fascinated, the Dane leaped up and shot into the corner, standing there alert and quiet, looking upward.

The mentalist slid his hand unobtrusively into his trousers pocket. "They know, sir. They can see. And now—I bid you good evening."

The house had grown full of unseen presences for the old judge; in thinking of some who might be near him now, his eyes grew wet. Slowly, elegantly, his shoulders straight, the Great Stanton ascended the stairs with the tread of an emperor, and the judge watched him go. A wonderful young man.

In the room with the tilted ceiling Molly was lying on the bed in her brassière and panties, smoking a cigarette. She sat up, hugging her knees. "Stan, for crying out loud, tell me why you got so mad at me when I wanted to stay for the party! Other private bookings we always stay and have fun and I don't get

lit on three champagnes, honest I don't, honey. You think I don't
know how to behave!"

He shoved his hands into his pockets, pulled out a slip of
paper and crushed it, then flung it into a corner of the room.
He spoke in a savage whisper. "For Christ's sake, don't go turning on the tears until we get out of here. I said *no* because it
wasn't the spot for it. We gave 'em just enough. Always leave
'em wanting more. We built ourselves up and I didn't see any
sense in knocking it all down again. For Christ's sake, we gave
'em a goddamned miracle! They'll be talking about it the rest of
their lives. And they'll make it better every time they tell it.
And what do we get for it? Three hundred lousy bucks and get
treated like an extra darky they hired to pass the booze around.
This is the big time, all right. Get your name in lights a foot
high and then come out to one of these joints and what do they
hand you—a dinner on a plate like a hobo at a back door."

He was breathing heavily, his face red and his throat working.
"I'll sweat it out of them. By Christ, that old guy downstairs
gave me the angle. I'll shake 'em loose from a pile of dough before I'm done. I'll have 'em begging me to stay a week. I'll
have 'em wondering why I take my meals in my room. And
it'll be because they're not fit to eat with—the bastards. I've been
crazy not to think of this angle before, but from now on I know
the racket. I've given 'em mentalism and they treat it like a dog
walking on his hind legs. Okay. They're asking for it. Here it
comes."

He stopped and looked down at the staring girl, whose face
was chalky around the lips. "You did okay, kid." He smiled
with one corner of his mouth. "Here's your ring, baby. I needed
it for a gag."

Frowning still, Molly slipped the diamond back on her finger
and watched the tiny specks of light from it spatter the dark
corner of the sloping ceiling.

Stan carefully unhooked the wires and got out of his clothes.
He went into the bathroom and Molly heard the bolt slammed
shut.

You never could tell why Stan did anything. Here he was,
madder than a wet hen, and he wouldn't say why and besides

she wouldn't have pulled any boners; she'd just have smiled and kept her voice low and made believe she was tired from being hypnotized. She hadn't muffed any signals. What was eating him?

She got up and retrieved the crumpled slip from the corner. That was when it all started, when the colored waiter handed it to Stan just before they went on. Her fingers shook as she opened it.

*"Kindly do not mingle with the guests."*

CARD VIII

# The Sun

*On a white horse the sun child, with flame for hair, carries the banner of life.*

"I'M NOT going to put on the light. Because we're not going to argue all night again. I tell you, there's not a goddamned bit of difference between it and mentalism. It's nothing but our old act dressed up so it will lay 'em in the aisles. And for real."

"Honey, I don't like it."

"In God's name, what's the matter with it?"

"Well, what if there are—what if people do come back? I mean, well, they mightn't like it. I can't explain it. I'm scared."

"Listen, baby. I been over this a hundred times. If anybody's going to come back they're not going to get steamed up because we fake a little. We'll be doing the marks a favor; we'll make 'em plenty happy. After all, suppose you thought you could really speak to your dad, now. Wouldn't that make you happy?"

"Oh, God, I wish I could. Maybe it's because I've wished so hard for just that and hoped that maybe someday I could."

"I know, kid. I know how it is. Maybe there's something in it after all. I don't know. But I've met half a dozen spook workers in the past year and they're hustlers, every one of them. I tell you, it's just show business. The crowd believes we can read minds. All right. They believe it when I tell them that 'the

115

lawsuit's going to come out okay.' Isn't it better to give them something to hope for? What does a regular preacher do every Sunday? Only all he does is promise. We'll do more than promise. We'll give 'em proof!"

"I—honey, I just can't."

"But you don't have to *do* anything! I'll handle all the effects. All you have to do is get into a cabinet and go to sleep if you want to. Leave everything else to me."

"But s'pose we got caught? I can't help it; I think it's mean. Remember how I told you once, the night you—you asked me to team up with you—about how I chalked on Daddy's tombstone 'He never crossed up a pal?' I was scared to death out there in that cemetery, and I was scared every minute until I touched Daddy's headstone, and then I started to cry and I said his name over and over, just as if he could hear me, and then somehow I felt like he really could. I was certain he could."

"All right. I thought you were his daughter. I thought you had guts enough to turn a trick that would get you the kind of life he'd want you to have. Give us a few years in this dodge and just one big job and then we can knock off. Stop jackassing all around the country and settle down. We'll—we'll get married. And have a house. And a couple of dogs. We'll—have a kid."

"Don't fib, honey."

"I mean it. Don't you think I want a kid? But it takes dough. A wad of dough. Then it'll be Florida in the winter and the kid sitting between us in the grandstand when the barrier goes up and they streak out, fighting for the rail. That's the kind of life I want and I've got my angles worked out, every one of them. Got my ordination certificate today. Baby, you're in bed with a full-blown preacher. I bet you never thought you'd bed down with a reverend! Last week I had a tailor make me an outfit— black broadcloth. I got a turn-around collar and everything. I can put on a pair of black gloves and a black hood and work in a red light like a darkroom lamp—and nobody can see a thing. I've even got cloth buttons so they won't reflect light. I tell you, it's a perfect setup. Don't you know a spook worker never takes a real rap? If anybody grabs, the chumps rally around him and start alibi-ing their heads off. Do you think I'm a feeblo to go monkeying around with scientific committees or any other wise guys that are likely to upset the works? Pick your crowd and you can sell 'em anything. And all *you* have to do is sit there with the old ladies admiring you and thanking you afterward for all the comfort you've brought 'em. But if you are yellow I can do it alone. You can go back to the carny and find yourself another kooch show and start all over."

"No, honey. I didn't mean—"

"Well, I do mean. I mean just that. One way is the big dough and plenty of class and a kid and clothes that will make you look like a million bucks. The other way is the carny, doing bumps and grinds and waggling your fanny for a bunch of rubes for a few more years. And then what? You know what. Make up your mind."

"Just let me think about it. Please, honey."

"You've thought about it. Don't make me do anything I don't want to do. Look, baby, I love you. You know that. No, don't pull away. Keep quiet. I said I love you. I want a kid by you. Get it? Put your other arm around me. It's like old times, eh, kid? There. Like it? Sure you do. This is heaven, kid. Don't break it up."

"Oh, honey, honey, honey."

"That's better. And you will do it? Say you will. Say yes, baby."

"Yes. Yes—I'll do anything."

In the old gray stone house near Riverside Drive, Addie Peabody (Mrs. Chisholm W.) answered the door herself. She had given Pearl the evening off and Pearl had gone willingly enough, in view of what was coming.

The first to arrive were Mr. and Mrs. Simmons, and Mrs. Peabody shooed them into the parlor. "Honestly, I was just dying for somebody to talk to, I thought the afternoon would never go by, I'd have gone to the matinee but I just knew I couldn't sit through one, I'd be so excited about tonight, they say this new medium is simply grand—and so young, too. They say she hasn't a speck of background, she's so spontaneous and natural, she used to be a show girl I hear but it really doesn't matter, it's one of the strangest things how the gift strikes people in all walks of life and it's so often among humble people. I'm sure none of us will ever develop full power although they do say the Reverend Carlisle is simply wonderful at developmental sittings. I have a friend who's been developing with him for nearly a year now and she has noticed some amazing phenomena in her own home when not a soul was there but herself. She's simply mad about Mr. Carlisle, he's so sincere and sympathetic."

In twos and threes the rest of the company gathered. Mr. Simmons made one or two little jokes just to liven things up, but they were all in good taste and not offensive, because, after all, you should approach a séance with joy in your heart and all the people have to be attuned or the phenomena are likely to be scarce and very disappointing.

The bell rang a steady, insistent note, full of command. Mrs. Peabody hurried out, taking a quick look in the hall mirror and straightening her girdle before she opened the door. Outside, the light above the door fell on the heads of two people, the first a tall, dramatic-looking woman in her late twenties, rather flashily dressed. But Mrs. Peabody's glance slid over her and came to rest on the man.

The Rev. Stanton Carlisle was about thirty-five. He was holding his black hat and the lamplight made his hair glisten golden —just like the sun, she thought. He made her think of Apollo.

Mrs. Peabody noticed in her first swift glance that he was dressed in street clericals with a black vest and a turn-about collar. He was the first spiritualist minister she had ever seen who wore clericals but he was so distinguished-looking that it didn't seem a bit ostentatious; anybody would have taken him for an Episcopalian.

"Oh, Mr. Carlisle, I just knew it was you. I got a distinct impression the minute you rang the bell."

"I am sure we shall establish an excellent vibrational harmony, Mrs. Peabody. May I present our medium, Mary Margaret Cahill."

Inside, Mrs. Peabody introduced them to the others. She served tea and it was so English—just like having the vicar over, she thought. Miss Cahill was a sweet-looking girl, and after all some people can't help being born on the wrong side of the tracks. She probably did the best she could with what she had to start with. Even if she did look a little cheap she was beautiful and had an odd, haggard expression about her mouth that touched Mrs. Peabody's heart. Mediumship takes so much out of them—we owe them such a tremendous debt.

Mr. Carlisle was charming and there was something about his voice that stirred you, as if he were speaking just to you even when he addressed the others. He was so understanding.

Finally Mrs. Peabody stood up. "Shall I play something? I always say there's nothing like having an old-fashioned family organ. They're so sweet-toned and so much nicer than a piano." She sat at the console and struck a gentle chord. She would have to get the pedal levers oiled; the left one squeaked a little. The first piece she turned to was "The Old Rugged Cross" and one by one the company picked it up, Mr. Simmons coming in with a really fine baritone.

The Rev. Carlisle cleared his throat. "Mrs. Peabody, I wonder if you recall that splendid old hymn, 'On the Other Side of Jordan.' It was a favorite of my sainted mother's, and I should dearly love to hear it now."

"Indeed I do. At least, it's in the hymnal."

Mr. Simmons volunteered to lead, standing by the organ, with the others humming:

> *On the other side of Jordan*
> *In the sweet fields of Eden*
> *Where the Tree of Life is blooming*
> *There is rest for me.*
> > *There is rest for the weary,*
> > *There is rest for the weary,*
> > *On the other side of Jordan*
> > *There is rest for me.*

Mrs. Peabody's eyes were wet when the hymn was finished, and she knew that this was the psychological moment. She sat silently on the bench and then closed her eyes and let her fingers find the chords. Everyone sang it softly.

*Shall we gather by the river,*
*The beautiful, the beautiful river.*
*Yes, we shall gather by the river*
*That flows by the throne of God.*

She played the "Amen" chords softly, drawing them out, and then turned to the Rev. Carlisle. His eyes were closed; he sat upright and austere with his hands resting on the knees of his black broadcloth trousers. When he spoke he kept his eyes closed.

"Our hostess has provided us with a fine cabinet. The niche between the organ and the wall will serve beautifully. And, I believe, there are hangings which can be lowered. Let us all compose ourselves with humble hearts, silently, and in the presence of God who hath hid these things from the wise and prudent and hast revealed them unto babes.

"I call upon the Spirit of Eternal Light, whom some call God the Father and some call the Holy Ghost; who, some believe, came among the earth-bound as our Lord and Savior, Jesus the Christ; who spoke to Gautama under the Bo tree and gave him enlightenment, whose praise was taught by the last of India's great saints, Sri Ramakrishna. Marvel not at what we shall attempt, for the hour is coming in which all that are in the graves shall hear his voice and shall come forth. Many of them that sleep in the dust of the earth shall awake, but some who did evil in their days upon the earth shall be reborn and remain among the earth-bound for yet another existence. No spirit who has ever returned speaks to us of hell fire but rather of rebirth and another chance. And when a man has done much evil he does not descend into a pit of eternal torment but wanders between the worlds, neither earth-bound nor liberated; for the Lord, being full of compassion, forgives their iniquity. He remembers that they were but flesh, a wind that passeth away and cometh not again until the prayers and faith of liberated and earth-bound alike cause their absorption into the Universal Soul of God, who is in all things and from which everything is made that was made. We ask that the Great Giver of Love enter our hearts and make us to become as little children, for without innocence we cannot admit those presences who draw near about us now, anxious to speak to us and make their nearness known. For it is written: 'He bowed the heavens also, and came down: and darkness was under his feet. And he rode upon a cherub, and did fly: yea, he did fly upon the wings of the wind.' Amen."

He opened his eyes and Mrs. Peabody thought she had never seen eyes as blue or with a glance so resembling an eagle's. Spiritual power flowed out of him; you could just feel it.

The spiritualist continued, "Let Mrs. Simmons sit nearest to the cabinet on the far side. Mrs. Peabody on the other side, before the organ which she plays so beautifully. I shall sit here, next to her. Mr. Simmons next to his wife."

An armchair was carried into the niche for Miss Cahill who sat tautly, her knees close together, her hands clenched. The Rev. Carlisle stepped into the niche.

"Are you sure you feel equal to it this evening, my dear?"

Miss Cahill smiled bravely up at him and nodded.

"Very well. You are among friends. No one here will break the circle. There are no skeptics to endanger your life by suddenly flooding you with light. No one will move from his chair when it is dangerous to the vibration lines. Any ectoplasmic emanations from your body will be carefully observed but not touched so you have nothing to fear. Are you perfectly comfortable?"

"Yes. Comfortable. Fine."

"Very well. Do you want music?"

Miss Cahill shook her head. "No. I feel so—so sleepy."

"Relax, my dear friend."

She closed her eyes.

Mrs. Peabody tiptoed about and extinguished all the lamps except one. "Shall I close the cabinet curtains?"

Carlisle shook his head. "Let us first have her with us. Without anything between us. Let us form the circle."

Silently they took their places. Minutes crept by; a chair creaked and outside a car passed. Behind the velvet drapes which shut off the street light it sounded out of key and impertinent. The Rev. Carlisle seemed in a trance himself.

Knock!

Everyone gasped and then smiled and nodded.

Knock!

Carlisle spoke. "Ramakrishna?"

Three sharp raps answered him.

"Our dear teacher—our loving *guru* who has never left us in spirit—we greet you in the love of God, which you imparted so divinely while you were earth-bound. Will you speak to us now through the lips of our dear medium, Mary Cahill?"

Miss Cahill stirred in her chair and her head drew back. Her lips opened and her voice came softly, as from a great distance:

"The body of man is a soul-city containing the palace of the heart which contains, in turn, the lotus of the soul. Within its blossom are heaven and earth contained, are fire and water, sun and moon, and lightning and stars."

Her voice came, monotonous, as if it were a transmitter of the words of another. "He, whose vision is clouded by the veils of maya, will ask of that city, 'What is left of it when old age covers it and scatters it; when it falls to pieces?' To which the enlightened one replies, 'In the old age of the body the soul ages not; by the death of the body it is not slain.' There is a wind that blows between the worlds, strewing the lotus petals to the stars."

She stopped and let out her breath in a long sigh, pressing her hands against the chair arms and then letting them drop into her lap.

"Our guide has spoken," Carlisle said gently. "We may expect a great deal tonight, I am sure."

Miss Cahill opened her eyes, then jumped from the chair and began to walk about the room, touching the furniture and the walls with the tips of her fingers. She turned to the Rev. Carlisle. "D'you mind if I get into something more comfortable?"

The reverend nodded. "My friends, it has always been my aim to present tests of mediumship under such conditions that the slightest suspicion of fraud is impossible. We must face it: there are fraudulent mediums who prey on the noblest and purest emotions known to man. And I insist that the gifts of Mary Cahill be removed from the category of ordinary mediumship. She is able, at an expense to her strength it is true, to work in a faint light. I should like a number of the ladies here tonight to accompany her when she changes her clothes and make sure that there is no chance of fraud or trickery, that nothing is concealed. I know that you do not for one moment harbor such thoughts, but to spread the gospel of Spiritualism we must be able to say to the world—and to our most hostile critics—I *saw*. And under test conditions."

Mrs. Peabody and Mrs. Simmons rose and Miss Cahill smiled to them and waited. Carlisle opened a small valise, drawing out a robe of white watered silk and a pair of white slippers. He handed these to the medium and the ladies filed out.

Mrs. Peabody led the way up to her own bedroom. "Here you are, dear. Just change your things in here. We'll be waiting downstairs."

Miss Cahill shook her head. "Mr. Carlisle wants you to stay. I don't mind a bit." The ladies sat down, tongue-tied with embarrassment. The medium slowly drew off her dress and slip. She rolled down her stockings neatly and placed them beside her shoes. When she stood completely stripped before them, leisurely shaking out the robe, a sadness gripped Mrs. Peabody, deep and nameless. She saw the naked woman, unashamed there in the frilly celibacy of her own bedroom, and a lump rose in her throat. Miss Cahill was so beautiful and it was all so innocent, her standing there with her mind, or certainly part of her mind, far away still in that mysterious land where it went voyaging. It was with regret and a feeling she had had as a little girl when the last curtain descended on a play, that she watched Miss Cahill finally draw the robe about her and tie the cord loosely. She stepped into the slippers and smiled at them; and Mrs. Peabody got up, straightening her dress.

"My dear, it is so good of you to come to us. We appreciate it so."

She led the way downstairs.

In the living room all the lights were extinguished, save for a single oil lamp with a shade of ruby-red glass which the clergyman had brought with him. It gave just enough light for each person to see the faces of the others.

The Rev. Carlisle took the medium by the hand and led her to the armchair in the niche. "Let us try first without closing the curtains."

They formed the circle, waiting patiently, devoutly. Mary Cahill's eyes were closed. She moaned and slumped lower in the chair, twisting so that her head rested against its back. A low whimper came from deep within her, and she twisted again and began to breathe heavily. The cord of the white robe loosened, the fringed ends fell to the carpet. Then her body suddenly arched itself and the robe fell open.

With a swift intake of breath the sitters leaned forward.

"Mrs. Peabody, do you mind?" The reverend's voice was like a benediction.

She hurried over, feeling the warmth in her face, and closed the robe, tying the cord firmly. She couldn't resist giving the girl's hand an affectionate little pat, but the medium seemed unconscious.

When she had regained her chair she looked over at the Rev. Carlisle. He sat upright, eyes closed, his hands motionless on his knees. In the dim red glow of the lamp his face, above the severe collar, seemed to hang in mid-air; his hands to float as motionless as if they were made of papier-mâché. Save for the indistinct circle of faces the only other thing visible in the room was the medium in her white robe. Her hair was part of the darkness.

Slowly and gently spirit sounds began. Gentle raps, then louder knocks. Something set the glass prisms of the chandelier tinkling, and their musical voices continued for several minutes, as if a ghostly hand were playing with them—as a child might play with them if it could float to the ceiling.

Mrs. Simmons spoke first, in a hushed, awed voice. "I see a light."

It was there. A soft, greenish spark hovered near the floor beside Mrs. Peabody and then vanished. Mrs. Peabody felt a breeze —the psychic breeze of which Sir Oliver Lodge had written. Then, moving high in the air across the room, was another light. She tilted her eyeglasses a trifle to bring it into sharper focus. It was a hand with the forefinger raised as if toward heaven. It vanished.

The shadows now seemed to flit with lights but some, she

knew, were in her own eyes. The next time, however, they all saw it. Floating near the floor, in front of the medium, was a glowing mass which seemed to unwind from nowhere. It took form and rose before her and for a moment obscured her face.

It grew brighter and Mrs. Peabody made out the features of a young girl. "Caroline! *Carol*, darling—is it you?"

The whisper was gentle and caressing. "Mother. Mother. Mother."

It was gone. Mrs. Peabody took off her glasses and wiped her eyes. At last Caroline had come through to her. The perfect image of the child! They seem to stay the age when they pass over. That would make Caroline still sixteen, bless her heart. "Carol—don't leave! Don't go, darling! Come back!"

Darkness. The oil lamp sputtered, the flame died down and pitch black enfolded them. But Mrs. Peabody did not notice it. Her eyes were tight shut against the tears.

The Rev. Carlisle spoke. "Will someone turn on the lights?"

Orange glow leaped out brilliantly, showing the reverend still sitting with his hands on his knees. He rose now and went to the medium; with a handkerchief he wiped the corners of her eyes and her lips. She opened her eyes and got to her feet swaying, saying nothing.

The spiritualist steadied her arm and then she smiled once at the company. "Let me go upstairs," she said breathlessly.

When she was gone they crowded around the Rev. Stanton Carlisle, pressing his hand and all talking at once from the release of the tension.

"My dear friends, this is not our last evening. I see many more in the future. We shall indeed explore the Other Side together. Now I must go as soon as Miss Cahill is ready. We must look after our medium, you know. I will go up to her now and I shall ask all of you to remain here and not to say good-bye. She has been under tremendous strain. Let us leave quietly."

He smiled his blessing on them and closed the door softly behind him. On the hall table was a blue envelope, "To our dear medium as a token of our appreciation." Inside was Mrs. Peabody's check for seventy dollars.

"Ten bucks apiece," Stan said under his breath and crushed

the envelope in his fingers. "Hang on to your hat, lady; you ain't seen nothing yet."

Upstairs he entered Mrs. Peabody's room and shut the door. Molly was dressed and combing her hair.

"Well, kid, we laid 'em in the aisles. And with the light on every minute and the medium visible. The robe business was terrific. Jesus, what misdirection! They couldn't have pried their eyes away even if they'd known what I was doing."

From under his clerical vest he drew two papier-mâché replicas of a man's hands and two black mittens. From a large flat pocket inside his coat came a piece of black cardboard on which was pasted a picture of a movie actress cut from a magazine cover and touched up with luminous paint. From his sleeve he took a telescopic reaching-rod made of blue steel. Bundling all the props into the white robe he stuffed them into the valise which he had brought upstairs. Then he lifted his shoe, pulled a luminous-headed thumbtack from the instep, tossed it in, and shut the bag.

"You all set, kid? You better endorse this before I forget it. It's only seventy skins, but, baby, we're just starting. I got it fixed so we can slip downstairs and out without a lot of congratulations and crap. Baby, next time we really turn the heat on the old gal."

Molly's lip was trembling. "Stan, Mrs. Peabody's awful sweet. I—I can't go on with this sort of stuff. I just can't. She wants to speak to her daughter so bad and all you could do was whisper at her a little."

The Rev. Stanton Carlisle was an ordained spiritualist minister. He had started by sending two dollars and an affidavit, saying that he had produced spirit messages, to the United Spiritual League, and had received a medium's certificate. To get his Minister's certificate he had sent five dollars and had been interviewed by an ordained minister who turned his rostrum over to Candidate Carlisle for a few minutes one Thursday night. Messages were forthcoming and the new minister of the spiritualist gospel was sworn in. He was now entitled to perform marriages, conduct services, and bury the dead. He threw back his head and laughed silently.

"Don't worry, kid. She'll hear from her daughter. And in something louder than a whisper. And she'll see her too. This routine with the lights on and the medium in view all the time was just the convincer. The next time we work with this bunch we'll work in a regular dark séance or a curtain over the cabinet. And do you know who's going to give Mrs. Peabody the big thrill of talking to her daughter? See if you can guess."

"No. Not me, Stan. I couldn't."

He was suddenly steely. "You don't want me to let on to all those nice old folks down there that I have been deceived by a fraudulent medium, do you, sugar? You've got 'em eating out of your hand, my little kooch dancer. And when the time comes—you're going to be one ghost that talks. Come on, kid. Let's beat it out of here. The sooner I ditch this bag of props the rosier life will get. You think you're the only one in this show that ever gets the shakes?"

The guests stayed late for a buffet supper. Mrs. Peabody had rallied from the shock of recognizing her daughter and was fully launched in praise of the new medium and her mentor, the Rev. Stanton Carlisle. "You know, I got a definite psychic flash the moment that man touched the doorbell, the very moment. And when I opened the door there he was with the light shining on his hair—just like a halo in the sun, it was a perfect halo effect. He's like Apollo, I said to myself. Those were the very words."

When the other sitters had gone Addie Peabody was too excited to sleep. At last she drew on a housecoat and came downstairs, feeling constantly the unseen presence of Caroline beside her. At the organ she let her hands fall on the keyboard in chords, and they sounded so spiritual and inspired. There was certainly a new quality about her playing. Then from beneath her fingers a melody took shape and she played with her eyes closed, from memory:

> *On the other side of Jordan*
> *In the sweet fields of Eden,*
> *Where the Tree of Life is blooming*
> *There is rest for me.*

# The Hierophant

*They kneel before the high priest, wearer of the triple crown and bearer of the keys.*

THE FACE floated in air, unearthly in its greenish radiance, but it was the face of a girl and when it spoke Addie could see the lips move. Once the eyes opened, heartbreakingly dark and empty. Then the glowing lids closed again; the voice came:

"Mother . . . I love you. I want you to know."

Addie swallowed hard and tried to control her throat. "I know, darling. Carol, baby—"

"You may call me Caroline . . . now. It was the name you gave me. You must have loved it once. I was so foolish to want a different name. I understand so many things now."

The voice grew fainter as the face receded in the darkness. Then its glow changed and diminished until it was a pool of light near the floor. It vanished.

The voice whispered again, this time amplified by the metal trumpet which had been placed in the cabinet with the medium. "Mother . . . I have to go back. Be careful. . . . There are bad forces here, too. All of us are not good. Some are evil. I feel them all around me. Evil forces . . . Mother . . . good-bye."

The trumpet clanged against the music rack of the organ and tumbled to the floor. It rolled against the leg of Addie's chair and stopped. Groping for it, she picked it up eagerly but it was silent and chill except at the narrow end where it was warm as if from Caroline's lips.

The raps which had disturbed them on the last two evenings now began and jumped from the walls, the organ, her own chair back, the floor, everywhere. They rapped in the mocking cadences and ridiculous rhythms that spiteful children use to torment a teacher.

A vase crashed from the mantelpiece and shattered on the tiles of the hearth. Addie screamed.

The tones of the Rev. Carlisle came from the darkness near her. "Let us have patience. I call upon the presence which has come here unbidden to listen to me. We are not hostile to you. We wish you no harm. We are here to help you attain liberation by prayer, if you can only listen."

A mocking rap on the back of his own chair answered him.

Mrs. Peabody felt the trumpet snatched from her hands. It clanged on the ceiling above her head and then a voice came from it and the rappings and rustlings stopped. The voice was low and vibrant and deeply accented.

"The way to God lies through the Yoga of Love." It was the control spirit, Ramakrishna. "You little, mischievous ones of the baser planes, listen to our words of love and grow in spirit. Do not plague us nor our medium nor the sweet spirit of the girl who has visited her mother and was driven away by you. Listen to the love in our hearts which are as mountain streams pouring out their love to the distant sea which is the great heart of God. *Hari Aum!*"

With the fall of the trumpet to the floor the room became still.

At the door, while he was saying good night, the Rev. Carlisle took Addie's hand firmly between his own. "We must have faith, Mrs. Peabody. Poltergeist disturbances are not infrequent phenomena. Sometimes it is possible for us, and our liberated dear ones, to overcome them by prayer. I shall pray. Your little girl, Caroline, may not be able to aid us very much but I am sure she will try—from her side of the River. And now, take courage. I will be near you even after I have gone. Remember that."

Addie closed the front door with dread of the vast, empty

house behind and above her. If only she could get a girl to live in. But Pearl had left and then the Norwegian couple and after them old Mrs. Riordan. It was impossible. And Mr. Carlisle had said it would do no good to go to a hotel; the elementals attached themselves to people and not to houses and that would be horrible. In a hotel before the maids and the bellboys and everybody.

Besides, this had been Caroline's home when they all had been alive—*in earth life*, she corrected herself. They had bought this house when Caroline was three. Just before Christmas it was. And she had had her Christmas tree in the niche where Miss Cahill always sat at the séances. Addie took a chiffon handkerchief from her belt and blew her nose. It was awful that all this had to start just when Caroline had begun to come through so wonderfully.

The armchair was still in the niche and Addie sat down in it gingerly. That corner was really Miss Cahill's now; she had sanctified it by her sacrifices and her suffering just to enable Caroline to speak to them and appear in full form. Addie sank deeper into the chair, trying to reason away the feeling that somehow this wasn't *her* home any more. She tried thinking back to Caroline's third Christmas and the gifts. There was a little wooden telephone, she remembered, and Caroline had spent all Christmas Day "calling up" people.

Now the house wasn't like home any longer—it belonged to a terrifying stranger. A stupid, jealous boor of a spirit that broke things and rapped on windowpanes until Addie thought she would lose her mind. It was everywhere; there was no escaping it. Even when she went shopping or took in a movie she seemed to feel things crawling under her skin. She had tried to tell herself it was just nerves but Mr. Carlisle had once mentioned a case he had helped to exorcise—where the poltergeist actually haunted a man's skin. And now she was positive of it. She broke into a fit of sobbing which made her sides ache. But it was a relief. You just couldn't feel any more miserable and that was a relief in a way.

The house was silent but on the long journey upstairs she felt herself watched. It was not by anything that had eyes, just an evil intelligence that *saw* without any eyes.

Addie Peabody braided her hair hastily and threw some water on her face, rubbing it a couple of times with a towel.

In bed, she tried to read one of the books the Rev. Carlisle had given her on Ramakrishna and the Yoga of Love but the words jumbled up and she found herself reading the same sentence over and over, hoping that the raps would not start again. They were only taps on her windowpane and the first time they came she had run to the window and opened it, thinking boys were throwing pebbles. But no one was there; the rooming houses across the street were all dark and asleep with their windows as black as caverns and the dingy lace curtains of one or two blowing out on the night wind. That was nearly a week ago.

Tap!

Addie jumped and looked at the bed-table clock. Ten minutes after one. She turned off the reading light and left on the night lamp in its opaque shade with the light glowing through the delicate cut-out letters: "God is Love."

Tap!

Addie switched on the light and looked at the clock. One-twenty. She gripped the leather traveling clock in her hands, straining her eyes until she could see the minute hand actually moving, slowly and inevitably, like life itself going by. She put the clock down and clutched the spread tightly with both hands and waited. It was one-thirty. Maybe it wouldn't come again. Oh, please, God, I have faith; indeed I do. Don't let it—

Tap!

She threw on her robe and hurried downstairs, snapping on the lights as she went. Then the emptiness of the illumined house made her flesh creep. She put out the upstairs lights by the hall switch and the blackness up the staircase seemed to smother her.

In the kitchen Addie filled a kettle, spilling water down her sleeve, and set it on the stove for tea. A crash from the pantry made her grab the robe together at her throat.

"Dear—" She addressed the air, hoping, willing to make it hear her. "I don't know who you are, dear, but you must be a little boy. A mischievous little boy. I—I wouldn't want to punish you, dear. God—God is love."

A crash from the cellar shook the floor under her feet. She was too frightened to go down to see but she knew that the big shovel by the furnace had fallen over. Then, through the still house, standing with its lights on in the midst of the sleeping city, she heard another sound from below, a sound which made her cover her ears and run back upstairs leaving the kettle humming on the stove.

From the cellar had come the metallic rasp of the coal shovel, creeping over the concrete in little jumps as if it had sprouted legs like a crab. An inch at a time. Scrape. Scrape.

This time she picked up the telephone and managed to dial a number. The voice which answered was muffled and indistinct but it was like a warm shawl thrown over her shoulders.

"I am sorry to hear it, Mrs. Peabody. I shall start an intensive meditation at once, spending the night in mental prayer, holding the thought. I don't believe that the phenomena will trouble you further. Or, at least, not tonight."

Addie fell asleep as soon as she got back in bed. She had made herself a cup of tea, and once she fancied she heard a sound from the cellar but even if she had she would not have been afraid, for the Rev. Carlisle was with her now, in spirit. If only she could persuade him to stay over for a few days at the house. She must ask him again.

The old gray stone house was dark and as silent as its neighbors. A milkman, driving on his lonely route, saw a man in a dark overcoat pulling what looked like a length of heavy fishline out of a cellar window. He wondered if he oughtn't to tell the cops but the guy was probably a wack. There were a lot of 'em in this territory.

Light was beginning to show at the window when Molly Cahill turned over and found Stan slipping into bed beside her. She buried her face in the hollow of his throat for a moment and then turned back and fell asleep. You can always smell perfume on them if they've been with another woman. That was what people said.

Addie Peabody got up late and called the Rev. Carlisle but there was no answer. She had the oddest feeling that the ringing she heard in her own telephone also came from one of the rooming houses across the street but she put it down to her nerves. Anyhow, nobody answered.

A little later when she opened the medicine cabinet to get the toothpaste one of those big brown roaches, about three inches long, was in there and flew out at her. She was sure the poltergeist had put it in there just to devil her.

And at breakfast the milk tasted like garlic and that she knew was the poltergeist because they always sour milk or make the cows' milk taste of garlic. And it was certified milk from the best company. She dressed hurriedly and went out. In the beauty parlor the chatter of Miss Greenspan and the heat of the dryer were restful and reassuring. Addie treated herself to a facial and a manicure, and felt better. She did some shopping and saw part of a movie before she got so restless she had to leave.

It was late afternoon when she returned. She had hardly taken off her things when she smelled smoke. For a moment she was paralyzed, not knowing whether to go and find out what was burning or call the fire department and she stood between the two ideas for several seconds while the smell got stronger. Then she saw that something was burning in the umbrella stand in the hall—evil-smelling and smoky. It wasn't doing any damage, just smoking and Addie carried the brass stand out in the back yard. The odor was like old-fashioned phosphorous matches. That was why the ancients always said the Evil One appeared in a burst of fire and brimstone—poltergeist fires smelled like phosphorus.

Minute by minute the evening drew on. The fire had set all her nerves on edge again; she had always been deathly afraid of fires. And then the raps started at the windows and even on the fanlight above the front door.

What a relief it was when she heard the doorbell ring and knew it was Mr. Carlisle and Miss Cahill. The Simmonses were not coming tonight, and with a little guilty pang Addie thought of it with elation—she would have Mr. Carlisle all to herself. That always seemed to get the best results. It was hard to get good results with so many different sets of vibrations even though the Simmonses were just as dear and devoted as any spiritualists she had ever known.

Miss Cahill seemed even more tired and run-down-looking than ever and Addie insisted on giving her a hot Ovaltine before the séance but it didn't seem to strengthen her any. The lines about her mouth grew deeper if anything.

After she had played "On the Other Side of Jordan" Mr. Carlisle asked her if Caroline had a favorite hymn. She had to answer truthfully that Caroline was not a religious child. She sang hymns in Sunday school, of course, but she never sang any around the house.

"Mrs. Peabody, what *did* she sing about the house? That is, what songs of a serious nature? An old love song perhaps?"

Addie thought back. It was amazing what she could remember when Mr. Carlisle was there; it was like being nearer to Caroline just to talk with him. And now she remembered. "Hark, hark, the lark at heaven's gate sings!" She turned and played it, gently at first and then more strongly until it filled the room and a metal dish vibrated in sympathy. She played it over and over, hearing Caroline's thin but true-pitched young voice through the blast of the organ. Her legs ached with pumping before she stopped.

Mr. Carlisle had already extinguished all the lights and drawn the curtain before the cabinet. She took her place in the straight-backed chair beside him and he turned out the last light and let the dark flow around them.

Addie started when she heard the trumpet clink as it was levitated. Then from a great distance came a shrill, sweet piping—like a shepherd playing on reeds. ". . . And Phoebus 'gins arise, His steeds to water at those springs . . ."

A cool breeze fanned her face and then a touch of something material stroked her hair. From the dark, where she knew the cabinet to be, came a speck of greenish light. It trembled and leaped like a ball on a fountain, growing in size until it stopped and unfolded like an opening flower. Then it grew larger and took shape, seeming to draw a veil from before its face. It was Caroline, standing in the air a few inches above the floor.

The green light that was her face grew brighter until Addie could see her eyebrows, her mouth and her eyelids. The eyes opened, their dark, cavernous blankness wrenched her heart.

"Caroline—baby, speak to me. Are you happy? Are you all right, baby?"

The lips parted. "Mother . . . I . . . must confess something."

"Darling, there isn't anything to confess. Sometimes I did scold you, but I didn't— Please forgive me."

"No . . . I must confess. I am not . . . not altogether liberated. I had selfish thoughts. I had mean thoughts. About you. About other people. They keep me on a low plane . . . where the lower influences can reach me and make trouble for me. Mother . . . help me."

Addie had risen from her chair. She stumbled toward the materialized form but the hand of the Rev. Carlisle caught her wrist quickly. She hardly noticed. "Caroline, baby! Anything— tell me what to do!"

"This house . . . evil things have entered it. They have taken it away from us. Take me away."

"Darling—but how?"

"Go far away. Go where it is warm. To California."

"Yes. Yes, darling. Tell Mother."

"This house . . . ask Mr. Carlisle to take it for his church. Let us never live here any more. Take me to California. For if you go I will go with you. I will come to you there. And we will be happy. Only when this house is a church can I be happy. Please, Mother."

"Oh, baby, of course. Anything. Why didn't you ask me before?"

The form was growing dim. It sank, wavering, and the light went out.

The pair in the cab was the usual stuff: gab, gab, gab. Jesus, what a laugh!—"they lived happy ever afterwards." The hackie slid between a bus and a sedan, grazing the car and making the driver mutter in alarm.

"G'wan, ya dumb son-of-a-bitch," he yelled back.

The couple were at it again and he listened in, for laughs.

"I tell you, we've got our foot in the door. Don't you see, baby, this is where it starts? With this house, I can gimmick it up from cellar to attic. I can give 'em the second coming of Christ if I want to. And you were swell, baby, just swell."

"Stan, take your hands off me."

"What's eating you? Get hold of yourself, kid. How about a drink before you hit the hay?"

"I said take your hands off me! I can't stand it! I can't stand it! Let me out of this cab! I'll walk. Do you hear? Let me out!"

"Baby, you better calm down."

"I won't. I won't go up there with you. Don't touch me."

"Hey, driver, let us out. Right here at the corner. Anywhere."

The cabbie took a quick look in his rear vision mirror. Before he got control of the wheel he had nearly piled the boat up against a light pole. Holy gees, the dame's face was glowing bright green right inside his own cab!

From Ed Wolfehope's column, "The Hardened Artery":

". . . She is a widow who owned a fine old mansion in the Seventies near the Drive. Her only child died years ago and she lived on in the house because of memories. Recently a pair of spook workers 'materialized' the daughter and she told her mother to give them the house and move to the West Coast. No one knows how much they took the widow for in cash first. But she left on her journey beaming and rosy—kissed both crooks at the train gate. And they put guys in jail for welching on alimony! . . ."

From "The Trumpet Voice":

"To the Editor:

"A friend of mine recently sent me a piece from a Broadway columnist, which is one lie from beginning to end about me and the Reverend Stanton Carlisle. I want to say it could not have been a practical joker with an air pistol who made the raps on my window. I kept my eyes open the whole time. And anybody who knows anything about Psychic Phenomena knows all about poltergeist fires.

"Miss Cahill and the Reverend Carlisle are two of the dearest people I have ever been privileged to meet and I can testify that all the séances they conducted were under the strictest test conditions and no decent person could even have dreamed of fraud. At the very first séance I recognized my dear daughter Caroline who 'died' when she was sixteen, just a few days before her high school commencement. She came back again and again in the other sittings and

I could almost have touched her dear golden hair, worn in the very style she wore it when she passed over. I have a photograph of her taken for her high school yearbook which shows her hair worn this way and it was something no one but I could have possibly known of.

"The Reverend Carlisle never said one word asking for my house. It was Caroline who told me to give it to him and in fact I had a hard time to persuade him to take it and Caroline had to come back and beg him before he would give in. And I am happy to say that here in California, under the guidance of the Rev. Hallie Gwynne, Caroline is with me almost daily. She is not as young as she was in New York and I know that means she is reflecting my own spiritual growth. . . ."

Sun beat on the striped awnings while six floors below them Manhattan's streets wriggled in the rising heat from the pavement. Molly came out of the kitchenette with three fresh cans of cold beer and Joe Plasky, sitting on the overstuffed sofa with his legs tied in a knot before him, reached up his calloused hand for the beer and smiled. "Sure seems funny—us loafing in mid-season. But that's Hobart for you—too many mitts in the till. Show gets attached right in the middle of the season."

Zeena filled an armchair beside the window, fanning herself gently with a copy of *Variety*. She had slipped off her girdle and was wearing an old kimono of Molly's, which hardly met in the middle. "Whew! Ain't it a scorcher? You know, this is the first summer I've ever been in New York. I don't envy you all here. It ain't quite this bad in Indiana. Say, Molly"—she finished the last swallow of beer and wiped her mouth with the back of her hand—"if they ever get this mess straightened out, why don't you come out with us and finish the season? You say Stan is working this new act of his solo."

Molly sat down next to Joe and stretched out her long legs; then she curled them under her and lit a cigarette, the match shaking just a little. She was wearing an old pair of rehearsal rompers; she still looked like a kid in them, Zeena noticed a little sadly.

Molly said, "Stan's awfully busy at the church. The folks are crazy about him. He gives reading services every night. I used to help him with those but he says a straight one-ahead routine

is good enough. Then he has development classes every afternoon. I—I just take it easy."

Zeena set down the empty can on the floor and took the full
one which Molly had put on the window sill. "Lambie-pie, you
need a good time. Why don't you get yourself slicked up and
come out with us? We'll get you a date. Say, I know a swell boy
with Hobart Shows this season—an inside talker. Let's hire a car
and get him and have dinner up the line somewheres. He's a swell
dancer and Joe don't mind sitting out a couple, do you, snooks?"

Joe Plasky's smile, turned on Zeena, deepened; his eyes grew
softer. "Swell idea. I'll call him now."

Molly said quickly, "No, please don't bother. I'm really fine.
I don't feel like going anywhere in this heat. Really, I'm okay."
She looked at the little leather traveling clock on the mantel,
which Addie Peabody had given her. Then she switched on the
radio. As the tubes warmed, the voice came through clearer. It
was a familiar voice but richer and deeper than Zeena had ever
heard it before.

". . . therefore, my beloved friends, you can see that our
claims for evidence of survival are attested to and are based on
proof. Men of the caliber of Sir Oliver Lodge, Sir Arthur Conan
Doyle, Camille Flammarion, and Sir William Crookes did not
give their lives to a dream, to a chimera, to a delusion. No, my
unseen friends of the radio audience, the glorious proofs of survival lie about us on every hand.

"We at the Church of the Heavenly Message rest content and
secure in our faith. And it is with the deepest gratitude that I
thank them, the splendid men and women of our congregation,
for their generosity, which has enabled me to bring you this
Sunday afternoon message for so many weeks.

"Some persons think of the 'new religion of Spiritualism' as a
closed sect. They ask me, 'Can I believe in the power of our dear
ones to return and still not be untrue to the faith of my fathers?'
My dearly beloved, the doors of Spiritual Truth are open to all—
it is something to cherish close to your heart *within* the church,
of your own faith. Whatever your creed it will serve simply to
strengthen it, whether you are accustomed to worship God in
meeting house, cathedral, or synagogue. Or whether you are one

of the many who say 'I do not know' and then proceed to worship unconsciously under the leafy arches of the Creator's great Church of the Out of Doors, with, for your choir, only the clear, sweet notes of the song sparrow, the whirr of the locust among the boughs.

"No, my dear friends, the truth of survival is open to all. It is cool, pure water which will gush from the forbidding rock of reality at the touch of a staff—your own willingness to believe the evidence of your own eyes, of your own God-given senses. It is we, of the faith of survival, who can say with joy and *certainty* in our heart of hearts, 'O death, where is thy sting? O grave, where is thy victory?' "

Joe Plasky's smile was now a faint, muscular imprint on his face; nothing more. He leaned across Molly and gently switched off the radio. "Got a deck of cards, kid?" he asked her, his face lighting up again. "I mean a deck of your own cards—the kind your dad would have played with. The kind that read from only one side."

CARD X

# The Moon

*Beneath her cold light howl
the dog and the wolf. And
creeping things crawl out of
slime.*

IN THE black alley with a light at the end, the footsteps followed,
drawing closer; they followed, and then the heart-stopping panic
as something gripped his shoulder.

". . . in about another fifteen minutes. You asked me to wake
you, sir." It was the porter shaking him.

Stan sat up as though a rope had jerked him, his pulse still
hammering. In the early light he sat watching the fields whip by,
trying to catch his breath, to shake off the nightmare.

The town looked smaller, the streets narrower and cheaper,
the buildings dingier. There were new electric signs, dark now
in the growing dawn, but the horse chestnuts in the square
looked just the same. The earth doesn't age as fast as the things
man makes. The courthouse cupola was greener with time and
the walls were darker gray.

Stanton Carlisle walked slowly across the square and into the
Mansion House, where Old Man Woods was asleep on the
leather couch behind the key rack. Knocking on the counter
brought him out, blinking. He didn't recognize the man with
the arrogant shoulders, the cold blue eyes; as the Rev. Carlisle

signed the register he wondered if anyone at all would recognize him. It was nearly seventeen years.

From the best room, looking out on Courthouse Square, Stan watched the town wake up. He had the bellboy bring up a tray of bacon and eggs, and he ate slowly, looking out on the square.

Marston's Drug Store was open; a boy came out and emptied a pail of gray water into the gutter. Stan wondered if it was the same pail after all these years—his first job, during high school vacation. This kid hadn't been born then.

He had come back, after all. He could spend the day loafing around town, looking at the old places, and catch the night train out and never go near the old man at all.

Pouring himself a second cup of coffee, the Rev. Carlisle looked at his face in the polished surface of the silver pot. Hair thinner at the temples, giving him a "widow's peak" that everyone said made him look distinguished. Face fuller around the jaw. Broader shoulders, with imported tweed to cover them. Pink shirt, with cuff links made from old opal earrings. Black knitted tie. All they could remember would be a kid in khaki pants and leather jacket who had waited behind the water tank for an open freight-car door.

Seventeen years. Stan had come a long way without looking back.

What difference did it make to him whether the old man lived or died, married or suffered or burst a blood vessel? Why was he here at all?

"I'll give it the once over and then highball out of here tonight," he said, drawing on his topcoat. Picking up his hat and gloves he took the stairs, ancient black woodwork with hollows worn in the marble steps. On the porch of the Mansion House he paused to take a cigarette from his case, cupping the flame of his lighter against the October wind.

Horse-chestnut leaves were a golden rain in the early sun, falling on the turf of the park where the fountain had been turned off for the winter. In its center a stained bronze boy smiled up under his bronze umbrella at the shower which wasn't falling.

Stan followed the south side of the park and turned up Main Street. Myers' Toy and Novelty Mart had taken in the shop next to it and expanded. In the window were construction kits for airplanes with rubber-band motors. Mechanical tractors. A playsuit of what looked like long red underwear, with a toy rocket-pistol. A new generation of toys.

Leffert's Kandy Kitchen was closed but the taffy still lay golden in metal trays in the window with almonds pressed in it to form flower-petal designs. Christmas was the time for Leffert's taffy, not autumn. Except the autumn when they had beaten Childers Prep; he had taken a bag of it to the game.

The wind whirled down the street, making store signs creak above him. The autumns were colder than they used to be, but the snow of winter wasn't as deep.

On the edge of town Stan looked out across rolling country. A farmhouse had stood on the ridge once. Must have burned down or been pulled down. Dark against the sky Mills' Woods lay over the rise, too far to walk; and what was the use of going through all that again. She was probably dead by now. It didn't matter. And the old man was dying.

Stan wondered if he could get a bus out of town before the night train left. Or he might load up with magazines and go to the hotel and read. It was well past noon but there was a lot of the day left.

Then a side street led him down familiar ways; here and there a lot stood empty, with a gaping cellar where a house had been.

He didn't realize he had walked so far when the sight of the school brought him up short. In a country of square, brick boxes some long-dead genius on a school board had made them build this high school differently: gray stone with casement windows, like a prep school or an English college. The lawn was still green, the ivy over the archway scarlet with the old year.

It was a cool June evening and Stan wore a blue coat with white pants; a white carnation in his lapel. Sitting on the platform he watched the audience while the speaker droned on. His father was out there, about ten rows back. And alone. Couples everywhere else, only his father, it seemed, was alone.

". . . and to Stanton Carlisle, the Edwin Booth Memorial medal for excellence in dramatic reading."

He was before them now but applause didn't register; he

couldn't hear it. The excitement under his ribs was pleasant. The power of the eyes upon him lifted him out of the black emptiness in which he had been sunk all evening. Then, as he turned, he suddenly heard the applause and saw his father, beaming, smashing his palms together, shooting quick looks left and right, enjoying the applause of the others.

"Taxi!" Stan saw the old limousine lumbering toward him and flagged it. The driver was Abe Younghusband, who didn't recognize him until he gave the address.

"Oh, say, you must be Charlie Carlisle's boy, ain't you? Ain't seen you around for some time."

"Sixteen—nearly seventeen years."

"That a fact? Well, guess there's lots of improvements since you left. Say, I heard you're a preacher now. That ain't true, is it?"

"Sort of half and half. More of a lecturer."

They turned off the car tracks, down the familiar street with the maples scarlet in the rays of the afternoon sun.

"I always figured you'd go on the stage. I still remember that show you put on at the Odd Fellows' Hall, time you borrowed Chief Donegan's watch and made believe you was smashing the hell out of it. His face was sure something to see. But I guess you got kind of tired of that stuff after a while. My boy's a great one on tricks. Always sending away for stuff. Well, here we are. I hear Charlie's pretty shaky these days. I hear he's turned worse during the last week."

The house looked tiny and run to seed. A wooden staircase had been built up one side of it, and a door cut into the attic floor. The yard was scuffed, with bare patches; the maples that used to shelter the house had been cut down. Where Gyp's kennel had stood there was still a rectangle in the ground. The earth forgets slowly.

The woman who answered the door was white-haired and stout, the lines about her mouth petulant. It was Clara Carpenter; but what a tub she had turned into!

"How do you do. Mrs. Carpenter?"

"Mrs. *Carlisle*. Oh." Her face lost some of its caution. "You must be Stan Carlisle. Come right in. Your dad's been asking me a dozen times an hour when you were coming." She lowered her voice. "He's not a bit well, and I can't make him stay in bed. Maybe you can persuade him to take it easy, a little. It's his heart, you know." She called upstairs, "Charlie, somebody to see you." To Stan she said, "I guess you know your way upstairs. The big bedroom. I'll be up directly."

The stairs, the newel post, the two ridiculous spouted urns on the mantelpiece, seen through the double doors. The metal fireplace covering. The wallpaper was different, and the upper hall looked different some way, but he didn't stop to find out why.

The old man was seated in a chair by the window, with a knitted afghan over his knees; seamed face, scrawny neck. His eyes looked frightened and sullen.

"Stanton?" Charlie Carlisle moved with difficulty, hands gripping the chair arms. "Stanton, come over here and let me take a good look. Gosh, you—you don't look so very different, son. Only you've filled out a lot. You're—you're looking all right, son."

Stan tried to throw his shoulders back. But a weight was pressing them, a deadly weight that made his knees tremble. The life seemed to be leaking out of him, flowing into the carpet under his feet. He took a chair on the other side of the window and leaned back in it, drawing his breath, trying to fight off the crushing weariness.

"I didn't know you'd married Clara," Stan said at last, getting a cigarette out and lighting it. He offered one to his father, who shook his head.

"Doctor's got me cut down to one cigar a day. Yes, I kept bachelor's hall for quite a spell after you left. I—I always figured I'd hear from you, boy, and then I'd tell you. Clara's a fine girl. Ever hear from your mother?"

The words had a hard time coming out, his lips were so tired. "No. Never did."

"I'm not surprised. Guess she didn't find us exciting enough. What do they call it now—glamour? That's what Cynthia wanted. Glamour. Well, if she found it I don't reckon she's got much of it now." The mouth came down in creases of bitterness. "But tell me what you been doing, Stan. I said to Clara, sure he'll come. I said, we had our differences, and I guess he's been busy, making his own way. I said, I know he'll come if I tell him I'm in bad shape. Feel a lot better today, though. I told the doctor I'd be back at the office in a month. Feel a lot better. What's this I hear you're a minister of the gospel, Stan? Clara heard you on the radio one day, she said. That's how we knew where to send that telegram."

The Rev. Carlisle uncrossed his legs and knocked the ashes from his cigarette into a jardiniere holding a fern. "I'm more of a lecturer. But I do have a Minister's certificate."

The elder Carlisle's face brightened. "Son, I'm gladder to hear that from you, and believe it, than any other news I've heard in a month of Sundays. You work your way through seminary? Why, son, I wanted you to go. I was willing to lay out cold cash to pay your way. You know that. Only you couldn't see it at the time. Always fooling with that magic nonsense. I'm glad you finally got that out of your system. It was your mother put those ideas in your head, Stan, buying you that box of tricks. I haven't forgotten it. But I don't even know your denomination."

The Rev. Carlisle closed his eyes. His voice sounded flat and toneless in his own ears. "It's not a big or a rich church, Dad. The United Spiritual League. It's devoted to preaching the gospel that the soul survives earthly death, and that those of us who still are earth-bound can receive intelligence—from those who have passed over to the higher spheres."

"You mean you're a spiritualist? You believe the dead come back?"

Stan forced a smile, his eyes wandering up to the ceiling where cracks made the outline of an old man's face. The sun was slanting through the window now and night was coming but not fast enough. He came back with a start.

"I'm not going to try converting you, Dad. I am secure in my faith. Many others share my views, but I am no proselytizer."

His father was silent for a time, swallowing uneasily. His head seemed to nod back and forth a fraction of an inch as he sat, a quick, rhythmic, involuntary nod of weakness. "Well, everybody to his own faith. I don't hold with spiritualism much. But if you're convinced, that's all that matters. Real estate is all shot, here in this town, son. If I was younger I'd pull out. Town's dying. I been trying to get the Civic Betterment Committee to put on a little campaign—make it a good, open-shop town and no nonsense. Attract industry. But they don't listen. Property values way down— Oh, here's Clara. Reckon it's most suppertime. We been talking so much."

"I'll wash up and be right down," Stan said. The load of weariness— There was a place where he might leave it, where it might slip from him like a weight cut from his neck.

In the hall he turned left and his hand was reaching for the knob when, with a cold flash, he realized that he was facing a smooth, papered wall. The attic door was not there! Looking down, he saw a single step at the bottom of the wall. So that was it—the stairs outside. It was an apartment now, cut off from the rest of the house. Strangers living in it, under the slope of the roof, around the brick chimney. The iron bed, the silk patchwork, smell of camphor and silk and lumber and the tight mesh of maple leaves below, seen through the narrow windows where you could make out the signboard on the lawn of the church. The house was dying, too.

Stan closed the bathroom door and locked it. The same taps on the washbowl anyhow, even though the walls were painted a different color. And the odd mix-up of tiles in the floor, where he used to find half-tiles and try to count them. The old-fashioned tub on its high legs; marble-topped commode with its old-fashioned mahogany drawers; shaving stand with its circular cabinet and a mirror on a swivel, where Dad kept his shaving brush, his mug and his soap, his hones.

Stan wondered if the water still made the sharp sucking gurgle in the tub when the stopper was pulled out—as it did when his mother had finished splashing and singing to herself. He recalled the day when he had fallen out of the tree, and Mother had picked him up in her arms and carried him upstairs, bleeding all down the front of her dress. She hadn't minded the dress getting messed up. He had made leggings of corrugated cardboard, like explorers wear in the jungle. One of them had been bloody; after the doctor had sewed up the cut in his forehead Mother undressed him, taking the cardboard leggings off carefully. She had put them on the marble top of the commode. They stayed there for a long time, until the blood stains became black. Jennie finally threw them out—said they gave her the jimjams.

If only they could all have stayed together a few more years. If Mother had not minded the town. If Dad had always been as weak and as friendly as he was now that he was dying. If only he could have been dying for twenty years, Stan might have loved him. Now there was nothing but the old things, and they were going past him and would soon be gone.

He drew his breath and tried again to strain his shoulders back. I mustn't forget to ask the old man about the church and how to go about selling it when it's time to pull out. But the Church of the Heavenly Message seemed too far away to matter, now. The old man was slipping into that dark hole where you fall and fall forever because there's no bottom to it. We are all creeping to its edge, some slowly, some, like the old man, balanced on the brink. And then what? Like the rush of wind past a bullet, probably, forever and ever. Gyp was dead all these years. Even the memories of him were dead and forgotten except in one mind. And when that was gone Gyp would be forgotten entirely. When the old man was dead and under ground Stan could forgive it.

Gyp never knew what hit him. They said the vet just put chloroform on a rag and dropped it in the box.

But that end of rope, tied to the leg of the workbench in the garage—it had been cut when Stan came home from school. Why did they tie Gyp up in there if they wanted to get rid of him? There was no they. Only he. Gyp had a chain on his kennel. Why the rope?

Oh, Christ, let me get to hell out of here. But the voice that had said "son" held him. The house was swallowing him. And they had sealed up the attic door; there was no way. All the years had dropped off, tearing with them his poise, so carefully built up tone by tone. They had taken his cleverness, his smile, his hypnotic glance, leaving him powerless and trapped inside the walls of old familiarity.

He had come back because Dad was dying and Mother was gone and the maples were cut down, the square still visible where

Gyp's kennel had stood, and the shaving stand on its smooth pillar of wood, still in the same place and still smooth under his hand, smelling sweetly of shaving soap.

The strop.

It hung from the brass hook where it had always hung. It was smooth, black with handling and with oil, shining.

The garage at night with the moonlight making bars of silver across the floor, silvering the workbench, sparkling on the bar of the vise and on the lidless coffee cans of nails and bolts. Shining blue and cold on the concrete floor. And the shadows hiding dread and shame.

"Take down your pants."

That was to add to the shame: nakedness.

Stan fumbled with the belt of his knickers, stalling for split seconds.

"Hurry up. I said drop 'em."

His knickers bound his feet about the ankles. He couldn't run. He had to take it. "Now bend over." A hand on his shoulder pushed him into the patch of moonlight, where his nakedness could show. Stan saw the shadow of the strop rise and braced himself. The pain split its way up to his brain in waves and he bit his lip, his breath catching at the bottom of his lungs. He pushed his knuckles in his mouth so they wouldn't hear him next door. The moonlight was a fuzzy blur of tears; and the strop, when it struck the roundness of his bare flesh, made a sound that got to his brain before the stab of pain—and the rope's end, tied to the leg of the workbench there in the smell of oil and gasoline on the day when the sun went out.

Downstairs Charlie Carlisle fidgeted with his napkin, pushing himself back in the chair by bracing his hands against its polished arms. "Confound it, Clara, what d'you s'pose the boy's doing up there? Oh, there you are, son. Sit right down."

When Charlie raised his glance to the man who entered the dining room he caught his old, quick breath at something he saw. It was Stan, much as he had appeared a few minutes before. Maybe with his face fresh-washed and his hair damped down a little. But in the set of the shoulders was something strange. And when old Charlie met his son's eyes they were a sharper blue than any he had ever seen before; as hard as a frozen pond.

The Great Stanton pulled back a chair and sat down swiftly and gracefully, opening his napkin with a single snap. Mrs. Carlisle brought in a platter of chicken. When rice and gravy arrived Charlie said, "Sit down, Clara. Quit running in and out. Stan'll pronounce the blessing."

The Rev. Carlisle ran his hands once over his hair and took a deep breath. His voice came resonantly:

"Almighty God, our heavenly father, we thank Thee from the bottom of our hearts for what we are about to receive. We come to Thee steeped in sin and corruption, our hearts black with guilt, knowing that in the river of Thy forgiveness they will be washed as white as snow."

His father had slid one heavily veined hand over his eyes.

"He who watches the sparrow's fall will hold us in the hollow of his hand to the end of our days, on earth and beyond."

Clara was frowning in bewilderment or worrying about the chicken getting cold.

". . . in the name of thy son, our Lord and Savior, Jesus Christ, we ask it. Amen."

The old man said "Amen" and then grinned weakly at his wife. "No matter what denomination, Clara, it's a proud day when we can have a son saying grace and him a preacher. Pass Stan the rice."

Clara was not one to eat in silence. She began a brief history of the community during the past sixteen years, full of hot summers, hard winters, deaths, births, weddings, and disasters.

Stan ate quickly and took a second helping of everything. At last he slid his plate away from him and lit a cigarette. He looked at Clara Carpenter Carlisle for a long minute; the penetrating blue glance made her conscious of the old apron over her good dress.

"My dear friend, have you ever thought that these persons whom you have mourned as dead will never die?"

Under that brilliant stare she began to simper and found it difficult to control her hands. "Why, Stan, I—I've always *believed*. But I think it's one of those things you just have to feel.

I never paid much attention. I took it for granted, about heaven."

The Rev. Carlisle wiped his lips with his napkin and took a swallow of water. "I have seen magnificent proofs that the spirit does not lie fallow until the Day of Judgment. The spirits of the liberated are around us every moment. How often have we said, in anguish, 'If only I could speak to him again. And feel the touch of his hand.' "

Both the older Carlisles looked embarrassed, eyed one another and then each took a sip of coffee.

Stan's mellow voice rolled on. "Yes. And the glorious truth is that it can be done. The spirits of the liberated are around us even now, as we speak." His eyes were still on Clara; he dropped his voice. "I feel one presence beside me now, distinctly. Insistently. Trying to get through."

On his father's face was the suggestion of a sly grin.

"It is one who loved me in its earth existence. But it is not human."

They stared at him.

"A small spirit, a humble presence. But brimming with devotion and loyalty. I believe it is the spirit of my old dog, Gyp." Charles Carlisle had slumped forward, his arms before him on the tablecloth, but now he sat up straighter, the bitter lines around his mouth deeper and more biting.

"Son, you don't believe that! That's blasphemous! You can't mean it—about a dog having a soul same as a man."

Stan smiled. "As I said before, I shall not try to convert you, Dad. Only the ones who have passed over into spirit life can do that. But I have communicated with Gyp—not in words, naturally, since Gyp did not speak in words. Yet this house is full of his presence. He has spoken to me, trying to tell me something." Watching his father keenly, Stan noticed a little flash of alarm on the wrecked face. He covered his eyes with his hand, watching his father's hands on the cloth before him, and bore in:

"Something about his last day on earth. I remember you told me, when I came home from school, that you had had a veterinary chloroform Gyp. But there's some contradiction, here. I get another impression . . ."

A pulse was beginning to pound in the shrunken wrist.

"Gyp has been trying to tell me something . . . wait a minute . . . the garage!"

His father's hands clenched into fists and then released the tablecloth, which they had seized.

"That's it . . . I see it clearly before me. Gyp is tied to the leg of the workbench in the garage. I see something rising and falling . . . in anger . . . faster and faster."

The clatter of a fork on the floor made Stan look up. The old man's face was ashy; he kept shaking his head, trying to speak. "No. No, son. Don't."

"That was the day—the day Mother left. With Mark Humphries. You came home and found her note. Gyp got in your way—you had to vent your temper on something. If I'd been home you'd have licked me. But Gyp got it. He died."

Old Carlisle had heaved to his feet, one hand clawing at his shirt collar. Stan turned, swaying a little, and walked stiffly through the doors into the living room, across it to the hall. When he took down his hat and coat his arms felt numb and heavy. One last glimpse of Clara shaking capsules from a bottle and holding a glass of water; the old man swallowing painfully.

The moon brightened concrete steps leading down the terrace where the grass was ragged. Stan's legs felt stiff as he descended to the street where the arching maples closed over him, moonlight showering through their leaves now black with night. A sound came from the house he had left, an old man weakly crying.

In a patch of silver the Rev. Carlisle stopped and raised his face to the full moon, where it hung desolately, agonizingly bright—a dead thing, watching the dying earth.

CARD XI

# The Lovers

*They stand between the Eden trees; winged Love hovers overhead while Knowledge lies in serpent coils upon the ground.*

WHEN Molly woke up the third time, Stan was dressing. She looked at the clock: four-thirty. "Where you going?"

"Out."

She didn't question him, but lay awake watching. His movements were so jumpy lately you didn't dare speak to him for fear he would bite your head off. Lately he had been sleeping worse and worse, and Molly worried about him taking so many sleeping pills all the time. They didn't have any more effect on him, it seemed, and his temper got worse and he looked like hell. She began to cry softly and Stan stopped in the middle of buttoning his shirt and came over.

"Now what?"

"Nothing. Nothing. I'm all right."

"What's eating you, kid?"

"Stan—" Molly sat up, holding the covers in front of her for warmth. "Stan, let's quit and go back to the old act."

He went on buttoning. "Where we going to book it? On street corners? Vaudeville's a dead pigeon. I know what I'm doing. One live John and we're set."

She drew the covers up tighter. "Honey, you look like hell.

Why don't you go see a doctor? I—I mean give you something for your nerves or something. Honest, I'm worried sick you're going to have a nervous breakdown or something."

He rubbed his eyes. "I'm going out for a walk."

"It's snowing."

"I've got to get out, do you hear? I'm going down to the church and look over the props. I've got an idea I want to try out. Go back to sleep."

It was no use. He would just keep going until he dropped and Molly prayed it wouldn't happen some time in the middle of a reading—or of a séance, where it would blow up the whole works. If anybody made trouble the cops would nail her along with Stan and in the shape Stan was in he couldn't talk his way out of a jam no matter how bad it was. Molly was worried sick and took half a sleeping pill herself when he had gone.

It was too early to go out and get a racing form, and all the magazines were old, and nothing was on the radio except platter programs, and they made her feel so lonesome—records being dedicated to the boys in Ed's Diner out on the turnpike. She wished she was in the diner with the truck drivers having a few laughs.

Stan let himself into the old Peabody house. He was glad he had banked the furnace the night before; down in the cellar he threw in more coal. Soon the fire was roaring and he stood with the heat on his face, watching blue flames feel their way up through the black coal.

After a moment he sighed, shook himself, and unlocked an old metal cabinet which had once held paint and varnish. Inside was a phonograph turntable which he switched on, placing a pickup arm into position above the aluminum record. Then he went upstairs.

The vast room which had been a parlor and a dining room before he knocked the partition out, was still chilly. Stan turned on the lamps. The bridge chairs sat in empty rows, waiting for something to happen to him—something to go wrong. Walking over to a lamp with a dead bulb, he snapped the switch, gave the amplifying tubes a minute to warm up, then crossed to the desk, where the trumpet usually lay at the developmental classes and trumpet séances.

Near the organ his foot, from long habit, found the loosened board beneath the carpet, and he put his weight on it. Ghostly, with the sound of a voice through a metal tube, came the deep tones of Ramakrishna, his spirit guide. "*Hari Aum.* Greetings, my beloved *chelas*, my disciples of earth life. You who have gathered here tonight." The voice stopped; Stan felt a crawling fear flowing over his scalp. The wiring must have broken again. And there was no time to rip it out. Or was it the loudspeaker? Or the motor? He ran down to the cellar; but the disc was still revolving. It must be in the amplifying unit. There was no time to fix it. The séance was scheduled for that evening. He could always blame it on conditions; a séance without phenomena was common enough for all mediums. But Mrs. Prescott was bringing two trusted friends, both social register. He had looked up all the dope on them and the recording was ready. They might not come back. They might be the ones who would bring in the live John he was waiting for.

Stan took off his coat and put on an old smock; he checked the tubes, the wiring. Then he went back upstairs and began to pry the panel loose. The loudspeaker connections were tight enough. Where was the break? And there was no time, no time, no time. He thought of a dozen stalls to tell a radio repairman, and threw them all out. Once he let anyone know the house was wired he was sunk. He thought of getting a repairman from Newark or somewhere. But there was no one he could trust.

Loneliness came over him, like an avalanche of snow. He was alone. Where he had always wanted to be. You can only trust yourself. There's a rat buried deep in everybody and they'll rat on you if they get pushed far enough. Every new face that showed up at the séances now seemed charged with suspicion and malice and sly knowledge. Could there be a cabal forming against him in the church?

Frantically he switched on the phonograph again and stepped on the board. "*Hari Aum.* Greetings, my beloved *chelas*, my disciples of earth life . . ." It wasn't broken! The last time he must have shifted his weight unconsciously off the loose board that closed the circuit. He stopped it now with a chilling fear that the next words the voice, his own voice, would say would not be words he had recorded on aluminum—the record would turn on him with a malevolent life of its own.

In the silence the house was closing in. The walls had not moved, nor the ceiling; not when he looked straight at them. He ran his hands over his hair once and took a deep breath. Hum the first eight bars of our opener. But it was no use.

Outside, across backyards, a dog barked.

"Gyp!"

His own voice startled him. Then he began to laugh.

He laughed as he walked into the hall, laughing up the stairs and in and out of bedrooms, now chastely bare. In the dark-séance room he snapped on the light. Blank white walls. Still laughing and chuckling he snapped the light off and felt for the panel in the baseboard where he kept the projector.

He aimed it at the wall; and there it was, jumping up and down crazily as his hand shook with laughing—the hazy image of an old woman. He twisted a knob and she vanished. Another twist and a baby appeared in a halo of golden mist, jumping crazily as his hand shook with laughing. "Dance, you little bastard," his voice thundered against the close walls.

He twisted the hand projector until the baby floated upside down, and he roared with laughter. He fell to the floor, laughing, and aimed the beam at the ceiling, watching the baby fly up the angle of the wall and come to rest overhead, still smiling mistily. Laughing and strangling, Stan began to beat the projector against the floor; something snapped, and the light went out.

He crawled to his feet and couldn't find the door and stopped laughing then, feeling his way around and around. He counted nine corners. He began to shout and then he found it and let himself out, dripping with sweat.

In his office the day was breaking gray through the Venetian blinds. The desk light wouldn't come on and he seized it and jerked it out of the wall plug and tossed it into a corner. The blinds got tangled with the cord; he gathered them in his arms and wrenched; the whole business came down on top of him and he fought his way free of them. At last the card index.

R. R. R. God damn it. Who had stolen the R's? Raphaelson, Randolph, Regan—here it was. *Woman psychologist, mentioned by Mrs. Tallentyre. Said to be interested in the occult. Has recommended that her patients take yoga exercises.* But the phone number, Jesus God, it wasn't there. Only her name—Dr. Lilith Ritter. Try the phone book. R. R. R.

The voice that answered the telephone was cool, low-pitched, and competent. "Yes?"

"My name is Carlisle. I've been having trouble sleeping—"

The voice interrupted. "Why not consult your physician? I am not a doctor of medicine, Mr. Carlisle."

"I've been taking pills, but they don't seem to help. I've been working too hard, they tell me. I want to see you."

There was silence for a long moment; then the cool voice said, "I can see you the day after tomorrow at eleven in the morning."

"Not before then?"

"Not before then."

Stan beat his fist once against the desk top, squeezing his eyes shut. Then he said, "Very well, Dr. Ritter. At eleven o'clock—Tuesday."

Whatever she might look like, the dame had a wonderful voice. And he must have pulled her out of a sound sleep. But Tuesday— What was he supposed to do until then, chew the rug?

The house grew warmer. Stan went over and pressed his forehead against the chill of the windowpane. Down in the street a girl in a fur coat and no stockings was walking an Irish setter. Stan's eyes followed the curve of the bare legs, wondering if she had on anything under the fur coat. Some of them run out that way—naked under their furs—to buy cigarettes or club soda or a douche bag.

Back in the flat Molly would be lying sprawled across the bed with her hair caught up on top of her head with a single pin. She would be wearing the black chiffon negligee but she might as well have on a calico wrapper. There was no one to look at her.

The Irish-setter girl turned, tugging at the leash, and the fur coat swung open, showing a pink slip. With a growl of frustration Stan twisted away from the window. He sat down at the desk and pulled out his appointment book. Message service that evening at eight-thirty. Monday morning, developmental class in trance mediumship and the Science of Cosmic Breath. God, what a herd of hippos. The Science of Cosmic Breath: in through the left nostril, on a count of four. Retain breath for count of sixteen. Exhale through the right nostril to count of eight. Measure the counts by repeating *Hari Aum, Hari Aum.*

Monday afternoon, lecture on the Esoteric Significance of the Tarot Symbols.

Stan took the Tarot deck from the side drawer and slowly his fingers began remembering; the front-and-back-hand palm, making the cards vanish in the air and drawing them out from under his knee. He paused at one card and laid it before him, holding his head in his hands, studying it. The Lovers. They were naked, standing in Eden with the snake down on the ground all ready to wise them up. Over their heads was the angel-form, its wings extended above the trees of Life and Knowledge. *Where the Tree of Life is blooming, there is rest for me.*

The lovers were naked. A wave of prickling crawled up over his scalp out of nowhere and, as he watched, the rounded hips and belly of the woman seemed to rotate. Jesus, if this is what I wanted I could have stayed with the Ten-in-One and been talker for the kooch show! There's a guy that always gets plenty.

He swept the cards to the floor and drew the telephone toward him, dialing. This time the voice said, "Yes, sir. I'll see if Mrs. Tallentyre's in."

She was in to the Rev. Carlisle.

"Mrs. Tallentyre, I spent most of last night in meditation. And from my meditation I drew a thought. I shall have to seek three days of silence. Unfortunately I cannot go to the Himalayas, but I think the Catskills will serve. You understand, I'm sure. I would appreciate it if you will take charge of the service tonight and notify class members that I have been called away. Just say that

I have gone in search of the Silence. I shall return, without fail, on the third day."

That was that. Now lock up. Lock the office door—time to clean up all the havoc later. Leave the appointment book downstairs on the hall table. Mrs. Tallentyre had a key to the outside door. Leave the inner door unlocked.

He put on his coat and a few minutes later was hurrying through the soft snow.

"Gee, honey, I'm glad you come back! Are you okay?"

"Yeah. Sure. How many times do I have to tell you I can take care of myself?"

"Want a couple of eggs? I'm starved. Let me fix you a couple. The coffee's all ready."

Stan stood in the kitchen door watching her. She was wearing the black chiffon negligee; against the early winter light from the window she might as well not have had on a stitch. Whoever figured out dames' clothes knew his onions. What made her seem so far away and long ago? The one dame who wouldn't cross him up. And the shape was still something you usually see behind footlights or in magazines.

Stan ran his hands once over his hair and said, "Come here." They stood watching each other for a moment, and he saw her take a deep breath. Then she turned off the gas under the skillet and ran over and threw her arms around his neck.

It was like kissing the back of your own hand but he picked her up in his arms and carried her into the bedroom. She clung to him and slid her hand under his shirt and he drew the chiffon open and started to kiss her shoulder but it was no use.

And now she was crying, looking up at him reproachfully as he threw on his jacket.

"Sorry, kid. I've got to get away. I'll be back Tuesday. I've—I've got to breathe."

When he had thrown some stuff in a keyster and locked it and hurried out Molly pulled the covers over her, still crying, and drew up her knees. After a while she got up and put on a robe and fried herself an egg. She didn't seem to be able to get enough salt on it, and in the middle of breakfast she suddenly took the plate and slammed it on the floor of the kitchen.

"Oh, God damn it, what's eating him? How can I know how to give him a party if I don't know what's the matter?"

After a while she got dressed and went out to have her hair washed and set. First she went around to the barber shop and saw Mickey, and he handed her sixteen dollars. The horse had paid off at seven to one.

With the wheels clicking past under him, Stan felt a little better. The Palisades had fingers of snow pointing up their slopes, and the river was rough with broken ice, where gulls sailed and settled. He read, sketchily, in Ouspensky's *A New Model of the Universe*, looking for tag lines he could pull out and use, jotting notes in the margin for a possible class in fourth dimensional immortality. Immortality was what they wanted. If they thought they could find it in the fourth dimension he would show them how. Who the hell knew what the fourth dimension was, anyway? Chumps. Johns.

A girl was having trouble getting her valise down from the rack and Stan leaped up to help her. Getting off at Poughkeepsie. His hand touched hers on the valise handle and he felt blood rising over his face. The kid was luscious; his eyes followed her as she walked primly down the car, carrying the bag before her. He crossed the train and watched her, out on the platform.

When he got to Albany he took a cab to the hotel, stopping off to buy a fifth of Scotch undercover from a saloon.

The room was good-sized and cleaner than most.

"You ain't been through lately, Mr. Charles. Territory been changed?"

Stan nodded, throwing his hat on the bed and getting out of his overcoat. "Bring some club soda. And plenty of ice."

The boy took a five and winked. "Like some company? We got swell gals in town—new since you was here last. I know a little blonde that's got everything. And I mean everything."

Stan lay down on the other bed and lit a cigarette, folding his hands behind his head. "Brunette."

"You're the boss."

He smoked when the boy had gone. In the ceiling cracks he could make out the profile of an old man. Then there was a tap on the door—the soda and ice. The boy scraped the collodion seal from the Scotch bottle.

Quiet again. In the empty, impersonal wilderness of the hotel Stan listened to noises coming up from the street. The whir of the elevator, stopping at his floor; footsteps soft in the corridor. He swung off the bed.

The girl was short and dark. She had on a tan polo coat and no hat, but there was an artificial gardenia pinned in her hair over one ear.

She came in, her nose and cheeks rosy from the cold, and said, "Howdy, sport! Annie sent me. Say—how'd ya know I drink Scotch?"

"I read minds."

"Gee, you musta." She poured two fingers' into a glass and offered it to Stan, who shook his head.

"On the wagon. But don't let that stop you."

"Okay, sport. Here's lead in your pencil." When she finished it she poured herself another and then said, "You better give me the fin now before I forget it."

Stan handed her a ten-dollar bill and she said, "Gee, thanks. Say, would you happen to have two fives?"

Silence. She broke it. "Lookit—radio in every room! That's something new for this dump. Say, let's listen to Charlie Mc-Carthy. D'you mind?"

Stan was looking at her spindly legs. As she hung the polo coat carefully in the closet he saw that her breasts were tiny. She was wearing a Sloppy Joe sweater and a skirt. They used to look like whores. Now they look like college girls. They all want to look like college girls. Why don't they go to college, then? They wouldn't be any different from the others. You'd never notice them. Christ, what a crazy way to run a world.

She was having a good time listening to the radio gags, and the whisky had warmed her. Taking off her shoes, she curled her feet under her. Then motioning Stan to throw her a cigarette, she stripped off her stockings and warmed her feet with her hands, giving him a flash at the same time.

When the program was over she turned the radio down a little and stood up, stretching. She drew off her sweater carefully, so as not to disturb the gardenia, and spread it over the chair back. She was thin, with sharp shoulder blades; her collar bones stood out starkly. When she dropped her skirt it was a little better but not too good. On one thigh, evenly spaced, were four bruises, the size of a big man's fingers.

She stood smoking, wearing nothing but the imitation gardenia and Stan let his eyes go back to the old man's face in the ceiling.

Tear-ass out of town, ride for hours, hotel, buy liquor, and for this. He sighed, stood up and slipped off his jacket and vest.

The girl was humming a tune to herself and now she did a soft-shoe dance step, her hands held up by her face, and spun around, then sang the chorus of the song that was coming over the loudspeaker. Her voice was husky and pleasant with power under control.

"You sing, too?" Stan asked dryly.

"Oh, sure. I only party to fill in. I sing with a band sometimes. I'm studying the voice." She threw back her head and vocalized five notes. "Ah . . . ah . . . AH . . . ah . . . ah."

The Great Stanton stopped with his shirt half off, staring. Then he seized the girl and threw her on the bed.

"Hey, look out, honey, not so fast! Hey, for Christ's sake, be careful!"

He twisted his hand in her hair. The girl's white, waxy face stared up at him, fearful and stretched tight. "Take it easy, honey. Don't. Listen, Ed McLaren, the house dick, is a pal of mine. Now go easy— Ed'll beat the hell out of any guy that did that."

The radio kept on. ". . . bringing you the music of Phil Requete and his Swingstars direct from the Zodiac Room of the Hotel Teneriffe. And now our charming vocalist, Jessyca Fortune, steps up to the mike with an old-fashioned look in her eye, as she sings—and swings—that lovely old number of the ever popular Bobbie Burns, 'Oh, Whistle and I'll Come to You, My Lad.' "

Ice in the river, piled against the piers of boat clubs, a dark channel in the middle. And always the click of the rail joints underneath. North south east west—cold spring heat fall—love lust tire leave—wed fight leave hate—sleep wake eat sleep—child boy man corpse—touch kiss tongue breast—strip grip press jet—wash dress pay leave—north south east west . . .

Stan felt the prickle crawl up over his scalp again. The old house was waiting for him and the fat ones with pince-nez and false teeth; this woman doc probably was one of them, for all the music of voice and cool, slow speech. What could she do for him? What could anybody do for him? For anybody? They were all trapped, all running down the alley toward the light.

The nameplate said, "Dr. Lilith Ritter, Consulting Psychologist. Walk In."

The waiting room was small, decorated in pale gray and rose. Beyond the casement window snow was falling softly in huge flakes. On the window sill was a cactus in a rose-colored dish, a cactus with long white hair like an old man. The sight of it ran along Stan's nerves like a thousand ants. He put down his coat and hat and then quickly looked behind a picture of sea shells drawn in pastel. No dictaphone. What was he afraid of? But that would have been a beautiful place to plant a bug if you wanted to work the waiting room gab angle when the doc's secretary came in.

Did she have a secretary? If he could make the dame he might get a line on this woman doc or whatever she was, find out how much overboard she was on occult stuff. He might swap developmental lessons for whatever she gave her patients—some kind of advice. Or did she interpret dreams or something? He lit a cigarette and it burned his finger as he knocked the ashes off. In reaching down to pick it up he knocked down an ashtray. He got on his hands and knees to pick up the butts and that was where he was when the cool voice said, "Come in."

Stan looked up. This dame wasn't fat, she wasn't tall, she wasn't old. Her pale hair was straight and she wore it drawn into a smooth roll on the nape of her neck. It glinted like green gold. A slight woman, no age except young, with enormous gray eyes that slanted a little.

Stan picked up the ashtray and put it on the edge of a table. It fell off again but he didn't notice. He was staring at the woman who stood holding the door open into another room. He weaved to his feet, lurching as he came near her. Then he caught a whiff of perfume. The gray eyes seemed as big as saucers, like the eyes of a kitten when you hold its nose touching yours. He looked at the small mouth, the full lower lip, carefully tinted but not painted. She said nothing. As he started to push past her he seemed to fall; he found his arm around her and held on knowing that he was a fool, knowing something terrible would strike him dead, knowing he wanted to cry, to empty his bladder, to scream, to go to sleep, wondering as he tightened his arms around her. . . .

Stan lay sprawling on the floor. She had twisted his shoulders, turning him until his back was toward her, and then planted one neat foot at the back of his knee. Now she knelt beside him on the carpet, gripping his right hand in both of hers, forcing it in toward the wrist and keeping him flat by the threatened pain of the taut tendons. Her expression had not changed.

She said, "The Rev. Stanton Carlisle, I believe. Pastor of the Church of the Heavenly Message, lecturer on Tarot symbolism and yogic breathing, a producer of ghosts with cheesecloth—or maybe you use a little magic lantern. Now if I let you up will you promise to be co-operative?"

Stan had thrown one arm over his eyes and he felt the tears slipping down his face into his ears. He managed to say, "Promise."

The deft hands released his and he sat up, hiding his face with his palms, thinking of a pillow that had been slept on and perfumed, with shame washing back and forth over him, the light too strong for his eyes, and the tears that wouldn't stop running. Something in his throat seemed to be strangling him from inside.

"Here—drink this."

"What—what is it?"

"Just a little brandy."

"Never drink it."

"I'm telling you to drink it. Quickly."

He felt blindly for the glass, held his breath and drank, coughing as it burned his throat.

"Now get up and sit over here in this chair. Open your eyes and look at me."

Dr. Lilith Ritter was regarding him from across a wide mahogany desk. She went on, "I thought I'd be hearing from you, Carlisle. You were never cut out to run a spook racket solo."

# The Star

*shines down upon a naked girl who, between land and sea, pours mysterious waters from her urns.*

"LIE BACK on the couch."

"I don't know what to talk about."

"You say that every time. What are you thinking about?"

"You."

"What about me?"

"Wishing you sat where I could see you. I want to look at you."

"When you lie down on the couch, just before you lean back, you run your hands over your hair. Why do you do that?"

"That's my get-set."

"Explain."

"Every vaudeville actor has some business: something he does in the wings just before he goes on."

"Why do you do that?"

"I've always done it. I used to have a cowlick when I was a kid and my mother would always be telling me to slick it down."

"Is that the only reason?"

"What difference does it make?"

"Think about it. Did you ever know anybody who did that—anybody else in vaudeville?"

"No. Let's talk about something else."

"What are you thinking about now?"

"Pianos."

"Go on."

"Pianos. People playing pianos. For other people to sing. My mother singing. When she sang my old man would go in the dining room and whisper all the time to one of his pals. The rest would be in the living room listening to my mother."

"She played the piano herself?"

"No. Mark played. Mark Humphries. He'd sit down and look up at her as if he was seeing right through her clothes. He'd run his hands once over his hair—"

"Yes?"

"But it's crazy! Why would I want to swipe a piece of business from that guy? After she'd run off with him I used to lie awake nights thinking up ways to kill him."

"I think you admired him."

"It was the dames that admired him. He was a great big guy with a rumbling voice. The dames were crazy over him."

"Did this Humphries drink?"

"Sure. Now and then."

"Did your father drink?"

"Hell, no. He was White Ribbon."

"The first day you were here I offered you a glass of brandy to help you get hold of yourself. You said you never drank it."

"God damn it, don't twist everything around to making it look as if I wanted to be like my old man. Or Humphries either. I hated them—both of 'em."

"But you wouldn't take a drink."

"That was something else."

"What?"

"None of your—I—it's something I can't tell you."

"I'm being paid to listen. Take your time. You'll tell me."

"The stuff smelled like wood alcohol to me. Not any more but the first time."

"Did you ever drink wood alcohol?"

"Christ, no, it was Pete."

"Pete who?"

"I never knew his last name. It was in Burleigh, Mississippi. We had a guy in the carny named Pete. A lush. One night he tanked up on wood alky and kicked off."

"Did he have a deep voice?"

"Yes. How did you know?"

"Never mind. What was he to you?"

"Nothing. That is—"

"What are you thinking about?"

"Damn it, quit deviling me."

"Take your time."

"He—he was married to Zeena, who ran the horoscope pitch. I was—I was—I was screwing her on the side I wanted to find out how she and Pete had done their vaude mental act and I wanted a woman and I made up to her and Pete was always hanging around I gave him the alky to pass him out I didn't know it was wood or I'd forgotten it he died I was afraid they'd pin it on me but it blew over. That's all. Are you satisfied?"

"Go on."

"That's all. I was scared of that murder rap for a long time but then it blew over. Zeena never suspected anything. And then Molly and I teamed up and quit the carny and it all seemed like a bad dream. Only I never forgot it."

"But you felt so guilty that you would never drink."

"For God's sake—you can't do mentalism and drink! You've got to be on your toes every minute."

"Let's get back to Humphries. Before he ran away with your mother you preferred him to your father?"

"Do we have to go over that again? Sure. Who wouldn't? But not after—"

"Go on."

"I caught him—"

"You caught him making love to your mother? Is that it?"

"In the Glade. We'd found it, together. Then I went there. And I saw it. I tell you, I saw it. All of it. Everything they did. I wanted to kill my old man. He drove her to Humphries, I thought. I wanted—I wanted—"

"Yes."

"I wanted them to take me with them! But she didn't, God

damn her, she left me with the old son-of-a-bitch to rot in his
goddamned hick town. I wanted to go away with her and see
something and maybe get into show business. Humphries had
been in show business. But I was left there to rot with that
Bible-spouting old bastard."

"So you became a Spiritualist minister."

"I'm a hustler, God damn it. Do you understand that, you
frozen-faced bitch? I'm on the make. Nothing matters in this
goddamned lunatic asylum of a world but dough. When you get
that you're the boss. If you don't have it you're the end man on
the daisy chain. I'm going to get it if I have to bust every bone
in my head doing it. I'm going to milk it out of those chumps
and take them for the gold in their teeth before I'm through.
You don't dare yell copper on me because if you spilled anything about me all your other Johns would get the wind up
their necks and you wouldn't have any more at twenty-five
bucks a crack. You've got enough stuff in that bastard tin file
cabinet to blow 'em all up. I know what you've got in there—
society dames with the clap, bankers that take it up the ass,
actresses that live on hop, people with idiot kids. You've got it
all down. If I had that stuff I'd give 'em cold readings that would
have 'em crawling on their knees to me. And you sit there out
of this world with that dead-pan face and listen to the chumps
puking their guts out day after day for peanuts. If I knew that
much I'd stop when I'd made a million bucks and not a minute
sooner. You're a chump too, blondie. They're all Johns. They're
asking for it. Well, I'm here to give it out. And if anybody was
to get the big mouth and sing to the cops about me I'd tell a
couple of guys I know. They wouldn't fall for your jujit
stuff."

"I've been shouted at before, Mr. Carlisle. But you don't really
know any gangsters. You'd be afraid of them. Just as you're
afraid of me. You're full of rage, aren't you? You feel you hate
me, don't you? You'd like to come off that couch and strike
me, wouldn't you?—but you can't. You're quite helpless with
me. I'm one person you can't outguess. You can't fool me with
cheesecloth ghosts; you can't impress me with fake yoga. You're
just as helpless with me as you felt seeing your mother run away

with another man when you wanted to go with her. I think you went with her. You ran away, didn't you? You went into show business, didn't you? And when you start your act you run your hands over your hair, just like Humphries. He was a big, strong, attractive man, Humphries. I think you have become Humphries —in your mind."

"But he—he—"

"Just so. I think you wanted your mother in the same way."

"God damn your soul, that's—"

"Lie back on the couch."

"I could kill you—"

"Lie back on the couch."

"I could— Mother. Mother. Mother."

He was on his knees, one hand beating at his eyes. He crawled to her and threw his head in her lap, burrowing in. Dr. Lilith Ritter, gazing down at the disheveled corn-colored hair, smiled slightly. She let one hand rest on his head, running her fingers gently over his hair, patting his head reassuringly as he sobbed and gasped, rooting in her lap with his lips. Then, with her other hand, she reached for the pad on the desk and wrote in shorthand: "Burleigh, Mississippi."

In the spring darkness the obelisk stood black against the sky. There were no clouds and only a single star. No, a planet; Venus, winking as if signaling Earth in a cosmic code that the worlds used among themselves. He moved his head a fraction, until the cold, brilliant planet seemed to rest on the bronze tip of the stone shaft. The lights of a car, winding through the park, sprayed for a moment across the stone and the hieroglyphics leaped out in shadow. Cartouches with their names, the boasts of the dead, invocations to dead gods, prayers to the shining, fateful river which rose in mystery and found the sea through many mouths, flowing north through the ancient land. Was it mysterious when it still lived? he wondered. Before the Arabs took it over and the chumps started measuring the tunnel of the Great Pyramid in inches to see what would happen in the world.

The spring wind stirred her hair and trailed a loose wisp of it across his face. He pressed her cheek against his and with his other hand pointed to the planet, flashing at the stone needle's point. She nodded, keeping silence; and he felt the helpless wonder sweep over him again, the impotence at touching her, the supplication. Twice she had given it to him. She had given it as she might give him a glass of brandy, watching his reactions. Beyond that elfin face, the steady eyes, there was something breathing, something that was fed blood from a tiny heart beating under pointed breasts. But it was cobweb under the fingers. Cobweb in the woods that touches the face and disappears under the fingers.

The hot taste of need rose in his mouth and turned sour with inner turmoil and the jar of forbidding recollection. Then he drew away from her and turned to look at her face. As the wind quickened he saw her perfectly molded nostrils quiver, scenting spring as an animal tastes the wind. Was she an animal? Was all the mystery nothing more than that? Was she merely a sleek, golden kitten that unsheathed its claws when it had played enough and wanted solitude? But the brain that was always at work, always clicking away behind the eyes—no animal had such an organ; or was it the mark of a superanimal, a new species, something to be seen on earth in a few more centuries? Had nature sent out a feeling tentacle from the past, groping blindly into the present with a single specimen of what mankind was to be a thousand years hence?

The brain held him; it dosed him with grains of wild joy, measured out in milligrams of words, the turn of her mouth corner, one single, lustful flash from the gray eyes before the scales of secrecy came over them again. The brain seemed always present, always hooked to his own by an invisible gold wire, thinner than spider's silk. It sent its charges into his mind and punished him with a chilling wave of cold reproof. It would let him writhe in helpless misery and then, just before the breaking point, would send the warm current through to jerk him back to life and drag him, tumbling over and over through space, to the height of a snow mountain where he could see all the plains of the earth spread out before him, and all the power of the cities and the ways of men. All were his, could be his, would be his, unless the golden thread broke and sent him roaring into the dark chasm of fear again.

The wind had grown colder; they stood up. He lit cigarettes and gave her one and they passed on, circling the obelisk, walking slowly past the blank, unfinished wall of the Museum's back, along the edge of the park where the busses trailed their lonely lights away uptown.

He took her hand in his and slid it into the pocket of his topcoat, and for a moment, as they walked, it was warm and a little moist, almost yielding, almost, to the mind's tongue, sweet-salty, yielding, musky; then in an instant it changed, it chilled, it became the hand of a dead woman in his pocket, as cold as the hand he once molded of rubber and stretched on the end of his reaching rod, icy from a rubber sack of cracked ice in his pocket, straight into the face of a believer's skeptical husband.

Now the loneliness grew inside him, like a cancer, like a worm of a thousand branches, running down his nerves, creeping under his scalp, tying two arms together and squeezing his brain in a noose, pushing into his loins and twisting them until they ached with need and not-having, with wanting and not-daring, with thrust into air, with hand-gripping futility—orgasm and swift-flooding shame, hostile in its own right, ashamed of shame.

They stopped walking and he moved toward a backless bench under the trees which were putting out the first shoots of green in the street lamp's glow, delicate, heartbreakingly new, the old spring which would bring the green softly, gently, like a young girl, into the earth's air long after they and the fatal, coursing city, were gone. They would be gone forever, he thought, looking down into her face which was now as empty as a ball of crystal reflecting only the window light.

The rush, the rocketing plunge of the years to death, seized hold of him and he gripped her, pressing her to him in a fierce clutch after life. She let him hold her and he heard himself moaning a little under his breath as he rubbed his cheek against the smooth hair. Then she broke away, reached up and brushed his lips with hers and began to walk again. He fell in behind her for a few steps, then came abreast of her and took her hand once more. This time it was firm, muscular, determined. It closed on his own fingers for a single reassuring instant, then broke away and she thrust her hands into the pockets of her coat and strode on, the smoke of her cigarette whirling back over her shoulder like a sweet-smelling scarf in the wind.

When she walked she placed her feet parallel, as if she were walking a crack in the sidewalk. In spite of high heels the ankles above them never wavered. She wore gunmetal stockings, and her shoes had buckles of cut steel.

Two ragged little boys, gleeful at being out after midnight, came bounding toward them, chasing each other back and forth across the walk by the wall where the trees leaned over. One of them pushed the other, screaming dirty words, and the one pushed caromed toward Lilith. Turning like a cat released in mid-air, she spun out of his path and the boy sprawled to the cinders, his hands slipping along, grinding cinders into the palms. He sat up and as Stan turned to watch, he suddenly sprang at his companion with his fists. Kids always play alike. Roughhouse around until one gets hurt and then the fight starts. A couple of socks and they quit and the next minute are friends again. Oh, Christ, why do you have to grow up into a life like this one? Why do you ever have to want women, want power, make money, make love, keep up a front, sell the act, suck around some booking agent, get gypped on the check—?

It was late and the lights were fewer. Around them the town's roar had softened to a hum. And spring was coming with poplar trees standing slim and innocent around a glade with the grass hummocks under one's hands—can't I ever forget it? His eyes blurred and he felt his mouth tighten.

The next moment Lilith's hand was through his arm, pressing it, turning him across the avenue to the apartment house where she lived, where she worked her own special brand of magic, where she had her locked files full of stuff. Where she told people what they had to do during the next day when they wanted a drink, when they wanted to break something, when they wanted to kill themselves with sleeping tablets, when they wanted to bugger the parlor maid or whatever they wanted to do that they had become so afraid of doing that they would pay her twenty-five dollars an hour to tell them either why it was all right to do it or go on doing it or think about doing it or how they could stop doing it or stop wanting to do it or stop thinking about doing it or do something else that was almost as good or something which was bad but would make you feel better or just something to do to be able to do something.

At her door they stopped and she turned to him, smiling serenely, telling him in that smile that he wasn't coming in to-night, that she didn't need him, didn't want him tonight, didn't want his mouth on her, didn't want him to kneel beside her, kissing her, didn't want anything of him except the knowledge that when she wanted him in the night and wanted his mouth on her and wanted him kneeling beside her, kissing her, she would have him doing all those things to her as she wanted them done and just when she wanted them done and just how she wanted them done to her because she had only what she wanted from anybody and she had let him do those things to her because she had wanted them done to her not because he could do them better than anyone else although he didn't know if there was anybody else and didn't want to know and it didn't matter and she could have him any time she wanted those things done to her because that was the way she was and she was to be obeyed in all things because she held in her hand the golden thread which carried the current of life into him and she held behind her eyes the rheostat that fixed the current and she could starve him and dry him up and kill him by freezing if she wanted to and this was where he had gotten himself only it didn't matter because as long as one end of the golden wire was embedded in his brain he could breathe and live and move and become as great as she wanted since she sent the current along the wire for him to become great with and live with and even make love to Molly with when Molly begged him to tell her if he didn't want her any more so she might get some man before she looked like an old hay-burner and her insides were too tight for her ever to have a kid.

All these things he saw in the full lower lip, the sharp cheek-bones and chin, the enormous eyes of gray that looked like ink now in the dark of the vestibule. He was about to ask her something else and he wet his lips with his tongue. She caught his thought, nodded, and he stood there, three steps below her with his hand holding his hat, looking up at her and needing and then she gave him what he was begging for, her lips for a full, warm, soft, sweet, moist moment and her little tongue between his like the words, "Good night" formed of soft moisture. Then she had gone and there he was for another day, another week, another month, willing to do anything she said, as long as she would not break the golden wire and now he had her permission, which she had pulled out of his mind, and he hurried off to take advantage of it before she changed her mind and sent him refusal, chilling along the invisible wire embedded in his brain, that would stop his hand six inches from his lips.

Three doors down was a little cocktail bar with a glass sign over it that was illumined some way from inside and said "BAR." Stan hurried in. The murals jagged crazily this way and that up the three-toned wall and a radio was playing softly where the bar man nodded on a stool at one end of the bar. Stan laid a dollar on the polished wood.

"Hennessy, Three Star."

" 'Inside, above the din and fray, We heard the loud musicians play The "Treues Liebes Herz" of Strauss—' "

"What's that?"

"It's from *The Harlot's House*. Shall we go in?"

They were walking down a side street in the early summer twilight; ahead of them Lexington Avenue was gaudy with neon. In the basement of an old brownstone was a window painted in primary blues and reds; above it a sign, "Double Eagle Kretchma." Gypsy music was filtering out on the heated air.

"It looks like a joint to me."

"I like joints—when I'm in the mood for dirt. Let's go in."

It was dark with a few couples sliding around on the little dance floor. A sad fat man with blue jowls, wearing a Russian blouse of dark green silk, greasy at the cuffs, came toward them and took them to a booth. "You wish drinks, good Manhattan? Good Martini?"

"Do you have any real vodka?" Lilith was tapping a cigarette.

"Good vodka. You, sir?"

Stan said, "Hennessy, Three Star, and plain water."

When the drinks came he offered the waiter a bill but it was waved away. "Later. Later. Have good time first. Then comes the payment—the bad news, huh? Have good time—always have to pay for everything in the end." He leaned across the table, whispering, "This vodka—it's not worth what you pay for it. Why you want to come here anyhow? You want card reading?"

Lilith looked at Stan and laughed. "Let's."

From the shadows in the back of the room a woman stepped out and waddled toward them, her bright red skirt swishing as her hips rolled. She had a green scarf around her head, a curved nose, loose thin lips and a deep, greasy crease between her breasts which seemed ready to burst from her soiled white blouse at any moment. When she wedged herself into the booth beside Stan her round hip was hot and burning against his thigh.

"You cut the cards, lady; we see what you cut, please. Ah, see! Good sign! This card called The Star. You see this girl— she got one foot on land, one foot on water; she pour wine out on land and water. That is good sign, lucky in love, lady. I see man with light hair going to ask you to marry him. Some trouble at first but it come out all right."

She turned up a card. "This one here— Hermit card. Old man with star in lantern. You search for something, no? Something you lose, no? Ring? Paper with writing on it?"

Against Lilith's blank, cold face the gypsy's questions bounded back. She turned another card. "Here is Wheel of Life. You going to live long time with not much sickness. Maybe some stomach trouble later on and some trouble with nervous sickness but everything pass off all right."

Lilith took a puff of her cigarette and looked at Stan. He pulled two bills from his wallet and held them to the gypsy. "That'll do, sister. Scram."

"Thank you, mister. But lots more fortune in cards. Tell lots of thing about what going to happen. Bad luck, maybe; you see how to keep it away."

"Go on, sister. Beat it."

She shoved the bills into her pocket along with the Tarot deck and heaved out of the booth without looking back.

"She'll probably put the hex on us now," Stan said. "Christ, what corn. Why the hell did I ever leave the carny? I could be top man in the mitt camp right now and tucking ten grand in the sock at the end of every season."

"You don't want to, darling." Lilith sipped her vodka. "Do you think I'd be sitting here with you if your only ambition was to be top man in a—what did you call it?"

"Mitt camp." He grinned weakly. "You're right, doctor. Besides I'd probably have pulled the switch once too often and gotten jugged." He answered her frown. "The switch is what the gypsies call *okana borra*—the great trick. You have the chump tie a buck up in his hanky. He sleeps on it and in the morning he has two bucks and comes running back with all his savings out of the teapot. Then when he wakes up next time he has nothing in the hank but a stack of paper and he comes back looking for the gypsy."

"You know such fascinating bits of folklore, Mr. Carlisle. And you think you could ever be happy using those very keen, crafty brains of yours to cheat some ignorant farmer? Even if you did make ten thousand a year and loaf all winter?"

He finished the brandy and signaled the waiter for a refill. "And when it rains you read mitts with your feet in a puddle and a river down the back of your neck. I'll stick to Mrs. Peabody's house—it's got a better roof on it."

Lilith's eyes had narrowed. "I meant to speak to you, Stan, when we got a chance. There are two women who will be introduced to your congregation, not directly through me, naturally, but they'll get there. One of them is a Mrs. Barker. She's interested in yoga; she wants to go to India but I told her not to uproot her life at this stage. She needs something to occupy her time. I think your Cosmic Breath would be just about right."

Stan had taken a slip of paper from his pocket and was writing. "What's her first name?"

"Give me that paper." She put it in the ashtray and touched her lighter to it. "Stan, I've told you not to write down anything. I don't want to have to remind you again. You talk very glibly about making a million with your brains and yet you continue to act as naïve as a carnival grifter."

He downed the drink desperately and found another in its place and finished that one as quickly.

Lilith went on. "The name is Lucinda Barker. There's nothing else you need to know."

There was silence for a minute, Stan sullenly rattling the ice in the chaser glass.

"The other woman is named Grace McCandless. She's single, forty-five years old. Kept house for her father until he died three years ago. She's gone through Theosophy and come out the other side. She wants proof of survival."

"Give—can you tell me something about the old man?"

"He was Culbert McCandless, an artist. You can look him up with the art dealers probably."

"Look, Lilith, give me just one 'test.' I know you're afraid I'll louse it up and they'll think back to you. But you've got to trust me. After all, lady, I've been in this racket all my life."

"Well, stop apologizing and listen. McCandless went to bed with his daughter—once. She was sixteen. They never did it again but they were never separated. Now that's all you'll get. I'm the only person in the world who knows this, Stan. And if your foot slips I shall have to protect myself. You know what I mean."

"Yeah. Yeah, pal. Let's get out of here. I can't stand the bum air."

Above them the summer leaves cut off the glow of the city in the night sky. By the obelisk they paused for a moment and then Lilith took the lead and they passed it. The back of the Museum seemed to leer at him, full of unspoken threats with doom straining at its leash in the shadows.

When she came out of the bathroom her hands gleamed white against the black silk robe as she tied the cord. On her feet were tiny black slippers. Lilith sat at the desk by the bedroom window and from its side compartment took a case containing several flat drawers, labeled "Sapphires," "Cat's Eyes," "Opals," "Moss Agates."

She said, without looking at him, "The notes wouldn't do you the slightest bit of good, Stan. They're all in my own shorthand."

"What do you mean?"

Her glance, raised to his for the first time, was calm and benevolent. "While I was in the bathroom you went into my office and tried out the key you had made for my file cabinet. I saw it on the dressing table after you had taken off your clothes. Now it's not there. You've hidden it. But I recognized the notches. You took the impression from my key the last time you went to bed with me, didn't you?"

He said nothing but smoked quickly; the ember of his cigarette became long and pointed and angry red.

"I was going to send you home, Stan, but I think you need a little lesson in manners. And I need my toenails fixed. You can help me with the polish. It's in the drawer of the bed table. Bring it over here."

Dully he stamped out his cigarette, spilling some of the embers and quickly sweeping them back into the tray. He took the kit of nail polish and went over to her, feeling the air against his naked flesh cold and hostile. He threw his shirt over his shoulders and sat down on the carpet at her feet.

Lilith had taken the drawer marked sapphires from its little cabinet and was lifting the stones with a pair of jeweler's forceps, holding them in the light of the desk lamp. Without looking at him she shook one foot free of its slipper and placed it on his bare knee. "This is very good for you, darling. Occupational therapy."

The Great Stanton twisted cotton on the end of an orangewood stick and dipped it into the bottle of polish remover. It smelled acrid and sharply chemical as he swabbed one tiny toenail with it, taking off the chipped polish evenly. Once he paused to kiss the slender foot at the instep but Lilith was absorbed in her tray of gems. Growing bolder, he drew aside the black silk and kissed her thigh. This time she turned and pulled the robe primly over knees, giving him a glance of amused tolerance. "You've had enough sinfulness for one evening, Mr. Carlisle. Be careful not to spill polish on the rug. You wouldn't want me to rub your nose in it and then throw you out the back door by the scruff of your neck, would you, darling?"

Bracing his hand against the curved instep he began to paint her nails. The rose-colored enamel spread evenly and he thought of the workbench out in the garage and its paint cans. Painting a scooter he had made out of boxes and old baby-carriage wheels. Mother said, "That's beautiful, Stanton. I have several kitchen chairs you can paint for me." The old man had been saving that paint for something. That meant another licking.

"Stan, for heaven's sake, be more careful! You hurt me with the orange stick."

He had finished the first foot and started on the other without knowing it.

"What would you do for a shoeshine if you didn't have me around?" He was startled at the amount of hostility in his own voice.

Lilith laid down a sapphire, narrowing her eyes. "I might have another friend of mine do them. Possibly someone who could take me to the theater, who didn't have to be so afraid of being seen with me. Someone who wouldn't have to sneak in and out."

He set down the bottle of polish remover. "Lilith, wait until we make a killing. One big-time believer—" But he didn't sound convinced himself; his voice died. "I—I want to be seen with you, Lilith. I—I didn't think up this setup. You were the one who told me to hang on to Molly. If I went back to the carny—"

"Stanton Carlisle. Pastor of the Church of the Heavenly Message. I didn't think you could be jealous. I didn't think you had that much of a heart, Stan. I thought all you cared about was money. And power. And more money."

He stood up, throwing off the shirt, his hands clenched. "Go on, pal. You can tell me about as many other guys as you want. This is fifty-fifty. I'm not jealous if another guy shakes hands with you. How's that so different from—the other thing?"

She watched him through eyes almost closed. "Not so very different. No. Not different at all. I shook hands regularly with the old judge—the one who set me up in practice when I was a court psychiatrist on a city salary. All cats have gray paws in the dark, you know, Stan. And I can vaguely recall, when I was sixteen, how five boys in our neighborhood waited for me one evening as I was coming home from night school. They took me into a vacant lot and shook hands with me one after the other. I think each came back twice."

He had turned as she spoke, his mouth hanging open idiotically, his hair falling over his face. He lurched over to the dressing table with its wing mirrors, gaped at his image, his eyes ravaged. Then in a spatter of desperate groping he seized the nail scissors and gouged at his forehead with them.

The stab of pain was followed instantly by a tearing sensation in his right wrist and he saw that Lilith stood beside him, levering his hand behind his shoulder until he dropped the scissors. She had not forgotten to pull up her robe and held it bunched under one arm to keep it from brushing her toes with their wet enamel.

"Put a drop of iodine on it, Stan," she said crisply. "And don't try drinking the bottle. There's not enough in it to do more than make you sick."

He let the cold water roar past his face and then tore at his hair with the rich, soft towel. His forehead wasn't bleeding any more.

"Stan, darling—"

"Yeah. Coming."

"You never do anything by halves, do you, lover? So few men have the courage to do what they really want to do. If you'll come in here and fuss over me a little more—I love to be fussed over, darling—I'll tell you a bedtime story, strictly for adults."

He was putting on his clothes. When he was dressed he pulled up a hassock and said, "Give me your foot."

Smiling, Lilith put the gems away and leaned back, stretching her arms luxuriously, watching him with the sweetest of proprietary smiles.

"That's lovely, darling. Much more accurately than I could do it. Now about the bedtime story—for I've decided to risk it and ask you to stay over with me. You can, darling. Just this once. Well, I know a man—don't be silly, darling, he's a patient. Well, he started as a patient and later became a friend—but not like you, darling. He's a very shrewd, capable man and he might do us both a lot of good. He's interested in psychic phenomena."

Stan looked up at her, holding her foot in both his hands. "How's he fixed for dough?"

"Very well-heeled as you would put it, darling. He lost a sweetheart when he was in college and he has been weighed down with guilt from it ever since. She died from an abortion. Well, at first I thought I'd have to pass him along to one of my tame Freudians—he seemed likely to get out of hand with me. But then he became interested in the psychic. His company makes electric motors. You'll recognize the name—Ezra Grindle."

# The Chariot

*holds a conqueror. Sphinxes draw him. They turn in opposite directions to rend him apart.*

GRINDLE, EZRA, industrialist, b. Bright's Falls, N. Y. Jan. 3, 1878, s. Matthias Z. and Charlotte (Banks). Brewster Academy and Columbia U. grad. 1900 engineering. m. Eileen Ernst 1918, d. 1927. Joined sales staff, Hobbes Chem. and Dye, 1901, head of Chi. office 1905; installed plants Rio de Janeiro, Manila, Melbourne 1908-10; export mgr. 1912. Dollar-a-year man, Washington, D. C. 1917-18. Amer. Utilities, gen. mgr. 1919, v.p. 1921. Founded Grindle Refrigeration 1924, Manitou Casting and Die 1926 (subsidiary), in 1928 merged five companies to form Grindle Sheet Metal and Stamping. Founded Grindle Electric Motor Corp. 1929, pres. and chairman of board. Author: The Challenge of Organized Labor, 1921; Expediting Production: a Scientific Guide, 1928; Psychology in Factory Management (with R. W. Gilchrist) 1934. Clubs: Iroquois, Gotham Athletic, Engineering Club of Westchester County. Hobbies: billiards, fishing.

From *The Roll Call*—1896, Brewster Academy:

EZRA GRINDLE ("Spunk") Major: Math. Activities: chess club, math club, manager of baseball 3 years, business manager of

*The Roll Call* 2 years. College: Columbia. Ambition: to own a yacht. Quotation: "By magic numbers and persuasive sound"— Congreve.

When the red-haired kid looked up he saw a man standing by the counter. The clerical collar, the dead-black suit, the panama with a black band, snapped him to life.

"My son, I wonder if you would be so kind as to help me on a little matter?" He slipped a breviary back into his pocket.

"Sure, Father. What can I do for you, Father?"

"My son, I am preparing a sermon on the sin of destroying life before birth. I wonder if you could find me some of the clippings which have appeared in your newspaper, recounting the deaths of unfortunate young women who have been led to take the lives of their unborn infants. Not the most recent accounts, you understand—of these there are so many. I want to see some of the older accounts. Proving that this sin was rampant even in our parents' time."

The kid's forehead was pulled up with the pain of thought. "Gee, Father, I'm afraid I don't getcha."

The smooth voice lowered a little. "Abortions, my son. Look under A-B."

The kid blushed and pounded away importantly. He came back with an old envelope. ABORTION, DEATHS—1900-10.

The man in the clerical collar riffled through them quickly. 1900: MOTHER OF TWO DIES FROM ILLEGAL OPERATION. SOCIETY GIRL . . . HUSBAND ADMITS . . . DEATH PACT . . .

## DEATH OF A WORKING GIRL
### By Elizabeth McCord

Last night in Morningside Hospital a slender young girl with raven tresses covering her pillow turned her face to the wall when a youth fought his way into the ward where she lay on the brink of death. She would not look upon him, would not speak to him although he begged and implored her forgiveness. And in the end he slunk away, eluding Officer Mulcahy who had been stationed in the hospital to watch for just such an appearance of the man responsible for the girl's condition and untimely death. He did not escape, however, before a keen-eyed little probationer nurse had noted the initials E.G. on his watch fob.

Somewhere in our great city tonight a coward crouches and trembles, expecting at any moment the heavy hand of the law to descend on his shoulder, his soul seared (let us hope) by the unforgiving gesture of the innocent girl whose life he destroyed by his callous self-interest and criminal insistence.

This girl—tall, brunette and lovely in the first bloom of youth—is but one of many. . . .

The man in black clucked his tongue. "Yes—even in our parents' time. Just as I thought. The sin of destroying a little life before it has been born or received Holy Baptism."

He stuffed the clippings back into the envelope and beamed his thanks on the kid with red hair.

In Grand Central the good father picked up a suitcase from the check room. In a dressing cubicle he changed into a linen suit, a white shirt, and a striped blue tie.

Out on Madison Avenue he stopped, grinning, as he turned the pages of a worn breviary. The edges were crinkled from rain; and on the fly leaf was written in faded, Spencerian script, "Fr. Nikola Tosti" and a date. The blond man tossed it into a trash can. In his pocket was a clipping, the work of a sob sister thirty years ago. *May 29, 1900.*

The morgue office of Morningside Hospital was a room in the basement inhabited by Jerry, the night attendant, a shelf of ancient ledgers, and a scarred wreck of a desk. There were two kitchen chairs for visitors, a radio, an electric fan for hot nights and an electric heater for cold ones. The fan was going now.

A visitor in soiled gray slacks and a sport shirt looked up as Jerry came back into the room.

"I borrowed a couple of shot glasses from the night nurse on West One—the little number with the gams. These glasses got markings on 'em but don't let that stop us. Fill 'em up. Say, brother, it's a break we got together over in Julio's and you had this bottle. I hadn't had a chance to wet the whistle all evening. I was dying for a few shots."

His new friend pushed a straw skimmer further back on his head and filled the medicine glasses with applejack.

"Here's lead in the old pencil, huh?" Jerry killed his drink and held out the glass.

Blondy filled it again and sipped his brandy. "Gets kind of dull, nights, eh?"

"Not so bad. I listen to the platter programs. You get some good records on them programs. And I do lots of crossword puzzles. Say, some nights they don't give you a minute's peace around here—stiffs coming down every ten minutes. That's mostly in the winter and in the very hot spells—old folks. We try not to get 'em in here when they're ready to put their checks back in the rack but you can't keep 'em out when a doctor says 'In she goes.' Then we got the death entered on our books and the city's books. It don't look good. Thanks, don't care if I do."

"And you got to keep 'em entered in all these books? That would drive me nuts." The blond man put his feet on the desk and looked up at the shelf full of ledgers.

"Naa. Only in the current book—here, on the desk. Them books go all the way back to when the hospital started. I don't know why they keep 'em out here. Only once in a while the Medical Examiner's office comes nosing around, wanting to look up something away back, and I dust 'em off. This ain't a bad job at all. Plenty of time on your hands. Say—I better not have any more right now. We got an old battle-ax, the night supervisor. She might come down and give me hell. Claim I was showing up drunk. I never showed up drunk on the job yet. And she never comes down after three o'clock. It ain't bad."

Cool blue eyes had picked out a volume marked *1900*.

Jerry rattled on. "Say, y'know that actress, Doree Evarts—the one that did the Dutch night before last in the hotel across the way? They couldn't save her. This evening, 'bout eight o'clock, I got a call to collect one from West Five—that's private. It was her. I got her in the icebox now. Wanna see her?"

The stranger set down his glass. His face was white but he said,

"Sure thing. I ain't never seen a dead stripper. Boy, oh, boy, but I seen her when she was alive. She used to flash 'em."

The morgue man said, "Come on. I'll introduce you."

In the corridor were icebox doors in three tiers. Jerry went down the line, unlatched one and pulled out a tray. On it lay a form covered by a cheap cotton sheet which he drew back with a flourish.

Doree Evarts had cut her wrists. What lay on the galvanized tray was like a dummy, eyes half open, golden hair damp and matted. The nostrils and mouth were plugged with cotton.

There were the breasts Doree had snapped by their nipples under the amber spotlight, the belly which rotated for the crowd of smoke-packed old men and pimply kids, the long legs which spread in the final bump as she made her exit. Her nail polish was chipped and broken off; a tag with her name on it was tied to one thumb; her wrists were bandaged.

"Good-looking tomato—once." Jerry pulled up the sheet, slid in the drawer and slammed the door. They went back to the office and the visitor knocked off two quick brandies.

Doree had found the end of the alley. What had she been running from that made her slice at her veins? Nightmare coming closer. What force inside her head, under the taffy-colored hair, pushed her into this?

The dank office swam in the heat of the brandy as Jerry's voice clattered on. "You get lotsa laughs some nights. One time —last winter it was—we had a real heavy night. I mean a real night. They was conking out like flies, I'm telling you. Lotsa old folks. Every five, ten minutes the phone'd ring: 'Jerry, come on up, we got another one.' I'm telling you, I didn't get a minute's peace all night. Finally I got the bottom row of boxes filled and then the second row. Now, I didn't want to go sticking 'em up in that top row—I'd have to get two ladders and two other guys to help me lift 'em. Well, what would you do? Sure. I doubled 'em up. Well, along about four o'clock the old battle-ax phones down and asks me where such-and-such a stiff is and I tell her— it was a dame. Then she asks about a guy and I look up the book and I tell her. Well, I'd shoved 'em into the same box. What the hell—they was dead people! She blows up and you shoulda heard her."

Good Christ, was this guy never going to shut up and get out for a minute? Just one minute would be enough. On the shelf over Jerry's head. *1900.*

"She was raising hell. She says, 'Jerry'—you shoulda heard her; you wouldn't believe it—'Jerry, I think you might have the decency'—those was her very words—'I think you might have the decency not to put men and women together in the same refrigerator compartment!' Can you beat that? I says to her, I says, 'Miss Leary, do you mean to insinuate that I should go encouraging homo-sex-uality amongst these corpses?'" Jerry leaned back in his swivel chair, slapping his thigh, and his companion laughed until tears came, getting the tightness worked out of his nerves.

"Oh, you shoulda heard her rave then! Wait a minute—there's the phone." He listened, then said, "Right away, keed," and pushed back his chair. "Got a customer. Be right back. Gimme a shot before I go."

His hard heels rang off down the corridor. The elevator stopped, opened, closed, and hummed as it went up.

*1900.* May 28th. Age: 95, 80, 73, 19 . . . 19 . . . Doris Mae Cadle. Diagnosis: septicemia. Admitted—hell, where was she from? No origin. Name, age, diagnosis. The only young one on the 28th and on the page before and after it. The elevator was coming down and he shoved the ledger back in its place.

Jerry stood in the doorway, swaying slightly, his face glistening. "Wanna give me a hand? A fat one! Jesus!"

"No. She ain't lived here in my time. 'Course, I only took over the house eight years ago. Mis' Meriwether had the house before me. She's been in the Home for the Blind ever since. Cataracts, you know."

A soft, cultured voice said: "Mrs. Meriwether, I hate to bother you with what is, after all, only a hobby of mine. I am a genealogist, you see. I am looking up the branches of my mother's family—the Cadles. And in an old city directory I noted that someone by that name lived at the house which you ran as a rooming house about thirty-five years ago. Of course, I don't expect you to remember."

"Young man, I certainly do remember. A fine girl she was, Doris Cadle. Remember it like it was yesterday. Some kind of blood poisoning. Took her to the hospital. Too late. Died. Buried in Potter's Field. I didn't know where her folks was. I would have put up the money to get her a plot only I didn't have it. I tried to get up a purse but none of my roomers could make it up."

"She was one of the Cadles of New Jersey?"

"Might a been. Only, as I recall, she come from Tewkesbury, Pennsylvania."

"Tell me, Mrs. Meriwether, are you related to the Meriwethers of Massachusetts?"

"Well, now, young man, that's right interesting. I had a grandmother come from Massachusetts. On my father's side she was. Now, if you're interested in the Meriwethers—"

"Mrs. Cadle, I thought I had all the data I needed but there are a couple of other questions I'd like to ask for the government records." The dark suit, the brief case, the horn-rimmed glasses over a polka-dot bow tie, all spoke of the servant of government.

"Come in. I been tryin' to find Dorrie's pitcher. Ain't seen it sence I showed it to you a while ago."

"Doris Mae. That was your second child, I believe. But you put the picture back in the Bible, Mrs. Cadle."

His voice sounded dry and bored. He must get awful tired, pestering folks this way all day and every day.

"Let's look again. Here—here it is. You just didn't look far enough. Did I ask you the date of your daughter's graduation from high school?"

"Never graddiated. She took a business course and run off to New York City and we never seen her no more."

"Thank you. You said your husband worked in the mines from the age of thirteen. How many accidents did he have in that time? That is, accidents that caused him to lose one or more days from work?"

"Oh, Lord, I can sure tell you about them! I mind one time just after we was married . . ."

The collector of vital statistics walked slowly toward the town's single trolley line. In his brief case was a roll of film recording both sides of a postcard. One was a cheap photograph of a young girl, taken at Coney Island. She was sitting in a prop rowboat named *Sea Breeze*, and holding an oar. Behind her was a painted lighthouse. On the message side was written in precise, characterless handwriting:

Dear Mom and all,
    I am sending this from Coney Island. It's like the biggest fair you ever saw. A boy named Spunk took me. Isn't that a silly nickname? I had my picture taken as you can see. Tell Pop and all I wish I was with you and hug little Jennie for me. Will write soon.
Fondly,<br>DORRIE

Conversation flattened out to an eager rustle as the Rev. Carlisle entered the room and walked to the lectern in the glass alcove, where ferns and palms caught the summer sun in a tumult of green. The rest of the room was cool and dark, with drawn hangings before the street windows.

He opened the Bible with the gold-plated clasps, ran his hands once over his hair, then gazed straight out above the heads of the congregation which had assembled in the Church of the Heavenly Message.

"My text this morning is from Ephesians Five, verses eight and nine: *'For ye were sometimes darkness, but now are ye light in the Lord: walk as children of light: for the fruit of the Spirit is in all goodness and righteousness and truth . . .'*"

Mrs. Prescott was late, damn her. Or was it the mark who was holding up the works? He must be the kind of bastard that always comes late—thinks the world will hold the curtain waiting for him.

Blue eyes lifted from the page and smiled their blessing on the faces before them. About twenty in the house with a few odd husbands dragged along; and a couple of male believers.

"Dearly beloved, on this day of summer, with God's glorious

sunlight illuminating the world, we find an object lesson in its brilliance . . ."

Where was Tallentyre? She was supposed to ride herd on Prescott and the mark.

". . . for we, who once walked in darkness of fear and ignorance and doubt, find our path through the earth-plane made bright and shining by the surety of our faith."

At the other end of the shadowy room the front door opened and closed. In the dim light two stout women in flowered print dresses came in—Tallentyre and Prescott. Son-of-a-bitch! Did the chump back out at the last minute? With a flash of anxiety Stan wondered if somebody might have wised him up.

Then in the doorway a man appeared, big, in a light gray flannel suit, holding a panama in his hand. A black silhouette in the gentle glow cast by the fanlight. The spread of shoulder spoke of arrogant ownership. The man was an owner—land, buildings, acres, machines. And men. Two round, owl-like saucers of light winked from the dark head—the light of the conservatory reflected from rimless glasses as he turned his head, whispering to Prescott. Then he sat down in the back row, pulling out one of the bridge chairs to make room for his legs.

The Rev. Carlisle drew breath and fixed his eyes on the gold-embossed Bible before him.

"My dear friends, let me tell you a story. There was a man who had been in the Great War. One dark night he was sent scouting into No Man's Land with one of his buddies—a star shell rose from the enemy trenches and illuminated the field. Well might he have prayed at that moment with David, '*Hide me from my deadly enemies who compass me about.*' The man of whom I speak dashed for the security of a shell hole, pushing his companion aside, while the machine guns of the Germans began to fill the field with death."

Ezra Grindle was fanning himself idly with his panama.

"The soldier who was left without cover fell, mortally wounded. And before the baleful glare of the star shell died, the other soldier, crouching in the shell crater, saw his companion's eyes fixed on him in a mute look of scorn and accusation.

"My dear friends, years passed. The survivor became a pillar of society—married, a father, respected in his community. But always, deep in his soul, was the memory of that dying boy's face—the eyes—accusing him!"

The panama was motionless.

"This man recently became interested in Spiritual Truth. He began to attend the church of a medium who is a dear friend of mine in a city out west. He unburdened his heart to the medium. And when they finally established contact with the 'buddy' whose earth life was lost through his cowardice, what do you suppose were the first words the friend in spirit uttered to that guilt-ridden man? They were, 'You are forgiven.'

"Picture to yourselves, my friends, the unutterable joy which rose in that man's tortured heart when the crushing weight of guilt was lifted from him and for the first time in all those years he was a free man—drinking in the sun and the soft wind and the bird song of dawn and eventide."

Grindle was leaning forward, one hand on the back of the chair in front of him. Mrs. Prescott whispered something in his ear; but he was deaf to it. He seemed caught and held by the voice of the man behind the lectern, a man in white linen with a black clerical vest, whose hair, in the shaft of summer sun, was as golden as his voice.

"My dear friends, there is no need for *God* to forgive us. How can we sin against the wind which blows across the fields of ripening grain, how can we injure the soft scent of lilacs in the spring twilight, the deep blue of an autumn sky or the eternal glory of the stars on a winter's night? No, no, my friends. We can sin only against mankind. And man, in his next mansion of the soul, says to us tenderly, lovingly, 'You are forgiven, beloved. When you join us you will know. Until then, go with our love, rejoice in our forgiveness, take strength from us who live forever in the shadow of his hand.'"

The tears had mounted to the clergyman's eyes and now, in the light of the alcove, they glistened faintly on his cheeks as he stopped speaking, standing erect with the bearing of an emperor in his chariot.

"Let us pray."

At the back of the room a man who had spent his life ruining competitors, bribing congressmen, breaking strikes, arming vigilantes, cheating stockholders, and endowing homes for unwed mothers, covered his eyes with his hand.

"Reverend, they tell me you bring voices out of trumpets."

"I have *heard* voices from trumpets. I don't bring them. They come. Mediumship is either a natural gift or it is acquired by devotion, by study, and by patience."

The cigars had cost Stan twenty dollars; but he pushed the box across the desk easily and took one himself, holding his lighter for the tycoon. The Venetian blinds were drawn, the windows open, and the fan whirring comfortably.

Grindle inhaled the cigar twice, let the smoke trickle from his nostrils, approved it, and settled farther back in his chair.

As if suddenly remembering an appointment, the spiritualist said, "Excuse me," and jotted notes on a calendar pad. He let Grindle smoke on while he made a telephone call, then turned back to him, smiling, waiting.

"I don't care about trumpet phenomena in *your* house. I want to see it in *my* house."

The clergyman's face was stern. "Mr. Grindle, spirit phenomena are not a performance. They are a religious experience. We cannot say where and when they will appear. They are no respecters of houses. Those who have passed over may reveal themselves in the humble cottage of the laborer and ignore completely the homes of wealth, of culture, and of education."

The big man nodded. "I follow you there, Carlisle. In one of your sermons you said something about Spiritualism being the only faith that offers *proof* of survival. I remember you said that the command 'Show me' is the watchword of American business. Well, you hit the nail right on the head that time. I'm just asking to be shown, that's all. That's fair enough."

The minister's smile was unworldly and benign. "I am at your service if I can strengthen your resolve to find out more for yourself."

They smoked, Grindle eyeing the spiritualist, Carlisle seemingly deep in meditation.

At the left of Grindle's chair stood a teakwood coffee table, a relic of the Peabody furnishings. On it sat a small Chinese gong of brass. The silence grew heavy and the industrialist seemed to be trying to force the other man to break it first; but neither broke it. The little gong suddenly spoke—a clear, challenging note.

Grindle snatched it from the table, turning it upside down and examining it. Then he picked up the table and knocked the top with his knuckles. When he looked up again he found the Rev. Carlisle smiling at him.

"You may have the gong—and the table, Mr. Grindle. It never before has rung by an exudation of psychic power—what we call the odylic force—as it did just now. Someone must be trying to get through to you. But it is difficult—your innate skepticism is the barrier."

On the big man's face Stan could read the conflict—the fear of being deceived against the desire to see marvels and be forgiven by Doris Mae Cadle, 19, septicemia, May 28, 1900: *But I tell you, Dorrie, if we get married now it will smash everything, everything.*

Grindle leaned forward, poking the air with the two fingers which gripped his cigar. "Reverend, out in my Jersey plant I've got an apothecary's scale delicate enough to weigh a human hair —just one human hair! It's in a glass case. You make that scale move and I'll give your church ten thousand dollars!"

The Rev. Carlisle shook his head. "I'm not interested in money, Mr. Grindle. You may be rich. Perhaps I am too—in a different way." He stood up but Grindle stayed where he was. "If you wish to arrange a séance in your own home or anywhere else, I can try to help you. But I should warn you—the place does not matter. *What matters is the spiritual environment.*" He had been speaking slowly, as if weighing something in his mind, but the last sentence was snapped out as if he had come to a decision.

"But God damn it—pardon me, Reverend—but I know all this! You'll get full co-operation from me. I've got an open mind, Carlisle. An open mind. And the men I'll pick for our committee will have open minds too—or they'll hear from me later. When can you come?"

"In three weeks I shall have a free evening."

"No good. In three weeks I'll have to be up in Quebec. And I've got this bee in my bonnet. I want to find out once and for all, Carlisle. Show me one tiny speck of incontrovertible evidence and I'll listen to anything else you have to say. Can't you consider this an emergency and come out to the plant tonight?" Stan had moved toward the door and Grindle followed him. "Mr. Grindle, I believe you are a sincere seeker."

They descended the carpeted stairs and stood for a moment at the front door. "Then you'll come, Reverend? Tonight?"

Carlisle bowed.

"That's splendid. I'll send the car for you at six. Will that be all right? Or how about coming out earlier and having dinner at the plant? We all eat in the same cafeteria, right with the men. Democratic. But the food's good."

"I shall not want anything very heavy, thank you. I'll have a bite before six."

"Right. The car will pick you up here at the church." Grindle smiled for the first time. It was a chilly smile, tight around the eyes, but was probably his best attempt. Stan looked at the big man closely.

Hair thin and sandy. Forehead domed and spattered with freckles. A large rectangle of a face with unobtrusive, petulant features set in the center of it. Habitual lines about the mouth as if etched there by gas pains, or by constantly smelling a faintly foul odor. Voice peevish and high-pitched, bluster on the surface, fear underneath. Afraid somebody will get a dime away from him or a dime's worth of power. Waistline kept in by golf and a rowing machine. Maybe with shoulder braces to lean against when troubles try to make him stoop like one of his bookkeepers. Hands large, fingers covered with reddish fur. A big, irritable, unsatisfied, guilt-driven, purse-proud, publicity-inflamed dummy —stuffed with thousand dollar bills.

The hand which the Rev. Carlisle raised as a parting gesture was like a benediction—in the best possible taste.

When Stan got back to the apartment it was two o'clock in the afternoon. Molly was still asleep. He jerked the sheet off her and began tickling her in the ribs. She woke up cross and laughing. "Stan, stop it! Oh—oh, honey, it must be good news! What is it?"

"It's the live One, kid. He's nibbling at last. Séance tonight out at his joint in Jersey. If it goes over we're set! If not, we're in the soup. Now go out and get me a kitten."

"A what? Stan, you feeling okay?"

"Sure, sure, sure. Fall into some clothes and go out and find me a delicatessen store that has a kitten. Bring it back with you. Never mind if you have to swipe it."

When she had gone he eased the eraser from the end of a pencil, wedged the pencil in the jamb of a door and bored into the shaft with a hand drill. Then he pushed the eraser back and put the pencil in his pocket.

The kitten was a little tiger tom about three months old.

"Damn, it couldn't be a white one!"

"But, honey, I didn't know what you wanted with it."

"Never mind, kid. You did okay." He shut himself and the kitten up in the bathroom for half an hour. Then he came out and said to Molly, "Here. Now you can take him back."

"Take him back? But I promised the man I'd give him a good home. Aw, Stan, I thought we could keep him." She was winking back tears.

"Okay, okay, kid. Keep him. Do anything you want with him. If this deal goes over I'll buy you a pedigreed panther."

He hurried back to the church, and Molly set a saucer of milk on the floor and watched the kitten lap it up. She decided to call him Buster.


"Here's where the Grindle property starts, sir," said the chauffeur. They had rolled through Manhattan, under the river with the tunnel walls gleaming, past the smoke of North Jersey and across a desolation of salt marshes. Ahead of them, over a flat waste of cinders and struggling marsh grass, the smokestack and long, glass-roofed buildings of the Grindle Electric Motor Corporation rose glittering in the last sunlight.

The car slowed down at a gate in a barbed fence around the top of which ran wire held by insulators.

The private cop on duty at the gate nodded to the chauffeur

and said, "Go right in, Mr. Carlisle. Report at Gatehouse Number Five."

They drove down a gravel road and came to another wire fence and Gatehouse Number Five. "Have to go in and register, sir," said the chauffeur.

Inside the concrete shack a man in a gray military shirt, a Sam Browne belt and a dark blue cap, was sitting at a desk. He was reading a tabloid; when he looked up Stan read his life history from the face: Thrown off some small city police force for excessive brutality; or caught in a shakedown and sent up—the face bore the marks of the squad room and the prison, one on top of the other.

"Carlisle? Waiting for you. Sign this card." It projected from a machine like a cash register. Stan signed. Then the cop said, "Pull the card out." Stan grasped its waxed surface and pulled. "Watch out—don't tear it. Better use both hands."

The Rev. Carlisle used both hands. But what was it all about? He handed the card to Thickneck, then realized that he had left them a record of his fingerprints on its waxed surface.

"Now step inside here and I'll go through the regulations."

It was a small dressing room.

"Take off your coat and hand it to me."

"May I ask what this is for?"

"Orders of Mr. Anderson, Head of Plant Security."

"Does Mr. Grindle know about this?"

"Search me, Reverend; you can ask him. Now give me your coat. Anderson is tightening up on regulations lately."

"But what are you searching for?"

Stumpy fingers felt in pockets and along seams. "Sabotage, Reverend. Nothing personal. The next guy might be a senator, but we'd have to frisk him." The examination included the Rev. Carlisle's shoes, his hatband and the contents of his wallet. As the cop was returning the vest a pencil fell out; he picked it up and handed it to the clergyman who stuck it in his pocket. On his way out Stan gave the cop a cigar. It was immediately locked up in the green metal desk, and the Great Stanton wondered if it was later tagged, "Bribe offered by the Rev. Stanton Carlisle. Exhibit A."

At the door of the plant a thin, quick-moving man of thirty-odd with black patent-leather hair stepped out and introduced himself. "My name's Anderson, Mr. Carlisle. Head of Plant Security." The left lapel of his blue serge suit bulged ever so slightly. "The committee is waiting for you."

Elevators. Corridors. Plaster walls pale green. A white spot painted on the floor in all the corners. "They'll never spit in a corner painted white." The hum of machines and the clank of yard engines outside. Then one glass-paneled door opening on a passage walled with oak. Carpets on the floor. The reception room belonged in an advertising agency; it was a sudden burst of smooth, tawny leather and chrome.

"This way, Mr. Carlisle."

Anderson went ahead, holding open doors. The directors' room was a long one with a glass roof but no windows. The table down its center must have been built there; certainly it could never be taken out now.

Grindle was shaking his hand and presenting him to the others: Dr. Downes, plant physician; Mr. Elrood of the legal staff; Dr. Gilchrist, the industrial psychologist, also on the plant staff; Professor Dennison, who taught philosophy at Grindle College; Mr. Prescott ("You know Mrs. Prescott, I believe, through the church.") and Mr. Roy, both directors of the company. With Anderson and Grindle they made eight—Daniel Douglas Home's traditional number for a séance. Grindle knew more than he let on. But didn't his kind always?

At the far end of the table—it seemed a city block away—stood a rectangular glass case a foot high; inside it was an apothecary's precision balance, a cross arm with two circular pans suspended from it by chains.

Grindle was saying, "Would you care to freshen up a little? I have an apartment right off this room where I stay when I'm working late."

It was furnished much like Lilith's waiting room. Stan shut the bathroom door and washed sweat from his palms. "If I get away with it this time," he whispered to the mirror, "it's the Great Stanton and no mistake. Talk about your Princeton audiences . . ."

One last look around the drawing room revealed a flowing cloud of blue fur, out of which shone eyes of bright yellow as the cat streamed down from a chair and floated along the floor toward him. Stan's forehead smoothed out. "Come to papa, baby. Now it's in the bag."

When he joined the committtee he was carrying the cat in his arms and Grindle smiled his tight, unpracticed smile. "I see you've made friends with Beauty. But won't she disturb you?"

"On the contrary. I'd like to have her stay. And now, perhaps you gentlemen will tell me what this interesting apparatus is and how it works." He dropped the cat gently to the carpet, where she tapped his leg once with her paw, demanding to be taken up again, then crawled under the table to sulk.

The head of Plant Security stood with his hand resting on top of the glass. "This is a precision balance, Mr. Carlisle. An apothecary's scale. The indicator in the center of the bar registers the slightest pressure on either of the two pans. I had one of our boys rig up a set of electrical contacts under the pans so that if either one is depressed—by so much as the weight of a hair— this electric bulb in the corner of the case flashes on. The thing is self-contained; flashlight batteries in the case supply current. The balance has been set level and in this room there are no vibrations to disturb it. I watched it for an hour this afternoon and the light never flashed. To turn on that light some force must depress one of the pans of the balance. Is that clear?"

The Rev. Carlisle smiled spiritually. "May I inspect it?"

Anderson glanced at Grindle, who nodded. The private police chief opened the doors of the case and hovered close. "Don't touch anything, Reverend."

"I'm afraid I don't understand much about electricity. But you're sure that this lighting device hasn't interfered with the free movement of the scale? What are these copper strips?" He pointed to them with the end of a pencil from which the eraser was missing, indicating two narrow metal strips leading from under the pans of the balance to insulated connections behind it.

"They're contact points. Two on each side. If either pan moves it touches these points, closes the circuit and the light goes on." Anderson swiftly shut the glass doors and latched them.

The Rev. Carlisle was not listening. His face had grown blank. Moving as if in a dream, he returned to the far end of the room and slipped down into the chair at the end of the table, thirty feet from the mechanism in its glass house.

Without speaking, Grindle motioned the others to their places —Anderson on Stan's left, Grindle taking a chair on his right, the rest on either side. The precision balance had half the long table to itself.

The Rev. Carlisle closed his eyes, folded his arms, and placed his head upon them as if trying to catch a nap. His breathing deepened, jerky and rasping. Once he stirred and muttered something incoherent.

"He's gone into a trance?"

The boss must have shut the speaker up with a look.

Silence grew. Then Grindle scratched a match to light a cigar and several others took courage and smoked. The room was in semi-darkness and the tension of the waiting men piled up.

The medium had been searched at the gate. Their eyes had been on him very second since he arrived. He had never touched the instrument—Anderson had been watching him for the slightest move. They had all been warned to look out for threads, or for attempts to tilt the massive table. Mr. Roy had quietly slipped from his chair and was sitting on the floor, watching the medium's feet beneath the table even though they were thirty feet from the balance. The scale was enclosed in glass; Anderson had latched the doors. And this medium claimed to be able to move solids without touching them! They waited.

On his right Stan could feel the great man, his attention frozen on the rectangular glass frame. They waited. Time was with the spiritualist. This was a better break than he had ever dreamed of. First the cat showing up, then this magnificent nerve-racking stall for the committee. Would it work after all?

He heard Grindle whisper, "Beauty—Beauty, come here!"

Stan raised his head, moaning a little, and from under one eyelid saw that the cat had wriggled from Grindle's lap and now stood gazing into the balance case.

A gasp ran around the waiting circle. The light had snapped

on, burning clear and ruby-red, a tiny bulb, Christmas-tree size, in an upright socket in one corner.

Stan moaned again, his hands closing into fists. The light went out; his fists relaxed.

Grindle cut short the buzzing whispers by a snap of his fingers.

Another wait. Stan's breath came heavier. He felt the saliva in his mouth thickening; his tongue was dry, the saliva like cotton; he forced it out over his lower lip. This was one time when he didn't have to fake the foam.

The light flared again and the medium's breathing became a whistling, agonizing battle.

Off again. Stan let out a sigh.

Silence. Time ticking by on someone's wrist watch. At the foot of the table the Persian looked back, frowning, at Grindle, saying in cat talk, "Let me get into that glass box."

The light again. This time it stayed on. Anderson slid from his seat while Stan's heart pounded but Grindle motioned him back and he compromised by standing in his place. From under folded arms Stan could see Anderson's lean hand, the nails softly polished, braced against the mahogany as he bent forward. The light went out.

This time the medium trembled and threw himself back in his chair, his head lolling. Thickly he said, "Open the case. Let the air into it! Take the cover off and examine the apparatus. Hurry!"

Anderson was already there. The Rev. Carlisle crumpled down in his chair, eyes closed, the foam thick on his lower lip and chin.

Through slit lids he could see Anderson and the psychologist taking the balance from its box. Beauty had stood close by and now was tapping with her paw at the metal contacts on the floor of the case. Grindle picked her up, squirming, and shut her up in the apartment.

Then Stan felt something touch his lips; he let his eyelids flick open. The doctor was standing over him, holding a bit of sterile gauze which he dropped into a flat glass culture dish, putting it back in his pocket. Go ahead, you goddamned wisenheimer townie, analyze it for soap! I could give you a good specimen right in the eye.

Now Grindle had Stan by the arm and was leading him toward the apartment. Over his shoulder he said, "Good evening, gentlemen. You may go."

With Grindle alone Stan began to recover. The industrialist offered him brandy and he drank it slowly. Beauty stared at him from hot, yellow eyes.

"I'll have the car take you back to New York, Mr. Carlisle, as soon as you feel up to traveling."

"Oh, thank you so much. I—I feel a little shaky. Did any phenomena occur?"

"The light in the cabinet went on three times." Behind the rimless glasses Grindle's gray, small eyes almost flashed. "That's proof enough for me, Mr. Carlisle. I shan't drag you all the way out here again. I told you I'm a hard-headed man. I needed proof. Well—" His voice broke with a tiny shading of emotion which habitual restraint could not hide. "I've seen something tonight that cannot possibly be explained by fraud or trickery. The conditions were absolutely air-tight. Some force inside the case depressed the pans of that balance and if anybody ever talks to me about magnets I'll laugh right in his face. The instrument is made of brass. This plant is miles from city vibrations—it's rooted in concrete. There were no threads. You never came near the thing; never touched it. . . ."

Grindle was pacing the carpet, smoking furiously, his face flushed.

The Rev. Carlisle finished his brandy and stretched out an affectionate hand to the Persian cat. Safe! This was the money-bags mountain and he stood, not on the top of it, but in sight of the top. He rose at last, rubbing his eyes wearily. The great man had been talking.

". . . ten thousand dollars. I told you I'd do it and I mean what I say. The check will reach you."

"Please, Mr. Grindle, let's not talk about money. If I have given you proof—"

"Well, you have. You have, man! Let me—"

"The church can always use donations, Mr. Grindle. You can

take care of that through Mrs. Prescott. I know she will be pleased. A fine, devoted woman. But for me it is enough to know that some little corner of the glorious truth has been revealed."

Beauty, lolling in the most comfortable chair in the room, suddenly started up and began to scratch her chin with her hind foot. Stan eased Grindle away toward the door. As it closed behind them he saw Beauty biting industriously at the fur over her ribs.

On the steps of the plant its owner paused. From his pocket he took out two envelopes, held them to the light and handed one to Stan. "Here—might as well give you this now, Carlisle. I was going to send it to Mrs. Prescott as you suggested, but you can save me the trouble. This other we won't need." He tore the envelope and its contents to bits.

"I don't understand, Mr. Grindle."

The smile broke out again with a glitter of white teeth. "It was a warrant for your arrest—in case you tried any fraudulent methods of producing phenomena. It wasn't my idea, Mr. Carlisle. I have to take advice once in a while, you know, from some of the boys who look after my interests."

Stan was erect and the blue eyes were hard. "That warrant was signed by a judge?"

"I presume so."

"And on what grounds was I supposed to be arrested—if you or one of your employees thought he detected trickery?"

"Why, with conspiracy with intent to defraud."

"And how would I have defrauded you, Mr. Grindle? Out of taxi fare from New York?"

The big man frowned. "You understand, I had nothing to do with it. Mr. Anderson—"

"You may tell Mr. Anderson," said the Rev. Carlisle tautly, "that I would be quite capable of suing for false arrest. I have never taken a penny for exercising gifts of mediumship. I never shall. Good night, sir."

He got into the waiting car and said coldly to the driver, "Just to the railroad station—don't drive me all the way in to New York."

Grindle stood gaping after him, then turned and went back to the plant.

Anderson was a good lad, devoted, devoted. Couldn't ask for more loyalty. But God damn it, he didn't understand. He just didn't understand the deeper, the spiritual things of life. Well, from now on Andy would be told to keep his nose out of psychic research.

The others had left the directors' room but Anderson was still there. He was attacking the end of the conference table with mighty heaves, trying to make the light flash.

"Give it up, Andy," the Chief said acidly. "On home. Go on."

"I'll find out how he did it! He did something."

"Andy, you can't find it in your soul anywhere to admit that it might have been an odylic force that you can't see or feel or measure?"

"Nuts, Chief. I know a hustler when I see one."

"I said go home, Andy."

"You're the boss."

As he was leaving Grindle called to him: "And fire the woman you had taking care of Beauty's coat. It's a disgrace—she's been neglected."

Anderson's voice was smoldering but weary. "What is it now, Chief?"

"It's disgusting—Beauty's coat is swarming with fleas."

"Okay, Chief. She gets the gate tomorrow." He walked quickly from the plant, found his car in the parking lot and rammed in the ignition key irritably. That goddamned phoney reverend. He would be just the one to weasel inside the Chief. And the Chief would protect him. But how in the jumping blue blazes of merry hell did he ever turn that light on and off inside the case? Odylic force, balls!

"Is that your odylic force, Reverend?"

"Yeah. That's it, babe. Like it?"

She chuckled, warm and enfolding, beneath him in the dark of the bedroom.

"Wait, lover. Let's rest."

They rested. Stan said, "He's going overboard, all right. He's not so tough—just another chump."

"Go easy with him, Stan."

"I'm easy. Every test a little stronger until he's fattened up for the full-form stuff. There's only one thing—"

"Molly?"

"Yeah, Molly. That dame's going to give us a lot of trouble."

"She can be handled."

"Yeah. But it wears you out, handling. Lilith, I'm sick of the dame. She's like a rock around my neck."

"Patience, darling. There's no one else."

They lay silent for a time, seeing each other with their finger tips and with their mouths.

"Lilith—"

"What, lover?"

"What does that guy really want? I've beaten him over the head with 'forgiveness' but I get only half a response. He doesn't gobble it. There's something else. Okay. We bring back the dead dame. She tells him he's forgiven and everything's jake. But where do we go from there?"

Dr. Lilith Ritter, at the moment in a very unethical but satisfying position in relation to one of her patients, laughed deep in her throat.

"What does he want to *do?* With his first love? Don't be so naïve, lover. He wants to do this . . . and this . . ."

"But—no; that's no good. Not with Molly. She'll never—"

"Oh, yes, she will."

"Lilith, I know that dame. She never stepped out of line once in all the years we been teamed up. I can't sell her on jazzing the chump."

"Yes, you can, darling."

"Christ's sake, *how?*"

The warm mouth closed his and he forgot Molly and the con game which kept him in a torment of scheming. Through their pressed lips Lilith murmured, "I'll tell you when the time comes."

The psychic lamp, provided by the Rev. Carlisle, shed no light except through a single dark-red disc in the center of its tin slide. The medium, dressed in a black silk robe, black silk pajamas and slippers, lay back in an armchair on one side of the billiard-room doorway. Grindle, in his shirtsleeves, sat opposite him, the lamp on a coffee table at his side. Dark curtains covered the door and a faint breeze tugged at them. Carlisle had raised one window in the inner room a few inches for ventilation. It was not open far enough for a man to stick his head through and it had been sealed. Grindle had pressed his signet ring into the hot wax. The other windows were sealed shut. There was a fifteen foot drop to the lawn outside, which sloped down to the river.

Beyond the darkened billiard room the two men waited. The medium's head was thrown back. His left wrist was fastened to Grindle's right by a long strand of copper wire, and he had poured salt water on their wrists.

The heel of the reverend's slipper was pressed tight against the leg of his chair.

Rap!

It seemed to come from the table bearing the red lantern.

Rap!

"Is there one in spirit life speaking?" The medium's words were a hoarse whisper.

Rap! Rap! Rap!

"We greet you. Are conditions favorable? May we turn up the lamp a little?"

Three more raps answered him. Grindle leaned over and raised the lamp's wick until a warning rap commanded him to stop. His big face was intent and ill at ease, but Stan detected no craft or outright skepticism. He was interested, moving in the right direction.

They waited. More silence. Then from beyond the dark draperies of the doorway came another knock—a hollow, musical sound, as if something had struck the window. Grindle started from his chair but the warning, upraised hand of the spiritualist stopped him. Carlisle's breathing came fast now, and heavy, and he seemed to lose consciousness.

The "sitter" began to sweat. Did he imagine a tingling discharge of current at his wrist where the wire was bound?

Another sound, a distinct click, from the billiard room. Then a whole chorus of clicks which he made out to be billiard balls, knocking against one another, sometimes in rhythm, as if they were dancing.

Sweat began to roll from the industrialist's forehead. It was a hot night, but not that hot. His shirt was sticking to his chest and his hands were dripping.

The ghostly billiard game went on; then a white ivory ball rolled out from under the curtains and hit the table-leg between him and the medium.

Carlisle stirred uneasily and a voice came from his stiff lips: "*Hari Aum!* Greetings, newcomer to the Life of Spiritual Truth. Greetings, our new *chela*. Believe not blindly. Believe the proof of the mind given you by the senses. They cannot give you the Truth but they point the Path. Trust my disciple, Stanton Carlisle. He is an instrument on which spiritual forces play as a lover plays his *sitar* beneath the window of his beloved. Greetings, Ezra. A friend has come to you from Spirit Life. *Hari Aum!*"

The resonant, accented chanting broke off. Grindle snapped his attention from the lips of the medium to the curtains before the darkened room. The clicks of billiard balls now sounded closer, as if they were rolling and knocking on the floor just beyond the curtains. He stared, his lips drawn back from his dentures, his breath whistling. A white ball rolled slowly from under the curtains and stopped six inches inside the room where they sat. The red cue ball followed it. Click!

While he watched, the hairs on the back of the big man's neck raised, the skin drew tight over his temples. For in the dim, ruby light a tiny hand felt its way out from under the curtains, groped delicately for the red ball, found it, and rolled it after the white one. Click! And the hand was gone.

With an unconscious shout Grindle leaped up and threw himself after the vanishing hand, only to spin around and claw at the curtains of the doorway to keep himself from falling. For his right wrist was firmly secured by copper wire to the wrist of the medium who was now groaning and gasping, his eyes half open and rolled up, until the whites looked as stark as the eyes of a blind beggar.

Then Grindle felt the room beyond them to be empty and still. He stood, fighting for breath, making no further attempt to enter.

The medium drew a long breath and opened his eyes. "We can remove the wire now. Were there any phenomena of note?"

Grindle nodded, still watching the doorway. "Get me out of this harness, Reverend! I want a look in there."

Stan helped unwind the wire and said, "One favor, Mr. Grindle —I wonder if you could get me a glass of brandy?"

His host poured him one and knocked off two straight ones himself. "All set?"

He drew the curtains and snapped the wall switch.

A reassuring glow fell from the hanging lamp above the billiard table. Stan's hand on his arm restrained him from entering.

"Careful, Mr. Grindle. Remember our test precautions."

The floor had been thickly sprinkled with talcum powder. Now it bore traces, and as Grindle knelt to examine them he saw with a chill that they were the unmistakable bare footprints of a small child.

He rose, wiping his face with a wad of handkerchief. The room had been the scene of grotesque activity. Cues had been taken from their racks and thrust into the open mouths of stuffed sailfish on the wall. The cue chalk had been thrown down and smashed. And everywhere were the tiny footprints.

Carlisle stood in the doorway for a moment, then turned back and sank into his chair and covered his eyes with his hand as if he were very tired.

At last the light in the billiard room snapped off and Grindle stood beside him, pale, breathing heavily. He poured himself another brandy and gave one to the medium.

Ezra Grindle was shaken as no stock-market crash or sudden South American peace treaty could have shaken him. For with a crumb of cue chalk a message had been written on the green felt of the billiard table. It held the answer to a vast, secret, shameful ache inside him—a canker which had festered all these years. Not a soul in the world could know of its existence but himself—a name he had not spoken in thirty-five years. It held the key to an old wrong which he would willingly give a million hard-earned dollars to square with his conscience. A million? Every cent he owned!

The message was in a characterless, copybook hand:

Spunk darling,
    We tried to come to you but the force was not strong enough. Maybe next time. I so wanted you to see our boy.
                                                              DORRIE

He drew the doors together and locked them. He raised his hand for the bell rope, then dropped it, and poured himself another brandy.

At his side stood the tall, silken figure in black, his face compassionate.

"Let us pray together—not for them, Ezra, but for the living, that the scales may fall from their eyes. . . ."

The train to New York was not due for half an hour and Mrs. Oakes, who had been visiting her daughter-in-law, had read the time table all wrong; now she would have to wait.

On the station platform she walked up and down to relieve her impatience. Then, on a bench, she saw a little figure stretched out, its head pillowed on its arms. Her heart was touched. She shook him gently by the shoulder. "What's the matter, little man? Are you lost? Were you supposed to meet mamma or papa here at the station?"

The sleeper sat up with a snarl. He was the size of a child; but was dressed in a striped suit and a pink shirt with a miniature necktie. And under his button nose was a mustache!

The mustachioed baby pulled a cigarette from his pocket and raked a kitchen match on the seat of his trousers. He lit the cigarette and was about to snap away the match when he grinned up at her from his evil, old baby face, thrust one hand into his coat and drew out a postcard, holding the match so she could see it.

Mrs. Oakes thought she would have a stroke. She tried to run away, but she couldn't. Then the train came and the horrible little creature swung aboard, winking at her.

CARD XIV

# The Tower

*rises from earth to heaven but
avenging lightning finds its
walls.*

BEYOND the garden wall a row of poplars rustled in the night
wind. The moon had not risen; in the gentle darkness the voice
was a monotonous, musical ripple, as soothing as the splash of a
fountain.

"Your mind is quiet . . . a lamp in a sheltered corner where
the flame does not flicker. Your body is relaxed. Your heart is
at peace. Your mind is perfectly clear but at ease. Nothing
troubles you. Your mind is a still, calm pool without a ripple . . ."

The big man had a white scarf knotted around his neck and
tucked into his tweed jacket. He let his hands lie easily on the
arms of the deck chair; his legs in tawny flannel trousers were
propped on the footrest.

Beside him the spiritualist in black was all but invisible under
the starlight.

"Close your eyes. When you open them again, stare straight
at the garden wall and tell me what you see."

"It's faint—" Grindle's voice was flaccid and dreamy. All the
bite had gone out of it.

"Yes?"

"It's growing clearer. It's a city. A golden city. Towers. Domes. A beautiful city—and now it's gone."

The Rev. Carlisle slipped back into his pocket a "Patent Ghost Thrower, complete with batteries and lenses, to hold 16 millimeter film, $7.98" from a spiritualists' supply house in Chicago.

"You have seen it—the City of Spiritual Light. My control spirit, Ramakrishna, has directed us to build it. It will be patterned after a similar city—which few outsiders have ever seen —in the mountains of Nepal. I myself was permitted to see it under Ramakrishna's guidance. I was teleported physically to the spot. I was leaving the church one snowy night last winter when I felt Ramakrishna near me."

The tycoon's head was nodding belief.

"I was walking through the snow when suddenly the street vanished; it became a stony mountain path. I felt light as air but my feet seemed heavy. That was the altitude. Then, stretching below me in a little valley, I saw the City—just as you have described your vision of it a few moments ago. And I knew that it had been revealed to me for a purpose. Once this realization dawned on me the mountains, the rugged outline of bare peaks and glaciers, softened. They seemed to close in and I was back on the doorstep of the Church of the Heavenly Message. But there, stretching away up the sidewalk, were my own tracks of a few minutes before! A few yards farther on they *stopped. I had dematerialized when I reached that spot.*"

Grindle said, "A wonderful experience. I've heard of such experiences. The holy men of Tibet claim to have them. But I never thought I'd ever meet a man who had reached such psychic heights." His voice was humble and old and a little foolish. Then he started up from his chair.

A vague light had drifted past on the garden wall. It had the shape of a young girl.

The medium said, "You must relax. No tension. All receptivity —all love."

Grindle settled back.

The sky clouded over; the darkness deepened. This time he did not stir but said hopefully, "I—I think I see something, out there by the sundial. Something moving—a spot of light."

It was true. By the shadows at the base of the sundial was a spot of greenish light. Expanding slowly, it moved toward them, a cloud of glowing vapor taking form.

This time the industrialist sat up in spite of Stan's reproving hand on his wrist.

The apparition drifted closer until they could see that it was a girl, dressed in shining garments which floated about her like a mist. Her dark hair was bound by a tiara in which seven bright jewels shone by their own cold light. She seemed to move a few inches above the ground, drifting toward them down a breath of night wind.

The believer's voice had become a feeble, despairing whisper. "Dorrie— Could it be Dorrie?"

"My dear . . ." The materialized form spoke in a voice which seemed part of the garden and the night. "It's Dorrie. But only for a moment. I can't stay . . . it's hard . . . hard to come back, darling."

The Rev. Carlisle's hand tightened on the older man's arm; but the clergyman himself seemed to have passed into a deep trance.

The ghostly figure was fading. It receded, lost outline, sank into a single dot of green glow and then vanished.

"Dorrie—Dorrie—come back. Please come back. Please—" He was on his knees now by the sundial, where the light had disappeared. His broad stern in the tawny slacks was toward Stan, who could have planted a kick right in the middle of it.

Grindle knelt for several seconds, then got to his feet heavily and dropped back into the deck chair, covering his face with his hands.

Beside him the Rev. Carlisle stirred and sat up. "Was there a full materialization? I 'went under' very rapidly. I could feel the force leaving me as the light grew. What happened?"

"I—I saw an old friend."

Molly was so happy she could cry. It had been a long time since they'd had anything like a holiday together. Stan had been acting so screwy she was afraid he was living on Queer Street. And then, all of a sudden, these three days—just driving anywhere, stopping at chicken-dinner shacks and roadhouses. Dancing and, in the daytime, going for a swim wherever a lake looked good. It was heaven; she got sad thinking about going back to the flat and starting all over again, doing nothing, just waiting for Stan to come home or something.

Stan was still awfully jumpy and sometimes you'd talk to him and he'd seem to be listening and then he'd say, "What was that, kid?" and you'd have to go through it all over again. But it was great to be getting around like this.

Stan looked nice in a bathing suit. That was something to be thankful for. Some guys were sweet guys but too skinny or with a pot. Stan was just right. She guessed they were both just right by the way other fellows ran their eyes over her chassis when she stepped out on a diving board. What hippos some girls her own age turned out to be!

The Great Stanton pulled himself out of the water and lay beside her on the float. They had the lake all to themselves except for some kids at the other end. He sat looking down at her and then leaned over and kissed her. Molly threw her arms around him. "Oh, honey, don't ever let anything bust us up, honey! All I want is you, Stan."

He slid his arm under her head. "Baby, how'd you like to do this every day in the year? Huh? Well, if this deal goes over we're set. And every day is Christmas."

Molly had a cold, sinking feeling inside her. He had said that so many times. Once it was "Get the house away from old Mrs. Peabody." Always something. She didn't really believe it any more.

He felt her go limp. "Molly! Molly! look at me! Honest to God, this is the thing I've been building toward ever since I started in this racket. I've run myself almost into the nut college building the guy. My foot's never slipped yet. And if you think that guy is easy to handle—"

She pressed her face against his chest and began to cry. "Stan, why do we have to be this way? He seemed like a nice sort of old guy—from what I could tell in the dark up there. I felt like an awful heel, honest. I don't mind taking some guy that thinks he's wise and is trying to be a cheater himself—"

He held her tighter. "Molly, we're in this deeper than you have any idea. That guy has millions. He has a whole private army. You ought to see that joint in Jersey. It's like a fort. If we step on the flypaper from now on they'll turn that bunch of private cops loose on us like a pack of bloodhounds. They'll find us no matter where we scram to. We've got to go into it all the way. I've put him in touch with his girl that died when he was a kid in college. He wants to make it up to her somehow. Money doesn't mean anything to that guy. He's willing to give anything—just to get square with his conscience. He's overboard on the spook dodge. He's letting his business run itself. He's living on Dream Street."

Stan had straightened the girl until she sat on the edge of the float, her feet in the cool water. He took both her hands. "Baby, from now on it depends on you. Whether every day is Christmas and I can get my nerves back in shape and act like a human being—or whether the wolves start howling for our blood."

Molly's eyes were big now and Stan bored in.

"Now, look. This is what we've got to do."

When she had heard it she sat for a moment with her hair falling over her face, looking down at her bare thighs and the bright yellow of the bathing suit. She ran her hands slowly from her crotch down to her knees. They felt cold and the water was cold around her feet; she raised them and drew them up, leaning her head on her knees, not looking at the man beside her.

"That's how it is, kid. I'll make it up to you. Honest to God, baby. Don't you see—this is the only thing that can put us back together again?"

Suddenly she stood up, throwing her hair back. Her fingers trembled as she drew on her cap. Then, without looking at him, she dived from the float and set out for the dock. Stan was churning the water with his legs, trying to overtake her. She reached the dock and raced up the ladder with him close behind. When they got to the cabin he bolted the door.

Molly whipped off her cap and shook out her hair. Then she slipped the bathing suit down and left it on the floor in a sodden pile, stepping out of it. Stan watched her, his heart thumping with anxiety. Now.

She said, "Stan, take a good look. Make believe you never saw me undressed before. I mean it. Now then, tell me, if I—if I—do it—will I look any different? To you?"

He kissed her so hard that her lip began to bleed.

Lilith opened the door for him and they went into her office. She sat behind the desk, where the contents of a tray of star sapphires lay spread out on a square of black velvet. She tumbled them back into the tray and swung out the false drawer fronts on the right-hand side of the desk, revealing the steel door of a safe. She put the gems away and spun the dial twice, then closed the panel and took a cigarette from the box on her desk.

Stan held his lighter. "She's hooked."

"The virtuous Molly?"

"Sure. It took some selling but she'll play ball. Now let's lay out the moves from here on in. I planted the City of Spiritual Light with him just before the first full-form job in the garden up at his place. Next séance, we'll start warming him up to the idea of kicking in some dough."

Stan had brought with him a portfolio. He drew the tapes and opened it, laying an architect's drawing before the woman who claimed to be a psychiatrist.

A bird's-eye view of a dream city, clustered about a central tower which rose from the desert amid a circling park of palms.

"Very pretty, Reverend."

"There's more." He lifted out the drawing. Beneath it was a Geodetic Survey map of an Arizona county. Drawn in red ink and carefully lettered was the location of the City.

Lilith nodded. "And this is the spot where you are going to take off into thin air? That's very well thought out, darling." She frowned, looking at the map. "Where are you going to hide the second car?"

"I'm going to leave it somewhere in this jerk town, marked over here."

"No good, darling. It must be hidden out of town—somewhere in the desert. Let's go through it again. You go out by train;

you buy a car in Texas and drive into this town of Peñas, where you put it in a garage. Then you hire a car in Peñas. You drive your new car outside the town and park it. You walk back, pick up the hired car, go to your own car, tow it to the spot near the site of the City and hide it well and drive back to Peñas in the hired car. You come back here by train. Correct?"

"Right. Then when we get ready to blow I drive out there, telling him to follow me in a day or two. I drive my car out to the site of the City and just off the highway. I get out, walk a hundred yards straight into the sand, then backtrack to the car, and from there follow the rock to the highway; hike on up the highway and pull out the new car. And drive like hell back east. And I've disappeared in the middle of the desert. He'll come along, following this map, and find the car. He'll follow the footprints—and blam! Gone! And me carrying all that dough. Ain't it a shame?"

She laughed softly at him over her cigarette. "It's complicated, Stan. But you'll probably be able to get away with it. I believe you could make a living selling spiritualism to other mediums."

"Say!" He leaned forward, his eyes narrow, thinking quickly; then he relaxed and shook his head. "No go. It's peanuts—they never have any real dough. Industry is the only place where dough is any more."

She looked back at the idealized drawing of the City of Spiritual Light. "There's one thing, Stan, that I wish you'd tell me."

"Sure, baby."

"How *did* you move that precision balance out at his factory?"

The Rev. Carlisle laughed. It was something he very seldom did; but now he laughed in a high key and was still bubbling when he spoke. "I'll tell you, doctor, as soon as we've got the chump cleaned. It's a promise."

"Very well. It was probably something ridiculous."

Stan changed the subject. "I'll get busy this week and rent a shack jammed right up next to his estate."

Dr. Lilith was filing a thumbnail. "Don't be so dramatic, darling. Yonkers is good enough. I agree that it should be in Westchester. The City of Light location will spread any hue and cry out in the southwest. But I don't think there will be any hue and cry. However, he may take the matter up with this Mr. Anderson. Don't forget that he has some very shrewd men working for him. Mr. Anderson would try to outthink you. He knows he is dealing with an ingenious man. He would start his hunt for you on his own hook, and it would begin at the country place and fan out from there. No. Yonkers is neither here nor there." She dropped the nail file back into the drawer. "How are you going to brush off the faithful Penelope?"

"Molly?" Stan was pacing the room, his hands in his pockets. "I'll give her a couple of grand and tell her to meet me some place in Florida. All she needs is a few bucks and a race track to keep her happy. She'll be in a daze as long as the dough holds out. If she wins a little she'll forget the day of the month and everything else. When she's broke she can go back to the carny and work the Ten-in-One. Or get a job as a hat check somewhere. She won't starve."

Lilith stood up and came over to him, stretching tailored gray arms up around his neck and giving him her mouth.

They swayed for a moment and Stan rubbed his cheek against the smooth hair. Then she pushed him away. "Run along, Reverend. I've a patient due in five minutes."

When Grindle got to the church he found the Rev. Carlisle in his study upstairs. On the desk, spread out under the lamp, were letters with currency clipped to them. Stan picked up one which held a ten-dollar bill and read aloud: " 'I know the wonderful future which the City holds for us all in the line of a pooling of our spiritual forces. What a joy it will be when our friends and loved ones in spirit life can be with us as often as we wish. God bless you, Stanton Carlisle.' Well, the rest of it is of no consequence." He smiled at the ten-spot. "It's very touching, Ezra, some of the letters. Many of them are from uneducated people—yet their faith is so pure and unselfish. The City will be a dream come true. They should thank Ramakrishna, though, for everything I do is done with the hand of that great spiritual leader on my shoulder."

Grindle sat staring at the ember of his cigar. "I'll do my share, Stanton. I'm pretty well fixed. I'll do what I can. This idea of pooling all the spiritual power in one spot makes sense to me. Same as any business merger. But my part isn't easy: I've built such a wall around myself that I can't get out any more. They're all devoted, loyal people. None better. But they won't understand. I'll have to think of some way . . ."

While the turntable revolved Stan leaned over the machine with a clothesbrush, keeping the blank record clear of acetate threads cut by the recording needle. Suddenly he raised the needle arm, tore the record from the turntable and slung it into a corner. "God damn it, kid, you've got to sound *wistful*. The dame and the old guy can be together forever, frigging like rabbits, only he's got to help the church build this City. Now take it again. And get in there and *sell* it."

Molly was almost crying. She turned back the pages of her script and leaned closer to the mike, watching Stan put on a new record blank.

I can't *act*. Oh, golly, I've got to try!

She started to cry, forcing the words out between catches of her breath, struggling through it and winking so she could still read the script. Toward the end she was crying so hard she couldn't see it at all and ad-libbed the rest. She was waiting any minute for Stan to blow up and bawl her out, but he let it ride.

When she was through he raised the recording arm. "That's the stuff, kid—plenty of emotion. Let's listen to it."

The playback sounded awful, Molly thought. All full of weepy noises and gasps. But Stan was grinning. He nodded to her and when he had heard it all he said, "That's the stuff, kid. That'll shake him loose. You wait and see. You think that sounds corny? Forget it. The chump's overboard. I could roll up my pants legs, throw a sheet over me, and he'd take me for his long lost love. But we're going to need one circus to nail him to the cross."

Moonlight struck through fern leaves in the conservatory; the rest of the church was in darkness. The minutes slid by—twenty of them by Stan's luminous-dial watch. He shifted his feet and found the floor board by the organ.

A tinkle came from the trumpet lying on the lectern, across the Bible. Grindle leaned forward, clenching his fists.

The trumpet stirred, then floated in air, moonlight winking from its aluminum surface. The chump moaned, cupping one hand behind his ear so as not to miss a single syllable. But the voice came thin and clear, a little metallic.

"Spunk darling . . . this is Dorrie. I know you haven't forgotten us, Spunk. I hope to materialize enough for you to touch me soon. It's wonderful . . . that you are with us in building the City. We can be together there, darling. Really together. We will be. Believe that. I'm so glad that you are working with us at last. And don't worry about Andy and the rest. Many of them will come to accept the truth of survival in time. Don't try to convince them now. And don't alarm them: you have some securities—some bonds—that they don't know about. That is the way out, dear. And let no one know how much you give, for all must feel that the City is their very own. Give your part to Stanton, bless him. And don't forget, darling . . . next time I come to you . . . I shall come as a bride."

It was late when Stan pressed the buzzer outside the apartment. Lilith opened the door, frowning. "I don't like your coming here so much, Stan. Somebody might see you."

He said nothing but hurried in and threw his brief case on her desk, tugging at the straps. Lilith closed the Venetian blinds a little tighter.

From the case he dug a helter-skelter of papers, the faked letters with currency still attached, which Lilith gathered up, pulling off the cash. She emptied them into the fireplace and put a match to them.

Stan was feverishly smoothing out bills and arranging them in stacks. "The convincer boodle did the trick, babe. I took every cent I had in the sock—eleven grand." He patted the piles of bills. "Jesus, what blood I've sweat to get it in this goddamned racket! But here's the payoff."

In two legal-sized brown envelopes were thick oblong packets.

He drew them out and broke confining strips of paper. "There it is, baby. How many people ever see that much cash in all their lives? *One hundred and fifty thousand!* Look at it! Look at it! And the McCoy. I never saw *one* five-yard note before. God almighty, we're lousy with 'em!"

The doctor was amused. "We'd better put them away, darling. That's a lot of money for one person to carry in his pocket. You might spend it foolishly."

While Stan gathered the crumpled bills of the convincer into a wad and slipped a rubber band around them Lilith assembled the "take" and placed it carefully back in the brown envelopes, sealing them. She swung open the dummy drawers of the desk and when she dialed the combination Stan automatically tried to get a peek but her shoulder was in the way. Lilith put the money away and spun the dial.

When she stood up the Rev. Carlisle was staring into the polished mahogany of the desktop, his face flushed. "Wounds of God! A hundred and fifty grand!"

She handed him a double brandy and poured one for herself. He took the glass from her hand and set it on the bookcase. Then he slid his arms around her roughly. "Baby, baby— God, this high class layout had me dizzy but I get it good and clear now. Baby, you're nothing but a *gonif* and I love you. We're a couple of hustlers, a pair of big-time thieves. How does it feel?"

He was grinning down at her, squeezing her ribs until they hurt. She took his wrists and loosened them a little, closing her eyes and raising her face to him. "You're wonderful, darling, the way you read my mind."

Dr. Lilith Ritter did not go to bed right away. After Carlisle had gone she sat smoking and drawing careful parallel lines on a scratch pad. Once she turned back to the file cabinet behind her and took out a folder identified only by a number. It contained a chart on graph paper, an idea with which she often played, an emotional barometric chart, marked with dates, showing a jagged rise and fall. It was an emotional diagram of Stanton Carlisle. She did not trust it entirely; but the curve had reached a high point, and on four other occasions such peaks had been followed by sudden drops into depression, instability, and black despair. Finally she put the folder away, undressed, and drew a tub of hot water into which she threw pine bath salts.

She lay in the water reading the financial section of the evening paper. Grindle Motors was off two points; it would go still lower before it started to rise again. Lilith's smile, as she tossed the paper to the floor and snuggled deeper in the comforting, scented warmth, was the smile of a well-fed kitten.

With a twist of triumphant glee her mind drew pictures of her two sisters as she had seen them last: Mina, spare and virginal, still proud of a Phi Beta key after all these years of beating Latin into the heads of brats. And Gretel—still looking like a wax angel off a *Tannenbaum*, with half a lung left to breathe with and a positive Wassermann.

Old Fritz Ritter had kept a State Street saloon called "The Dutchman's." His daughter Lille smiled. "I must be part Swedish," she said softly to a bar of pink soap, molded in the form of a lotus. "The middle way."

For two days Ezra Grindle had dropped from sight. His legal staff, his chauffeur-bodyguard, and his private chief of police, Melvin Anderson, had conferred again and again as to where the boss might be, without getting anywhere. Anderson knew little about the Old Man's activities lately and was afraid to stick a tail on him for fear he would find out about it. The Chief was cagy as hell. The lawyers learned that Grindle had not touched his checking accounts. Nothing, at least, had cleared. But he had been into one of his safe-deposit boxes. It was difficult to find out what securities the Chief had liquidated or how much. And where was he? He had left word: "I shall be away on business."

The lawyers went over the will. If he had made a new one they would have drawn it. All his faithful employees were remembered, and the rest was distributed to his pet colleges, medical foundations, and homes for unwed mothers. They would just have to wait.

In a tiny bedroom, lit only by a skylight, on the top floor of the Church of the Heavenly Message, the great man sat with his glasses off and his dentures in a glass of water beside him. He was wearing the yellow robe of a Tibetan lama. On the pale green wall of his cell was painted in Sanskrit the word *Aum*, symbol of man's eternal quest for spiritual At-One-ness with the All Soul of the Universe.

At intervals Grindle meditated on spiritual things but often he simply daydreamed in the cool quiet. The dreams took him back to the campus, and her lips when he kissed her for the first time. She wanted to see his college and he was showing her the buildings which stood there in the night, illumined, important. Afterward they strolled in Morningside Park, and he kissed her again. That was the first time she let him touch her breast . . .

He went over every detail. It was amazing what meditation could do. He remembered things he had forgotten for years. Only Dorrie's face eluded him; he could not bring it back. He could recall the pattern of her skirt, that day at Coney Island, but not her face.

With the pleasure of pressing a sore tooth, he brought back the evening, walking on the Drive, when she told him what she had been afraid of; and now it was true. It seemed that no time had passed at all. His frantic inquiries for a doctor. He had exams the very time she was supposed to go; she went by herself. Afterwards, up in the room, she seemed all right, only shaky and depressed. What a hellish week that was! He had to put her out of his mind until exams were through. Then the next night—they told him she was in the hospital and he ran all the way over there and they wouldn't let him in. And when he did get in Dorrie wouldn't speak to him. It went around and around in his head—like a Tibetan prayer wheel. But it was slowing down. Soon it would stop and they would be Joined in Spirit.

The skylight had grown a darker blue. The Rev. Carlisle brought him a light supper and gave him further Spiritual Instruction. When the night had come there was a tap at the door and Carlisle entered, carrying with both hands a votive candle in a cup of ruby-red glass. "Let us go to the chapel."

Grindle had never seen that room before. A large divan was piled with silk cushions and in an alcove was a couch covered with black velvet for the medium. The entire room was hung in folds of dark drapery. If there were any windows they were covered.

The clergyman led his disciple to the divan; taking his hand he pressed him back against the cushions. "You are at peace. Rest, rest."

Grindle felt foggy and vague. The bowl of jasmine tea which he had been given for supper had seemed bitter. Now his head was swimming lightly and reality retreated to arm's length.

The medium placed the votive candle in a sconce on the far wall; its flickering light deepened the shadows of that dead-black room and, on looking down, the bridegroom could barely make out the form of his own hands. His eyesight blurred.

Carlisle was chanting something which sounded like Sanskrit, then a brief prayer in English which reminded Grindle of the marriage service; but somehow the words refused to fit together in his mind.

In the alcove the medium lay back on the couch and the black curtains flowed together by their own power. Or was it the medium's odylic force?

They waited.

From far away, from hundreds of miles it seemed, came the sound of wind, a great rushing of wind or the beating of giant wings. Then it died and there arose the soft, tinkling notes of a *sitar*.

Suddenly from the alcove which served as a cabinet came the trumpet voice of the control spirit, Ramakrishna, last of India's saints, greatest of *bhakti* yogis, preacher of the love of God.

"*Hari Aum!* Greetings, my beloved new disciple. Prepare your mind for its juncture with the Spirit. On the seashore of endless worlds, as children meet, you will join for an instant the Life of Spirit. Love has made smooth your path—for all Love is but the Love of God. *Aum.*"

Ghostly music began again. From the curtains before the alcove a light flashed, then a sinuous coil of glowing vapor poured from between them, lying in a pool of mist close to the floor. It swelled and seemed to foam from the cabinet in a cascade. Its brilliance grew, until on looking down Grindle could see his own figure illumined by the cold flaming brilliance of the light. It rose now and pulsated, glowing bright and then dimming slightly. The air was filled with a mighty rhythm, like the heart of a titan, roaring and rushing.

The pool of luminous matter began to take form. It swayed as a cocoon might sway from a moth's emerging. It became a cocoon, holding something dark in its center. Then it split and drew back toward the cabinet, revealing the form of a girl, lying on a bed of light, but illumined only by the stuff around her. She was naked, her head resting on one bent arm.

Grindle sank to his knees. "Dorrie—Dorrie—"

She opened her eyes, sat up and then rose, modestly drawing a film of glowing mist over her body. The old man groped forward awkwardly on his knees, reaching up to her. As he drew near, the luminous cloud fell back and vanished. The girl stood, white and tall, in the flicker of the votive candle across the room; and as she gazed down at him her hair fell over her face.

"Dorrie—my pet—my honey love—my bride . . ."

He picked her up in his arms, overjoyed at the complete materialization, at the lifelike smoothness of her body—she was so heartbreakingly earthly.

Inside the cabinet the Rev. Carlisle was busy packing yards of luminous-painted China silk back into the hem of the curtains. Once he put his eye to the opening and his lips drew back over his teeth. Why did people look so filthy and ridiculous to anyone watching? Christ!

The second time in his life he had seen it. Filth.

The bride and bridegroom were motionless now.

It was up to Molly to break away and get back to the cabinet. Stan turned the switch and the rhythmic, pounding heartbeat filled the room, growing louder. He tossed one end of the luminous silk through the curtains.

The quiet forms on the divan stirred, and Stan could see the big man burrowing his face between Molly's breasts. "No—Dorrie—my own, my precious—I can't let you go! Take me with you, Dorrie—I don't want earth life without you . . ."

She struggled out of his arms; but the bridegroom seized her around the waist, rubbing his forehead against her belly.

Stan grabbed the aluminum trumpet. "Ezra—my beloved disciple—have courage. She must return to us. The force is growing weaker. In the City—"

"No! Dorrie—I must—I—once more . . ."

This time another voice answered him. It was not a spiritual voice. It was the voice of a panicky showgirl who has more than she can handle. "Hey, quit it, for God's sake! Stan! Stan! *Stan!*"

*Oh, bleeding wounds of Christ, the dumb, stupid bitch!*

The Rev. Carlisle tore the curtains apart. Molly was twisting and kicking; the old man was like one possessed. In his pent-up soul the dam had broken, and the sedative Stan had loaded into his tea had worn off.

Grindle clutched the squirming girl until she was jerked from his hands.

"Stan! For God's sake *get me out of here! Get me out!*"

Grindle stood paralyzed. For in the dim, red, flickering light he saw the face of his spiritual mentor, the Rev. Stanton Carlisle; it was snarling. Then a fist came up and landed on the chin of the spirit bride. She dropped to the floor, knees gaping obscenely.

Now the hideous face was shouting at Grindle himself. "You goddamned hypocrite! Forgiveness? All you wanted was a piece of ass!" Knuckles smashed his cheekbone and Grindle bounced back on the divan.

His brain had stopped working. He lay looking stupidly at the red, jumping light. A door opened somewhere and somebody ran out. He stared at the leaping red flame, not thinking, not living, just watching. He heard something stir near him but couldn't turn his head. He heards sounds of crying and somebody say "Oh, good God," and then the faltering slap of bare feet and a girl's voice sobbing and a fumbling for a door and a door opening and staying open against a hallway where there was a dim yellow light but it all made no sense to Ezra Grindle and he preferred to watch the little flame in its ruby-red glass cup flickering and dancing up and down. He lay there a long time.

Below him the front door slammed once. But it didn't seem to matter what happened. He groaned and turned his head.

One arm—his left one—numb. And all one side of his face frozen. He sat up and stared about him. This dark room—there had been a girl's body. Dorrie's. She was a bride. It was his wedding. The Rev. Carlisle—

Slowly he remembered things in little snatches. But was it the Rev. Carlisle who hit Dorrie? Or was it an evil spirit impersonating him?

Grindle stood up, having trouble balancing. Then he shuffled over to the door. One leg was numb. He was in the hallway of a house. There was a room upstairs.

He held onto the banister and took a step but he fell against the wall and sank to his knees. He crawled, step by step, dragging his left leg, which felt wooden and dead. He had to get upstairs for some reason—his clothes were upstairs—but everybody had gone—dematerialized.

He found the cell with the green walls and hauled himself to his feet, his breath whistling. What had happened? His clothes were still in the closet. Have to put them on. There was a wedding. There was a bride. Dorrie. They had been together, just as Stan had foretold. Stanton— Where was he? Why had Stanton left him this way?

Grindle was annoyed with Stanton. He struggled to get his trousers on and his shirt. Have to sit down and rest. Dorrie was there in spirit. Who else could it be but Dorrie, his Dorrie, come back again? Had she lived after all? And come back to him? A dream—?

But they had gone.

Glasses. Wallet. Keys. Cigar case.

He limped back into the hall. Stairs again, a mile of them going steeply down. Hold on. Have to hold on tight. Andy! Where was Andy and why had he let him get caught this way in a house with so many stairs and what had hurt his leg? With a sudden surge of anger Grindle wondered if he had been kidnapped. Shot? Slugged over the head? There were desperate men who might—*the mob rule grows ever more menacing, even as we sit here tonight, gentlemen, enjoying our cigars and our . . .* That was from a speech.

And the door to that black room open.

Grindle felt as if twenty years had fallen over him like a blanket. Twenty more years. He stood looking into the dark. There was a cabinet over there, and a single splash of green light still lay on the floor.

"Stanton! Dorrie! Stanton, where are you!"

Halfway across the room he stumbled and crawled the rest of the way to the pool of light. But it wasn't moist and musky, like Dorrie. It felt like fabric.

"Stanton!"

Grindle struck a match and found a wall switch. The light revealed that the patch of luminous vapor was a piece of white silk sticking out from the bottom hem of the black curtains in the alcove.

But Stanton had struck Dorrie!

He drew aside the curtains. There was the couch, all right. Maybe Stanton had fallen behind it when the evil presence— this was Thursday? I've missed the board meeting. They would hold it without me; too important. I should have been there, to act as a sea anchor on Graingerford. But Russell would be there. Dependable man. But could Russell convince them by himself of the soundness of the colored-labor policy? The competition was doing it—it was a natural. Graingerford be damned.

On the floor by the couch lay a control box with several switches on its bakelite panel. Grindle turned one.

Above him began the faint, ghostly music of a *sitar.* Another turn of the switch and it stopped.

He sat on the medium's couch for a moment, holding the box on his knees, the wire trailing from it underneath the black velvet cover toward the wall. A second switch produced the cosmic heartbeat and the rushing wind. Another—*"Hari Aum!"*

At the sound of Ramakrishna's voice he snapped it off. The click of the switch seemed to turn on his own reason. In one jagged, searing flash he saw everything. The long build-up, the psychic aura, the barrage of suggestion, the manufactured miracles.

Dorrie— But how, in heaven's name, did that sanctimonious devil find out about Dorrie? I've never spoken her name all these years—not even to Dr. Ritter. Even the doctor doesn't know about Dorrie or how she died.

The villain must be genuinely psychic. Or some debased telepathic power. A fearful thought—such a black heart and such uncanny powers. Maybe Dr. Ritter can explain it.

Downstairs. Got to get downstairs. Telephone. In that devil's office—

He made it.

"Andy? I'm perfectly all right—just can't talk very plain. Something's the matter with one side of my face. Probably neuralgia. Andy, for the Lord's sake, stop fussing. I tell you I'm all right. It doesn't matter where I am. Now keep quiet and listen. Get Dr. Samuels. Get him out of bed and have him up home when I get there. I'll be there in two hours. I want a checkup. Yes, this evening. What time is it? Get Russell up there too. I've got to find out what happened at the meeting this morning."

The voice at the other end of the wire was frantic. Grindle listened for a time and then said, "Never mind, Andy. I've just been—away."

"One question, Chief. Are you with that spirit preacher?"

The Chief's voice grew clearer. "Andy—I forbid you ever to mention that man's name to me again! That's an order. You and everyone else in the organization. Is that clear? And I forbid anyone to ask me where I've been. I know what I'm doing. This is final."

"Okay, Chief. The curtain is down."

He made two more calls. One was for a cab and the other was to Dr. Lilith Ritter. There was one chamber in his brain that wasn't functioning yet. He didn't dare open it until he was safely in Dr. Ritter's office.

Molly had not stopped for clothes. She pulled on her shoes, threw a coat around her, grabbed her purse, and ran from that awful house. She ran all the way home.

In the flat Buster miaowed to her, but she gave him a quick pat. "Not now, sugar. Mamma has to scram. Oh, my God!"

She heaved a suitcase onto the bed and threw into it everything small and valuable she could see. Still crying in little bubbling starts, she drew on the first panties and bra that came out of a drawer; she got into the first dress she touched in the closet, shut the keyster, and put Buster in a big paper bag.

"Oh, my God, I've got to hurry." Play dumb and give them an Irish name. "I've got to hurry, somewhere. Stan—oh, damn you, damn you, damn you, I *don't* feel dirty! He was just as clean as you, you damn cheap hustler. Oh—Daddy—"

The hotel people were nice about Buster. She expected cops any minute but nothing happened. And the address she found in the *Billboard* was the right one. A reply to her telegram got back early the next morning:

SENDING DOUGH NEED GIRL SWORD CABINET ACT COME
HOME SWEETHEART

ZEENA

# Justice

*holds in one hand a balance, in the other a sword.*

LILITH opened the door; she said nothing until they were in the office and she had seated herself behind the desk, asking softly, "Did she?"

Stan had discarded clerical bib and collar. He was sweating, his mouth cottony. "She went all the way. Then she blew up. I —I knocked out the pair of them and left them there."

Lilith's eyes half closed. "Was that necessary?"

"Necessary? Wounds of God! Don't you think I tried to weasel out of it? The old bastard was like a stallion kicking down a stall to get into a mare. I dropped both of them and beat it."

Lilith was drawing on her gloves. She took a cigarette from her purse. "Stan, it may be some time before I can meet you." She swung open the panel and dialed the safe combination. "He may come to me—I'll try to persuade him not to hunt for you." She laid the convincer wad and the two brown envelopes on the desk. "I don't want to keep this any longer, Stan."

When he had stuffed the money into his pockets Lilith smiled. "Don't get panicky. He won't be able to start any action against you for several hours. How hard did you hit him?"

"I just pushed him. I don't think he was all the way out."

"How badly is the girl hurt?"

"For God's sake, she isn't *hurt!* I just dropped her; she'll come out of it quick. If she stays groggy it will give the chump something to worry about: what to do with her. If she gets clear she'll head straight back to the flat and wait for me. She'll have a good long wait. I've got the keyster parked uptown in a check room. The phoney credentials and everything. If Molly had any brains she could put the con on that mark for hush money: claim he attacked her in the dark séance room. Christ, why didn't I think of that angle sooner? But it's sour now. I'm on my way."

He lifted Lilith's face and kissed her, but the lips were cool and placid. Stan was staring down into her eyes. "It's going to be a long time, baby, before we get together."

She stood up and moved closer to him. "Don't write to me, Stan. And don't get drunk. Take sedative pills if you have to, but don't get drunk. Promise me."

"Sure. Where you going to write to me?"

"Charles Beveridge, General Delivery, Yonkers."

"Kiss me."

This time her mouth was warm.

At the door he slid his arm around her, cupping her breast with his hand, and kissed her again. Suddenly he drew up, his face sharp with alarm. "Wait a minute, baby. He's going to start thinking back on who tipped me to that abortion. And he's going to think straight to you! Come on, sweetheart, we've both got to scram."

Lilith laughed: two sharp notes like the bark of a fox. "He doesn't know that I know that. I worked it out from things he *wouldn't* say." Her eyes were still laughing. "Don't tell me how to look out for myself, lover. Tell me—" A black-gloved hand pressed his arm. "Tell me how you made that precision balance move!"

He grinned and said over his shoulder, "Yonkers," as he walked swiftly out of the door.

Mustn't use the car. Cab drivers remember people. Subway to Grand Central. Walk, do not run, to the nearest exit. One hundred and fifty grand. Christ, I could hire a flock of private cops myself.

In a dressing room under the station he opened the traveling bag and pulled out a shirt and a light suit. There was a fifth of Hennessy; he uncapped the bottle for a short one.

A hundred and fifty grand. Standing in his underwear he fastened on a money vest with twelve pockets. Then he took up the roll of currency—one handful—his profits from the church racket. Take a fifty and a few twenties and stash the rest away.

Snapping off the rubber band from the fat roll he peeled off the fifty. The next bill was a single. And the one after it. But he hadn't cluttered up the convincer boodle with singles! Had he added any money to the pile that night in Lilith's office? Singles!

He spread out the wad, passing the bills from one hand to the other. Then he turned so that the light above the wash bowl would fall on them and riffled through them again. Except for the outside fifty the whole works was nothing but ones!

Stan's eyebrows began to itch and he dug at them with his knuckles. His hands smelled of money and faint perfume from bills carried by women.

The Great Stanton took another pull of brandy and sat down carefully on the white dressing stool. What the hell had gone sour now? Counting over showed three hundred and eighty-three dollars in the boodle. There had been eleven thousand—and the "take"? Good Christ!

He let the dollars fall to the floor and snatched at one of the brown envelopes, cutting his thumb as he tore it open.

There was a shuffle of feet outside and the attendant's white duck trousers appeared beneath the door. "You all right in there, sir?"

"Yeah, yeah, sure."

This pile ought to be all five-century notes—

"You ain't feeling faint, is you, mister?"

*Oh, good God, leave me alone.* "No. I'm okay, I tell you."

"Well, that's fine, sir. I just thought I heard noise like some gentleman having a fit. Gentleman have a fit in here last week and I had to crawl under the door and hold him down. Had to get the porter, mop up all the blood where he cut his self."

"For God's sake, man, *let me get dressed!*" Stan grabbed a dollar from the scattered bills at his feet and held it under the door.

"Oh—oh! Thank *you*, sir. Thank *you*."

Stan tore off the brown paper. Singles!

The other envelope was tough; he ripped into it with his teeth. Again—the thick packet contained nothing but one-dollar bills!

The pastor of the Church of the Heavenly Message crushed a handful of them in his fist, his eyes traveling along the black lines between the tiles of the floor. He let out an explosive sound like a cough; lifting his fist he beat the crumpled paper against his forehead twice. Then he fired the money into a corner and turned on both faucets of the washbowl. In the roaring water he let himself go; he sank his face in the basin and screamed, the sound bubbling up past his ears through the rush of water. He screamed until his diaphragm was sore and he had to stop and sit down on the floor, stuffing a towel in his mouth and tearing it with his teeth.

At last he hoisted himself up and reached for the brandy, swallowing until he had to stop and gasp for breath. In the mirror's merciless light he saw himself: hair streaming, eyes bloodshot, mouth twisted. Bleeding wounds of Christ!

The gypsy switch.


He stood, swaying, his hair falling damply over his eyes.

Dr. Lilith Ritter said, "Sit down, Mr. Carlisle."

Her voice was cold, kind, and sad—and as professional as the click of a typewriter.

His head began to shake as if he were saying no to a long series of questions. It went on shaking.

"I've done everything I can," said the sad voice through cigarette smoke. "When you first came to me you were in bad shape. I had hoped that by getting at the roots of your anxiety I could avert a serious upset. Well—" The hand gestured briefly with its star sapphire. "I failed."

He began rubbing his fingers along the top of the desk, listening to the small whimpering noise of sweat against mahogany.

"Listen to me, Mr. Carlisle." The doctor leaned forward earnestly. "Try to understand that these delusions are part of your condition. When you first came to me you were tortured by guilt connected with your father—and your mother. All of these things you think you have done—or that have been done to you lately—are merely the guilt of your childhood projected. Do I make myself clear?"

The room was rocking, the lamps were double rings of light, sliding back and forth through each other while the walls billowed. His head shook: no.

"The symbolism is quite obvious, Mr. Carlisle. You were filled with the unconscious desire to kill your father. You picked up somewhere—I don't know where—the name of Grindle, an industrialist, a man of power, and identified him with your father. You have a very peculiar reaction to older men with a stubble of white beard. It makes you think of fungus on the face of a corpse—the corpse you wanted your father to be."

The doctor's voice was very soft now; soothing, kind, unanswerable.

"When you were a child you saw your mother having intercourse. Therefore tonight in hallucination you thought you saw Grindle, the father-image, in intercourse with your mistress—who has come to represent your mother. And that's not all, Mr. Carlisle. Since I have been your counselor you have made a transference to me—you see me also as your mother. That explains your sexual delusions with regard to me."

He slid his hands over his face, mashing the palms into his eyes, gripping strands of hair between his fingers and wrenching until pain freed his frozen lungs and let him draw a breath. His thoughts ran over and over, playing the same words until they became meaningless: grindle grindle grindle grindle mother mother mother stop stop stop. The voice didn't stop.

"There is one thing more you must face, Mr. Carlisle: the thing that is destroying you. Ask yourself why you wanted to kill your father. Why was there so much guilt connected with that wish? Why did you see me—me, the mother-image—in hallucinations both as your mistress and as a thief who had cheated you?"

She was standing up now and leaning across the desk, her face quite near him. She spoke gently.

"You wanted intercourse with your mother, didn't you?"

His hand went up to cover his eyes again, his mouth opened to make a wordless noise that could have been anything, a yes, a no, or both. He said, "Uh—uh—uh—uh." Then it seemed that all the pain in him was concentrated in the back of his right hand in a sudden, furious stab like a snake bite. He dropped it and stared at the doctor, momentarily in focus again. She was smiling.

"One other thing, Mr. Carlisle." She blew cigarette smoke. "The man you claimed to have killed in Mississippi—I thought at first that was merely another delusion involving the father-image. On investigation, however, I discovered there really was such a death—Peter Krumbein, Burleigh, Mississippi. I know you'll be glad to know *that*, at least, really did happen. It was quite easy to trace. Not so many years ago, was it, Mr. Carlisle?"

She turned away suddenly and picked up the telephone, the smooth voice brisker now. "Mr. Carlisle, I've done all I can for you, but you *must* have hospital care. These hallucinations— We can't have you wandering about and getting into trouble. Just put yourself in my hands; you can trust me absolutely.

"Bellevue Hospital? Psychiatric Division, please."

The buzzer hummed; a latch clicked in the foyer. Then the door into the waiting room opened and closed. Someone coming.

He backed away, looking at her, his mouth hanging open, his eyes bulging. Door. Have to get out. People. Danger.

"Psychiatric Division? This is Dr. Lilith Ritter. Please send an ambulance . . ."

The door, rushing behind him, shut off her voice.

Get out. Street. Hide. He clung to the knob, holding the door shut so she couldn't follow him.

Dream. Nightmare. Delusion. Nothing . . . nothing real. Tongue . . . naked . . . talk . . . money . . . dream . . . nightmare.

Dimly, through wood, he heard the telephone click into its

cradle. Snap of a latch . . . waiting room. Then her voice. "Will you come in, please?"

Silence.

He sucked without thinking at the back of his right hand, where there was a red, smarting mark like a cigarette burn.

Safe? People coming! Got to get—

Another voice beyond the panels, high-pitched. Man. "Doctor —a ghastly mess . . ."

"Lie straight on the couch, please. Let me take your glasses, Mr. Grindle."

# The Devil

*Beneath his bat-wings the lovers stand in chains.*

THERE was a plate of glass shaped like a star in the floor where the dancers swayed and shuffled. When the band went into a sweet one the house lights dimmed out and the star glowed, shining up the girls' skirts, leaving their faces in darkness, but X-raying their clothes from the hips down. They screamed and giggled as their partners pushed them across the star and back into obscurity.

In one corner of the room the mentalist rose from his chair, steadying himself by a hand on its back. "Thank you, sir, and your charming girl friend, for your interest and for the drink. You understand, folks, I've got other people waiting . . ."

The drunk slid a silver dollar along the table and the mind reader took it in his finger tips. It vanished in a quick movement. He bowed and turned away.

The girl snickered, the noise bubbling in her glass as she drank. "Daddy, isn't he spooky?" She kept on chuckling. "Now, then, sweetheart, you heard what he said! He said, 'A man who has a good head for business will give you the thing nearest to your heart, something which once lived in a wire cage.' You heard him, daddy. What d'you s'pose he meant?"

236

The man said thickly, "Anything you say, kid, goes. You know that. Anything. Gee, honey, you got the prettiest lil pair of—" He remembered the slip of paper that the mind reader had told him to tuck under the strap of his wrist watch and he pulled it out, unfolding it and trying to focus on it. The girl struck a match.

In her affected scrawl, using small circles for dots, was written, "Will Daddy buy me that red-fox jacket?" He stared at the slip and then grinned. "Sure, kid. Anything for you, kid. You know that. Le's get outa here—go up t'your place. C'mon, honey, 'fore I'm too lit—too lit t'enjoy"—he broke wind but never noticed it —"anything."

At the bar Stan knocked off another quick one on the house. Even through the curtain of alky the maggot in his mind kept burrowing. How long will this joint last? They get crummier and crummier. That shiny-haired bastard—private. Private. Private information. Private investigations. Private reports, private shellackings. Private executions?

The thought turned and twisted in his mind, burning the alcohol out of it. Jesus, why did I ever have to tangle with that old crumb? How was I to know that Molly— Oh, God, here we go again.

A waiter stepped close and said, "Table eighteen, bud. The gal's named Ethel. Had three husbands and the clap. The guy with her is a drummer. Plumbers' supplies."

Stanton finished his drink and dropped a quarter in the waiter's vest pocket as he brushed past him.

On his way to the table Stan saw the boss, his navy-blue shirt sleeves rolled up and canary yellow tie pulled down, talking to two men in rumpled suits. They had not removed their hats. Both necks were thick.

A cold ripple slipped down his back. Wind seemed to whistle inside his undershirt. Cold. Oh, Jesus, here they come. Grindle. Grindle. Grindle. The old man's power covered the country like a pair of bat-wings, flapping cold and black.

Stan walked slowly to the back of the room, ducked behind a partition and squeezed his way through the kitchen and out

into the alley at the rear of the Pelican Club, breaking into a
run when he was clear of the building. He didn't dare go back
for his hat. Christ, I ought to hang it on a nail right by the back
door. But they'll block that the next time.

Always different faces, different guys. They must hire private
dicks in every state, all of them different. Anderson sits inside
that barbed-wire fort and spins it out like a spider, millions of
bucks to smash one guy. Mexico. I've got to jump the border
if I'm ever going to shake them. Three thousand miles of this
damn country and no hole to duck into. How do those goons do
it so quick? Mind readers—they must chase after every guy
doing a mental act and take a sample of his hair, see if it's blond.

Across the dark rooftops a train whistled, long and mourn-
fully. Stan ducked down another alley and leaned against the
wall, listening to the roaring jolt of his own heart, fighting to
get his breath. Lilith, Lilith. Across two thousand miles stretched
the invisible golden wire still, and one end was buried in his
brain.

Back in the Pelican Club the boss said, "Now you fellas run
along. You tell McIntyre I'm not putting in no cig or novelty
girls and I'm holding on to the hat check myself. It ain't for
sale."

# The Hermit

*An old man follows a star
that burns in his lantern.*

IN THE light of the fire the cards fell, forming the pattern of a cross. Stan dealt them slowly, watching them fall.

The gully was shielded from wind, the fire hidden from the tracks a quarter of a mile away across fields standing high with brittle weed-stalks. Weeds grew to the edge of the gully, the fire turning them yellow against the sky where stars hung, icy and remote.

*The Empress.* She smirked at him from beneath her crown of stars, holding a scepter with a golden ball on its end. The pomegranates embroidered on her robe looked like strawberries. Beyond her, trees stood stiffly—like the trees on a theater backdrop in a tank town. At her feet the ripening wheat-heads. Smell of ripening wheat. Venus sign on the couch where she sat. Smell of ripening wheat.

What did they think, the wriggling bugs of the scum, jetting into the world to meet acids, whirling douches, rubber scum bags, upholstery of cars, silk drawers, clotted handkerchief . . . two hundred million at a shot . . .

Across the fire the fat man lifted a steaming can from the embers with a pair of pliers. "Got yourself a can, bud? Java's done."

239

Stan knocked tobacco crumbs from a tin and twisted a rag around it. "In there, pal."

The coffee set his stomach churning again. Christ, I need a drink. But how to snake out the bottle without that bastard cutting himself in?

He eased the bottle neck from his coat and pretended to be studying the cards while the white mule trickled into the steaming can.

The squat hobo raised his face. "My, *my!* What is this that gives off so heavenly an aroma?" His voice was like sandpaper. "Could it be *Odeur de Barleycorn?* Or is it a few drops—just the merest suggestion behind the ears—of that rare and subtle essence, 'Parfum Pourriture d'Intestin— You never know she wears it until it's . . . too late'? *Come on, blondy, gimme the bottle!*"

Through his smile Stan said, "Sure. Sure, pal. I was going to break it out later. I'm waiting for another pal of mine. He's out trying to get a lump."

The fat man took the bottle of rotgut, measured it by eye, and very accurately drank half of it, handing it back and returning to his coffee. "Thanks, bud. The only pal you got is right in there. You better soak it up before some other bo muscles in on us." He shifted his weight, crossed his legs, and took a long drink of coffee, which trickled down the shiny blue surface of his jowls. A two days' growth of beard made him look like a pirate.

He rested the can on his knee and wiped his chin, running his tongue around between his lips and gums. Then he said, "That's right, bud—kill the bottle. How would you like it if we had an unexpected guest?" His voice took on a reedy, mincing tone and he held his head coyly on one side, lifting bushy eyebrows. "He'd find us in a dither—it being the maid's day off. All we'd have to offer him would be a drink of that fine, mellow, wood-aged polecat piss." The jowls swayed as he shook his head in mock concern. Then the dark face brightened. "Or perhaps he would be that priceless gem—the guest-who-always-fits-in—ready at a moment's notice to don an apron (one of your frilly best, naturally, kept just for those special people) and join you in the kitchen, improvising a snack."

Stan brought the bottle to his mouth again and tilted it; the raw whisky found holes in his teeth and punished him, but he finished it and heaved the bottle into the weeds.

The fat man threw another branch on the fire and squatted beside Stan. "What kind of cards are those, bud?"

The man's shirt was almost clean, pants cuffs scarcely frayed. Probably rode the plush a lot. In his lapel was a tiny steering-wheel emblem of a boat club.

Stan gazed up into his face. "My friend, you are a man who has seen life. I get the impression that somewhere in your life has been an office with a broad carpet. I see a window in an office building with something growing in it. Could it be little cedar trees—in a window box?"

The fat hobo stood up, swishing the coffee in his can. "Everybody had cedars. I had a better idea—an inspiration. Grass hummocks—just plain grass tufts. But this will show you the *genius*. What do you think I put in them? *Katydids!* I'd bring up a client late at night—town all dark there below us. Tell him to step back from the window and listen. You couldn't believe you were in the city." He looked down and his face tightened. "Wait a minute, bud. How'd you know about them grass tufts?"

The Great Stanton smiled thinly, pointing to the cards before him. "This is the Tarot of the Romany cartomancers. A set of symbols handed down from remote antiquity, preserving in their enigmatic form the ancient wisdom through the ages."

"What d'you do with 'em? Tell fortunes?" The gravel voice had lost its hostility.

"I receive impressions. You have two children. Is that correct?"

The fat man nodded. "Christ knows, I had once. If that bitch hasn't let 'em kill themselves while she was out whoring around."

"Your third wife?"

"Yeah, that's right. Wait a minute. How'd you know I was a three-time loser?"

"I drew the impressions from your mind, my friend, using the cards of the Tarot as a concentrative. Now, if you wish me to continue, I shall be glad to. The fee will be twenty-five cents, or its equivalent in merchandise."

The hobo scratched his scalp. "Okay, bud. Go ahead." He threw a quarter beside the cards and Stan picked it up. Five shots.

Gathering the cards he shuffled them, having the fat man cut them with his left hand.

"You see, the first to appear is the *Hermit*. An old man, leaning on a staff, follows a star that burns in his lantern. That is your quest—your journey through life, always seeking something just out of your reach. Once it was wealth. It became the love of women. Next, you sought security—for yourself and others. But misfortune descended on you. Things inside you began to tear in opposite directions. And you would have five or six drinks before you took the train home at night. Isn't that right?"

The glowering, dark face nodded.

"The *Hermit* is the card of the Search. The Search for the Answer."

"Come again, bud." The fat man's tone was subdued and hopeless. "What brains I ever had was knocked loose by yard dicks years ago."

Stan closed his eyes. "Man comes into the world a blind, groping mite. He knows hunger and the fear of noise and of falling. His life is spent in flight—flight from hunger and from the thunderbolt of destiny. From his moment of birth he begins to fall through the whistling air of Time: down, down into a chasm of darkness . . ."

The hobo stood up cautiously and edged around the fire. He watched the cartomancer warily. Nuts can blow their tops easy —and this one still held a can of hot coffee.

The Great Stanton spoke aloud to himself. The jolt of whisky had loosened his stomach and drawn it out from his backbone. Now he rambled; with a foolish, drunken joy he let his tongue ride, saying whatever it wanted to say. He could sit back and rest and let his tongue do the work. Why beat my brains out reading for a bum that was probably too crooked and phoney even for the advertising racket? The tongue does the work. Good old tongue, man's best friend—and woman's second best. What the hell am I talking about?

". . . we come like a breath of wind over the fields of morning. We go like a lamp flame caught by a blast from a darkened window. In between we journey from table to table, from bottle to bottle, from bed to bed. We suck, we chew, we swallow, we lick, we try to mash life into us like an am-am-*amoeba* God damn it! Somebody lets us loose like a toad out of a matchbox and we jump and jump and jump and the guy always behind us, and when he gets tired he stomps us to death and our guts squirt out on each side of the boot of All Merciful Providence. The son-of-a-bitch!"

The world began to spin and he opened his eyes to keep his balance. The fat man wasn't listening. He was standing with his back to the fire, throwing pebbles at something beyond the circle of light.

When he turned around he said, "A goddamned, mangy, flea-bitten abortion of a *dog* was trying to horn in on our fire. The stinking abomination. I hate 'em! They come up to you, smell-ing, groveling, please-kick-my-ass-mister. I *hate* 'em! They slaver all over you. You rub 'em behind the ears and they practically come in your face out of gratitude."

Stanton Carlisle said, "My friend, at some time a dog did you an injury. I think the dog was not yours but that it belonged to another—to a woman."

The bo, moving agilely with the grace of an athlete gone fat, was standing beside him now, fists working, the knuckles rip-pling as he spoke. "Sure it was a dog—a toadying, cringing, vomit-eating, goddamned abortion of a dog! Sure he belonged to a woman, you crazy bastard! And the dog was *me!*"

They held the pose like figures in a tableau. Only the firelight moved, jumping and flickering on the weeds and on the two faces, the pudgy one dark and tormented, the gaunt face of the blond hobo a blank.

There was a whining scuffle from the bank overhead and both men turned. An emaciated dog slid down and tremblingly ap-proached the warmth, tail flattened between his haunches, eyes rolling.

Stan chirped between his teeth. "Come here, boy. Here. Over here by me."

The dog bounded toward him, yelping with delight at the sound of a friendly voice. He had almost reached Stan when the squat hobo drew back his foot. The kick lifted the animal, squirming and squealing, into the air; it fell, legs spraddled, in the middle of the fire, screamed, and shot away into the dark, trailing sparks from singed fur.

Stan swept the coffee in a curve; it glistened in the firelight, a muddy arc, and caught the fat man in the eyes. He stumbled back, wiping his sleeve across them. Then he lowered his head, resting his jowl on his left shoulder and stepping in with a rocking motion, left fist forward, right hand half open, ready to defend his face. In a soft, cultured voice he said, "Get your hands up, brother. You are in for a very unpleasant three minutes. I'll play with you that long and then send you off to dreamland."

The Rev. Carlisle had doubled in the middle, as if taken by a violent stomach cramp. He moaned, bending over, and the fat man dropped his guard an inch. It was low enough.

When Stan sprang he carried a thick faggot from the fire and with one lunge caught the hobo with its burning point just below the breast bone. The man went down limply and heavily, like a dummy stuffed with sand.

Stan watched him gape, fighting for breath. Then he smashed the torch into the open mouth, feeling the teeth crush under it.

The alcohol was draining out of his mind. He was alone and cold, under an immensity of sky—naked as a slug, as a tadpole. And the shadow of the crushing foot seemed to move closer. Stan began to run.

Far away, up on the drag, he heard the hoot of a whistle and he ran faster, staggering, a stitch in his side. Oh, Jesus—the Tarot. I left it by the fire. One more signpost pointing to the Rev. Carlisle.

A freight was slowing. He ran, his breath scorching, looking ahead, through the dark, for obstructions on the line. An iron step came whipping by him and he reached for it, but it tore from his fingers. The job was picking up speed.

A wide-open boxcar door slid up to him and he leaped.

Then, with the scalding panic rushing over him, he knew that he had missed and was swinging under.

A hand from the car gripped his shoulder and held him, half inside the car and half out, while under his feet the earth flew past.

The freight high-balled along.

CARD XVIII

# Time

*One foot on earth and one on water, an angel pours eternity from cup to cup.*

In the parking lot the Maryland sun beat down, flashing from rows of windshields, from chromium handles and the smooth curves of enameled mudguards.

Cincinnati Burns eased the battered convertible into line while Molly, standing out on the gravel, shouted, "Cut her left, honey. More left."

He drew out the ignition key and it was suddenly snatched from his hand and hurled out between the cars. Cincy said, "You little devil! You're mighty sassy. Ain't you? Ain't you?" He boosted the child high in the air while it screamed with joy.

Molly came running up. "Let me hold him, Cincy, while you get the key." He passed the baby to her and it grabbed a damp handkerchief from the gambler's coat pocket and waved it triumphantly.

"Come on, precious. Let's let Daddy get the key. Hey, quit kicking me in the tummy."

The big man set the boy on his shoulder, handing Molly his hat for safekeeping, and they headed for the grandstand. The gambler shifted the baby and looked at the stop watch on his wrist. "Plenty of time, kitten. The third race is our spot."

245

They stopped to buy paper cups of raspberry sherbet and Cincinnati whispered suddenly, "You hold the bambino, Molly. There's Dewey from St. Louis."

Treading softly, he approached from the rear and squatted down behind a glum, lantern-jawed man in a seersucker suit. Cincy took a pack of matches and holding his thick fingers, knuckles covered with red hair, as delicately as if he were threading a needle, he stuck a match between Dewey's shoe sole and the upper. Lighting the match, he sneaked back a few steps and then strolled over to where his wife and son were watching from behind the refreshment stand.

When the match burned down the long-faced horse player shot into the air as if hoisted by a rope and began smacking at his foot.

Molly, Cincy, and young Dennis, peeking around the corner of the stand, began to shout in unison. Molly dropped her cup of sherbet, and Dennis Burns, seeing it fall, threw his after it gleefully.

"Hey, what goes on?" Cincy rattled change in his pocket and said, "You go on. I'll catch up to ye's."

When he joined them he held four cups of sherbet. "Here, kids—one to suck on and one to drop. Dewey is sure a sucker for the hotfoot. This must be a thousand times somebody gives him the hotfoot. It's a dozen times, at least, that I give him the hotfoot myself. Let's get up in the stand, kitten. I'll get you organized and then I've got to get the roll down on that hay-burner in the third; he shouldn't drop dead, kennahurra. You wouldn't know that, that's Gaelic. If he breaks a leg we're going to have to talk fast back at that fleabag. What the hell, it's time we was pulling out of that trap anyhow. Every time I wake up in the morning and get a glim full of that wallpaper I feel like I ought to slip you five bucks."

CARD XIX

# The Wheel of Fortune

*spins past Angel, Eagle, Lion, and Bull.*

STAN lay on the splintery boards, feeling the vibration against his elbows, smelling the acrid odor of machine oil rising from the planks. The freight thundered along, gaining speed.

The hands drew him further in and then slid under his armpits and helped him to sit up. "You all right, son? You sure come near swinging yourself into Kingdom Come." The voice was soft and friendly.

Now they were passing the outskirts of a town, lonely street lamps sending bars of light winking through the door. The man who had dragged him in was a Negro, dressed in denim overalls and a denim work coat. Above the bib of the overalls a white shirt was visible in the shadows. His smile was the only part of his face Stan could see.

Getting to his feet he braced himself against the sway of the car under him and worked his fingers and arms, easing the strain out of them. "Thanks, pal. It was too dark for me to put on any speed myself—couldn't see what was ahead of me on the drag."

"It's tough, dark night like this. You can't see the grab-irons. You can't hardly see *nothing*. How about a smoke?"

Stan felt a bag of tobacco pressed into his hand. He twisted

247

himself a cigarette and they shared the match. The Negro was a young fellow, slim, with smooth, handsome features and close-cropped hair.

Stan drew in smoke and let it dribble from his nose. Then he began to shake, for the steady pound of the wheels under him brought back the stab of that hopeless, desperate fear, "This is it," and he trembled harder.

"You cold, mister? Or you got a fever?"

"Just shaken up. I thought I was going to hand in my checks."

Their cigarettes perfumed the darkness. Outside the rising moon rode with them, dipping beyond treetops.

"You a working stiff, mister, or just on the road?"

"On the road."

"Plenty fellows likes it that way. Seem like I'd rather work than knock myself out hustling."

"What kind of work do you do?"

"Any kind. Porter work, handyman. I run a freight elevator once. I can drive pretty good. Biggest old truck you can find, I'll drive her. I've shipped out: cook's helper and dishwasher. I can chop cotton. Reckon there ain't anything you can't do, you set your mind on it."

"Bound north?"

"New Jersey. Going to try and get me a job at Grindle's. What I hear, they taking on men. Taking on colored."

Stan braced his back against the closed door on the other side of the car and drew a final puff from the cigarette, sending the butt flipping through the open door, trailing sparks.

Grindle. Grindle. Grindle. To drown out the chatter of the wheels he said, "Why are they hiring guys all of a sudden? Business must be picking up."

The youth laughed a little. "Business staying right where she is. They hiring because they done a whole mess of firing a while back. They hiring all colored, this new bunch, what I hear."

"What's the idea of that?" Tame lawyers, tame psychologists, tame muscle-men. Bastards.

"What you s'pose? They get all the colored boys in there, and then they stir up the white boys, and pretty soon they all messing around with each other and forget all about long hours and short pay."

Stan was only half listening. He crawled into the corner next to the Negro and sat down, stretching his legs out in front of him. "Hey, bud, you wouldn't happen to have a drink in your pocket, would you?"

"Hell, no. All I got is four bits and this bag of makings. Traveling fast and light."

Four bits. Ten shots of nickel whisky.

The Great Stanton ran his hands over his hair.

"My friend, I owe you a great debt for saving my life."

"You don't owe me nothing, mister. What you expect me to do? Let you slide under and make hamburg steak out of yourself? You forget all about it."

Stan swallowed the cottony saliva in his mouth and tried again. "My friend, my ancestors were Scotch, and the Scotch are known to possess a strange faculty. It used to be called second sight. Out of gratitude, I want to tell you what I see in the future about your life. I may be able to save you many trials and misfortunes."

His companion chuckled. "You better save that second sight. Get it to tell you when you going to miss nailing a freight."

"Ah, but you see, my friend, it led me to the very car where I would find assistance. I *knew* you were in this car and would help me."

"Mister, you ought to play the races and get rich."

"Tell me this—I get a decided impression that you have a scar on one knee. Isn't that so?"

The boy laughed again. "Sure, I got scars on *both* my knees. I got scars on my ass, too. Anybody got scars all over him, he ever done any work. I been working since I could walk. I was pulling bugs off potato plants, time I quit messing my britches."

Stan took a deep breath. He couldn't let this wisenheimer townie crawl all over him.

"My dear friend, how often in your life, when things looked bad, have you thought of committing suicide?"

"Man, you sure got it bad. Everybody think they like to die sometime—only they always wants to be hanging around afterwards, watching all the moaning and grieving they folks going to do, seeing them laid out dead. They don't want to die. They just want folks to do a little crying and hollering over 'em. I was working on a road gang once and the captain like to knock me clean out of my skin. He keep busting me alongside the head whether I raise any hell or not—just for fun. But I didn't want to kill myself. I wanted to get loose. And I *got* loose, and here I am—sitting here. But that captain get his brains mashed out with a shovel a couple months later by a big crazy fellow, worked right next to me on the chain. Now that captain's dead and I ain't mourning."

A fear without a form or a name was squirming inside Stanton Carlisle. Death and stories of death or brutality burrowed under his skin like ticks and set up an infection that worked through him to his brain and festered in it.

He forced his mind back to the reading. "Let me tell you this, friend: I see your future unrolling like thread from a spool. The pattern of your days ahead. I see men—a crowd of men—threatening you, asking questions. But I see another man, older than yourself, who will do you a good turn."

The Negro stood up and then squatted on his haunches to absorb the vibration of the car. "Mister, you must of been a fortuneteller sometime. You talk just like 'em. Why don't you relax yourself? You last a lot longer, I'm telling you."

The white hobo jumped to his feet and lurched over to the open door, bracing his hand against the wall of the car and staring out across the countryside. They roared over a concrete bridge; a river flashed golden in the moonlight and was gone.

"You better stand back a little, son. You go grabbing scenery that way and somebody spot you if we pass a jerk stop. They phone on ahead, and when she slow down you got the bulls standing there with oak towels in their hands, all ready to rub you down."

Stan turned savagely. "Listen, kid, you got everything figured out so close. What sense does it all make? What sort of God would put us here in this goddamned, stinking slaughterhouse of a world? Some guy that likes to tear the wings off flies? What use is there in living and starving and fighting the next guy for a full belly? It's a nut house. And the biggest loonies are at the top."

The Negro's voice was softer. "Now you talking, brother. You let all that crap alone and come over here and talk. We got a long run ahead of us and ain't no use trying to crap each other up."

Dully Stan left the doorway and crumpled into the corner. He wanted to shout out, to cry, to feel Lilith's mouth again, her breasts against him. Oh, Jesus, there I go. God damn her, the lying, double-crossing bitch. They're all alike. But Molly, the dumb little tomato. Quickly he wanted her. Then disgust mounted—she would leech on to him and drain the life out of him. Dull, oh, Christ, and stupid. Oh, Jesus . . . Mother. Mark Humphries, God damn his soul to hell, the thieving bastard. Mother . . . the picnic . . .

The Negro was speaking again and the words filtered through. ". . . take on like that. Why don't you tell me what you moaning about? You never going to see me again. Don't make no difference to me what you done. I mind my own business. But you'll feel better a hundred per cent, get it off your mind."

The prying bastard. Let me alone . . . He heard his own voice say, "Stars. Millions of them. Space, reaching out into nothing. No end to it. The rotten, senseless, useless life we get jerked into and jerked out of, and it's nothing but whoring and filth from start to finish."

"What's the matter with having a little poontang? Nothing dirty about that, 'cept in a crib you likely get crabs or a dose. Ain't anything dirty about it unless you feels dirty in your mind. Gal start whoring so as to get loose from cotton-chopping or standing on their feet ten, eleven hours. You can't blame no gal for laying it on the line for money. On her back she can rest."

Stan's torrent of despair had dried up. For a second he could draw breath—the weight seemed to have been lifted from his chest.

"But the purpose back of it all—why are we put here?"

"Way I look at it, we ain't put. We growed."

"But what started the whole stinking mess?"

"Didn't have to start. It's always been doing business. People ask me: how this world get made without God make it? I ask 'em right back: who make God? They say he don't need making; he always been there. I say: well then, why you got to go bringing him in at all? Old world's always been there, too. That's good enough for me. They ask me: how about sin? Who put all the sin and wickedness and cussedness in the world? I say: who put the boll weevil? He growed. Well, mean people grow where the growing's good for 'em—same as the boll weevil."

Stan was trying to listen. When he spoke his voice was thick and flat. "It's a hell of a world. A few at the top got all the dough. To get yours you got to pry 'em loose from some of it. And then they turn around and knock your teeth out for doing just what they did."

The Negro sighed and offered Stan the tobacco, then made himself another cigarette. "You said it, brother. You said it. Only they ain't going have it forever. Someday people going to get smart *and* mad, same time. You can't get nothing in this world by yourself."

Stan smoked, watching the gray thread sail toward the door and whip off into the night. "You sound like a labor agitator."

This time the Negro laughed aloud. "God's sake, man, labor don't need agitation. You can't agitate people when they's treated right. Labor don't need stirring up. It need squeezing together."

"You think they've got sense enough to do it?"

"They *got* to do it. I *know.*"

"Oh. You *know.*"

The lad in denims was silent for a moment, thinking. "Looky here—you plant four grains of corn to a hill. How you *know* one going to come up? Well, the working people, black *and* white—their brains growing just like corn in the hill."

The freight was slowing.

God, let me get out of here . . . this damn, slap-happy darkie, whistling in the lion's den. And Grindle . . . every second, moving closer to the fort . . .

"Hey, watch yourself, son. She's still traveling."

The train lost speed quickly. It was stopping. Stan jumped to the ground and the Negro followed, looking left and right. "This ain't good. Got no business stopping here. Oh—oh—it's a frisk."

At either end of the train, lights appeared, brakemen walking the tops carrying lanterns; flashlights of railroad bulls playing along the body rods and into open boxcars.

The young hobo said, "Something funny—this division ain't never been hostile before. And they frisking from both' ends at once . . ."

On the other side of the freight a train whistled in, hissing, glowing, the red blaze of the engine shining under the boxcar and throwing the hoboes' shadows across the cinders ahead of them.

"Hey, son, let's try and jump that passenger job. You a fast rambler?"

The Rev. Carlisle shook his head. The furies were drawing close, Anderson's web was tangling him. This was the end of it. Dully he clambered back into the boxcar and sank down into a corner, burying his face in his bent elbow, while with hoarse voices and a stamp of feet the furies moved in . . .

"Hey, bo—" The whisper through the door barely penetrated. "Come on—let's nail that rattler. We make better time too."

Silence.

"So long, boy. Take it easy."

Doom had stepped onto the roof; then a light stabbed into the car, searching the corners. Oh, Jesus, this is it—this is it.

"Come on, you bastard, unload. And get your hands up."

He stood, blinking in the glare of the flashlight, and raised his arms.

"Come on, hit the grit!"

Stan stumbled to the door and sat down, sliding his feet into darkness. A big hand gripped his arm and jerked him out.

From the top of the car the head-end shack peered over, holding his brake club under one arm. "You got him?"

A voice behind the flashlight said, "I got one. But he ain't no coon. Way we got the tip, the guy was a coon."

The brakeman above them signaled with his lantern and from the dark came the chug of a gasoline-driven handcar. It sped up and Stan could see that it was crowded with men—dark clothes—it was no track gang. When it stopped the men piled off and hurried across the rails.

"Where is he? On the freight? Who's shaking down the rattler?"

"We got boys frisking the rattler, don't worry."

"But we got it from Anderson . . ."

This is it. This is it. This is it.

". . . that the guy was colored." One of the newcomers came closer and brought out a flashlight of his own. "What's that in your pocket, bud?"

Stanton Carlisle tried to speak but his mouth was gritty.

"Keep your hands up. Wait a minute. This isn't a weapon. It's a Bible."

His lungs loosened; he could draw half a breath. "Brother, you hold in your hand the most powerful weapon in the world—"

"Drop it!" Big Hand shouted. "Maybe it's a pineapple made to look like a Bible."

The other voice was cool. "It's just a Bible." He turned to the white hobo. "We're looking for a colored lad. We know he boarded this train. If you can give us information which might lead to his arrest, you would be serving the forces of justice. And there might be something in it for you."

Justice. *Something in it* could mean folding money. Justice. A buck—ten cans of alky . . . justice. White-stubble justice . . . a buck—twenty shots . . . oh, frig them with their razorstrops, their *brake clubs* . . .

He opened his eyes wide, staring straight ahead in the light-beam. "Brother, I met a colored brother-in-God when I was waiting to nail this job. I tried to bring him to Jesus, but he wouldn't listen to the Word. I gave him my last tract—"

"Come on, parson, where did he go? Was he riding here in the car with you?"

"Brother, this colored brother-in-God nailed her somewhere up at the head-end. I was hoping we could ride together so I could tell him about our Lord and Savior Jesus Christ who died for our sins. I've rode from coast-to-coast a dozen times, bringing men to Christ. I've brought only a couple thousand so far . . ."

"Okay, parson, give Jesus a rest. We're looking for a god-damned nigger Red. You saw him grab her up front? Come on, guys, let's spread out. He's here someplace . . ."

The man with big hands stayed with Stanton while the others swarmed over the freight, swung between the cars and moved off into the darkness. The Rev. Carlisle had slipped into a low mutter which the yard dick made out to be a sermon, addressed either to an invisible congregation or to the air. The goddamned Holy Joe had thrown them off; now the coon had a chance of getting clear.

At last the freight whistled, couplings started and clanked, and it groaned off. Beyond it the passenger train, sleek and dark, waited while flashlights sprayed into the blinds, the side boxes of the diner, and along the tops.

Then it too began to move. As the club car slid past, Stan glimpsed through long windows a waiter in a white coat. He was uncapping a bottle while an arm in a tweed coat held a glass of ice.

A drink. Good Christ, a drink. Could I put the bite on this bull? Better not try it, no time to build it.

The railroad detective spat between his teeth. "Look here, parson, I'm going to give you a break. I ought to send you over. But you'd probably have the whole damn jail yelling hymns. Come on, crumb, take the breeze."

The big hands turned Stan around and pushed; he stumbled over tracks and up an embankment. In the distance the light of a farmhouse glowed. A drink. Oh, Jesus—

The passenger flyer picked up speed. In the club car a wrist shot from a tweed sleeve, revealing a wrist watch. Ten minutes' delay! Confound it, the only way to travel was by plane.

Under the club car, squeezed into a forest of steel springs, axles, brake rods and wheels, a man lay hidden. As the rattler gained speed, Frederick Douglass Scott, son of a Baptist minister, grandson of a slave, shifted his position to get a better purchase as he rolled on toward the North and the fort with its double fence of charged wire.

Shoulders braced against the truck frame, feet against the opposite side, he balanced his body on an inch-thick brake rod which bent under him. Inches below, the roadbed raced by, switches clawing up at him as the car pounded past them. The truck hammered and bucked. A stream of glowing coals, thrown down by the engine, blew over him and he fought them with his free hand, beating at the smoldering denim, while the train thundered on; north, north, north.

A specter was haunting Grindle. It was a specter in overalls.

CARD XX

# Death

*wears dark armor; beside his horse kneel priests and children and kings.*

THE PITCHMAN rounded a corner, looking both ways down the main street for the cop, and then slid into the darkened vestibule of the bank building. If the rain held off he might get a break at that. The movie theater was about to let out; fellows would be coming out with their girls.

As the first of the crowd drifted past him he drew a handful of gaudy envelopes from a large pocket inside his coat and fanned them in his left hand so that the brightly printed zodiac circle and the symbols stood out, a different color for each sign.

He ran his free hand once over his hair and took a breath. His voice was hoarse; he couldn't get it much above a whisper. "My friends if you'll just step this way for a single moment you may find that you have taken a step which will add to your health happiness and prosperity for the rest of your lives . . ."

One couple stopped and he spoke directly to them. "I wonder if the young lady would mind telling me her birth date it costs you nothing folks because the first astrological chart this evening will be given away absolutely free of charge . . ."

The young fellow said, "Come on." They walked on past. The goddamned townies.

Need a drink. Jesus, I've got to pitch. I got to unload five of them.

"Here you are folks everybody wants to know what the future holds in store come in a little closer folks and I'll tell you what I'm going to do I'm going to give each and every one of you a personal reading get your astronomical forecast which shows your lucky numbers, days of the month and tells you how to determine the right person for you to marry whether you've got anybody in mind or not . . ."

They moved by him, some staring, some laughing, none stopping.

Hideous. Their faces suddenly became distorted, like caricatures of human faces. They seemed to be pushed out of shape. Some of them looked like animals, some like embryo chicks when you break an egg that is half incubated. Their heads bobbed on necks like stalks and he waited for their eyes to drop out and bounce on the sidewalk.

The pitchman started to laugh. It was a chuckle, bubbling up inside of him at first, and then it split open and he laughed, screaming and stamping his foot.

A crowd began to knot around him. He stopped laughing and forced out the words. "Here you are folks while they last." The laugh was fighting inside of him, tearing at his throat. "A complete astrological reading giving your birthstones, lucky numbers." The laugh was hammering to get out. It was like a dog tied to the leg of a workbench, fighting to get free of a rope. Here it came. "Whah, whah, whah, whah! Hoooooooooooooo!"

He beat the handful of horoscopes against his thigh, leaning his other hand against the stone lintel of the vestibule. The crowd was giggling at him or with him, some wondering when he was going to stop suddenly and try to sell them something.

One woman said, "Isn't it disgusting! And right in the doorway of the bank! It's indecent."

The pitchman heard her and this time he sat down limply on the marble steps, letting the horoscopes scatter around him, holding his belly as he laughed.

Something hit the crowd at its edge and mashed it forward and to each side. Then the blue legs moved in.

"I told you to beat it out of town."

The face of the cop seemed a mile above him, as if it were looking over the rim of a well.

Same cop. Two-dollar fine and get out of town.

"Wheeeeeeee! Ho—ho. Hah. Officer . . . officer . . . whah-hoooooooo!"

The hand that jerked him to his feet seemed to plunge out of the sky. "I told you to scram, bum. Now you going to walk down to the lockup or you going on a stretcher?"

A quick thrust and his hand was twisted halfway up his back; he was walking bent over to keep from getting his wrist broken. Through waves of laughter the world seeped in, coming in slices, as if the laughter split at the seams and showed a little raw and bloody reality before it closed up again.

"Where we going, officer? No, no, don't tell me. Let me guess. Down cellar?"

"Shut up, bum. Keep walking or you'll get your arm broke. I've got a good mind to work you over before we get down there."

"But, officer, they've seen me once down there. They'll get awfully tired of seeing me. They'll think it ridiculous, me show-ing up there so often. Won't they? Won't they? Won't they? You've got no rope around my neck. How can you be sure I won't run? Wait for the moon—it's coming out from under the rain pretty soon; any minute now. But you don't understand that. Officer, wait . . ."

They had left the crowd and cut down a side street. To the left was an alley, dark, but with a light at the other end of it. The cop shifted his grip on the prisoner's hand, letting go for a fraction of a second, and the pitchman spun free and began to run. He was sailing through air; he couldn't feel his feet touching the stones. And behind him the heavy splat of shoes on cobbles. He raced toward the light at the end of the alley, but there was nothing to be afraid of. He had always been here, run-ning down the alley and it didn't matter; this was all there was any time, anywhere, just an alley and a light and the footsteps spanging on the cobbles but they never catch you, they never catch you, they never catch— A blow between his shoulders knocked him forward and he saw the stones, in the faint light ahead, coming up toward him, his own hands spread out, fingers bent a little on the left hand, thumbs at an eager angle, all spraddled out as if he were making shadows on a wall, of two roosters' heads, the thumbs forming the beaks and the spread fingers the notches of the combs.

The nightstick had struck him, whirling through the space between the two men. It bounded off, hitting a brick wall with a clear, wooden ping as the cobbles met his hands and the jar of the fall snapped his neck back. He was on his hands and knees when the foot caught him in the ribs and sent him sprawling on his side.

The great oval face ducked out of sight. The cop had bent to pick up the nightstick and the top of his cap cut off the sight of the face, above its V of shirt and black tie. That was all you could see.

He heard the shattering crack of the nightstick across his shoulders before the pain fought its way down the clogged nerves and went off, spraying around inside his brain like a hose jet of hot steel. He heard his own breath pop out between his teeth and he drew his feet under him. He was halfway erect when the stick knocked the rest of the breath out of him, smashing against his ribs.

It was somebody else's voice. "Officer . . . oh, Jesus . . . I ain't done nothing . . . gimme a break . . . oh, Jesus . . ."

"I'll give ye a break. I'll break every bone in your head, you stinking crumb. You as'd for it. Now you're gonna get it."

The stick landed again and the pain was white and incandescent this time as it slowly slid up his spine toward the brain on top.

The world came back and Stanton Carlisle, his mind sharpened to a point, saw where he was. He saw the lift of the cop's upper lip, revealing a gold crown. And in the faint light, behind him now, he noticed that the cop needed a shave. He was not over forty; but his hair and the beard beginning to sprout over the jowls were pearly. Like fungus on a corpse. At that instant pain from the blow across his buttocks reached his mind and a thousand tumblers fell into place; a door swung open.

Stan closed in, clamping one hand on the cop's lapel. His other hand crossed it, under the jowls, seizing the opposite lapel in its fist. Then, twisting sideways to protect his groin, Stanton began to squeeze. He heard the nightstick drop and felt the big hands tearing at his forearms, but the harder they pulled the tighter his fists dug into the throat. The day-old beard was like sandpaper on the backs of his hands.

Stan felt the wall of the alley jar against his shoulder, felt his feet leave the ground and the dark weight fall on him; but the only life in him now was pouring out through his hands and wrists.

The mountain on him wasn't moving. It was resting. Stan got one foot free and rolled both of them over so he was on top. The massive body was perfectly still. He tightened the choke still more, until his knuckles felt as if they would burst, and he began to tap the cop's head against the cobbles. Rap. Rap. Rap. He liked the sound. Faster.

Then his hands let go of themselves and he stood up, the hands falling to his sides. They wouldn't work any more, wouldn't obey him.

A bundle of astro-readings had fallen out and lay scattered on the stones, but he couldn't pick them up. He walked, very straight and precise, toward the light at the other end of the alley. Everything was sharp and clear now and he didn't even need a drink any more.

The freights would be risky. He might try the baggage rack of a long-haul bus, under the tarpaulin. He had traveled there once before.

Nothing more to bother about. For the cop was dead.

I can kill him again. I can kill him again. Any time he starts after me I can keep killing him. He's mine. My own personal corpse.

They'll bury him, just like you bury a stiff, clotted handkerchief.

I can kill him again.

But he won't come again. He's a dead pigeon.

I can kill him again.

But he's dead from a bum ticker.

I can kill him.

CARD XXI

# Strength

*A rose-crowned woman closes
a lion's jaws with her bare
hands.*

IN THE evening light a tall figure, gaunt, with matted yellow hair, leaned over the top fence rail, watching a man and woman planting corn. The woman thrust a hoe handle into the earth and the man, who seemed to have no legs, hopped along on his hands, dropping grains of corn into the hills and smoothing the earth over them.

"Wait a minute, Joe. There's somebody wants us."

The big woman strode over plowed ground, pulling off her gloves. "I'm sorry, bud, but we ain't got nothing in the icebox to give you for a lump. And I ain't got time now to fix you a sit-down. You wait till I get my pocketbook from the house and I'll let you have four bits. There's a lunch wagon down the road." She stopped and caught her breath, then said hoarsely, "Glory be, it's Stan Carlisle!" Over her shoulder she called, "Joe! Joe! Come here this minute!"

The hobo was leaning on the fence, letting it carry his weight. "Hi, Zeena. Saw your ad—magazine."

The man drew near them, hopping along on his hands. His legs, twisted into a knot out of the way, were hidden by a burlap sack which he had drawn over them and tied around his waist.

He swung up and sat looking at Stan silently, smiling as Lazarus must have smiled, newly risen. But his eyes were wary.

Zeena pushed back her straw hat and recovered her voice. "Stanton Carlisle, I swore if I ever set eyes on you again I'd sure give you a piece of my mind. Why, that child was pretty near out of her head, time she got to the carny. Everybody there thought she was touched, way she'd stumble around. I had her working the sword-box layout and she could just about step in and out of it, she was that bad. You sure done yourself proud by that girl, I must say. Oh, you was going to be mighty biggety—make a star out of her and everything. Well, you got there. But what good did it ever do her? Don't think I've ever forgot it." Her voice faltered and she sniffed, rubbing the back of a work-glove across her nose. "And what do you do but end up putting that kid, that sweet kid, on the turf—same as any two-bit pimp. It ain't any fault of yours that the kid pulled out of it so good. Oh, no. I hope she's forgot every idea she ever had about you. It ain't your fault she's married now to a grand guy and's got the cutest little kid of her own you ever laid eyes on. Oh, no, you done your best to land that girl in a crib house."

She stopped for breath, then went on in a different tone, "Oh, for God's sake, Stan, come in the house and let me fry you a slice of ham. You look like you ain't had a meal in a week."

The hobo wasn't listening. His knees had sagged; his chin scraped the fence rail and then he sank in a heap, like a scarecrow lifted from its pole.

Zeena dropped her gloves and began to climb the fence. "Joe, go down and hold the gate open. Stan's passed out. We got to get him in the house."

She lifted the emaciated body easily in her arms and carried it, legs dangling, toward the cottage.

Morning sun struck through the dotted curtains of the kitchen, falling on the golden hair of a man at the table, busy shoveling ham and eggs into his mouth. He stopped chewing and took a swallow of coffee.

". . . that skull buster was known all the way up and down the line. He beat two old stiffs to death in the basement of the jug last year. I knew when he got me up that alley that the curtain was going down."

Zeena turned from the stove with a skillet in one hand and a cake turner in the other. "Take it easy, Stan. Here's some more eggs. I reckon you got room for 'em." She filled his plate again.

Near the door Joe Plasky sat on a cushion, sorting mail into piles by states. It came in bundles; the mailman left it in a small barrel out on the road. On the barrel was painted: "ZEENA–PLASKY." They had outgrown an R.F.D. box long ago.

"He started working me over with the club." Stan paused with a forkful of egg in the air, looking at Joe. "So I let him have it. I clamped the *nami juji* on him and hung on. He went out for good."

Zeena stopped, holding the cake turner. She said, "Oh, my God." Then her eyes moved to Joe Plasky, who went on calmly sorting mail.

Joe said, "If it happened the way you tell it, kid, it was him or you. That Jap choke is a killer, all right. But you're a hot man, Stan. You've got to move quiet. And fast."

Zeena shook herself. "Well, he ain't moving till we get him fed up some. The boy was starved. Have some more coffee, Stan. But, Joe, what's he going to do? We can't—"

Joe smiled a little wider but his eyes were dark and turned inward, thinking. Finally he said, "They got your prints up there?"

Stan swallowed. "No. They don't print you on vag and peddling falls. Not in that town, anyway. But they know it was a blond pitchman working horoscopes."

Joe thought some more. "They didn't mug you?"

"No. Just a fine and a boot in the tail."

The half-man acrobat pushed aside the piles of letters and hopped over to the stairway, which led to the attic bedrooms. He swung up the stairs and out of sight; overhead they could hear a scrape as he crossed the floor.

Stan pushed back his plate and took a cigarette from the pack on the window sill. "Zeena, I've been living in a goddamned nightmare—a dream. I don't know what ever got into me. When vaudeville conked out we could have worked the night clubs.

I don't know yet how I ever got tangled up with the spook racket."

The big woman was piling dishes in the sink. She was silent.

Stanton Carlisle's voice went on, getting back something of the old resonance. "I don't know what ever got into me. I don't expect Molly ever to forgive me. But I'm glad the kid got herself a good spot. I hope he's a swell guy. She deserves it. Don't tell her you ever saw me. I want her to forget me. I had my chance and I fluffed, when it came to Molly. I've fluffed everything."

Zeena turned back to him, her hands shining from the soapy water. "What you going to do, Stan, when you leave here?"

He was staring at the ember of his cigarette. "Search me, pal. Keep on bumming, I guess. The pitch is out. Everything's out. Good God, I don't know—"

On the stairs Joe Plasky made a scraping noise, coming down slowly. When he entered the kitchen he held a large roll of canvas under his arm. He spread it on the linoleum and unrolled it in two sections—gaudily painted banners showing enormous hands, the mounts and lines in different colors with the characteristics ascribed to each.

"Sophie Eidelson left these with us last season," he said. "Thought maybe you could use 'em. McGraw and Kauffman's is playing a town down the line from here—be there all this week. There's worse places to hole up in than a carny."

Zeena dried her hands hastily and said, "Stan, give me a cigarette, quick. I've got it! Joe's got the answer. You could work it in a Hindu makeup. I've got an old blue silk kimono I can fix over for a robe. I reckon you know how to tie a turban."

The Great Stanton ran his hands over his hair. Then he knelt on the floor beside the half-man, pulling the palmistry banners further open and examining them. In his face Zeena could see the reflection of the brain working behind it. It seemed to have come alive out of a long sleep.

"Jesus God, this is manna from heaven, Joe. All I'll need is a bridge table and a canvas fly. I can hang the banners from the fly. They're looking for a pitchman, not a mitt reader. Oh, Jesus, here we go."

Joe Plasky moved away and picked up a burlap sack containing outgoing mail. He slung it over his shoulder and held the top of it in his teeth, setting off for the door on his hands. "Got to leave this for the pickup," he said, around the burlap. "You folks stay here—I've got it."

When he had gone Zeena poured herself a cup of coffee and offered one to Stan, who shook his head. He was still examining the banners.

"Stan—" She began to talk as if there was something which had to be said, something which was just for the two of them to hear. She spoke quickly, before Joe could return. "Stan, I want you to tell me something. It's about Pete. It don't hurt me to talk about him now. That was so long ago it seems like Pete never hit the skids at all. Seems like he died while we were still at the top of the heap. But I got to thinking—a kid will do an awful lot to lay some gal he's all steamed up about. And you were a kid, Stan, and hadn't ever had it before. I expect old Zeena looked pretty good to you in them days, too. Pete wouldn't ever have drank that bad alky. And you didn't know it was poison. Now come clean."

The Great Stanton stood up and thrust his hands into his pockets. He moved until the sun, shining through the window of the kitchen door, struck his hair. Soap and hot water had turned it from mud to gold again. His voice this time filled the kitchen; subtly, without increasing in power, it vibrated.

"Zeena, before you say another word, do me one favor. You remember Pete's last name?"

"Well— Well, he never used it. He wrote it on our marriage license. Only I ain't thought of it for years. Yes, I can remember it."

"And it's something I could never guess. Am I right? Will you concentrate on that name?"

"Stan— What—"

"Concentrate. Does it begin with *K?*"

She nodded, frowning, her lips parted.

"Concentrate. *K . . . R . . . U . . . M*—"

"Oh, my God!"

"The name was *Krumbein!*"

Joe Plasky pushed at the door and Stan moved aside. Zeena

buried her mouth in the coffee cup and then set it down **and** hurried out of the room.

Joe raised his eyebrows.

"We were cutting up old times."

"Oh. Well, in that outfit I know McGraw a little—only **you** better not use my name, Stan. A guy as hot as you."

"What's calluses on the ends of the fingers, left hand?"

"Plays a stringed instrument."

"What's a callus here, on the right thumb?"

"A stonecutter."

"How about a callus in the bend of the first finger, right hand?"

"A barber—from stropping the razor."

"You're getting it, Stan. There's lots more that I forget—I ain't read mitts steady in many a year. If Sophie was here she could give you hundreds of things like that. She's got a whole notebook full of stuff. It locks with a key. But you'll make out all right. You always could read."

Zeena and Joe were sitting in the shade of the porch, opening letters and shaking out dimes. The woman said, "Hand me some more Scorpios, hon. I'm fresh out."

Joe ripped open a carton. The astrological booklets came in stamped-and-sealed envelopes. They addressed them quickly with fountain pens and threw them in a wire basket to be bundled up later for the postman.

Zeena said, "Beats all, Stan, how this mail-order business snowballs up. We put in one little ad and plowed back the dimes into the business. Now we got five chains of magazines covered and we can't hardly stop shaking out dimes to tend to the place here."

The Great Stanton reached into a saucepan by the side of the steamer chair where he lay in the sun. Taking a handful of dimes he counted out five batches of ten and rolled them into a red paper wrapper—five dollars' worth. The little red cylinders piled up in a china bowl on the other side of the chair, but he had carelessly allowed several to fall beside him. They were hidden between his thigh and the canvas chair-seat.

Joe hopped off the porch and over toward Stan, holding a

basket of dimes in his teeth. He emptied them into the saucepan, smiling. "Little more and we're going to buy another place—farm next to this one. We've pretty near got this place mortgage-free. Long as people want horoscopes, I mean, astro-readings—you can't call 'em horoscopes through the mail unless they're drawn to the hour and minute of birth—long as they keep going like this we're set. And if they slack off, we've still got the farm."

Stan leaned back and let the sun strike through his eyelids. He was gaining. A week had filled him out. Almost back to his old weight. His eyes had cleared and his hands hardly shook at all. He hadn't had anything but beer in a week. A guy who's good at the cold reading will never starve. When Joe turned back to the porch Stanton slid the red cylinders from the chair to his pants pocket.

The truck bounced off the side road in a cloud of dust, white under the full moon, and turned into a state highway. Zeena drove carefully to spare the truck and Joe sat next to her, one arm on her shoulders to steady himself when they stopped suddenly or slowed down. Stan was next to the door of the cab, his palmistry banners in a roll between his knees.

Town lights glittered ahead as they topped a gradual rise. They coasted down it.

"Almost there, Stan."

"You'll make it, kid," Joe said. "McGraw's a hard cookie, but he ain't a nickel-nurser once you got him sold."

Stan was quiet, watching the bare streets they were rolling through. The bus station was a drugstore which kept open all night. Zeena stopped down the block and Stan opened the door and slid out, lifting out the banners.

"So long, Zeena—Joe. This—this was the first break I've had in a hell of a while. I don't know how—"

"Forget it, Stan. Joe and me was glad to do what we could. A carny's a carny and when one of us is jammed up we got to stick together."

"I'll try riding the baggage rack on this bus, I guess."

Zeena let out a snort. "I knew I'd forgot something. Here, Stan." From the pocket of her overalls she took a folded bill and, leaning over Joe, pressed it into the mentalist's hand. "You can send it back at the end of the season. No hurry."

"Thanks a million." The Great Stanton turned, with the rolled canvas under his arm, and walked away toward the drugstore. Halfway down the block he paused, straightened, threw back his shoulders and then went on, holding himself like an emperor.

Zeena started the truck and turned it around. They drove out of town in a different direction and then took a side road which cut into the highway further south, turning off it to mount a bluff overlooking the main drag. "Let's wait here, snooks, and try to get a peek into the bus when it goes by. I feel kind of funny, not being able to see him to the station and wait until it came along. Don't seem hospitable."

"Only smart thing to do, Zee. A fellow as hot as him."

She got out of the cab and her husband hopped after her; they crossed a field and sat on the bank. Above them the sky had clouded over, the moon was hidden by a thick ceiling.

"You reckon he'll make it, Joe?"

Plasky shifted his body on his hands and leaned forward. Far down the pale concrete strip the lights of a bus rose over the grade. It picked up speed, tires singing on the roadbed, as it bore down toward them. Through its windows they could make out the passengers—a boy and a girl, in a tight clinch on the back seat. One old man already asleep. It roared below the bank.

Stanton Carlisle was sharing a seat with a stout woman in a gay flowered-print dress and a white sailor straw hat. He was holding her right hand, palm up, and was pointing to the lines.

Joe Plasky sighed as the bus tore past them into darkness with a fading gleam of ruby taillights. "I don't know what'll happen to him," he said softly, "but that guy was never born to hang."

# The
# Hanged Man

*hangs head downward from
the living wood.*

IT WAS a cheap straw hat, but it added class. He was the type of guy who could wear a hat. The tie chain came from the five-and-ten, but with the suit and the white shirt it looked like the real thing. The amber mirror behind the bar always makes you look tanned and healthy. But he was tanned. The mustache was blackened to match the hair-dyeing job Zeena had done.

"Make mine a beer, pal."

He took it to a table, put his hat on an empty chair and unfolded a newspaper, pretending to read it. Forty-five minutes before the local bus left. They don't know who they're looking for up there—no prints, no photo. Stay out of that state and they'll look for you till Kingdom Come.

The beer was bitter and he began to feel a little edge from it. This was all right. Keep it at beer for a while. Get a stake, working the mitt camp. Get a good wad in the grouchbag and then try working Mexico. They say the language is a cinch to learn. And the damn country's wide open for ragheads. They advertise in all the papers down there. Give that mess with the cop time to cool and I can come back in a few years and start working California. Take a Spanish name maybe. There's a million chances.

A guy who's good at the cold reading will never starve.

He opened the newspaper, scanning the pictures, thinking his way along through the days ahead. I'll have to hustle the readings and put my back into it. In a carny mitt camp you got to spot them quick, size 'em up and unload it in a hurry. Well, I can do it. I should have stayed right with the carny.

Two pages of the paper stuck and he went back and pried them apart, not caring what was on them, just so as not to skip any. In Mexico . . .

The picture was alone on the page, up near the top. He looked at it, concentrating on the woman's face, his glance merging the screen of black dots that composed it, filling in from memory its texture, contour, color. The scent of the sleek gold hair came back to him, the sly twist of her little tongue. The man looked twenty years older; he looked like a death's head—scrawny neck, flabby cheeks . . .

They were together. They were together. Read it. Read what they're doing.

### PSYCHOLOGIST WEDS MAGNATE

In a simple ceremony. The bride wore a tailored . . . Best man was Melvin Anderson, long-time friend and advisor . . . Honeymoon cruise along the coast of Norway . . .

Somebody was shaking him, talking at him. Only it wasn't any grass tuft—it was a beer glass. "Jees, take it easy, bud. How'd ya bust it? Ya musta set it down too hard. We ain't responsible, you go slinging glasses around and get cut. Why don't ya go over to the drugstore. We ain't responsible . . ."

Darkness of street darkness with the night's eyes up above the roof cornices oh Jesus he was bleeding suitable for a full evening's performance gimme a rye and plain water, yeah, a rye make it a double.

It's nothing, I caught it on a nail, doc. No charge? Fine, doc. Gimme a rye—yeah, and plain water better make it a double rye and plain water seeping into the tire tracks where the grownups were everywhere.

I ain't pushing, bud, let's have no hard feelings, I'm your

friend, my friend I get the impression that when you were a lad there was some line of work or profession you wanted to follow and furthermore you carry in your pocket a foreign coin or lucky piece you can see Sheriff that the young lady cannot wear ordinary clothes because thousands of volts of electricity cover her body like a sheath and the sequins rough against his fingers as he unhooked the smoothness of her breasts trembling pressing victory into we'll make a team right to the top and they give you a handout like a tramp at a back door but the doors have been closed, gentlemen, let them look for threads till Kingdom Come and the old idiot gaping there in the red light of the votive candle oh Jesus you frozen-faced bitch give me that dough yeah make it a rye, water on the side . . .

You could hardly see the platform for the smoke and the waiter wore a butcher's apron his sleeves were rolled up and his arms had muscles like Bruno's only they were covered with black hair you had to pay him every time and the drinks were small get out of this crummy joint and find another one but the dame was singing while the guy in a purple silk shirt rattled on the runt piano the old bag had on a black evening dress and a tiara of rhinestones

> *Put your arms around me, honey, hold me tight!*

She drew the mike toward her and her tits bulged on each side of the rod Christ what an old bag . . .

> *Cuddle up and cuddle up with all your might!*

She rubbed her belly against the microphone . . .

> *Oh! Oh! I never knew*
> > *any boy*
> > > *like*
> > > > *you!*

"Waiter—waiter, tell the singer to let me buy her a drink . . ."

*When you look at me my heart . . . begins to float,*
*Then it starts a-rocking like a . . . a motor boat!*
*Oh! Oh! I never knew*
*Any boy . . . like . . . you!*

"Whew, I'm all winded. Ya like that number? The old ones always the best, ain't they? Thanks, sport—same as ever for me, Mike. Ain't I seen you in here before, honey? Gee, you been missin' a good time . . ."

All hallways look alike and the lights burning black dressers and yellow bedspreads kiss me "Yeah, sure, honey, keep your pants on long enough for me to catch my breath. Them stairs—whew!"

Smell of face powder sweat perfume "Yeah, honey, I'll peel. Wait a minute, can't you? Never mind a chaser, just lean on the bottle, sport. Boy, this ain't bad. C'mon over and get friendly, honey, mamma's going to treat you right. Gee, ain't you the handsome one! Hey, honey, how about giving me my present now, huh? Where'd you get all them dimes? Holy gee, you musta stuck up a streetcar company. No more jumpsteady for me, honey, let's 'make a baby'—I got to get back."

Groping in the dark he found it, lying on its side there was still a drink in it oh Jesus I got to get out of here before they see this room . . .

The sun blinding him, feel in the lining, maybe some of them slipped down . . . one more roll of dimes . . . tie them in the tail of the undershirt this damn fleabag's a fleabag but the bottle don't need any corkscrew and to hell with water I fixed 'em all, the bastards, they'll never find me . . . covered my tracks too smart for 'em the bastards I bashed him right in the face and he fell back on the divan with his mouth hanging open the old bastard never knew what hit him but I'll slip them yet and work it in a Hindu outfit with dark makeup but there was one more drink the damn thieves somebody sneak in here and lap it up let me out of here got to get air oh Jesus the goddamned chairs are sliding back and forth back and forth and if I hold on tight to the carpet I won't slide and hit the wall with his fist beating away

on the mantelpiece she sits straight up on the edge of the sofa
looking at herself in the glass sign in front of the church when
they boarded up the attic door and his hands bunching up the
tablecloth as I rammed it into him, Gyp. That fat bastard I hope
I blinded him following the star that burns in his lantern head
down from the living wood.

In the office trailer McGraw was typing out a letter when he
heard a tap on the screen door. He shaded his eyes against the
desk lamp and said out of the side of his mouth, "Yeah, what?"

"Mis'er McGraw?"

"Yeah, yeah. What d'ya want? I'm busy."

"Wanna talk t'you, 'bout a 'traction. Added 'traction."

McGraw said, "Come on in. What you got to sell?"

The bum was hatless, shirt filthy. Under his arm he carried a
roll of canvas. "Allow me t'introduce myself—Allah Rahged, top-
money mitt reader. Got m'banners all ready t'go t'work. Best
cold reader in the country. Lemme give you demonstration."

McGraw took the cigar out of his mouth. "Sorry, brother, I'm
full up. And I'm busy. Why don't you rent a vacant store and
work it solo?" He leaned forward, rolling up the paper in the
typewriter. "I mean it, bud. We don't hire no boozers! Jesus!
You smell like you pissed your pants. Go on, beat it!"

"Jus' give me chance make a demonstration. Real, old-time,
A-number-one mitt reader. Take one look at the mark, read past,
present—"

McGraw was letting his cold little eyes slide over the man
whose head came within an inch of the trailer roof. The hair
was dirty black, but at the temples and over the forehead was a
thin line of yellow. Dyed. A lammister.

The carny boss suddenly smiled up at his visitor. "Take a seat,
bud." From a cupboard behind him he lifted a bottle and two
shot glasses. "Have a snort?"

"I thank you, sir. Very refreshing. I'll need only a fly and a
bridge table—hang my banners on the edges of the fly."

McGraw shook his head. "I don't like a mitt camp. Too much
trouble with the law."

The bum was eyeing the bottle, his red eyes fastened on it.

"Have another? No, I don't like mitt camps. Old stuff. Always got to have something new. Sensational."

The other nodded absently, watching the bottle. McGraw put it back in the cupboard and stood up. "Sorry, bud. Some other outfit, maybe. But not us. Good night."

The rum-dum pushed himself up, hands on the chair arms, and stood, swaying, blinking down at McGraw. Then he ran the back of his hand across his mouth and said, "Yeah. Sure." He stumbled, reached the screen door, and pulled it open, gripping it with his hand to keep his balance. He had forgotten the soiled canvas banners with their gaudily painted hands. "Well, so long, mister."

"Hey, wait a minute."

The lush was already back in the chair, leaning forward, his hands spread against his chest, elbows on the chair arms, head lolling. "Hey, mister, how 'bout 'nother li'l shot 'fore I go?"

"Yeah, sure. But I just happened to think of something. I got one job you might take a crack at. It ain't much, and I ain't begging you to take it; but it's a job. Keep you in coffee and cakes and a shot now and then. What do you say? Of course, it's only temporary—just until we get a real geek."

# OTHER NEW YORK REVIEW CLASSICS*

*\*For a complete list of titles, visit www.nyrb.com or write to:*
*Catalog Requests, NYRB, 435 Hudson Street, New York, NY 10014*

**LEONARDO SCIASCIA** The Day of the Owl
**LEONARDO SCIASCIA** Equal Danger
**LEONARDO SCIASCIA** The Moro Affair
**LEONARDO SCIASCIA** To Each His Own
**LEONARDO SCIASCIA** The Wine-Dark Sea
**VICTOR SEGALEN** René Leys
**PHILIPE-PAUL DE SÉGUR** Defeat: Napoleon's Russian Campaign
**VICTOR SERGE** The Case of Comrade Tulayev
**VICTOR SERGE** Unforgiving Years
**GEORGES SIMENON** Dirty Snow
**GEORGES SIMENON** The Engagement
**GEORGES SIMENON** The Man Who Watched Trains Go By
**GEORGES SIMENON** Monsieur Monde Vanishes
**GEORGES SIMENON** Red Lights
**GEORGES SIMENON** The Strangers in the House
**GEORGES SIMENON** Three Bedrooms in Manhattan
**GEORGES SIMENON** Tropic Moon
**GEORGES SIMENON** The Widow
**CHARLES SIMIC** Dime-Store Alchemy: The Art of Joseph Cornell
**VLADIMIR SOROKIN** Ice
**VLADIMIR SOROKIN** The Queue
**ADALBERT STIFTER** Rock Crystal
**THEODOR STORM** The Rider on the White Horse
**A.J.A. SYMONS** The Quest for Corvo
**HENRY DAVID THOREAU** The Journal: 1837–1861
**TATYANA TOLSTAYA** The Slynx
**EDWARD JOHN TRELAWNY** Records of Shelley, Byron, and the Author
**LIONEL TRILLING** The Liberal Imagination
**LIONEL TRILLING** The Middle of the Journey
**IVAN TURGENEV** Virgin Soil
**ELIZABETH VON ARNIM** The Enchanted April
**EDWARD LEWIS WALLANT** The Tenants of Moonbloom
**ROBERT WALSER** Jakob von Gunten
**ROBERT WALSER** Selected Stories
**REX WARNER** Men and Gods
**SYLVIA TOWNSEND WARNER** Lolly Willowes
**SYLVIA TOWNSEND WARNER** Summer Will Show
**ALEKSANDER WAT** My Century
**C.V. WEDGWOOD** The Thirty Years War
**SIMONE WEIL AND RACHEL BESPALOFF** War and the Iliad
**GLENWAY WESCOTT** The Pilgrim Hawk
**REBECCA WEST** The Fountain Overflows
**EDITH WHARTON** The New York Stories of Edith Wharton
**PATRICK WHITE** Riders in the Chariot
**JOHN WILLIAMS** Stoner
**EDMUND WILSON** To the Finland Station
**RUDOLF AND MARGARET WITTKOWER** Born Under Saturn
**GEOFFREY WOLFF** Black Sun
**FRANCIS WYNDHAM** The Complete Fiction
**JOHN WYNDHAM** The Chrysalids
**STEFAN ZWEIG** Chess Story
**STEFAN ZWEIG** The Post-Office Girl